IN THE
BARREN
GROUND

ALSO BY LORETH ANNE WHITE

In the Waning Light
A Dark Lure

Snowy Creek
The Slow Burn of Silence

Wild Country
Manhunter
Cold Case Affair

Shadow Soldiers
The Heart of a Mercenary
A Sultan's Ransom
Rules of Engagement
Seducing the Mercenary
The Heart of a Renegade

Sahara Kings
The Sheik's Command
Sheik's Revenge
Surgeon Sheik's Rescue
Guarding the Princess
"Sheik's Captive," in *Desert Knights* with Linda Conrad

More by Loreth Anne White
Melting The Ice
Safe Passage
The Sheik Who Loved Me

LORETH ANNE WHITE

IN THE BARREN GROUND

Montlake
Romance

Text copyright © 2016 Loreth Beswetherick

Published by Montlake Romance, Seattle

www.apub.com

Amazon, the Amazon logo, and Montlake Romance are trademarks of Amazon.com, Inc., or its affiliates.

ISBN-13: 9781503936232
ISBN-10: 1503936236

Cover design by Jason Blackburn

Printed in the United States of America

Thank you once again, Pavlo, for unwavering support, and love, even in the dark deadline hours.

THE HUNGER

And there carried upon the night wind an odor that was both fetid and fragrant. So subtle was this scent, that had Cromwell not noticed the queer change that came suddenly upon his Voyageur guide as the draft stirred the flames to brightness, he'd not have noticed it himself. But his man, Moreau, who was squatting in his furs before the campfire smoking his pipe, abruptly snapped his eyes toward the dark forest. It was then that Cromwell became aware of the gentle but malodorous scent. Moreau's nostrils flared, as though he might be a creature of the woods catching the carrion stink of a predator upwind. And as the flames settled back to embers, Cromwell saw a look in the Voyageur's dark face that deeply disquieted him. His man was scared, to the very quick of his soul . . .

~ Fort Resolution, 1849

The Reader closes the book and sits in silence for a while, like a shadow, just staring at the jars upon the shelf that contain the floating human heart and eyeballs. The Reader feels good. Powerful. For the Reader owns this Story now. The Reader likes, very much, the idea that a Story is alive—a dynamic dialogue between creator and consumer—an act of copulation. And an author can never claim his Story is complete until it has been read by a reader, and only then can the circle be closed. A Story can never remain static, either. For each new reader brings to the Story afresh his own unique set of past experiences, giving him a peculiar lens through which to conjure different emotions out of the very same words . . .

The Reader flexes a hand that is stiff and still stained with blood. The Reader holds all the power. It is the Reader who breathes life into these words on the page, makes them whole and tangible and frightening in the real world.

The Reader is in control . . .

CHAPTER 1

Friday, November 2. The Barrens. Two degrees south of the Arctic Circle. Day length: 8:06:38 hours.

As the sun cracked over the horizon a quiet befell the five occupants of the bright yellow AS355 Eurocopter Twin Squirrel, the words "Boreal Air" printed in bold black letters beneath the craft's belly. They'd entered the land of desolation. Only the sound of thudding rotors reached into their earphoned cocoons of private awe. Selena Apodaca watched the trees unfolding below—black spruce, tamarack—growing more sparse and stunted the farther north they flew. Like grizzled old crones, the conifers bent and marched resiliently forward into the frigid winds blasting down from the arctic—the dwindling survivors of the dense boreal forests that lay farther south. Only to disappear. For soon there were no trees. Just whalebacks of scarred bedrock that bloomed with rust-red lichen and sphagnum mosses, muskeg bogs pocked with tussock, and silvery threads of river strung with beads of dark blue lakes.

A herd of migrating caribou suddenly lifted their antlers, alerted by the sound of the chopper. An invisible current seemed to spark through the herd. It exploded into two groups, half the animals splashing into a river and up the opposite bank. The rest cascading down an esker ridge.

The Barren Lands.

It was a primordial place, Selena thought—the last, vast, uninhabited frontier of the North American continent, still being formed in front of her eyes in slow geologic motion. Oblivious to insignificant mankind.

An old caribou bull struggled, lagging behind his herd, and she wondered if he'd survive the night. This place was as hostile as it was breathtakingly beautiful, and winter was relentless. Already it lurked like a dark, constant shadow along the horizon, coming a little closer each day, and the air was turning brittle—the ice of the tundra creeping down from the north.

Marcie Della, one of the elders of the Twin Rivers First Nations community, had told her that this land was called the *hosi*—the treeless place. And that it was no-man's-land. Marcie was one of the remaining few who still knew the old names for some of these lakes, and where the "dreaming places" lay—sacred areas where terrible visions would afflict travelers who dared rest weary limbs there. Marcie also told of a cadaverous creature of the cold—a hateful shape-shifter that lived in the tundra winds and snows, a wolflike thing whose hunger for human meat and whose rage could never be sated. She had a name for this thing that meant "the spirit of lonely places."

"It doesn't get old, does it?" Selena jumped at the sudden intrusion of the voice in her headset. She shot a glance at Raj Sanjit, who was strapped into the seat beside her. His liquid black eyes met hers. His breath condensed into clouds around his face—even inside the chopper it was frigid. He grinned. "It's like we're entering a kingdom where everything is sacred, don't you think? And that we ought to hold a special passport that admits us, or else we shall be punished by death."

Selena wasn't sure what to make of this oddly maudlin comment from her teammate. She glanced at Veronique and Dean, their fellow wildlife biologists seated with their K9s to Raj's left, to see if she was once again being mocked for her newfound fascination with the lore and locals of this place. The light of mirth twinkled in Veronique's eyes, but her features remained studiously benign. Dean looked hostile. Irritation snapped through Selena.

During these last few weeks of their university co-op, she'd been getting on fine with her crew, in spite of Dean's earlier, unwelcome sexual advances. Now it seemed he was back to his brooding. He looked away and stroked the head of Buddy, the black Lab pressed between his knees. Selena's gaze went to the other K9, Pika, an Australian shepherd lying patiently at Veronique's boots. Both animals were scat sniffers, trained to search specifically for the feces of wolverine—the elusive "death eater" of the north—now extinguished almost everywhere else in North America. Once collected, the scat samples were shipped back to a lab at the University of Alberta where DNA and other markers told scientists about the existing populations and health thereof. They'd been doing this all summer as part of a massive environmental study required of WestMin Diamonds before the territorial government would consider approving an open-pit mine at the south tip of Ice Lake.

Selena and Raj were focused on the local grizzly bear populations, but they were collecting DNA old-school style, with bait and wire traps designed to snag the hair of *ursus arctos horribilis,* which in turn was also sent to a lab for analysis.

As Selena opened her mouth to snap back a retort, the voice of their pilot, Heather MacAllistair, came through their headsets. "Looks like the storm might hit before the day's out." She pointed a gloved hand toward a black band on the horizon, and cast a glance over her shoulder, eyes invisible behind mirrored aviator shades. Her hair hung in a thick blonde braid down the center of her back. "You guys equipped for an overnight or two? Because if that keeps coming at that speed, I might not be able to get in for the scheduled pickup."

Sunset today would be at 4:21 p.m. Heather was slated to meet Selena and Raj for pickup at 4:00 p.m.

"Yeah, we're good to hunker down if the weather hits," Raj said. He turned to Selena and said softly, "You good?"

She nodded, but her nerves jangled. This was their last week. She was due back at school before the end of November, where she was working on her master's. But the sight of that storm brought a strange foreboding. Perhaps it was guilt. She pulled her backpack closer between her knees, as if to guard the secret she had hidden in there.

The chopper banked sharply and Heather lowered her bird over the WestMin exploration camp—a tiny huddle of canvas tents, yurts, and Quonset huts of galvanized steel, plus a drilling station, an ore-processing shed, and an airstrip of scarred earth.

The few men dotting the camp looked up as the chopper buzzed over. One waved. Another made a crude sign. A dog on a chain lunged and barked. Heather opened her side window, and flipped a gloved finger at the men. One made a jerking-off motion in response, and she laughed before banking her Twin Squirrel out over the ruffled water of Ice Lake. She aimed for the north tip where she would drop off Selena and Raj.

"Look." Heather pointed suddenly. "Three o'clock. Wolves."

Four of them. *Canis lupus*. The gray wolf. The largest member of the wolf family. Paws as big as a man's fist. The carnivores loped single file right along the water's edge. The lead wolf was black. A huge specimen. He was followed by a white one, and two smaller animals with pelts of mottled gray.

Selena turned in her seat to watch the wolves as they flew past. But she leaned suddenly forward as something else caught her eye—a movement up on the ridge. She squinted, trying to make out what she'd seen, but the low-angled light glancing off iced rocks blinded her.

"What is it?" Raj's voice came through her earphones.

"I . . . thought I saw a man. Wearing furs. He disappeared behind that boulder there." She pointed.

"Fur?" Raj leaned over Selena, trying to see. "Maybe it was a bear, because there's no quad, floatplane, or any form of transport in sight."

"Maybe he's like us—going to be picked up later. Some hunter. Or geologist."

"In fur? Yeah. Right." He wiggled his thick black brows at her. "Going bush are we, Selena? The old lady's stories about monsters getting to you, are they?"

She cursed softly and turned away.

At the north tip of Ice Lake, Heather brought her Squirrel down and set the skids gently atop the spine of an esker. She kept the rotors going. She was on the clock—had several more crews to fly out of Twin Rivers that day.

Selena said her thanks, removed her headset, opened the door, and climbed out with her pack and shotgun. Raj handed down the rolls of fine wire, stakes, and two jerry cans of bear lure they'd need for the day. He hopped out himself. They ran in a low crouch, the downdraft snapping hair against Selena's face and drawing tears from her eyes as the Twin Squirrel took off.

Selena shrugged into her pack as she watched the chopper shrinking to a tiny yellow speck before simply disappearing into the endless sky. Her gaze went to the band of black weather that seemed to loom larger and closer now that they were on the ground. Usually she measured size in relation to her own body, but out here, the reverse seemed to apply. Out here she measured herself in relation to the sheer size and scope of everything else. And in the Barrens, she was tiny. Irrelevant to geography and time.

"At least there's no blackfly swarm today," Raj said, securing the rolls of barbed wire and the bundle of stakes to his pack. They got to work, covering ground quickly.

As was their routine, Raj hammered in stakes while Selena unraveled and strung a single strand of wire between the stakes at a bear's shoulder height. Both remained vigilant for wildlife but it was Selena who insisted on carrying the gun. She felt that Raj's attention tended to wander, while she remained ever conscious of the fine line between being a scientist or being prey. Drawing a mask up over her nose and mouth to avoid the stench, she uncapped one of the containers of bear lure and began pouring a blackened sludge of rotted moose blood, fish guts, and vanilla over a pile of dead sphagnum moss at the center of the wire enclosure they'd just created.

Ursus arctos horribilis would be attracted by the pungent odor as it carried down the valley. Unable to resist, the bears would go under the wire to investigate, snagging tufts of hair on the barbs in the process. She and Raj would return one last time this season to remove, bag, and document the clumps of hair. Selena stilled as a shadow passed over them. She looked up. Gyrfalcon. North's America's largest and most powerful. It wheeled silently in the air high above them. As she watched the bird, another movement entered her peripheral vision. Her gaze shot to the ridge. Her heart kicked. A man. On the cliff. Dead still. Watching them.

Selena rose slowly to her feet, shielding her eyes against the glare.

"Raj," she said quietly, "on the cliff."

He glanced up, also wearing his mask.

"Over there." She pointed. "Someone's watching us."

Raj squinted into the sun, then opened his pack, took out his binoculars. He focused his scopes into the sunlight. And burst out laughing.

"What!?"

"Inukshuk," he said, cackling even louder. "Whooo hooo. The stone man is coming to *get* yoooo, Apodaca," he said.

She grabbed the scopes from him. He was right. It was an inukshuk—made from slate-gray tundra rocks stacked one upon another to form the image of a man. The longer arm of an inukshuk pointed down toward them. Selena panned the binoculars slowly across the rest of the ridge. "I swear I saw something move," she snapped.

She'd felt it, too. A sense of being watched. The same eerie sensation had been dogging her back in the village for the last few weeks. But she could see nothing up there.

She handed the scopes back to Raj and repositioned her 12-gauge pump action shotgun so it was within easier reach on her pack. Flagging their most recent trap on their GPS device, they set out to cover more miles and lay more traps. Some time around lunch they heard a helicopter nearby. Then the world fell silent again. It was around 3:30 p.m. when the sky suddenly turned black. The temperature drop was instant.

Dense fog rolled in from the lake and tiny snowflakes materialized in the cloud. They donned merino-wool hats. Selena zipped her jacket up to her chin and drew her hood over her hat. She disliked the way the hood and fur ruff dulled her awareness. It made her feel vulnerable. Disquiet began to hum inside her.

Another few miles into their hike and the snow started coming down heavily, settling fast on the ground. Visibility was near zero. Wind whipped and moaned through rocks. Tension twisted in Selena. She kept glancing up at the top of the cliff, but it was hidden by fog. They reached a slight basin near the rock face, and halfway across it, Selena stopped and took off her gloves to check her GPS. This was the place. This was where he'd said she must do it.

Ahead of her, Raj halted, waiting for her to catch up.

"Go ahead," she called. "I'll just be a moment."

It was their unspoken signal for a bathroom break. Raj hesitated, then moved forward, cloud swallowing him almost instantly.

Selena set down her gear. Hurriedly, she fumbled to open her pack. She removed the bag inside, emptied the contents into the snow. She then took a second bag from her pack, and did the same a little closer to the cliff face, allowing parts of the contents to fall between big rocks. Her mouth was dry. Her hands trembled.

A trickle of stones down the cliff face suddenly made her freeze.

She looked up, listened.

Just wind. Making a soft susurration in the rock formations. It sounded like words . . . *Sssin . . . ssssave you . . . sssssave Selenaaa . . .* Snow whirled in a sudden gust around her. Wet flakes touched her face. Her heart boomed against her rib cage.

Marcie Della's words slithered through her brain . . .

They are shape-shifters, part wind, part wolf, part man . . . merciless with hearts of ice. They come on the breath of winter . . . fly at you like a sudden, screeching storm . . .

She shook herself. Marcie's stories *were* getting to her.

The wind whispered again . . . *ssssave you, Ssseleeena . . .* and with the sound came a strange smell. So subtle she could barely detect it. She snapped around to face it, search for it, drawing air deeper into her nasal passages with sharp sniffs. She caught it again. Sweet. Yet putrid.

Then she heard it. Another clatter of rocks.

Sweat prickled her skin.

Something was definitely up there. Very slowly, her eyes fixed on the spot where she'd heard the rocks, Selena reached for the gun on her back. She clicked off the safety.

She aimed blindly at the spot. Fog thickened. Snowflakes grew fatter. Fear, raw, rose up her throat. She waited for the warning huff of a grizz, the swipe of a clawed paw against earth.

But nothing moved.

Even the air seemed to grow more still.

Yet she could feel it—a crawling damp, a presence.

"Raj!" she yelled. Then, "Go away, bear!" She rose to her feet. *Make yourself look big.* "I'm not fucking going to be eaten by you, you hear me, bear! Raj!! Where in the hell are you!?" Her voice cracked as something sounded *behind* her. She spun around, muzzle leading. "Where the fuck are you, you damn animal?"

She opened her mouth to scream for Raj again, but before she could utter a sound, it hit her like the blow of a baseball bat to the base of her head. Her skull cracked and her body whipped forward. She tasted coppery blood leaking from her nasal passages. She seemed to hang for a moment in air as time stretched, then she crumpled to the snow like a puppet with snipped strings. Her face smashed into the ground. The impact sparked her vision with pinpricks of light and blackness. The shotgun slipped from her limp hand. Her brain told her to grab it back, roll over, curl into a ball, protect her soft organs, but her body was disconnected from her mind. Another blow thumped down on her back. Air exploded from her compressed lungs. She felt the sharpness of claws raking open her jacket, tearing her flesh off in ribbons. She felt the wetness of her own blood. But no pain. With every ounce of her will she tried to move. But she was paralyzed. Neck broken. Her body was pulled backward, her face being dragged through snow and dirt. Her mouth filled with dirt, blood. Her teeth scraped against rocks.

Then she was being rolled over like a limp doll. Her head flopped back. Her eyes faced the sky.

Confusion screamed through her brain as she saw what had attacked her. And as she registered it, she knew. She knew with every remaining fiber of her being. That Evil was real. And it could come at you in ways you could never imagine. The next blow crushed down, tearing open her throat. Blood and froth bubbled out of the hole as she fought to breathe, but couldn't. With her eyes she beseeched for mercy, but knew none would be forthcoming. Another clawed swipe shattered her cheekbone, ripping open her cheek and nose, gouging out her eye.

It was 3:48 p.m.

Nearly ten minutes away from pickup time. Only five more days before she was due back at school. With her friends. Her mom. But as Selena slid into oblivion, she realized she would not make her twenty-second birthday. Perhaps, she thought in an absurd final moment of consciousness, this basin in which she lay beneath the cliff face was one of those "dreaming places" where she should never have stopped to rest, or to empty what she had from those bags . . .

CHAPTER 2

Sunday, November 4. Twin Rivers. Day length: 7:54:59 hours.

Constable Tana Larsson ate her supper in front of the television—leftover moose stew with baby carrots warmed in the microwave. The meat had been a thank-you gift from Charlie Nakehk'o for saving his grandson's life. The day after her arrival almost a month ago, Tana had been learning her way around this isolated, fly-in community when she'd found nine-year-old Timmy Nakehk'o passed out drunk and hypothermic in the rocky shallows of the Wolverine. A local teen had been bootlegging to minors, among others. She'd arrested and charged him, which had made her an enemy of the town's youth right out of the gate, so she was relieved to have at least scored some brownie points with Timmy's grandfather.

Charlie Nakehk'o was a Twin Rivers elder—a spiritual leader with a brown face like a shriveled apple doll. He wore his lank, gray hair in two long braids, each secured with a leather thong. And yeah, he went the whole hog and even tucked a kestrel feather into the end of each braid. A renowned trapper and hunter, Charlie was well respected in this community, and he held sway with the chief and local band council who governed Twin Rivers much in the way an elected mayor and town councilors would. He also contracted as a hunting guide for the swank Tchliko Lodge downriver. Tana figured she'd be in moose meat for months—she still had a freezer full of the stuff. At least her dogs would be happy.

They lay asleep at her feet, one an irascible old Karelian bear dog named Toyon, the other, Maximus, a giant of a malamute-wolf hybrid she'd rescued from a trapper she and her old partner had found dead while on a call north of Yellowknife.

Outside the night was black as pitch, but at least the snow had stopped. It lay about an inch deep on the ground and was developing a fine crust of ice. By solstice next month they'd be lucky to get over four hours of daylight total, depending on cloud cover. She was good with that. She wanted the peace of the dark, the remoteness of the far north. She'd fucked up her life, needed to work some things out, and Twin Rivers had seemed a good place to start fresh. She wasn't so sure now.

This place seemed to possess a sentience, a maleficence, that was conspiring against her efforts to belong. Perhaps it sensed the badness, the shame, in her, and she had yet to prove her worth before she could be redeemed for the big-ass mistakes that had driven her north into the Barrens, to the very edge of civilization.

For starters, this police detachment to which she'd been posted was supposed to be staffed by two full-time Mounties, plus a civilian clerk, but Tana had suddenly been left the lone cop out here. Two nights ago her station commander, Corporal Hank Skerritt, had been medevaced to Yellowknife after shooting off his foot with a 12-gauge pump action. By the time she'd gotten the call and managed to reach Skerritt on the other side of the river, he'd lost a lot of blood. Even so, he'd been manic—ranting gibberish, eyes feverish. She'd had to physically subdue and restrain him before she could call for assistance.

And until the Royal Canadian Mounted Police brass in Yellowknife sent a replacement for Skerritt, that left Tana alone with Rosalie Nitah—the civilian dispatcher—to police a population of three hundred and twenty in a jurisdiction that covered 17,500 square miles. Most of that population lived in the town of Twin Rivers, and a few in Wolverine Falls, a settlement a little farther upriver. But to access the rest of the area, there was only one mode of transport—air—until snow and ice made parts accessible via snowmobile.

Rosalie had told Tana that Corporal Skerritt—unbeknownst to HQ in Yellowknife—had been going quietly and progressively crazy since last winter. It was the near twenty-four-seven darkness and cold that did it, said Rosalie. Followed by the incessant sunlight of summer combined with blackfly swarms that had made him insomniac and driven him totally over the top.

And then there was the larger-than-life lore that dogged the station commander from three years back—Sergeant Elliot Novak. "He's still out there, in the woods," Rosalie had said. "He's gone bush. It's the white-man cops," she'd said. "This place messes with their white-man heads."

Tana, however, might stand half a chance, according to Rosalie, given that Tana had only "half a white-man head," her Scandinavian prospector father's half. Her mother had been Dogrib, a people of the Dene First Nations from the shores of Great Slave Lake. And because of it, Tana spoke North Slavey, which is probably why she'd been given this accursed outpost even though she was pretty much still a rookie. That, and no one else seemed to want it.

Strange things, Tana thought as she stared at the reality dating game show on TV, *are done in the lands of the midnight sun, by men who moil for gold. Or diamonds . . .*

The bachelor on the show held a box containing a massive solitaire diamond as he approached the two final, shivering contestants. Onto which finger would he slip that sparkling stone? Both women appeared as though they might faint awaiting his final choice.

Tana stilled her spoon as the camera panned right in on the diamond. The hard gem winked rainbows. *The enduring symbol of love.* Her eyes suddenly grew hot as her own little diamond ring that she wore on a chain under her uniform seemed to burn against her skin. Her jaw tightened. It was a farce, that shit, a marketing coup if ever there was one—eternally linking a cold, hard stone to love, and guilting every man into buying his woman one. Why was she even watching this crap? Because it was on TV, that's why, and there wasn't a remote to be found in this tiny police building apartment, and she was too exhausted to get up and change the channel manually. Plus . . . it did have that voyeuristic, salacious thing going on. The voiceover was saying how this solitaire was as "pure as the cold Canadian tundra from whence it was mined."

"Now, that right there is another marketing coup," she said to her dogs.

Toyon cocked an ear, but Max didn't bother.

Diamonds were expensive to mine in the frozen north. The terrain was vast and inaccessible. Labor was expensive. Yet the stones that came out of this tundra had to compete on the same global market as diamonds that were produced far more cheaply in places like Africa, India, Vietnam, or China, so local entrepreneurs had sought ways to add "value" to the Canadian gems. The result was a government mandate that ten percent of all diamonds mined in the Northwest Territories must be cut and polished here, instead of being shipped to India, which processes about eighty percent of the world's diamonds.

This had brought jobs and a huge diamond-related industry to Yellowknife, Tana's hometown on the shores of Great Slave Lake.

Somaba'ke—the Money Place—Yellowknife was now called. And today, at the end of the small airport runway in Somaba'ke, sat Diamond Row—a series of low buildings that housed artisans who hunkered at long benches, shaping and polishing the rough stones, putting facets on them that turned them into brilliant, sparkling gems. These folk were employed by jewelers like Tiffany & Co., and they came from around the world, places like Tanzania, Mauritius, Armenia, India. Most became Canadian citizens.

And onto every gem polished locally, microscopic images such as polar bears and maple leaves were laser-branded, and each of those branded diamonds was then given a serial number, along with a government certificate, stating that it had been mined, cut, and polished in the Canadian north and was thus "conflict free."

No blood on *these* stones for your loved ones.

No horrific wars financed with *that* engagement ring on your finger.

No child labor. *And* you had a piece of paper to "prove" it.

Diamonds were also the choice of currency for terrorism and organized crime. Which is why Tana knew about diamonds. When the first big mines started producing in the Territories, a special RCMP division had been set up in Yellowknife to police the international crime it had started attracting.

Now there was going to be a mine just north of here, at Ice Lake. And come January, for the first time in Twin Rivers's history, the community would be connected for a short while each year to Yellowknife by an ice road.

And with the ice road would likely come the associated crime.

Already, just the appearance of engineers and WestMin geologists had brought trouble and protests to town. A road would have its pros, though. The police station desperately needed supplies, and a new truck. If you wanted a vehicle out here, you had to Hercules it in at huge cost. The town also needed new equipment for the diesel generator plant that kept them powered off-grid.

But right now, until January, they remained locked in the past. A place where myth and superstition could still crawl out with the winter shadows.

Telling herself that she needed the nourishment, Tana delivered the last spoonful of stew to her mouth. But as she did, her stomach clenched. Quickly, she set the bowl on the side table and put her head back. She closed her eyes, focused on breathing slowly, on keeping her food down. A heavy blanket of exhaustion swamped over her—the kind of bone-weary, mind-fuzzing fatigue that made you feel as though you were trying to drag your limbs and brain through molasses, unlike anything she was accustomed to. Her dogs had already been fed, thank goodness. One less chore.

She rested her socked feet on the back of Maximus and was slowly sucked down into a deep, drug-like sleep. When her mobile beeped through into her consciousness, she woke in a sweat. The room was cold. The television flickered with some wildlife documentary. Confusion chased through her brain. Her phone beeped again.

She leaned over, clicked on the lamp. Her phone was on the kitchen counter. Next to her gun belt. Beside the bar stool over which she'd draped her bullet-suppression vest. Apart from her boots, belt, jacket, and vest, she'd been too tired to remove the rest of her uniform. She shoved herself up onto her feet, but before she could take a step toward the kitchen, her stomach heaved. Tana stumbled wildly to the bathroom and hung over the toilet bowl, where she threw up in racking heaves, holding her hair back. Her phone bleated again in the kitchen. She swore. Grabbing a towel, she wiped her mouth and made for the kitchen counter and snatched up her phone. The call had been routed through the emergency dispatch number downstairs, part of an automated phone tree system if someone needed a cop outside regular office hours. Even at full staff complement, Twin Rivers RCMP did not offer twenty-four-hour policing.

"Constable Larsson," she said.

"This . . . Markus Van . . . security manager at West . . . camp."

"Can you speak up?" she said loudly. "You're cutting out."

The voice came louder, slower. "Marcus Van Bleek. There's been a wolf mauling. North end of Ice Lake." The accent was thick and guttural. Afrikaans. It had become a common sound in Yellowknife ever since De Beers arrived. She'd heard it here in Twin Rivers, too—De Beers prospectors snooping around the WestMin claim and staking out adjacent land, no doubt.

"One victim?" she said.

"Two. Biologists. Both dead. Pilot found them, but couldn't land . . . thick fog in Headless Man Valley. Bodies . . . still out there."

"And he's *certain* there were no survivors?"

"She. Pilot is a she. And Jesus, not a chance. I went in there myself on ATV with one of our camp guys. Four wolves were scavenging what was left. We shot the wolves dead. But the place . . . like a slaughterhouse. Bodies eviscerated. Head torn off the female—face half eaten. I reckon the attack happened at least a day ago, if not two. The kids had been forced to overnight because of the fog."

Her stomach lurched again. She eyed the bathroom, beads of perspiration pricking on her forehead. "Did you leave anyone out there to guard the bodies, protect them from further predation?"

"All due respect, ma'am, there's nothing left to protect."

Shit.

There was *always* something left to protect. Her brain raced. She was going to need a coroner. That would take hours from Yellowknife. Even longer if the fog held up. While she waited she'd have to secure what was left of the remains herself, assess the scene, file her own police report.

"You got a GPS location for the site?" she said.

Van Bleek gave the coordinates. Tana managed to reach for a pen and paper and jot the details down without throwing up again.

"Look," Van Bleek said, "you might be able to fly into camp tonight. Cloud cover is high, and we can light up the airstrip for you, but no pilot is going to fly you into Headless Man Valley. Fog is socked in there like frozen pea soup."

She glanced at the window. Black outside—the kind of complete darkness that could only come in wilderness miles away from any urban lighting. "What about ATV? You said that you got in there on quads?" she said.

"Ja, we can get you partway in on ATV, but the last couple of miles you'll need to hike. Too steep, rocky, narrow for wheels. Slick with ice, new snow. I can have some four-wheelers gassed up and ready to go. I'll guide you in myself. But you better bring backup firepower because that gore is going to bring in more animals. We've been having a problem with some of those wolf bastards getting aggressive with guys at our camp."

Probably because you've been feeding them . . .

Tana signed off and dialed Oskar Jankoski, a local pilot under contract to fly for the RCMP.

No answer.

She cursed, killed the call. She'd have to go out to his place and find him. There was only one other fixed-wing pilot in town, Cameron "Crash" O'Halloran, a rough, commando-style bush cowboy whom she suspected was behind the booze smuggling and all other manner of minor legal transgressions. Possibly major, too—local rumor had it he'd once killed a man, and that's why he was hiding up north. He wasn't even her last resort.

Her heart thumped a steady drumbeat as she buckled on her duty belt and strapped on her bullet-suppression vest. She retrieved her sidearm from the small gun safe in the adjoining bedroom, checked her rounds, and holstered it. Never again would she leave her sidearm unsecured. She'd learned the hard way, was lucky to still have a job, but had lost everything else.

She whistled for her dogs, flicked off the upstairs lights, and started down the wooden steps to what served as the police station.

She opened the outside door and let out her dogs. While they did their business, she filled their water bowls, and grabbed her to-go backpack, which included survival gear. She selected a rifle, shotgun, and ammunition from the gun room plus bear bangers, air horn, flares. Mentally she ran through her checklist while pulling snow pants over her uniform and stuffing her arms into her fur-ruffed down jacket. Donning her lined boots and regulation muskrat hat with warm earflaps, she snagged her gloves off the side table. She opened the door to call for her dogs. They came bounding in, fur cold to the touch.

Before leaving, she called the RCMP operational communications center in Yellowknife, reported the attack, gave coordinates, and requested a coroner's team. Twin Rivers was connected to the outside world via a North-Tel satellite communications system. A large dish in the communications enclosure outside received satellite signals that were then converted and relayed to a small cell tower, which in turn broadcast to a tiny cellular network in town. Outgoing calls operated in reverse. Internet, television, and radio signals were transmitted the same way. However, their local network remained only as good as a clear line of sight from the dish to satellites in orbit. Heavy snow, seriously foul weather, technical malfunction could all knock them off-grid entirely.

"Be good now, boys," she said, giving each one a ruffle and a kiss. "When Rosalie comes in she'll feed and walk you, okay?"

Hurriedly, she gathered her gear, clicked off the lights, and locked up behind her.

When she'd arrived in Twin Rivers they'd given her a tiny log cabin closer to the river, which she'd really liked, but when it became apparent that she'd have to man the fort herself until reserves arrived, she, Toyon, and Maximus had moved into the apartment above the station usually reserved for the station commander.

Outside the air was brittle. High clouds obliterated the stars. It was minus eleven Celsius. She fired up the truck, loaded her gear, and headed for Jankoski's cabin on the outskirts of what passed for town. Her wheels crunched through the frozen snow crust, headlights poking twin yellow beams into the blackness.

CHAPTER 3

"Jankoski," Tana yelled as she banged on his door with the base of her gloved fist. No answer. She banged again, louder. "Jankoski!" A dog barked somewhere.

Tana tried the door. It was unlocked. She creaked it open, stepped inside. The place was hot, reeked of stale booze. She flicked on the living room light. And there he lay, passed out on the sofa. Shirtless, hair mussed. A day or two's worth of growth on his face.

Two whiskey bottles on the floor. One empty.

She swore. "Wake up, you loser." She prodded him with her snow boot. He cracked open an eye. It took him a moment to pull her into focus. "Tana, hey, whassup?"

"You're shit-faced." She kicked at the empty bottle, sending it spinning across the wood floor. Fury rode her hard. Memories, bad ones, reared ugly heads. "No bloody respect for yourself, you know that? Or the job. You're supposed to be on fucking standby. We got a call."

He struggled into a sitting position. His skin was slick with sweat. He stank. Tana winced as her stomach did a dangerous little lurch.

"What call?" he said.

"Fucking loser," she muttered as she stormed toward the door.

"Wait!" He scrambled to his feet, swayed, and grabbed for the back of a chair. "I can handle it. I'm coming—"

"Like hell you are." She slammed his cabin door shut in his face, stomped down the wood stairs, and climbed into her idling truck. The cabin door was flung open behind her. "Tana!" he called into the night. "It's a one-off, okay, no need to report this, right?"

She gassed the engine and spun her wheels, kicking up a spray of snow crystals as she took off in the direction of the airstrip. Anger thumped through her veins. Along with all sorts of other feelings and fears she did not want to articulate. A guy just didn't sit down and consume a bottle and a half of spirits and was then still able to talk if it was a "one-off." She had no time for that. Wanted to have no sympathy for him. Bastard was putting her head in a place she did *not* want to be.

The tree-lined track that led to the small airstrip and hangars was eerily silent, shadows lurching in her headlights. She caught the occasional glimpse of animal eyes glowing green in the dark. She drew up outside Crash O'Halloran's house behind the "airport."

Tana sat for a moment in her truck, watching his house, thinking of Timmy, feeling as though she was about to strike a deal with the devil. But it was either him, or fail to get out to the wolf attack site tonight.

Tana banged on O'Halloran's door, praying she'd find him in a better state than Jankoski. The door opened almost immediately, startling her. Warm light spilled out into the night. His dark-blond hair stood on end. He wore a tight, long-sleeve tee. Tattoos poked out from the base of his sleeves. His jeans slung low on his hips. He grinned, and it put dimples into his rugged, weather-browned cheeks, amusement into his light-green eyes. He reminded her of a scarred and cocky junkyard dog. An edginess crackled through her. Because he intimidated her. Just a little.

Then she glimpsed Mindy Koe in the room behind him, snuggled on the sofa, watching TV. Mindy saw Tana's keen and sudden interest.

The girl gathered a blanket around her shoulders, got off the sofa, and exited the living room.

Fuck.

Tana glared at him. "You sober?"

"Unfortunately."

"'Unfortunate' is exactly what I'd use to describe both you and Jankoski," she said. "I need a flight. WestMin mining camp. Can you get me in, stat?"

He studied her face for a moment. His eye contact was brazen, intimate. Tana held her ground, resisting the urge to blink, or swallow.

He glanced skyward, scratched lazily at his stubbled chin and neck, and then looked toward the small wind sock billowing gently at the end of his porch.

"It'll have to be a straight in and out," he said. "Several storm fronts approaching. First wave could punch through before morning."

"You can leave me there, fetch me tomorrow once it's clear."

"*If* it's clear," he said. "What's with Jankoski?"

"He's unavailable."

A slow, sly smile creased his face. "Let me get changed. Then I'll get the ol' Beaver girl warmed up." He closed the door in her face.

Tana cursed under her breath, removed her gloves, and fumbled with her cell phone. Wind was already increasing, tiny crystal flakes beginning to prick her cheeks. Coyotes yipped in the woods, their cries rising in pitch and excitement. She wondered what had been killed as she pressed the Dial button. When her call picked up, Tana said, "Rosalie, I'm flying out with O'Halloran—been a fatal wolf mauling north of the WestMin camp." She gave Rosalie the details, then said, "I might not make it in tomorrow. Can you look after my boys, let them out, feed and water them? Their kibble is in the kitchen upstairs, moose meat in the fridge. I've left the door to upstairs unlocked."

"No problem." A pause. "So, where's Jankoski?"

"He no longer works for us."

"Was he wasted again?"

"Again? So he's a drunk? Why did no one tell me?"

"Most people out here run into trouble with liquor now and then, Tana. Who's going to take his contract—Crash?"

The man who likely flew in the illegal alcohol that almost killed Timmy Nakehk'o. The man who has an underage woman in his house right now. Not on her life.

"We'll find someone. This is a one-off. He can send you the bill."

Crash exited his door dressed in an antique leather bomber jacket lined with shearling. He wore an old leather flight cap and metal-rimmed goggles perched across his brow. He brushed past her. Not a word. She turned in his wake and saw that the back of his jacket sported a faded cartoonlike image of a big-breasted, naked woman with wings. *He was dressed like a freaking World War II pilot?* She watched as he made for the airstrip and unlocked the gates that opened into the fenced-off runway area. He paused.

"Coming, Constable? You can park next to the hangar."

Tana muttered another curse under her breath and crunched toward her truck. She drove around to the hangar while he ran through his exterior flight check and opened the cargo door. He folded the back passenger seat forward, hopped in, and helped load her gear up into the barrel chest of the de Havilland Beaver. It was mustard yellow with a fat burgundy stripe down the side. Cartoon teeth had been painted around the prop. It looked heavy. It looked capable of eating a smaller Cessna or Super Cub for snacks.

"You sure the WestMin strip is long enough to land this thing?" she said.

"You want to take all this gear, you're going to need this plane," he said as he took the bag containing the electric fencing from her and stuffed it into the back. He held out his hand for her backpack, to which she'd strapped her shotgun and rifle. "Might not have quite the short-takeoff or landing performance of a smaller bird, but it handles comparably to a Super Cub or Helio." He met her gaze. "You can of course use Jankoski, if you prefer."

She hefted her pack up toward him in silence. He stashed it, and said, "Go around to the passenger side and jump in. Headgear is on the seat." He closed the cargo door in her face.

Tana inhaled deeply and went around the plane. She climbed in, seated herself in the copilot seat, and put on the earphones she found there. The cockpit was tiny, spartan, and cold. When he took the pilot's chair his arm butted up against hers.

He began to work the wobble pump manually in order to pressurize the fuel lines. It clunked like a primitive crank. Then he pressed the start button. The engine whined and coughed like a car engine struggling against a flat battery to turn over before it caught. He gave it throttle and the whole plane shuddered and rattled to life. Tana wondered if Jankoski, even in his state, might have been a better bet with his Cessna.

O'Halloran taxied out into position at the end of the runway.

"So, where's the old flying outfit from?" she asked with a nod toward his jacket, trying to distract herself as the engine built rpms and the Beaver shook at the seams to be let go.

"My grandfather's. He was shot down over Holland."

"How'd you get his gear, then?"

"They gave it to my dad, after my grandfather's body and wreck were found by some Dutch school kids. My dad also became a pilot. Taught me to fly when I was fourteen."

"That's her age, you know?" she said.

"Who?"

"Mindy. She's only fourteen. Did you know that?"

He glanced at her, something dark and fleeting in his face caught by the cockpit lights. A slow grin curved his mouth, setting those dimples back into his weather-beaten cheeks. "Is *that* what you think?"

She said nothing.

"Mindy and I are just friends." He drew his goggles down over his eyes and suddenly looked every bit the Black Devil, or the Blond Knight. Or whatever a battle-worn, World War II flying ace was supposed to be named. All he needed was a silk scarf. "Besides, you don't look a whole lot older than her yourself, Constable."

"If I catch you," she said quietly into her mouthpiece, "I swear, I'll put you away. Statutory rape."

He shot her another glance. Heat seemed to crackle off his body. It was tangible. A warning. "Is that right?" he said.

"That's exactly right," she said into her mouthpiece.

"What happened at the mining camp—why do they want you?" he said as he let his plane rip onto the snow-covered runway.

"Wildlife incident," she said, pressing her hands tight against her thighs.

"What kind?"

"I'll know when I get there."

He watched her face for a moment, as if measuring her mettle, and she wished to God he'd just watch where he was going.

"Ready, Constable?"

"As I'll ever be."

And the Beaver lifted, barely, just getting enough height for her fat belly to miss the tips of the black spruce that lined the end of the runway.

"So here's the safety drill," he said as they chugged higher into the sky and banked north into the black, endless emptiness. "Survival equip is stashed in back. Unless it's scattered all over the ground." He gave a dark chuckle.

Tana closed her eyes and concentrated on not throwing up. And she tried not to think about where he might have gotten his charming nickname.

CHAPTER 4

Out of the blackness a smattering of lights emerged at the tip of a lake that gleamed like a sheet of dark glass. Below that inky water lay the kimberlite cores of diamonds, and on the south shore perched the WestMin exploration camp.

O'Halloran brought his Beaver in low, aiming for a strip of lights demarcating the runway. The wings wobbled wildly in a sudden downdraft that blasted from the cliffs to the east. Tana's heart surged into her throat. Her grip tensed on her thighs as the ground yawed toward them, snowflakes hurtling like asteroids into the windshield, the prop sending a staccato beat across their line of vision. But O'Halloran steadied his plane just in time. Wheels touched frozen whiteness with a *snick* and they bounced, and bumped and slid down the runway.

At the end of the strip, near two Quonset hangars, a man and a woman huddled in jackets beside an ATV, their faces ghostly under the harsh, white lights of a generator-powered, portable floodlight tower that stood nearby.

O'Halloran taxied off to the side and brought his chunky Beaver to a stop. It was snowing lightly, wind currents from their plane making flakes shimmy in laughing circles as if in celebration of their landing alive.

Tana removed her headset, opened the passenger side door, jumped down. O'Halloran went into the back, opened the cargo door, and started to hand her gear to her. As she took her heavy pack, rifle, and shotgun from him, a small, wiry man approached with a spiderlike stride that made him appear canted to one side.

"Harry Blundt," he called in a high-pitched voice, thrusting his hand forward as he neared. Tana set her pack down, shook his hand. His grip was cold, dry, vise tight. He vibrated with an electrical intensity. The woman he'd been waiting with remained near the quad. She'd turned to watch a big, burly guy who was carrying gear out of the hangar.

"I'm the camp boss," Blundt said, moving from foot to foot as if cold, or simply unable to keep still. He stood a head shorter than Tana, far shorter than she'd expected for a man preceded by such larger-than-life tales. But she recognized him immediately from the media. Blundt had been variously described in reports as awkward, hyperactive, uber-intense, ADD, but a brilliant geologist–treasure hunter from the interior of BC. He was the man who'd discovered the diamonds beneath Ice Lake while De Beers and other major mining outfits had deemed this area barren of the precious gems. If Blundt's WestMin mine panned out, if he managed to secure all the requisite government approvals and investment backing, he was on his way to becoming a very, very rich little man. His intense, dark eyes bored up at her from inside their deep-set caves below a thatch of gray brow. He reminded her of a beetle.

"Constable Tana Larsson," she said, pulling on her gloves. Her breath clouded in front of her face. She reached up and took her pack with the electric fencing from O'Halloran, set it down on the hard-packed snow with the rest of her gear.

"Markus is prepping to take you in," Blundt said. "A terrible thing to have happened. Terrible. Markus has one quad all juiced up and safety checked already, busy on the other. He's my security man, top guy, good, very good, ex-African mines, here, can I carry something for you?" Words shot out of Blundt's mouth and tripped over each other at a machine-gun clip. Tana had read about his idiosyncratic, staccato-like speech, how he jumped from one topic to another as if his mouth couldn't keep up with the speed of the ideas firing in his brain. It could drive a person nuts, she'd been told.

She'd heard also about how ruthlessly Blundt drove his crews. He never tired himself, and he expected no less of others. He'd even worked his fourteen-year-old son to the breaking point. The resulting clash had been legendary. Harry Blundt was quite simply a Northwest Territories and Yukon diamond legend, not much different from the idiosyncratic characters of old.

Tana hefted her pack onto her shoulders, and glanced up at O'Halloran. He still had another bag of hers to hand down.

"Go ahead," he said. "I'll bring over the last of this stuff."

She hesitated, then said, "Thanks."

"The attack site is about three hours north of here on quad," Blundt said as he led Tana in his crablike scuttle toward the waiting ATV and hangars. The woman stood smoking, watching them approach.

"Northeast side of the lake is the only really navigable route up Headless Man Valley. Bit rocky, some swampy muskeg halfway in, where a river feeds into the lake. That part can be tricky, but it should be mostly frozen by now. Then it gets steep. Big boulders up to the esker ridge. Slick with snow and ice right now. Will have to trek the last section up to the cliff base where Heather found them. Terrible, terrible thing. My guys shot four of the wolves. Probably more scavengers there now." Blundt's gaze darted up to Tana, then went to her shotgun and rifle. "You came alone?"

"I'm all there is."

"Terrible thing," he said, again, and Tana wasn't sure whether he meant the attack, or the fact she was solo.

Hard snow squeaked under their boots. The air was sharp, a brisk breeze coming off the water, trailing wisps of mist in behind it.

"Did you know the victims?" Tana said. "Anything you can tell me about them?"

"Selena Apodaca and Raj Sanjit. Both early twenties. Working on the grizzly bear DNA study for EnviroTech, part of the environmental assessment study required of us before the territorial government will sanction construction of a full-scale mining operation here. Regs have gotten tighter since the big Ekati and Diavik finds. We'll have to drain most of Ice Lake for the open pit, see? Best way to get at those kimberlite pipes. They're wide pipes, open pit is the way to go with those. Could affect habitat, wildlife movement through the Headless Man corridor. Selena and Raj were flown out Friday morning by Heather—that's her waiting just up there by the four-wheeler—with a K9 team doing a wolverine study. Elusive things those wolverine. Legendary creatures of the boreal forests. Like ghosts—you know they're out there. You see evidence. Hardly ever see them, though. A vicious predator and scavenger belonging to the weasel family. Known for physical power and quick temper. This is the last place in North America you find them, up here. The Barrens. Extinguished everywhere else farther south. Incapable of adapting to habitat loss, see?"

"You mean, these environmental teams could be finding evidence of rare wolverines, grizzly habitat, which would impact your application?"

"Something like that. Everyone either wants their chunk of a new and potentially massive diamond op, or they want to stop it, so no one else can have anything. Bastard business this. Funny people, humans. Now it's the natives, the aboriginals; they're saying there's old burial sites out there somewhere, bones of cultural significance, but you know what? They won't say *where* the goddamn sites are. Claim they are family secrets to be held close to family chests. How are we to protect *secret* sites, eh? Just take their word for it that they're there? Back in the dark ages, when an Indian on the trail of a caribou herd got sick, they just left the poor bugger to die. He could try to catch up, of course, otherwise he kicked the bucket, and the wolverines ate him. Nature's recyclers—eaters of the dead is what they're called in the indigenous languages of this area. Bones. Christ almighty. Probably bones all over the goddamn Barrens."

Tana winced inwardly. PC was something Harry Blundt had apparently never been accused of.

"This is Heather MacAllistair," Blundt said as they reached the woman and ATV. The burly guy was now inside the hangar using a jerry can to gas up a second quad. He glanced up, met Tana's eyes, but gave no nod of greeting.

"You must be the new cop," MacAllistair said, dropping her cigarette butt to the snow. She ground it out with her boot and reached forward to shake Tana's hand. "Nice to meet you. Sorry about the circumstances."

Heather was tall and striking. Thick blonde hair. Wide-set blue eyes, wide mouth, chiseled cheekbones. The kind of features cameras made love to. But she was also visibly shaken, her complexion sheet white. Her hand was dry, cold. Strong grip.

"You're the one who found them?" Tana said.

She nodded and tucked her bare hands one under each armpit of her down jacket, shivering slightly. "The teams were forced to overnight both Friday and Saturday. I couldn't get in for the scheduled pickup Friday afternoon. Heavy fog. Zero visibility. It's a tricky area with the cliffs if you can't see where you're going." She cleared her throat, her blue eyes watering in the sharp air. Tana noticed they were bloodshot. Her breath smelled of booze. "Selena and Raj were good to hunker down and wait out the weather—had gear. It's EnviroTech protocol, and the teams had done it several times before." She cleared her throat again. "The first weather gap, a tiny one, came around noon today, and I took it. I managed to get in and collect the K9 team first—Veronique and Dean and their two dogs. We then flew to the lake site, but Selena and Raj weren't there. I tried to raise them via two-way radio. No answer. No response from their satellite two-way text system, either. So we went in low, looking—" Her voice caught. She wiped her nose with the back of her hand. Tana noticed they were work hands. Calloused and chapped from the cold. Something about those hands made her like this woman. "That's when we found them."

"What time was that?" Tana asked.

"Before 1:00 p.m."

"And what did you see?" Tana said, guiding her forward.

"They . . . blood all over the snow. Entrails, body parts, ripped clothing. A pack of four wolves was feeding on them. I tried to buzz the animals off. They retreated, but returned right away."

"And you didn't land?"

"No," she said. "There was nothing we could do for them at that point, anyway. And the weather window was closing rapidly, fog coming in dense again." She looked down at her boots, taking a moment, then her gaze met Tana's and held. "I feel terrible. If I'd landed, yes, we might have been able to kill the animals, but we'd also have been stuck out there, until who knows when. And without contact. Our radios are two-way—range is minimal. So, I thought it best to fly straight here with the K9 crew. Get them warmed up. And I knew Harry had satcom equipment that could reach you guys so we could report it. We couldn't get a signal right away because of the weather, so Markus and Teevak went out there themselves. Markus managed to get a call through after they returned—the very dense, low cover had lifted a bit by then." She rubbed her hand hard over her mouth. "They were two of the nicest kids."

"And there was absolutely no chance there was a survivor when you first reached the attack site?"

"Shit, no. No fucking way. Those kids were ripped apart, gutted, disemboweled. The head was off the . . . Selena's head had been ripped right off. I . . ." Her eyes gleamed. "Sorry." She swiped hard at her eyes with the base of her wrist. "I've seen action, horrible death in Iraq, Afghanistan. Libya. Men and women blown apart after stepping on an

IED. I've transported them out of the heat of battle. But this . . . something about wild animals tearing you apart like that. Just meat. Eaten while still alive. Bears will do that—start eating you before you're dead. Wolves, too, while you're still conscious of the fact."

A chill snaked down Tana's spine at the thought. "You're ex military?"

"US Army. Medic. Got my pilot's license there. Flew several tours. Afghanistan, Iraq. Libya. Quit and came north about seven years ago."

PTSD, Tana wondered. She was constantly looking for signs of it, since Jim.

"Has their employer, EnviroTech, been notified?" she said.

"Yeah," Blundt interjected. "I managed to get hold of their project manager about an hour ago."

"And the K9 team—where are they now?"

"They flew back to Twin Rivers already. I had a supply plane leaving, so we put them on it. It was their last week on the job."

"Have you got a way to contact them for me while I head out?" Tana said to Blundt. "Ask them to remain in town until I can get a statement from them?"

Blundt and MacAllistair exchanged a glance. "Sure. No worries," he said.

"And which WestMin employee went with Markus Van Bleek to check out the site—who shot the wolves?"

"Teevak Kino," Blundt said.

"And where is Kino now?"

"Flew out with the rest of my crew about thirty minutes ago," Blundt said. "Whole bloody lot has gone, apart from our camp cook, and Markus, and me. One of my guys is getting married, see? So I let them all have a few days to go blow off some steam in Yellowknife. We'd already downscaled the camp for winter mode, and we're all basically in a holding pattern until the new ice road punches through in January.

Then we kick into full gear and can start hauling in major equipment, vehicles, supplies we'll need come spring."

The quad inside the Quonset hangar grumbled to life. Markus revved the engine, and drove it over. "Constable," he said, dismounting. His eyes were dark, unreadable. He possessed a watchful, animal stillness, a guardedness that Tana found slightly unnerving.

"You're the one I spoke to on the phone?" she said.

"Ja. Markus Van Bleek." He did not offer his hand. "I'll be taking you in." He reached for her pack. She hesitated, then handed it to him. He dumped it onto the carry rack of the quad he'd brought over, then reached for the bag of electric fencing that Blundt was holding. He began to secure it all to the rack with straps.

"I'm afraid I haven't got anyone else to go with you right now," Blundt said, watching Van Bleek. "You sure you don't want to wait for daylight?"

"The bodies of two kids are being scavenged as we speak," Tana said crisply. "I need to preserve what remains of them until the coroner can get in."

The trio exchanged glances, and Tana felt distinctly unwelcome.

"I'll come with you," MacAllistair offered suddenly. But Tana took her arm and drew her quietly aside.

"You been drinking, Heather?" She spoke low.

"Jesus, just a few whiskies. Who *wouldn't* after seeing that shit? Like I said, military is one thing, but those kids—"

"Get some rest, okay?" Tana said. Civilian safety was her priority, and although MacAllistair seemed stable on her feet, she definitely smelled like she'd had one too many. Eyes showed it, too. "I'll need an official statement from you, too. Please remain at the camp until I return. If the forecast holds, the coroner should be able to get in by daybreak—"

"Forecast is irrelevant." Irritation laced her tone now. "Headless Man has its own weather. It's the topography, the cold lake, the warmth from the muskeg swamps, the cliffs—it can make for dense fog where the skies are clear everywhere else."

"We'll hope for the best, then."

MacAllistair eyed her, a wariness showing in her features, a subtle hostility in her eyes at being challenged. Tana got this a lot. She was a very young, female cop in a vast wilderness that rewarded independence, freedom of spirit, that attracted a rough breed of cowboy—women as well as men—strong people who tended to eschew bureaucracy, including the arm of the law. Civic trappings like running water, sewer, electricity, grocery stores, and the security of calling 9-1-1 for help were not high on a true northerner's radar.

"Fine," MacAllistair said quietly. "I'll wait. But if you're trapped out there for any length of time . . . I got work to do. I fly for Boreal Air, and there's a last rush on before the serious meteorological stuff hits in a few days and we'll be socked in for God knows how long. My base is in Twin Rivers. I rent a place from Crow TwoDove. You can find me there."

As MacAllistair spoke, O'Halloran approached them with the last of Tana's gear, snowflakes settling on his World War II jacket.

"Thanks," Tana said, taking her bag from him. "You can clear out if you want. I might be a while."

"Gee, thank you, officer."

"I need your number, though. To call for a return flight. Otherwise, I might be able to catch a ride with the coroner's crew."

He inhaled deeply, stuck his hands in his pockets and looked away for a moment, as if debating something, then said, "Look, I don't fly for the Mounties. I got my own living to make."

"This'll pay."

"I don't need *your* pay."

Damn him. He was going to make her beg. "Could be a long-term contract," she lied. She doubted he'd even clear the criminal record check required for him to become a contracted civilian to the RCMP.

But she sure as hell could use him until they did send someone up here to replace Jankoski.

"Told you, don't want it."

Their gazes locked. Wind, snow gusted. She needed to get going. She could hear Markus firing up his quad. Seconds were ticking. "Send me your invoice for tonight, then." She turned and walked toward the waiting ATVs. As she did, she heard MacAllistair say to O'Halloran, "I saw you out there Friday, Crash. Saw your bird parked just on the other side of the cliff from where those kids were working. Around lunchtime when I was flying another crew."

"Wasn't me."

Tana slowed, her interest suddenly piqued.

"An AeroStar 380E—bright red? How many of those around?"

"I said, it wasn't me."

"*Had* to be. I tried to raise you on the radio."

Tana set her bag down, lowered herself into a crouch. She began to retie her bootlaces, straining to catch the rest of their conversation.

"Like I said, must've been someone else, maybe hunting, prospecting. An AeroStar is one of the most economical ways of getting around."

"I know. I bought a kit myself, secondhand off a guy up in Inuvik. Untouched. I'm pretty much done building the thing, but I'm having issues with the sprag clutch. I was hoping to bounce some ideas off you."

Tana moved on to her other bootlace. Van Bleek was revving his engine, getting impatient. Urgency crackled through her.

"Well, give me a shout when you're back in town," O'Halloran said. "We're probably going to be grounded in a few days. I'll come out, take a look then."

"We ready to roll, Constable?" Van Bleek yelled.

Snow was coming down heavier now. Swirling fat flakes, dense mist creeping up from the lake, strangling lights with ghostly halos.

She gave a thumbs-up sign, got to her feet, hurried over. Strapping her last bag onto the quad, she removed her muskrat hat, tucked it down the front of her jacket, and donned the helmet and goggles Van Bleek had left on her seat. He'd also left the engine warming for her.

He pulled out ahead of her quad, his headlights bouncing off fog. "Stay right up my ass," he yelled. "Some tricky navigational shit ahead."

They trundled toward the black lake, mist swallowing them. Something made Tana glance back over her shoulder.

O'Halloran was standing like a ghostly silhouette against the brightly lit maw of the hangar. Hands in pockets. Just watching her.

Unease feathered into her chest.

Crash watched the young Constable Tana Larsson disappearing into the fog with Van Bleek and a dark, inky feeling sank through him. With it came tension. Resentment. A strange sense of time running out.

Van Bleek was dangerous, depending on who was asking, and who was paying. But so far as Crash knew, if his information was correct, the cop should be safe alone with him in the wilderness, at least for tonight. And as long as she wasn't stepping into Van Bleek's scummy pond.

He swore, spun around, and marched back to his plane. Last thing he wanted—needed—was to worry about some rookie cop's little ass.

He was long done worrying about people.

Besides, she was a law enforcement officer. It was her choice. She needed to handle the work that came with the territory. And yeah, sometimes cops lost. And got killed.

Part of the job.

Not his problem.

CHAPTER 5

Tana picked her way carefully up the slick incline that led to the esker's south ridge. Her breath rasped in her chest and it billowed like smoke in the glow of her headlamp. Temperatures had been falling steadily as she'd followed Van Bleek's ATV into the silent maw of Headless Man Valley. And they continued to drop as she stepped gingerly into the boot prints left by Van Bleek as he hiked ahead of her through the snow-covered boulders like a silent Cyclopean monster with his head-mounted spotlight leading the way.

A cliff loomed somewhere in the fog to her right. She couldn't see it, but felt its skulking presence.

Despite the cold, sweat pearled and trickled between her breasts. Her pack was heavy. Her regulation flak vest underneath her down jacket, secured tightly with Velcro strips, did not offer good breathability. It had a dense, claylike consistency, and with each step up the hill it pinched the flesh between the bottom edge of the jacket and her gun belt where her stomach was growing chunky. The vest alone added an extra five to ten pounds to the overall weight she was lugging. She'd been fatigued and feeling off-color to start with.

They'd abandoned the quads down along the shoreline when the trail had narrowed and grown too steep to negotiate with wheels.

According to her Garmin, they should be reaching the top of the esker ridge any moment now. From there they should be able to see down into a valley that lay at the base of a cliff where the bodies had been found.

She stilled suddenly as her hairs prickled up the back of her neck. Something was off.

Then she heard it. A faint, rising howl. Distant. She listened as it rose into the primordial darkness. It was joined by others, escalating in a crescendo. A sound so wild, so haunting, it never failed to ripple chills over Tana's skin. Especially now, thinking of what they were eating out there. Her pulse quickened as the howls were answered by several yips, then a long, drawn-out moan from the opposite direction. She felt as if they were surrounded by wolves out there in the dark somewhere.

Van Bleek, up ahead, also stilled to listen.

"Must be another pack or two, coming in for the kill," he called down to her.

Tana turned in a slow circle, her headlight making shadows leap and snowflakes attack out of the dark. There was something else giving her the chills, not just the howls. She could feel it—something right here. Watching them from the fog. Something heavy and silent and malicious.

She swallowed.

Van Bleek resumed his hike up the trail. Tana studied his hulking silhouette as he moved into the distance, trying to catch her breath, to recapture her calm, her control. The man moved with the quiet, coiled, watchful efficiency of a hunter, she thought. A predator himself—as if completely unafraid and in tune with this wild terrain. Tana didn't trust people who had no fear. Fear was normal, a survival tool. She knew the wilderness, too. She could hunt with the best—had learned from her dad, on those occasions that he'd saved her from her mother and taken her with him, before vanishing for months again, years even. Tana knew fear. Of many kinds. And out here, she was keenly aware that she was a fragile human, with limited night vision, vulnerable against a pack of wolves working in concert from the fringes of darkness. Or any other animal that could see in the night.

She started after Van Bleek before he vanished entirely into the mist, and she mentally channeled her thoughts onto the tasks that lay ahead. It bolstered her, gave her a renewed sense of purpose.

Another ten minutes or so into the hike, and a small stone clattered noisily down the rocks to her right. Tana froze, breathing hard. Her heart thumped a steady *whump whump whump* of blood against her eardrums. Slowly she moved her head, panning her headlamp over the area where she'd heard the noise. But her beam was useless. It bounced back off the fog instead of penetrating it. The sense that something was out there, hidden just behind the wet curtain of mist, intensified.

Another rock clattered down the slope. She jumped, and became acutely aware of her rifle and her 12-gauge pump action on her pack.

"You okay down there?" Van Bleek called.

"Heard something."

He ran his headlight across the slope. Twin orangey-red glows suddenly bounced back. *Shit.* Tana's stomach jerked.

"Bear!" she yelled, reaching for her shotgun. She shook free her gloves, put gun stock to shoulder, heart jackhammering. She curled her finger around the trigger. Mist swirled, and the hot orange orbs vanished.

But it was still there. Just hidden.

She sighted down the barrel at the spot where the glowing eyes had disappeared, her body anticipating the explosive impact of the bear. If a grizz charged now, she was toast. At this distance, with this visibility, she was unlikely to stop the animal before it was on her, even if she did place her slug just right. Stones clacked to her left.

She swung her gun after the sound, sweat breaking out on her brow under her hat.

"Can you see it?" she yelled.

Van Bleek panned his light slowly across the slope again. Silence was suddenly suffocating. Bears were cunning predators. It could have stalked around behind them. Could be anywhere.

Time stretched.

"I think it's gone!" Van Bleek called from above. Tana waited another moment, then reluctantly lowered her weapon and put her gloves back on. But as she did, out of her peripheral vision, she caught a shadow. She tensed, spun. Her movement caused her boot to slip on a layer of ice underfoot and she went down hard, smacking her elbow into rock. Pain speared up her arm, stealing her breath. Her gun dropped and slid down onto a lower boulder. *Fuck.*

Van Bleek turned his spotlight on her.

"You need a hand?"

"I'm fine," she snapped, blinking like a mole into Van Bleek's beam. "Get that light off me so I can see." She reached down to retrieve her shotgun, frustration riding her hard. She held onto that emotion, used it to beat back fear before it beat her. "Rocks are slick," she said as she heaved herself back onto her feet under the weight of her pack. "Why don't you aim that damn thing where the danger is instead of at me, huh?" Van Bleek was watching her, waiting for her to gather herself.

"I'm fine." She dusted snow off her pants.

He hesitated. "You sure you're not hurt?"

"What part about 'fine' did you not hear?"

He eyed her a second longer, then turned and resumed his climb. But he'd dropped his pace noticeably.

"No need to slow down on my account," she yelled after him. "I said I'm *fine.*"

He had the audacity to chuckle softly. Smug asshole.

It was 11:40 p.m. and snow had stopped falling by the time they crested the ridge. They heard them first. A wet snarling, snapping, growling. Crunching. The sound of animals feeding on flesh. Bones.

Human flesh and bones.

Van Bleek made a rapid sign for her to lower herself. She crouched slowly to the snow beside him.

"See?" he whispered, pointing. "Over there." Tana blinked, her brain trying to process what she was seeing in the darkness.

Shapes. Shadows. Animals—the wolves, she couldn't tell how many—were fighting and tearing at what she reckoned were the bodies of Selena Apodaca and Raj Sanjit. Bile rose up into her gullet. "Sweet Jesus," she whispered.

"What do you want to do?" Van Bleek said.

"Scare them off those kids," Tana said without hesitation. From her breast pocket, she removed two little pencil rocket launchers, gave one to Van Bleek. She handed him flare cartridges. "Take these. I want to see how many animals are down there, and what kind." She screwed a flare cartridge into her own launcher, using the light of her headlamp to see what she was doing. "You go first," she said. "Try to fire into the air right above them. Then I'll shoot mine."

Van Bleek shot off his flare. He aimed true. It exploded into a mushroom of bright pink cloud above the massacre. There was a yelp, squeals. Some of the wolves retreated, but two big ones stood their ground over their kills—wet, foaming, bloody mouths as glowing eyes looked in their direction. A kick of fear shot through Tana's adrenaline at the aggression she saw in the alphas' postures. She fired her own flare farther to the right of the one Markus had expelled, in the direction several animals had run. Her flare exploded with a massive crack above them, frizzing brightly into the mist. The canines cowered, but this time they did not flee. Five in total that she could see. One of the two alphas and a smaller wolf slinked back to the carcasses.

"They're not going anywhere," she said quietly. "They've been emboldened by the blood."

"And the taste of human meat," Van Bleek said quietly.

Tana slid her rifle out from her pack. "You take those two big ones on the left," she said, focusing through her sight on the carnage below. "I'll start with the animals on the right."

They fired, reloaded, fired, and launched more flares. Like soldiers on a ridge they worked in concert to slaughter the pack. Below, wolves cried, yelped. Snapped. And fell. The killing was over in minutes. Silence was suddenly deafening. She could smell the sulfurous powder from the flares. Tana's heart boomed. Sweat slicked her body. A kind of pain burned behind her eyes. "We had to do it," she whispered more to herself than Van Bleek. "They'll need those animals for necropsy. They've eaten from those kids' bodies—they've been acclimated to human flesh. We had to kill them all."

Van Bleek remained silent beside her, just staring down into the valley as the light from their flares dwindled and flickered out. Darkness closed around them. Tana swiped the back of her glove over her mouth. Her hand was shaking. "We need to get down there," she said. "Before more scavengers come. Need to secure the remains of those poor kids."

CHAPTER 6

"Looks like a bloody butcher's shop," Van Bleek said, panning his beam over the slaughter.

Or big game kill . . . apart from clothing and other gear that had been shredded to ribbons and littered the site. The snow had turned pink and red and was all chunked up. Wolf carcasses lay among the remains of the two humans. Rib bones gleamed through dark red, wet flesh. Bits of human meat and innards congealed in the subzero temperature. Entrails tangled across the snow.

Tana moved toward the closest human body, careful to minimize her own tracks by making only one line of footprints both in and out of the main kill area. But it might prove futile since the entire site appeared to be tracked out with both boot and animal prints, along with other drag and pull and scuffle marks. The boot prints were likely Van Bleek's and Kino's, left when they came to shoot the first pack of wolves.

The stink in the air was thick, heavy. It smelled of sweetish, raw meat, and it was underlaid with the corroded green copper tang of blood. An odor of violent death, never forgotten once you'd smelled it before. A memory slammed into Tana—finding Jim in the bathroom. She inhaled sharply at the impact of it. Mistake. It forced a whiff of punctured bowel deep into her nostrils, and her stomach heaved violently.

She doubled over, trying to control herself.

"Here," called Van Bleek. "This is it. The decapitated head." He bent down to take a closer look.

"Step back," she commanded.

He glanced at her, blinding her with the spotlight on his head.

"Christ, keep that thing out of my eyes. Stand up, and get away from that. Don't touch or step on *anything*. Back out the way you walked in. Go around to the base of that cliff over there," she said. "Keep guard from there in case any animals come."

Her brain reeled. Assess. Contain. Control any further contamination until daybreak. After which she could inventory the whole thing—photograph and document it.

He stood in balky silence for a moment, his breath heavy white steam under the glow of his headlamp.

"And you?" he said.

"I'm going to string two electric fences up. One around each body."

"Body parts are fucking all over the place."

"The . . . main parts." She cleared her throat. "Go, please. Now."

He hesitated a moment longer. "Yes ma'am."

She watched until he'd made his way to the base of the cliff. When he'd positioned himself and was panning his light into the fog in search of animals, she returned her attention to the massacre.

What was left of the body closest to her she determined to be Raj Sanjit, although most of his face had been chewed off. His hair was matted with gore, but it appeared to be black and cropped short. A hand, partially torn from an arm still attached to the body, looked dark-skinned in the light of her headlamp.

His stomach was gone, vital organs rich in nutrients hollowed out, leaving a cavernous, glistening maw beneath his rib cage. Tana moved to the other body. Her stomach recoiled violently.

Only a ragged stump with bone and gristle remained where the head had been. The rest of the torso was mostly eaten. Inside the ripped-open rib cage, the body cavity was empty. The heart gone, just a bit of lung left.

Tana panned her light over to the decapitated head.

It lay facedown. Ragged neck stump. Skull gleamed through torn scalp. Long hair, lighter in color. Frizzy looking.

Selena Apodaca.

Near the head was something pale blue. Part of a woolen hat. An eyeball was stuck to it.

Tana puked almost at once, stumbling to the side. She tried to stop herself, but nature's urge was uncontrollable. Seized by cramps, she bent over, bracing her hands on her knees, and she threw up again, and again. Until all she had was the acid burn of bile in her throat and mouth, which made her stomach clench all over again. Heaving, sweating, she waited for the cramps to pass.

"You okay out there, ma'am?" came Van Bleek's voice.

She swore like a trooper and swiped the back of her sleeve across her mouth. "Fine."

I've gone and puked my DNA all over a fucking scene—so, yeah, I'm great. I'm doing fucking just swell . . .

"Want me to come over?"

"Stay where you are. Keep covering for us."

She retched one more time. Tana cursed again. She could usually control herself. But her body was no longer her own. She was being commandeered by this tiny thing growing inside her womb. Even out here, even among all this blood and death and pointless gore, it was asserting its presence, reaching determinedly for life. And Tana's own will to survive—for her baby—was so sudden and sharp and fierce that it stole her breath.

She took a moment to marshal herself, planning how best to tackle this.

One of her fences would cover an area of about twenty-seven square feet. Not much. But it was better than nothing, because if the wolves, or bear, returned before dawn, the electrical jolt would give them pause. Enough so that she or Van Bleek could shoot.

And in case of more snow, she'd need to get the small tarps in her pack covering those torsos at least.

The fencing was going to take a while to set up. Which was fine—better than sitting and doing nothing but staring at this mess in the dark and waiting for more predators. Carefully, she retraced her footsteps, retreating to an area where she could set down her pack. Shadows leaped in the mist as her head moved with the lamp. A bird, probably an owl, swooped low, *fwopping* wings in the dark. Tana glanced up, saw the big shadow, then it was gone into the darkness.

A feeling of cognizance hung in its wake, a sense of being watched by unseen eyes.

She glanced at the cliff. Van Bleek's shape hulked at the base under his headlamp. A chill snaked down her back. That man felt no safer than a wild predator. Tana shook herself. It was fatigue. Hormones. Blood sugar. It was the violence that seemed to scream in the silence. The fact that she'd been forced to slaughter so many beautiful wolves who'd just been doing what they were programmed to do—stay alive. Hunt. Eat meat.

She first unpacked the two small tarps. Tana walked carefully back to the bodies, and covered them gently. She returned to her gear, crouched down, removed her gloves, pocketed them. Fiddling with bare fingers in the cold, she unstrapped the bags of electric fencing and assembled the poles.

When she had all the poles assembled, she carried them to the gutted torsos and poked the first pole into the ground, struggling to find a soft spot between rock and stones. She got it in at a good thirty-degree angle, moved on to plant the next stake. Once they were all in place, she unspooled the thin wire and affixed it pole to pole with clips. It was finicky work and her fingers grew painful from the cold.

An hour passed before she was able to connect the batteries and make her two fences live.

Once she'd finished, Tana circled around to join Van Bleek, who sat on a rock under the cliff face, gun resting in his arms. His hunting spotlight was planted on a boulder beside him, pointing out into the dark night.

She clicked off her own spotlight to conserve batteries, and seated herself beside him. It was almost 1:00 a.m. Monday morning. They had another seven hours at least until the beginnings of faint dawn light. If and when the batteries from Van Bleek's spotlight failed, she'd have hers as a backup.

Hours ticked by. The night grew colder. Quieter. No more animals came. It was as if word had gotten out—this was a bad place.

"First time you seen real blood and gore, Constable?" Van Bleek said quietly.

"I've got a bug."

Silence.

"Flu or something," she said. "It's going around. Rosalie—our dispatcher—her grandkid has it." Why was she even justifying herself? She didn't have to lie to anyone. She needed to embrace this, feel proud. But holy crap, she'd thought the "morning" sickness would have quit by now. She was five months in. And heaven forbid that *anyone* should ever grow so inured as to *not* be sickened by a scene like this. Or was it just a sign she'd never be a good cop? Never make homicide detective someday?

And it made her wonder about Van Bleek.

"How about you?" she said.

"I lived in Africa." He offered nothing more, and she didn't press.

She leaned back against the cold rock face, wrestling with her doubt demons. The night always brought the demons. They got off on mocking her lack of self-worth. They laughed in her face, and said, *ha ha, little half-breed, you think a badge and uniform and gun will prove to the world that you're not the abused offspring of a drunk hooker? You think people won't know how your mother beat you when she was wasted? You think you are* worth *something, you little slut—apple never falls far from the tree, Tana Bee . . .*

She cleared her throat. "You want to catch some sleep while I keep first watch?" she said.

"Don't think either one of us wants to risk sleep tonight," he said quietly.

He was right. Even though no scavenger had approached, there was a sense of them lurking, just beyond sight—wolves. Bears. Coyotes, maybe. Foxes. Wolverine, even. She'd throw out another flare in about an hour, just to see what was out there. Warn whatever off. She had several flare cartridges ready. Bear bangers, pepper spray, an air horn, too.

Wind soughed, moaned in the rocks. A wolf howl came over the hills. Answering cries sounded from a far-off pack. Communication. Wild style. Informing of the kill in Headless Man Valley. As the world tilted toward dawn, air currents began to shift, as if the earth was stirring, getting ready to wake.

"You do hunt, right?" Van Bleek said after a long period of silence. "Your sort all hunts."

She shot him a look. "My *sort*?"

There was a glimmer in his eye. He was toying with her. "Oh, you mean Natives."

He chuckled.

She let it slide. Gallows humor took odd shapes.

"I hunted with my father," she said after a while. "Since I was five. That was the first time he took me away."

"Away?"

"I mean, out into the wilderness, for several months. I don't know exactly how long." The image of her dad filled her mind. Big, strapping

Norwegian. Bushy beard. He seemed so very large in her mind's eye. So strong. Even now. She quickly blocked out the other memories that she knew would follow—the reason he'd taken her away that year. "He taught me how to track. He was a prospector, an illegal trapper. He did whatever kept him off grid and alive in the bush."

"So, the daughter of a man who walked on the wrong side of the law becomes a cop."

She said nothing.

"And your mother?" he asked.

"She was Dogrib, the Native, yeah."

He waited for her to say more, but Tana kept quiet, thoughts churning unwillingly, inexorably, back toward her mother.

"So," he said after a long period of silence, and she almost briefly liked him for distracting her, "I take it that you've seen enough animal kills over your lifespan, at least—what's your read here. Something a bit . . . off about this one?"

"Off?"

"Like . . . weird. Like not normal."

"Never seen a human mauling. Nothing normal about that."

"You know why they call this place Headless Man?"

"I'm sure you're about to tell me."

"Two prospectors were found a few miles southeast from here, in the twenties, sitting with their backs leaned up against a cliff face, just like we're doing. Fully dressed. Boots on, packs and picks and guns at their sides. Only trouble—no heads. Just gone. Just the two torsos propped there like they were having a good old chat. Still had diamonds in their bags."

She turned to him. "They ever find the heads?"

"Nope."

"How'd the heads been removed?"

"Ripped. Clean off. Bodies all intact, just those heads torn off their stumps."

She swallowed. "Legends," she said, voice thick. "They have a way of growing larger than the reality that inspired them."

"I dunno. I tell you, there's bad juju in this valley. In these rocks. I can't explain it, but you can feel it. Even in the hot summer sun, you press your bare palm to these stones, and you can feel it. Like it's transferring into you. Cold shit. Black shit."

"I wouldn't have taken you for superstitious, Van Bleek."

He snorted. "Lived long enough in central Africa, some very deep and dark places, to know that there is sometimes more than meets the eye. On those edges of civilization, the Congo, sometimes . . . boundaries are crossed that you don't understand."

"What did you do in Africa?"

"Diamond mines. Security for De Beers."

"Is that what brought you out here—De Beers?"

"Ja. Worked up at Snap Lake."

"And then what, you defected to Harry Blundt? He recruit you?"

"Something like that."

"Blundt isn't worried about having potentially inserted a De Beers spy into his midst?"

He gave a low, guttural chuckle. "Everyone in this business worries about spies, Constable. It's diamonds. Canadian ones, at that—the cleanest currency in the world. It's why Blundt hired me to head up a security team from the get-go, before he's even got approval for the mine. That kimberlite core he's testing, if you watch the industry news, you'll know that he's onto some of the strongest pipes in the north. This whole place is going to change."

Yeah, starting with that new ice road come January.

Tana's thoughts turned reluctantly to the tiny diamond ring she wore on a chain under her uniform, the futility of it all.

Around three in the morning Van Bleek's spotlight failed, and Tana clicked hers on. Temperatures dropped even lower. She was grateful for the earflaps on her muskrat hat, the big hood of her parka, her long-john underwear, and her insulated waterproof pants. Even her bullet-suppression vest was welcome now. Wind came up, carrying scents from miles across the arctic. It whispered in the rocks above them, telling stories of other kills. Downwind, noses would be rising to meet it, and waffling softly, catching and reading the scents.

She drew her knees in, trying to keep out the creeping cold. At least the mounting wind would clear the fog out of the valley.

"Death by dogs," Van Bleek said softly, staring at the small tarps Tana had draped over what was left of the bodies. "One of the worst ways to go, if you ask me, being ripped apart while alive like that. At least a lion will break your neck and kill you, quick and quiet, before it starts eating you."

"Maybe the wolves didn't kill them," Tana said quietly. "Maybe something else got them first, a bear perhaps, then the wolves chased it off and took over. We'll know more after the autopsies."

CHAPTER 7

Monday, November 5. Day length: 7:49:11 hours.

Crash took his Beaver low, following the silvery course of the Wolverine River to Tchliko Lodge. The day had dawned cold, clear. It was 8 a.m., the sun twenty minutes out from cresting the horizon and painting the snow in shades of gold and pink and orange. Everything was fucking perfect, but even so, he struggled to get the feel of his old Zen back. He felt a niggle, a darkness closing in, something coming. And he was thinking of Tana Larsson out there in Headless Man Valley, alone with Van Bleek and those dead biologists. She—the whole attack thing—had knocked him off kilter. It was nothing he cared to articulate beyond the fact that he was just not as free to do as he pleased before she'd come bashing on his door asking for a ride.

    I swear, I'll put you away. Statutory rape . . .

He gave a snort. *That's the least of your troubles, hon . . .*

    The lake stretched up ahead, gunmetal gray against the snow. Clouds of steam roiled from hot tubs set into wooden decks outside log cabins that were strung along the lakeshore. Smoke coiled from two of the main lodge building's stone chimneys. Everything about the Tchliko estate was designer rustic. Super high-end.

Crash brought his chunky baby in, touching her wheels down neatly on the airstrip that was better maintained than most he'd landed on in the north. Prevailing winds came off the lake. And far out on the water, beyond a peninsula of forested land, he saw whitecaps. A sign of the coming weather, the first big-ass snowstorms of winter. He'd have to get the plane's skis on soon.

As he taxied to a stop, he saw Alan Sturmann-Taylor making his way down to the strip to meet him. Sturmann-Taylor was a giant of a man with a shock of prematurely white hair atop a handsome, angular face with striking, deep-set blue eyes. He came to a halt at the edge of the strip and stood facing square into the icy wind, a colorful Nepalese scarf flapping about his neck. A trophy from one of his Everest trips, no doubt. We all had them—trophies. Whether they were stuffed animal heads, scarves, trinkets, Instagram photographs, locks of human hair, kids' baby teeth. They all said: I was there. I did this. This is *my* Story. My triumph. My bravery. My ownership of this thing. We considered serial killers creepy when they kept mementos from their victims, like body parts, and when they touched those mementos again and again in order to relive the emotional thrill of their kills. But really, it was no different for the rest of us.

As his prop slowed to a halt, Crash removed his headset, opened the door, and jumped down onto the hard-packed snow of the runway.

Two employees in lodge uniforms came running to unload the delivery he'd brought for the lodge. Crash threw the guys a salute, and opened the cargo door for them.

"How are you, mate?" Sturmann-Taylor said as he approached, arms open wide. He hugged and backslapped Crash with manly bravado, his hands big as hams, muscles like a logger's. His dress was "Patagucci," as Crash liked to call it—technical designer adventure gear. Expensive.

"Good, good," Crash lied. "Chamonix trip worth it? Decent skiing?"

"Some of the best I've had. Lost one of our guides to an avalanche, but Christ, what an experience. C'mon up to the lodge while the boys offload. You had breakfast?"

"Coffee would be great."

Sturmann-Taylor led the way up to the lodge building with his hearty stride. Whether it was conquering the Amazon, fly-fishing in Patagonia, tracking with the San bushmen in the Kalahari, crossing the Sahara on camel, or racing in the Dakar, Sturmann-Taylor drummed the beat of Adventurer, and he walked the walk. He was a psychologist turned big-shot investor with a passion for all things fine, and an intellect to match his bank accounts. It didn't hurt that he'd come from serious money to start with.

"Got a new group in, I see," said Crash, nodding toward where he could see Charlie Nakehk'o near the shooting range with several men in keffiyehs atop their camo hunting gear.

"Two new groups, in fact. The Saudis have come for grizzly bear. The other group is here for our new cultural experience. It was a huge success last year, everything from wild cuisine, foraging in the forest with our gourmet chef, locals demonstrating traditional ways and crafts. Sweat lodges and drumming. A lot of the wives are signing up while their better halves go after the blood experience." He chuckled and held open the big door. "Of course Charlie is our main draw for the hunts. That man makes a small fortune in tips."

They entered the lodge, and Sturmann-Taylor ordered espressos from his "butler," who Crash pegged as his bodyguard. The man was a cipher. Expressionless. Ex-Israeli special forces. Built like a street fighter. He had a quiet physicality, and he was carrying concealed—that much Crash had deduced some time ago. Not legal in this country—not without complicated permits, or professional reason. Like being a cop. But then, this part of the world was out of sight enough that it operated by its own rules. Or rather, it was neglected enough that it *had* to forge its own rules. Wild style.

It's why he liked it.

It's why a man like Sturmann-Taylor had built his lodge here. Why he flew his international clients in here—his sheiks, and businessmen and their prostitutes, his political players, actors, financiers, dealers of darker arts. Out here they could indulge their fancies—a private gentleman's hunt club, so to speak. And discuss business. Sturmann-Taylor showed Crash into the library. A row of French doors looked out over Tchliko Lake. Most of the wall space was lined floor to ceiling with bookshelves, many of which held antique leather-bound first editions. A fire crackled in the hearth. Persian rugs in rich, red tones covered the polished wood floor, and the heads of dead animals mounted on the remaining wall space watched with glass eyes.

The butler delivered the coffees. Sturmann-Taylor closed the door behind him.

"You've never told me his name," Crash said.

"Yes, well, I like my staff to remain in the background. It's an integral part of the lodge experience. Did you manage to secure it?"

Crash opened the lapel of his jacket and removed a packet. He set it on the antique table, picked up a small espresso cup and saucer. He took a sip. It was rich and bitter. Turkish and very good. He perused the bookshelves, sipping his coffee while Sturmann-Taylor opened his packet and crushed the buds of dried cannabis between thumb and forefinger. He inhaled the aroma.

"Ah," he said. "Perfect."

Crash said nothing. He angled his head, reading the titles of several hardbacks. Collectors' items. All of it had been flown in. He imagined this place was insured to the hilt. Security was top of the line, and very discreet. He'd been checking it out bit by bit on each visit, building a picture.

Sturmann-Taylor opened a drawer, took out his cigarette rolling papers. He began to fashion himself a joint, grinding the buds between his fingers and picking out stalks. He'd said before that he found this old-school process meditative, preferable to using trendy vaporizers. Crash set his cup and saucer down beneath a photo of Sturmann-Taylor and his second wife. He removed a book titled *The Minotaur*.

"Careful with the spine, don't pull the books out by the spine."

Crash rolled his eyes in the privacy of his turned back. He flipped through the pages.

Sturmann-Taylor licked the end of the paper, sealed his joint. He flicked his lighter and lit his joint, inhaling deeply. He held his breath.

Keeping himself busy, Crash replaced *The Minotaur* and selected a book titled *The Hunger* from the shelves. He opened the cover. On the title page was an old-fashioned ink drawing depicting a creature that looked like a man crossed with a wolf. Cadaverous body with prominent ribs and hollowed-out stomach. Huge, blackened teeth that dripped blood. Gnarled talons for fingers held a decapitated woman's head up by the long hair. Blood dripped from the ripped neck of the head. The head's eyes were missing from the sockets and part of the cheek had been clawed off.

He turned the page, read the poem.

> *In the Barren ground of the soul*
> *nothing can grow.*
> *For here is bitter and cold where*
> *the sun hangs low.*
> *Where a midnight caribou mutilation*
> *awakens a howl of emptiness with ice*
> *where once there was heart.*
> *And it comes with hunger*
> *for blood in its mouth.*
> *For, in the Barrens of the soul*
> *monsters take toll . . .*

Crash frowned, and flipped through the rest of the pages while Sturmann-Taylor exhaled slowly, then grinned like an old movie star who'd never lost his star quality or mojo. "Really is the good shit. I'll need more. Lots more."

Crash snorted. "Might have to play it low-key for a while. New cop in town. She's already been on my ass for flying in liquor. Damien, the jerk, flogged it to a kid who nearly died."

"A female cop?"

"On a lone crusade to clean up Twin Rivers, God knows why. Few enough pleasures out here as it is for some of these guys. She's made herself some enemies right out the gate."

Crash read some random text in the middle of the book about a small hunting party in the Barrens with a Voyageur guide.

"This is set locally," he said with surprise.

"It is, and it's set in the past. A horror novel written right in this lodge, by one of my first and subsequently most regular guests. He comes each winter now, to polish his final draft-of-the-year."

Crash glanced at the name on the spine. "Drakon Sinovski?"

"Pseudonym. His real name is Henry Spatt. Not so romantic—or *horrible*—as Drakon, eh?" He took another suck on his joint. "Just seeing him in the flesh, you'd never guess he had this dark shit in his brain. Then again, you never can tell a killer just by looking in his eyes." He exhaled smoke around his words, pointed his joint at the book. "Sold over one million copies worldwide that one did. Next ones never took off quite so well. And those masks above the fireplace there—" He motioned to several wooden masks all painted in bold reds with black and white, gaping mouths, and reeds for hair. One was a double-headed crow with a squarish beak almost the length of a short man's arm. Another looked as though it might be sporting real human hair.

"They're gifts from Henry," he said. "All from the West Coast. They depict various cannibalistic creatures of North American indigenous lore, like the *Tsonoqua*. Or the secretive *Hamatsa* cannibal society's terrible man-eating beast with the unpronounceable name of *Baxbaxwalanuksiwe*. Interesting mythos around those, really, because there is often an element of complicity among the victims. And of course, if bitten, they become cannibals themselves. Reminiscent of the modern vampire trope, no?"

The weed was making Sturmann-Taylor loquacious.

"Yeah," Crash said absently, replacing the book. It was not his thing, books.

Sturmann-Taylor chuckled—a kind of self-indulgent, guttural sound that was contagious, and usually made others smile. He took another deep drag, closing his eyes as he held the smoke in his lungs. He breathed out leisurely. "Sure you don't want some?" he said, offering the joint to Crash.

"I quit sucking smoke into my lungs when I quit heroin."

Sturmann-Taylor's eyes turned serious. He held Crash's gaze for several beats. The fire cracked, and a log ember fell in a powdery crash.

"Well, I like it," he said, finally. "Reminds me of my university lecturing days. Got the best pussy during those years. Can I tempt you with another java?"

Crash glanced out of the window. The guys had finished offloading. "I still need to make another run before dark. Yellowknife and back. And one more tomorrow again. Hopefully before that series of storms sock us in. Reckon we're going to be grounded for a week or two."

"We should talk," Sturmann-Taylor said, nipping the live end off his joint. His voice had changed. He was all business. "I might need transport for . . . shall we say, a more sensitive haul than usual."

Crash's pulse quickened. He remained outwardly cool. "Sure. Whenever you're ready, you know where to find me." He returned his coffee cup and saucer to the tray, made for the door. Sturmann-Taylor moved to show him out, but Crash held up his hand. "No worries. I know the way."

The "butler," however, emerged from the shadows outside the door and tracked him to the exit. The man stood silently watching as Crash made his way over the snow-covered lawn to his plane. Crash had walked by the open door of the lodge gym once, and seen the butler with the punching bag. Krav Maga trained, he'd deduced.

Crash readied his plane and taxied into position on the runway. As he gave his Beaver throttle, making her quiver at the seams, he saw Sturmann-Taylor watching from the library window. A sober coolness filled Crash.

It was going to require several more trips out here before he gained tacit entrance into Sturmann-Taylor's inner circle. But he could taste it now—he was getting close.

And if he was right, the ultimate prize would be the raw blood stones heading for laundering at WestMin when the mine opened.

CHAPTER 8

Tana checked her voice recorder and pinned the mic to her collar. It was easier to speak her observations out loud than to try writing them down with frozen fingers. She'd transcribe it all later. It was just after 8:15 a.m. and the sun was struggling like a pale lemon trapped behind glass to rise off the horizon. It wouldn't get far. Its arc would only get shallower and shallower until it barely peeped over at all in late December.

A cold wind pushed through the valley, the sound crisp and sibilant on ice crystals that had grown on snow during the night. The breeze had cleared the skies and she'd managed to transmit a satellite call. She'd been told the coroner's ETA was a few hours out. Her goal was now to document the scene while she waited.

She'd left Van Bleek at the cliff and climbed the opposite esker ridge. From up here she surveyed the scene below with a bird's eye. In the stark light of dawn, the carnage was surreal.

On the cliff ridge opposite her, above Van Bleek, stood an inukshuk. These stone figures were common throughout the tundra. One arm of the inuk was usually created longer than the other, and it would point travelers in the direction they should go, either to find water, or a mountain pass, that kind of thing. Nothing weird there. She took a photo anyway, in an attempt to capture the whole scene. She snapped a couple of the cliff, then of the slaughter below. Wolves lay in a sea of churned-up red and pink snow that was littered with bits of meat, viscera, clothing. Apodaca's head.

Apodaca's and Sanjit's bodies were lumps under tarps inside the electric fences. She captured it all, checked her watch, activated her mic. She stated time and weather conditions, and that she was present at the scene with Markus Van Bleek. In bullet point fashion she detailed how they'd arrived, how they'd killed the wolves, and what measures she'd taken to protect the scene.

"There are nine dead wolves," she said. "Five were shot by myself and Van Bleek around 11:40 p.m., Sunday, November fourth. According to Van Bleek, four were killed by himself and WestMin employee Teevak Kino earlier on Sunday afternoon. Kino was not present at the WestMin camp when I arrived on Sunday night. Boreal Air pilot Heather MacAllistair witnessed four wolves feeding on the victims when she attempted to pick them up on Sunday before 1:00 pm. She believed the wolves could have been the same four that the team saw moving north along the lake shore when she'd flown her clients in on Friday morning."

Tana paused, then added for her own reference. "MacAllistair also apparently saw a red AeroStar helicopter on the other side of the cliff around lunchtime on Friday, before the storm and fog moved in. She believed it belonged to pilot Cameron 'Crash' O'Halloran." She made a mental note to follow up.

Tana studied the scene, trying to develop a mental picture of what had happened.

She imagined the biologists being dropped off not far north of this point. She pictured them working their way to this valley, then the fog and snow moving in. She noted there was no sign from up here that a tent had been erected.

Tana activated her mic again. "There is no immediate evidence that the victims had set up camp for the night. This could mean the attack occurred some time before nightfall on Friday, November second. The animal predation is extensive, and would appear to support that timeline."

She clicked one more photo, then made her way slowly down the ridge.

She stopped at a trail of grizzly bear prints still evident under a fine layer of newer snow that dusted them. Massive bear. Claws as long as her middle finger. The prints led right into the kill area. Some of the grizz prints were atop wolf prints. Others had been covered by canine prints. She was unable to tell which animals had come first, especially given the very fine layer of snow that dusted the trace. She laid a small forensics ruler in the snow beside the tracks, and photographed them. She also documented the various boot prints.

Working in a concentric circle, meticulously recording and photographing as she went, she gradually made her way inward toward ground zero—the bodies. Something made her look up, a sense of being watched—with intent. By the eyes of something hungry. Her gaze went to the cliff, to Van Bleek.

He was regarding her. Still as a stone statue. The hairs on the back of her neck prickled.

The man unsettled her on some very primitive level. Even so, she was grateful for his help. Without him, she would not have gotten in here. There'd have been nothing left of these kids at all.

Tana moved in closer to the bodies, and came to where she'd thrown up. Shame washed through her. She'd fucked up again, gotten her DNA all over the scene. She swallowed her distaste and photographed what she'd done, the words of her old instructor going through her mind— *take pictures of everything, and I mean everything, no matter your thoughts. Something seemingly irrelevant could become important after the fact. In court. Lawyers will pick you apart . . .*

A raven cawed. Tana glanced up. A giant gleaming black bird had perched itself on the outstretched arm of the inukshuk, something long dangling from its beak. She took her field binoculars from her belt, zeroed in on the bird. A ribbon of pale meat flapped from the bird's beak. As she watched, a gunshot cracked the air in the valley. Shock rippled through her body. The feathers exploded from the bird, and it tumbled down dead to the ground.

She lowered her binoculars, heart thumping. Van Bleek stood under the cliff, gun still raised.

"What in the hell did you do that for?" she yelled.

Slowly, he brought his rifle to waist level, and reseated himself on his rock. He glared at her.

Sweat prickled over her body. She glanced at her watch, willing the sound of a chopper to appear in the distance.

Focus. He's not going to shoot a cop . . . you're just getting twitchy . . .

Tana re-centered on her task. She snapped photos of the shredded blue woolen hat with the ripped-out eyeball congealing to the fabric, and then she crouched down to get a better look. Clumps of scalp and long strawberry blonde hair also stuck to the wool. Selena Apodaca's eye, hair. Tana's gaze followed drag marks, prints, what looked like arterial spurt, toward the hump under the blue tarp. Near the hump lay a shotgun in red snow amongst bits of backpacks, a bloodied boot, shredded clothing, plastic, a can of bear spray. And two ripped jerry cans with black stuff on them. The black contents also stained snow around the cans.

What happened here, girl? You were attacked by what? Bear? Or circled by wolves coming in closer for nips as you tried to fight them back? You were still alive—your heart still pumping when your blood spurted like that. Did the animals drag you down, tear at you from all directions as they fought for your flesh while you were still clinging to life?

Tana photographed the weapon, then examined it. Twelve gauge, Mossberg 500A. One round in the chamber, two in the mag. No sign the gun had been fired. She thought of herself last night, those orange eyes staring at her through the fog. Judging by the height of the eyes from the ground and the distance between them, she was pretty sure it had been a big bear. And if it had charged from that distance, she would probably be dead, but she would have fired as it came at her. So what happened here? Something took the biologists by surprise? If the unarmed victim had been attacked first, the other could have fired. Into the air, at least. Perhaps the biologist carrying the weapon was attacked first. Perhaps they'd frozen in fear.

Tana turned in a slow circle, a dark feeling leaking into her. Everywhere wolf tracks crisscrossed big-ass brown bear prints through blood. And then there were the human tracks. She'd need to take a record of Van Bleek's and Kino's boot treads for her report. And her own. And Apodaca's and Sanjit's.

She moved to the decapitated head. Closing her eyes for a second to force her mind into gear, she then photographed it, before getting down to examine it more closely. Tana adjusted her crouching position slightly to ease the irritating pinch of her bulletproof vest under her jacket.

Reengaging her mic, she cleared her throat and said, "The head has been chewed, and ripped off the female victim's body. It's lying about three meters out from the torso. Face down. The tissue at the neck is ragged. It looks as though part of the spinal column is crushed." She cleared her throat again. "The back of the head has been partially scalped, and there is a significant concave depression at the base of the skull. The long hair is matted with blood and clumped with what appears to be viscera. The color of the hair is strawberry blonde, very curly." With a gloved hand, Tana turned the head over, and reeled back.

Her breathing turned rapid. "Down the side of the face are four deep symmetric gouges, or rips. Like a claw mark. The right cheek is . . . has . . . been eaten, and the right cheekbone is crushed. The . . ." She paused, wiped her brow with the back of her sleeve. The teeth grimaced at her like those of a skeleton with no soft tissue to make it seem human. "The right brow bone has been crushed inward. Both eyes are missing."

Just bloody, dark sockets.

Tana stared at the head, once Selena, now grinning sightlessly up at the pearlescent sky. It was unnerving. We were biologically programmed to respond to the emotions in the face of another person, she thought. A smile could be contagious. Grief in the features of another was the same—we could physically feel it. Watching someone cry could make us cry, too. Without the soft tissues of the lips, the expression of the eyes, the essence of what had once made Selena Apodaca human was gone. Tana's thoughts turned to the victim's parents. Family. Friends. Her jaw tightened. She looked away for a moment and sucked in a deep breath of air, thankful for the frigid wind. It helped her breathe without taking in the smell of meat.

Once she'd gathered herself, Tana made her way over to the live electric fence around Raj Sanjit's body. After taking photos of the snow-covered tarp, she disconnected the batteries and climbed over the wire. Tana drew back the tarp, and shock whipped through her.

THE HUNGER

For, in the Barrens of the soul,

monsters take toll . . .

With bloodstained fingers the Reader caresses, oh so gently, the printed words of the poem at the beginning of *The Hunger*. It is night. Candles flicker on either side of the new jar where a fresh eye swims in red liquid. It was such a pretty eye when alive. Sort of mossy green.

A fire burns fierce in the kiln-like stove. The room is a cavern, a dark sweat lodge. Hot.

The Reader sits naked.

The Reader is sated.

For in the Reader's belly is roast heart.

A treat.

For the Reader's birthday. The second of November. A time to lure. The cur. When winter does stir . . . and how perfect that Nature's Gods shined on the exact same day this cycle around. Usually it would be thereabouts. The closest window to the day the Reader was born, ripped from a mother's womb, destroying that which had given birth in the process. Death-Life. Hand-in-hand. A yin and yang . . .

CHAPTER 9

Raj Sanjit's cloudy eyes gazed vacantly up at Tana. His face had also been partially eaten. A section of his arm was gone. Near his thigh lay part of his left hand. His clothes had been shredded away in ribbons and strips, along with skin. One of his boots was off. He'd been disemboweled—the soft and nutritious inner organs likely instinctively eaten by animals first. Tana's gaze followed the loops of intestine trailing away from his body. In the wilds, she knew, especially in the heat of summer, a predator's consumption of the bowels and stomach first would naturally slow a kill from spoiling too fast. It was where the bacteria set in first.

Sanjit had the same symmetrical clawlike gouges down the side of his head, and along his thighs. Tana engaged her mic.

"The animal predation on the male is extensive," she said. "And consistent with the possibility the biologists were killed on Friday afternoon." Whatever had been eating him had been at it for some length of time. She described what she was seeing, and took more photos.

Then she noticed a black substance on parts of his body.

Her attention went to the ravaged jerry cans. She picked her way over to them, and gagged, quickly covering her nose and mouth with her arm before she threw up again. The black sludge appeared to be some kind of lure made of rotted fish and whatever else.

She surveyed the scene again, trying to picture it. The couple had been working with this rotted sludge, likely what they were using to coax grizzlies. It could have attracted a bear, who then stalked them. Or it could have brought in wolves that were habituated to associating humans with a food source.

The wolves might have become bold . . . going for the biologists themselves . . .

Before heading over to Apodaca's headless torso, Tana crouched down and went through the remains of the backpacks.

There was one tent between them, some plastic bags that had been ripped apart for what seemed like nuts and granola. Clothing. Water bottles. A small portable propane burner with a pot. Two mugs. Some ready-to-eat dehydrated camping meals. Notebooks. GPS device, an inReach satellite two-way texting device. Two-way radio. Lip balm with a hint of pink. Tana inhaled, thinking of the young woman who'd brought this vanity with her into the bush. The couple also had with them bear spray and bangers. But none of these defensive tools had been used.

Near the packs lay coils of fine, barbed wire, baggies of what appeared to be bear hair with GPS locations recorded on them.

Tana documented it all, then worked her way over to Selena Apodaca's torso under the tarp.

The first rays of sun washed over the cliff. They held no warmth, but the presence of sun was more welcome than Tana cared to admit.

She stepped over the electric fencing, and photographed the tarp in situ. Not covered by the tarp was part of an arm. A silver cuff inlaid with a jade eagle encircled the wrist.

Tana knew that jewelry. It was the distinctive work of Twin Rivers local Jamie TwoDove. She'd first seen several pieces just like it the day she'd arrived in town, on display under the glass counter at the General Store and Diner. Old Marcie Della had caught her looking, and proudly explained that the jewelry was now being sold in Yellowknife, and in Calgary and Edmonton. American tourists were also buying it in the port city of Vancouver where the big cruise ships left to sail up the inside passage to Alaska.

After documenting the silver cuff, Tana carefully slid it off the wrist. On the inside, a bloodied inscription read: *To Selena, with love, JT.*

JT. That could refer to Jamie TwoDove. She glanced at the tarp. Could he and Selena Apodaca have been romantically involved? Her chest tightened. She'd need to speak to Jamie, break this news before it reached him in other ways.

Carefully Tana drew back the tarp. Her breath caught and her stomach balled instantly.

So badly had it been ravaged, Selena Apodaca's headless body was barely recognizable as human.

The stomach cavity was completely gutted. Pubic area eaten. Thighs had been ripped and clawed apart. Her ribs had been picked of flesh. There was some lung left.

But her heart was gone.

Tana spun around and doubled over as her stomach heaved. Thank God nothing came up—she'd had nothing to eat, barely anything to drink. It heaved again, and sweat broke out over her face. She panted lightly, straining for self-control. She waited for the sound of Van Bleek yelling to ask if she was okay, if only to highlight the fact he could see she was struggling.

To his credit he remained silent.

Taking a slow breath, Tana came erect again. She turned to face the torso. Or what was left of it. Engaging her mic, she described what she was seeing.

". . . Signs of the same symmetrical claw rips on what remains of the body. These marks would appear to indicate a violent bear attack, rather than a bear simply feeding off bodies. It would appear to indicate that the victims fought to their death. It's possible a bear stalked, surprised, and killed them first, then wolves, lured by the scent of the kill, chased off the bear to feed." She was stepping over the line of pure documentation into theory, but to hell with it. There'd been no manual for this shit at depot division. She was not a trained detective. She had very little experience. She was basically a first responder, just covering all bases to the best of her ability under the remote and unusual circumstances.

As in many fatal bear maulings where there were two victims, a bear would commonly attack a first victim, while the second attempted to beat off the animal. The bear then often turned on the second victim, killing him, or her, before returning to the injured first victim.

It was possible the biologist carrying the gun had been hit first. The second tried to help, but had no gun.

A noise chopped into her thoughts. It grew louder in the sky. Her pulse jumped. *Helicopter.* Coroner and body retrieval. Thank heavens. This would become the Office of the Chief Coroner's case now. These remains would be flown to Edmonton for autopsy. The wolves would be taken to wildlife officials for necropsy. Her eyes burned in relief. Her job here was done.

As Tana turned to make her way up the ridge to wave in the chopper, something odd caught her eye.

She bent down.

A bone. Lying partially under Selena Apodaca's torso. Completely devoid of flesh. Porous and white, except where it had been stained with blood.

What the . . .

Tana quickly photographed it. Then, with gloved hands she tried to move the torso. More bones lay beneath it. Old bones—very old bones. Nothing to do with this attack.

The thud of the chopper grew louder.

Tana recorded her find. The bones looked human to her. Femur, tibia. A piece of pelvis? *Shit.* Had these two biologists been killed where others had died before?

The air in the valley started to reverberate with the pulse of approaching rotors, and after being stranded out in the wilderness overnight, in dark and cold, it was the most welcome and human sound in the world.

Tana left the torso and moved quickly to get up the ridge, but she stalled again near the periphery of the slaughter scene. A mottled gray wolf lay dead at her feet. Female. Stomach baggy and teats distended. A mother. Who'd recently given birth. Tana's gaze was held transfixed. There were little pups out there somewhere, waiting in a den for this mother that she'd killed to come home. Emotion ripped through Tana's chest. Her jaw tightened as a fierce passion to survive, to do right by her own child, by all that felt wrong here, seared through her.

Breathing hard, her blood pumping through her veins with an unarticulated anger and drive, she scrambled up the rest of the esker slope, crested the ridge, and shaded her eyes against the low-angled glare of the sun. A red bird, all shimmer and metal and polycarbonate windshield, came in. She could see the pilot in his headgear and mirrored shades, behind the controls. She waved her arm in a slow wide arc, then crouched low, downdraft pummeling her as the pilot brought his craft in. He gently set skids down on the ridge.

Rotors and engine slowed.

The door opened, and a woman jumped out onto the sugary crust of snow. She wore a down parka with fur ruff and a coroner's office logo. Behind her were two guys—body retrieval assistance, Tana guessed.

"Constable Larsson," Tana said, coming forward. "Thank you for coming so soon."

CHAPTER 10

It was already dark by the time Tana and Markus Van Bleek returned to the WestMin camp. Beyond exhausted and starving, Tana hauled her gear off the back of the ATV she'd parked outside the WestMin hangar. Harry Blundt came scurrying toward them.

"How'd it go, how did it go?" Blundt said, taking a bag from her. "You must be hungry. Cook is in the mess—that big yurt over there. Got some stew going. Coffee's on."

"I am famished," Tana said. "Just don't tell me it's moose stew."

"It's moose stew," he said. "Yes, it is. Of course it is."

She laughed in spite of herself, and felt a spurt of affection for this funny little man.

"This way, this way," Blundt said, taking off at a trot. Tana suspected the geologist had only two speeds: High. And off. Like Toyon when he was a pup. She hefted her pack and guns up onto her shoulder, and cast a backward glance at Van Bleek. He was offloading his own ATV.

"Coming?" she said.

"No."

She hesitated. "Thanks."

He grunted. "Any time you need help at a slaughter, Constable, I'm your man."

She held his gaze for a moment, disquiet rustling through her, then she turned to follow Blundt. The sky was that eerie indigo peculiar to northern nights. A green and yellow aurora pulsed softly along the horizon. Her feet ached as she walked. Her lower back felt as though it had been hit with a mallet. Her headache didn't help.

"Your pilot left," said Blundt as she caught up. "But Heather is still here. She's probably sobered up enough to fly you back tonight, unless you want to bunk at camp."

Tana crooked a brow. "Good. I need a statement from her. From you, too. I already got one from Van Bleek." She'd taken impressions of his boots as well. "I'll also need to talk to Teevak Kino."

Blundt stalled in his tracks, looked up at her. "Why? It's a natural death, an accident. Nothing criminal. Is there?"

She looked into his eyes. It was hard to read him, too. Especially in this light. He seemed to be constantly moving, agitated, even while stationary. "I need to file my police report," she said. "Standard procedure in a death that occurs outside of a hospital or doctor's care. The coroner's office will investigate further. There will most likely be a set of recommendations that comes out of it, to help prevent similar attacks in the future."

"Hmm," he declared, then he turned and continued his crab-like scuttle toward the yurt. The circular tent structure was set upon a wooden platform to accommodate the depth of the coming snows. Smoke came out a metal flue vented through the top of the yurt. Tana could smell food. Her stomach growled.

"Where is Heather now?" she said.

"One of the cabins. Sleeping. I'll go rouse her and send her over to the mess."

"She was on a bit of a bender?"

"Could say."

"Regular occurrence?" Tana asked.

"Anything you want to know about Heather, you can ask her yourself." Blundt stomped up onto the wooden deck and reached for the door. Tana followed.

"Your chef didn't go with the rest of the crew to Yellowknife?" she said.

"Cook?" Blundt snorted. "That man thinks he's above them all, he does. Doesn't drink. That's the main problem. All full of native mysticism and whatever other mumbo-jumbo stories. But he can cook, I'll hand him that. And he holds his own as a bouncer when things get rowdy out here. Happens every now and then, when you mix a bunch of guys who've been in the bush too long with some good strong booze. Got a powerful left hook, that Indian."

Blundt opened the door. Steamy warmth rushed out to meet Tana.

"Go on in," he said, putting her bag inside the door. "I'll go rattle Heather's cage. When you're done eating and interviewing her, come find me."

It was hot inside, pots steaming away on an industrial-sized gas stove. She dumped her gear on the wood floor near the door and removed her down jacket. She needed a shower. But more than anything she needed some food and something to drink.

A man stood with his back to her, stirring a pot. He was about six two, wide shoulders. A long, skinny, black ponytail hung down the middle of his chef's jacket.

"Hey," Tana said.

He turned. His face was broad. Flared cheekbones. Pocked, reddish-brown skin. Black eyes. Those eyes consumed her in silence. The pot behind him bubbled noisily.

"Officer," he said, slowly, wiping his hands across his apron.

"Tana Larsson," she smiled. It felt weak. *Everything* about her felt weak.

He observed her a moment longer. She noted a fresh cut and bruising across his jaw. Scratches on his knuckles.

"Harry Blundt said I might be able to find a cup of coffee and something to eat in here," she offered.

"Got moose stew warmed up. Coffee's on the boil. You must be cold. You've been out a while. Take a load off—I'll bring you some grub."

With relief, she pulled out a metal chair and seated herself at the table closest to the counter where he worked. "Whatever you've got will be great."

He reached for a bowl, started spooning in slop. Steam curled. She watched his hands, wondering whom he'd had a dustup with.

"You didn't go with the rest of the crew to Yellowknife, then?"

He dumped the steaming bowl and a spoon in front of her, along with a mug of coffee. "Cream and sugar are on the table, there. And no, not my thing. Big piss-up. Don't do the booze anymore." He paused. "Bad shit, that wolf stuff."

"Yeah." Tana adjusted her sitting position to relieve the pinch from her vest. She shoveled a spoonful into her mouth, closed her eyes for a second, just letting the warmth fill her. "Holy crap," she said, looking up at him. "This is actually amazing."

"Moose."

"Not like the moose stew that *I* make."

He grinned. It made him look scarier.

"So what do I call you?" she asked, delivering another spoonful to her mouth.

"Indian."

He looked serious.

"You must have a name."

"Big Indian. That's my name."

Tana chewed slowly as she weighed him. "Your legal name?"

"Yup."

"Your parents had a sense of humor, then?"

"I had it changed."

"What was it before?"

"I don't say the old name. It belonged to another man. The old me. This—" He prodded his considerable chest with the tips of all ten fingers. "*This* is the new me. Big Indian."

"So . . . I should call you Big, or Indian—which do you prefer?"

"Either." He went back behind his counter, emptied garbage, peels, bones into a pail. "Or both."

She watched the garbage. "Where does that go?"

"Landfill."

"Fenced?"

"Nope."

"So, wild animals—"

"Yup. They scavenge in the dump."

"Wolves, too?"

He swung suddenly around to face her. Intensity smoldered in his eyes. The interior of the yurt seemed to shrink. Tana stopped her spoon halfway between bowl and mouth.

"Yup," he said slowly, quietly. Deep voice. "Wolves. Bear. Coyotes. Fox. Ferrets. Eagles. You name it—those noble creatures—they *all* eat the garbage dumped in there. The men, they been feeding those same four wolves by hand, too. Last summer, when the crew sometimes ate on the deck outside, when the bugs weren't so bad, they'd toss scraps to the animals right from where they sat. And at night, I seen those animals slinking between the cabins and tents sniffing for more."

"And you believe those are the same wolves that attacked those two biologists?" Her spoon remained suspended.

"Yu-up."

"What makes you think they're the same?"

"From what Teevak said. Matched the description. And they've tried to bite humans before."

She lowered her spoon. "When?"

"'Bout a week ago. Two of Harry's guys went to look at the old plane wreck behind the airstrip, back near the dump. It was getting dark. Wolves came out of the trees and circled them. Then the big black one moved in on one of the guys. He kicked at it. It snapped and snarled, and retreated, but then one after the other, they came, trying to bite the men, like they was testing to see if they'd be easy prey. Had to beat 'em back with broken branches and throwing rocks. The men thought it was a good laugh after they'd calmed themselves with mugs of whiskey." He yanked open the gas-powered refrigerator, hauled out a hunk of red meat, slapped it onto a board. He reached for a carving knife, waved the tip at her. "Those wolves probably followed those biologist kids to the north end of that lake. Those kids had the stink of the lure on them to start with. And the wolves probably did the same thing as they did with those two guys looking at the plane wreck. Only this time they were bolder."

Tana thought of the deep clawlike gouge marks on the bodies. The bear prints. She wasn't so sure.

He sliced into the meat. "It's like with those other two girls who were killed. Bad shit, that. Happening all over again."

"*What* other two?"

He cubed the chunk of meat that he'd sliced, and scraped the pieces of flesh into a pot. "Three, four years ago. The Mountie's kid was the first. Mauled to death up a tributary of the Wolverine."

"What Mountie?"

"Elliot Novak."

Her pulse quickened. "Wolves?"

"Maybe bear, maybe wolf. They never could tell for sure. Maybe something else—but wolves and a bear ate parts of her, for sure. They shot a female grizz and a pack of wolves nearby. There was human flesh in all their bellies. Ripped her head clean off her body."

Tana went cold.

He started slicing off another cut of meat.

"What, exactly, happened?"

"Don't rightly know. No one does. Elliot took his daughter, Regan, ice fishing for the weekend. Early November it was. Somehow Regan left the tent during the night. Her dad found her body the next morning, being torn apart by wolves in the forest, just upriver from where they were sleeping. He hadn't heard a thing."

Rosalie's words curled through Tana's brain. *He's still out there, in the woods. He's gone bush. It's the white-man cops. This place messes with their white-man heads* . . . Jesus Christ. Is *that* what happened to him? He lost his daughter to wolves?

"You said there was another one."

"Following year. Also just at the start of the snows—first week of November. Dakota Smithers. She was only fourteen years old." He cubed the next slab of meat as he spoke. Tana could smell it. She pushed her bowl aside, appetite gone.

"Dakota was part of the culture camp that the Twin Rivers School used to hold every year out at Porcupine Lake, to help the kids stay in touch with their indigenous roots. She and some others went out with their dogsleds one afternoon. Dakota got separated from the group when fog rolled in. Dogs came back with the sled. No Dakota. Found her three days later. Eaten by wolves, bear, other scavengers. Couldn't say what killed her, though."

Tana felt ill.

"So it wasn't the same wolves that—"

"Nope. I told you. Those wolves and the bear that fed off Regan were killed by wildlife officers. It was Regan's DNA in their bellies." He pointed the bloodied knife at her again. "See, now, *that* is where Elliot went truly mad. He believed some*one* had killed his kid, and left her in the forest for the animals. He got to convincing Dakota's mother, Jennie, that the same person had gotten her daughter, too. Made him totally nuts, looking for some monster, when it was just the way of the wild. Wife left him. He went into the bush in the end."

"And he's still out there?" she said.

"Yup."

"You sure?"

"So I hear."

"From who?"

He shrugged. "Here and there."

"Where is he?"

"Badlands. Nobody from town will go in the badlands." His gaze locked with hers, and he fell silent. Tana had a bizarre sensation that he was transferring things, thoughts, into her head with his intensity. And she was seized by an absurd sense of time warping, as if this place had been shifted slightly. Into another realm. Where different laws of physics and logic applied. She needed sleep. Bad.

The door swung open suddenly, and in blew a bluster of ice crystals off the snow. Tana jumped.

"Sorry to spook you," MacAllistair said, stomping her boots, and closing the door behind her. She wore shades in spite of the darkness. She stilled upon sensing the tension in the yurt. "What?" she said. "Did I interrupt something?"

CHAPTER 11

Heather poured a coffee and seated herself opposite Tana.

"Big Indian messing with minds again?" she asked, stirring sugar and cream into her mug. She pushed her shades onto the top of her head, exposing a puffy black eye.

"Bad night?" Tana said.

"Probably not worse than yours. What can I tell you?" She took a deep draft from her mug, cradling it with both hands.

"How'd you hurt your eye?"

"Happens when you get so shit-faced that you can't stand up." She held Tana's gaze, daring the cop to say something, to pass judgment. Then she smiled. It lit her bloodshot eyes, and she still looked pretty. "Ever been in that state, officer? Where you just need to block it all out. Ever done something stupid like that?"

A memory washed into Tana's chest. With it, shame. She took a sip of her own coffee, and said, "So, I guess you wouldn't be up to flying me home tonight."

"Hell no, I'm good." MacAllistair took another hit of caffeine, leaned back in her chair, smiled again, and looked halfway normal. "I'm practiced. We work hard up here. Play harder. Keeps us busy long dark nights. I'll take you home once you've wrapped up here—regular rates for the RCMP. Sky is good and clear. Won't be for long. Besides, I need to get back to base. Only stayed 'cause you asked me to. What do you need?"

Tana removed her notebook and pen from her pocket. She flipped the book open. "Run the times, dates by me again—when did you pick Selena Apodaca and Raj Sanjit up from Twin Rivers?"

MacAllistair related her memories of Friday, from when she'd taken off with the crews in the early morning, the route she'd flown, buzzing over the camp, seeing wolves along the lake—repeating much of what she'd already told Tana the night they'd met.

While she spoke, Tana took notes, and Big Indian listened, a sullen shadow in the kitchen, stirring his pot.

"And after you dropped the K9 crew off on Friday morning, what did you do then?"

"I flew back to Twin Rivers, and ferried other folk back and forth—surveyors for the ice road. Hydro guys. Until the weather blew in."

"You couldn't get in all day Saturday, either?"

"I could fly a few other areas, but definitely not Headless Man. The fog sits like a soup on that lake. Cliffs hold it in like a basin. First window was Sunday afternoon. And it was hardly a break, but the wind had turned, and usually when that happens some of the fog clears off the north end of Ice Lake, so I gave it a shot. I got Dean and Veronique and their dogs first. They were farther up the valley, along the river. And then we flew in to Selena and Raj's pickup location. They weren't there. Like I said, we tried to raise them on radio, and via their inReach satellite texting system. No reply. So I flew back a little way along the route they would have been working, and . . ." She cleared her throat. "That's when we saw the wolves feeding on them." She wiped her mouth. Her hand trembled slightly.

"I heard you mention seeing a red chopper on the other side of the cliff before the weather blew in on Friday."

Heather stilled her mug en route to her mouth, then lowered it slowly back to the table. She cupped her hands around it, a wariness entering her eyes.

"Yeah," she said finally. "A red AeroStar. It's a tiny two-seater thing—barely two people can squish in. You build them from a craft kit. They come out of the Balkans. I'm making one myself."

"Do you know whose it was?"

She moistened her lips. "No."

Tana glanced up. "Are there many around like it?"

"Could have come in from a hundred miles any direction. Illegal hunters, diamond guys, engineers, prospectors, who knows."

"But is there anyone that *you* know in this region with one?"

Her mouth tightened. "Crash."

Big Indian looked up sharply.

"Wasn't his, though," MacAllistair said.

"How do you know?"

"He said so." A pause. "Look, why do you need to know, anyway? What difference does it make to what happened to those kids?"

"Maybe the pilot of the red AeroStar saw something that could aid with the coroner's recommendations."

She nodded slowly. "So . . . it's not like it's a police matter."

Tana closed her book. "It's standard procedure for police to file a report in an event like this. Thanks. You still on for the ride after I've checked in with Blundt?"

"For sure." She slugged back the rest of her coffee, grabbed the packet of smokes she'd left on the table, and pushed to her feet. "I'll be in the hangar, waiting for you."

Tana shrugged back into her jacket. When she stepped out, an aurora pulsed high across the sky.

CHAPTER 12

Tana had barely landed back in Twin Rivers and was feeding her dogs when the call came in—*big fight at the Red Moose*. She wheeled her RCMP truck into the frozen parking lot, slammed on the brakes, sending her vehicle skidding to an angle in front of the stairs that led up to the old-style saloon. She killed her siren, left her light bar strobing, and flung open her door. Loud music, yelling reached her instantly.

"Stay here!" she commanded her dogs, and she ran toward the stairs, hand ready near her sidearm.

Pine trees swirled and swayed in the wind. Aurora borealis danced in the sky.

She took the wooden stairs two at a time. As she reached the porch of the Red Moose, the double doors swung open. A man came hurtling backward out of the doors. His arms windmilled as he flailed wildly to keep balance, and rolled down the stairs. She sidestepped him, pushed through the doors.

"Oh man, this is going to be good," said someone bashing in through the doors behind her. "Cops are even here."

It was hot inside. Smelled like a locker room, sour with sweat, spilled beer, and wine. Music pounded. It took a moment for her eyes to adjust to the light. It was all dark wood inside. The caricature of a neon red moose lit the bar area in reddish light.

The fight was centered near the bar counter. Around two big young guys in particular, one laying into another, who was trying to defend himself against the attack. Men were yelling. A chair went flying, hit the mirror behind the counter. Glass shattered. A woman shrieked.

Oh, Jesus—when was she going to cut a break?

Pulse racing, Tana shoved through the people massing around the fight. Another chair went flying. Glass tinkled. It crunched beneath her boots. The floor was slippery with spilled drink.

"Step aside, RCMP."

No one seemed to hear her.

"Police!" she yelled. "Step aside!"

As she got deeper into the fray she recognized the two men at the center of the melee. The big young gun on the attack, his long black hair flying loose, eyes psychotic, sweat gleaming, was Jamie TwoDove—the man she reckoned had made the bracelet Selena Apodaca had been wearing when she was killed. Like a lunatic he was laying into Caleb Peters, the band chief's son. Blood oozed from a cut on TwoDove's brow. Peters was trying to defend himself while two guys grappled to pull TwoDove off him. A row of glasses went smashing across the bar. A woman screamed. The bartender bellowed. He was waving a baseball bat and looked red enough in the face to use it at any moment. Bar stools went crashing. A man crawled along the floor. Tana tripped over him and went down hard. She halted her fall with bare hands. A shard of glass sliced her left palm. She slipped again in beer, cursing as she shoved herself off all fours and back onto her feet, being jostled in the crowd. Several guys were now yelling: *fight, fight, fight, fight!*

She heard the sickening crunch of a fist connecting with flesh and cartilage.

Adrenaline exploded through her. She grabbed the guy in front of her by the collar, yanked him aside. He spun around, and threw her a left hook. His knuckles cracked across her cheekbone before she saw it coming. She was blinded for a moment, sparks of light firing through her brain, the blow resounding against the inside of her skull. A coppery taste leaked down the back of her sinuses. She grabbed her baton, and swung it across his shoulder. "Police! Everyone stop. Stand down. Put that music off!" she yelled at the barkeep.

He didn't seem to hear.

A guy with a massive beard got TwoDove into a stranglehold. TwoDove kicked wildly to free himself, going purple in the face. More stools went flying as his boots connected with them. Someone grabbed TwoDove's legs. He started to howl, spittle foaming onto his lips, chin.

"He's gonna die if you cut off his air like that—let him go," a woman screeched.

Tana muscled into the fray, going for her pepper spray, but before she got off a blast, an explosion rocked the air. Sound slammed against her eardrums. Deafness began to ring in Tana's ears. Her eyes watered.

Everyone fell silent in shock.

Dust, bits of wood wafted down from the ceiling where the deer-horn chandelier swung.

"Turn that music off!" she yelled, pointing at the barkeep. She spun around, heart thumping, looking for the source of the gunshot.

O'Halloran stood just inside the doorway, shotgun in hand, eyes narrowed, body stiff.

"Put that down," she commanded him. She was shaking, blood leaking down her cheek. Everyone was silent, watching. Apart from TwoDove, who was being muffled while his legs thumped against the bar counter.

"You heard the officer," O'Halloran said. "Everyone step back. Party's over." He did not put the gun down.

Tana hesitated. She didn't trust him. Her brain raced. Civilian safety was her number-one priority. TwoDove was in medical distress. She needed to get him out of here. She swallowed, holding O'Halloran's gaze, silently warning him to stay in check, then she turned and pushed through to TwoDove, going for her cuffs.

As she got one of his wrists cuffed, he flung her off with superhuman strength, like nothing she'd ever experienced. She went flying like a small flea, backward and into the wall. The impact punched the breath out of her lungs, and for a second she was winded, immobile.

TwoDove bent over double, and like a bull he barreled full-bore for Tana's stomach. She went for her baton again and swung her hips sideways in an attempt to avoid the impact, but his massive shoulder connected hard with her waist. She grunted. TwoDove crashed into the wall as Tana smashed her baton down across his shoulders. He staggered, and dropped to all fours on the glass-littered floor. He panted, struggling to regain his breath, drool stringing down from his mouth. She grabbed his hair, yanking his neck back as she pulled his cuffed arm behind his back. She reached for his other arm, pushing him flat to the ground with her knee. Shoving his head to the floor, she cuffed his other wrist.

Breathing heavily, she said near his ear, "Jamie, can you hear me?"

He gasped for breath.

"Listen to me, Jamie. Focus." She snapped her fingers in front of his eyes. "I'm not here to hurt you. I don't want anyone to hurt you. I know about Selena, okay? I know you're having a hard time. Jamie?"

He stilled at the sound of Selena's name. "Jamie, can you *hear* me? Nod if you can hear me."

He gave a small nod, started crying. "I'm Constable Larsson. I was with Selena and Raj earlier today. I was coming to find you, to talk to you. It's okay, I know you hurt. I know you're mad at the world that this could happen. But I'm going to help you through this, okay? Did you hear me, Jamie?"

He nodded.

"You're coming with me. I'm going to take you where you can sleep this off. I'll get someone to look at the eye of yours, okay?"

He began to sob deeply. His muscles, the iron-like tension in them, easing.

She got off him, helped him to his feet. She was shaking inside. Adrenaline pounding. "Okay, we're going to my truck outside, nice and easy. You understand?"

Tana steered him toward the door. People stepped back in silence, watching. Some dude near the pool table whistled. Others laughed. She knew they were judging her. Testing her. She knew she'd made a mistake going into the fray like that on her own. But shit, what in the hell . . .

O'Halloran remained standing in the doorway, blocking her way. She reached him. His gaze locked with hers, and a smile curved slowly across his mouth. "Not bad, officer."

"Put that thing away, understand?" she said quietly to him.

The grin tugged deeper at his lips, and his eyes danced. "That your way of saying thank you?"

"I was doing fine."

"Were you?"

She pushed TwoDove past him, and out of the doors, started down the stairs with him. The cold air was bracing and welcome. Her dogs yipped and whined in the back of her truck.

TwoDove broke loose suddenly and ran, hands behind his back. She took off after him, slipping on ice, her dogs barking like crazy. Maximus launched out of the truck bed and chased, his teeth latching onto TwoDove's pant leg as Tana reached and grabbed him.

TwoDove kicked at Max, who growled and shook the pant fabric. "Fucking dog—get that fucking dog off me!"

"Hey, hey, listen to me, I'm on your side. Jamie."

"Get those fucking wolves off me. Fucking wolves . . ." He began to sob again, and Tana realized he was amped up on far more than just booze and grief. She propelled him toward the truck. The light bar on top was still pulsing red and blue into the night, chasing garish color over the snow. She yanked open the back passenger door, placed her palm at the back of his head. "Get inside. Mind your head."

She shut him in, where he was safely behind the grid in the rear of her truck cab.

"Max, come here, you okay, bud?" She crouched down, and felt along his ribs. He squiggled and licked her face. He seemed fine. "Thank you," she whispered. "But next time you better stay in the truck, or you're going to get me in big trouble, okay, boy? Come, hop." She opened the tailgate for him, hooked her arms around his belly, and hefted the big old guy into the truck bed where Toyon wiggled with glee.

She slammed the tailgate shut.

Music had started back up inside the Red Moose. Northern lights danced softly in the sky, above the speared tips of an army of black spruce. Her lights continued to strobe the night air.

Great big judders suddenly took hold of her. Then dizziness. She grasped the top of the cold tailgate with both hands, gripped hard, and rested her head on the backs of her hands for a moment, catching her breath and orientation.

"You okay?" She jumped. Her gaze shot toward the sound. O'Halloran. He stood outside the saloon, on the porch of the Red Moose. Studying her. Shotgun in hand. Her police lights throwing the craggy shape of his face into flickering relief.

No smile now. Something very still about him.

"You okay?" he said, again.

"Fine." Angry for allowing him to have witnessed her moment of weakness, she started around her truck for the driver's-side door.

He thumped down the stairs in his heavy boots, came crunching over ice toward her. She reached for the door handle, but he clamped his hand firmly over her wrist. She froze. Glared at his hand.

Wind caught her hair and she realized it must have come loose from the neat bun at the nape of her neck.

"You're bleeding," he said, so softly it threw her. "Look at me."

She did, slowly.

He hesitated. Then cupped the side of her face, and angled her head to the light. "Needs a stitch, or five." She felt his warmth, his breath, the cold roughness of his palm. He smelled like soap. His calloused thumb wiped a trail of blood off her cheek. He seemed to come closer, even though his body made no movement at all.

"I'm fine."

"You're very fine, Constable Larsson."

"Step back." She yanked open her door, and wavered, dizzy. She clutched onto the door for balance, wishing to hell he'd just go away. Damn him for coming out here, for zeroing in on her weak, lonely moment. For seeing her like this.

"I saw you take quite a blow to your gut. Your hand is hurt, too."

She breathed in, deeply, then out, nice and slow, taking a moment to commandeer her balance, her focus. But a sudden raw fear sliced across her mind. A new fear. Her baby. *Was her baby all right?* Emotion burned sharp into her eyes.

He touched her elbow, and she snapped her body tight and upright, heart racing back up to speed. "Stay clear, please. Do not touch me."

"Get into the passenger seat," he said. "I'm driving you back—"

"Not on your life, bud."

But his touch on her elbow remained steady. "Come."

"You need to step back, sir. This is an RCMP vehicle. A civilian does not drive this vehicle."

"So says the officer of the law," he said quietly. "A strong Mountie who can stand against the wild, wild northwest all by herself. Well, let me tell you something, Constable, the rules, they don't quite apply out here. Do they?"

Another wave of dizziness seized her. She braced her palm against the truck, feeling sick suddenly, sick as a dog. She hung her head down, trying to get the nausea to pass.

She felt his hand move to her shoulder.

"Get in. I'm taking you to the doc."

"There is no doctor in town," she said.

"Figure of speech. The clinic. Nurse."

"I need to get TwoDove into lockup. He needs medical attention. You can't drive this vehicle. You can't—"

"Then we'll get him into lockup, and I'll bring the nurse to you both."

She closed her eyes. *God help me. I need to do this—I do need to see a nurse. I need to tell someone I am pregnant.* Wind wafted the tendrils of hair that had come loose across her face. She felt her vision going. She felt the gentle touch of her gran's hand in the soft sough of the breeze, a Dogrib elder who'd helped raise her when her father had finally taken Tana away from her mother . . .

You can't do everything alone, Tana, my child. You need to learn how to ask for help. You need to let people help you. Everyone needs a tribe. Man is not strong without tribe . . .

But allowing a civilian to drive a police-issue vehicle? She'd be in such shit. She was already in shit. She started to pass out. Low blood sugar. She needed something sweet. Food. She'd hardly had any of Big Indian's stew. No sleep for days, really . . .

He caught her as her knees buckled. "Come." He took her arm, led her around the truck, helped her into the passenger seat of her own cop truck. And there she sat, with her prisoner in the back who'd fallen asleep and was snoring noisily. O'Halloran closed the passenger door. The window was open at the top and she was grateful for the cool air. He turned his back to the truck and stood a moment with his shotgun at his side. It was as though he was fighting something inside himself—a rugged, lone, northern cowboy silhouetted against the eerie pulse of red and blue light outside. And she heard him say, *"Fuck it!"*

Then he whirled around, marched across the front of her truck, climbed into the driver's seat, and slammed the door.

He sat silent for a moment, then reached across and flicked off the bar lights like it was something he did every day. He fired the engine.

As he drove, Tana put her head back and closed her eyes as she tried to fight off the rolling waves of dizziness. The way her body was taking control frightened her. It made her feel so damn vulnerable.

"So, you don't want to fly cops, but you're okay to drive them?" she said with her eyes closed.

He didn't reply.

Tana realized that the last time she'd let someone care for her, just given over to him in a way that had made her vulnerable, was with Jim. It had been the first time in her life that she'd truly trusted a man *would* care for her. With respect. With love. And he had. And look where that had gotten her.

Her head pounded.

"*Sin!* Sin, sin, sin . . . Selena . . . sinned!"

Her eyes shot open. She spun around. TwoDove was babbling in his sleep. Drool shone down the side of his mouth. His eyes fluttered open suddenly and then seemed to roll back inside his skull before his lids shuttered closed again. Worry pinged through her. She glanced at O'Halloran.

"What's he on? Do you know?"

"'Shrooms."

"*Mushrooms?*"

"They're occasionally hallucinogenic. Especially if combined with tons of alcohol."

"I suppose you supply those, too?"

No mirth toyed across his mouth now.

"The locals gather them in the fall," he said. "They dry them, make tea. Old Twin Rivers tradition." They neared the tiny Twin Rivers church, a peeling, white clapboard building with a small wooden spire and a cross on top—legacy to the Catholic missionaries who had once tried to save the indigenous peoples of this place. O'Halloran turned the wheel, taking the truck into what passed for Main Street. In summer it was a wide strip of gray, glacial dirt and gravel. It was now white, hard-packed snow and ice, flanked by clapboard buildings, a portable library, cabins, the clinic, the Twin Rivers General Store and Diner. The diner windows were ablaze with yellow light, and a rainbow of Christmas lights twinkled along the eaves. A group of youngsters huddled outside, smoking, cigarette tips flaring orange in the night.

"They'll have my badge for this," she said softly, watching the kids as the studded truck tires crunched down the snowy street.

"You try to police urban style out here, Tana, on your own like this, it's going to break you," he said, as quietly.

She turned to him in shock at his use of her first name. His profile was rugged, harsh. His hands strong on the wheel.

"Like it broke the others," he said.

CHAPTER 13

Crash helped Tana shuffle Jamie TwoDove up the stairs. Jamie was a big-ass dude, his weight heavy on their shoulders. They managed to maneuver him into the police station, and toward the small lockup wing that contained two cells. Her dogs followed them in, nails clicking on the wooden floors.

Jamie stumbled and Tana paused, breathing hard.

Crash glanced at her.

She was quite bloodless and strained-looking under dusky skin. Soft, dark hair escaped messily from what had once been a controlled bun at the nape of her neck. Her eyes, he noticed, were a warm mahogany brown. Up close, her lashes looked very soft and thick and long.

"Let me do this," he said softly.

"I need to get him into the cell myself. You stay here."

He snorted. Stubborn woman. Feisty as all hell. Showed no fear. He let her take Jamie, watching closely as she battled to manipulate the massive young man into the cell. The room was tiny with a narrow cot and a small barred window up near the roof on the back wall. Through the bars Crash could see the undulating green light in the sky. Tana edged Jamie backward and onto the small bunk. She guided him down onto the mattress and into a prone position with his head turned side-ways on the thin pillow so that he wouldn't choke on his own drool, or vomit, should he throw up.

"You okay there, Jamie?" she said, smoothing hair off his face.

Crash was struck by the gentleness in her touch, the compassion in her tone for a guy who'd just tried to beat the shit out of her. And whom she'd just whacked with her baton.

"I'm going to lock that cell door, okay, and fetch the nurse to take a look at you. Then you can sleep it off and we'll talk in the morning."

Crash leaned against the wall, folded his arms, crossed one boot over the other, and studied her through the cell bars, intrigued. He told himself part of the reason he was still standing here right now was because he'd made it his business to know exactly what was going down in this area of the north, and who was playing and buttering up whom. He was also interested in learning what, exactly, had triggered TwoDove—why he'd laid into the chief's son like that. Ordinarily Jamie was a pretty docile guy. Plus, it wouldn't hurt to get a good read on how capable a cop she was going to be in town, and how that might screw with his own plans.

Jamie moaned, then muttered, "Never have, she shouldn't have . . . place of bones . . . Bad . . . Bad, mess with the lonely ones. Told Caleb. Bad shit. Bad move . . . lovely bones . . ."

Crash frowned.

"What did you say, Jamie?" Tana said, leaning forward.

Jamie groaned, his eyelids fluttering. Another stream of drool crawled out of his mouth. "Sin, sin, Sinlina. . . . the hungry ones . . . dead ones came . . . Took her away to the other side . . . dark side . . ."

She looked up, caught Crash's eyes.

"Like I said, they can be hallucinogenic, the mushrooms. He'll be fine in the morning."

She came out, closed the cell door, and locked it. He followed her into the area that served as an office. It contained three metal desks behind a counter with a door in it. The desk closest to the counter was used by their admin clerk, Rosalie. One was clearly occupied by Tana. The other sat empty, still awaiting a new officer. At the far end of the room, set into an alcove, was a kitchenette area. Near the back, a cast-iron stove glowed with embers. Three doors led off the main office. Crash knew that through the first he'd find a passageway to the gun room, storerooms, evidence locker, and a tiny room with a bunk bed. The second door opened to stairs that climbed to the small apartment usually occupied by the station commander. The third door opened into an interview room.

Tana shucked out of her jacket, and held for a moment onto the back of a chair.

"I'm going to get Addy—the nurse," he said.

"Why were you there?"

"What?"

"At the Red Moose. Why were you there with a shotgun?"

"I was in the diner when word came there was a fight, and that you'd rushed off to—" He smiled. "To stop it."

"So you came to save me."

"Came to stop the fight. I've seen how these things can go."

She held his gaze, measuring him, profiling him. She was so pale right now that her eyes looked like black holes. The cut on her cheek needed attention. She was going to have one helluva shiner come morning. He wondered what she'd seen out at the north tip of Ice Lake, how she was coping. At the same time he had no interest. Did not want to know a goddamn thing. Wanted to feel nothing. No desire to look into this station, police life, the bad feelings it gave him. Yeah, he knew he had issues. Big-shit ones. Knew also that some things you just never came back from, never healed . . . and that was your lot.

"Why was TwoDove going for Caleb Peters?" she said.

"No idea. I arrived after you did." He hesitated, then said, "What did you mean, when you said that you knew what Jamie was going through? With Selena?"

Her gaze locked with his a moment longer, as if she was deciding how much to tell him, just how far to let him in. And Crash knew what she was seeing. A jaded old bastard. Someone who flouted the law and sold booze to kids. Someone capable of sleeping with a fourteen-year-old girl. Distaste filled his mouth—for himself. He had to have at least fifteen years on Tana, and right now, looking into her fresh, earnest rookie face, he felt every minute of those years. And just as jaded as she was guileless.

"Do you know if Jamie and Selena were an item—were they seeing each other?" she said.

Her big wolfish dog, the one who looked as grizzled as Crash felt, came up to his leg and nudged him. He leaned down, scratched the animal behind the ear, feeling scars. "I dunno. Maybe."

"What kind of mushrooms are they?"

"Don't know the botanical name," he lied. "The locals call them by a Slavey word, which means something like *fighting men*. Marcie Della from the diner says that warriors of old, or members of a bear hunting party, would drink the tea before going out. It's also used in spirit quests for young boys." He turned and made for the door. "I'll send Addy. She can tell you more about the narcotic properties of the plants locals use. Any overdoses or poisonings tend to head her way."

As he opened the door to the cold, he said, without looking back at her, "Want me to bring some food? You look like you could use some."

She was silent. He glanced over his shoulder. Her eyes were gleaming. She wiped her mouth, and her hand was shaking. "Yeah," she said very quietly. "Thanks."

He stepped out of the door and shut it behind him. *Oh, fuck, you asshole. What the fuck are you doing?* Outside, the wind was picking up. The foul weather was on its way.

He crunched over frosted snow on his way to the clinic feeling as though he'd just crossed some Faustian line.

And that he was going to be real sorry he had.

CHAPTER 14

"He'll have one hell of a headache in the morning," Addy Armstrong said as she packed up her emergency medical bag. "But it's nothing Jamie TwoDove hasn't seen before."

"You know him well, then?" Tana said, watching closely from the door of the cell, for Addy's safety, in case Jamie TwoDove woke up and went ballistic again. Addy was the public health nurse for Twin Rivers. Tana had met her briefly at the small welcome barbecue Chief Dupp Peters and the local band councilors had held upon her arrival. Apart from a local admin assistant, Addy worked alone in the clinic, and lived behind it. A local volunteer filled in on Addy's days off, but she was always on call while she was in Twin Rivers. When she left for her several-weeks-long vacation, a temp nurse was sent to fill in. A doctor flew in for a period once a month. So did a social worker. A dentist and psychologist less often.

Addy gave a half shrug and came to her feet. "When you're the only medical service in town, you tend to get to know pretty much everyone quite intimately." Tana stepped back, allowing Addy to exit. She locked the cell door behind Addy, and the nurse followed her into the office.

"It's a little tough," Addy said, preempting Tana's next questions. "In a closed community like this, there's a very fine line between patient confidentiality, friendship, other considerations. But it *is* there, and my patients trust me—they all know I won't cross that line."

Tana got her drift. The nurse wasn't going to just freely offer up Jamie TwoDove's medical or drug-use history. But if TwoDove had been arrested before, or had a criminal record, that would be in the police database. She'd follow that up in the morning, as well as file her report on the wolf attack.

"How about you?" Addy said, meeting Tana's eyes. "Shall I sew up those gashes of yours now? Crash said that you also took a head butt to the stomach at the Red Moose."

Anxiety tightened Tana's jaw. "I . . . yeah. I—"

"Shall we go through to the little bunk room?" Addy said with a smile, but her eyes revealed that she was reading something deeper in Tana's hesitation. "There's good lighting in there. I've done this a few times." She smiled again.

"Ah, yeah. Sure." Tana led the way down the hall, and into the small room with a cot. Her dogs followed.

"You guys stay out here," she ordered. Tails sagged. Toyon flopped down in the passage with a groan. Maximus just stood there.

Tana showed Addy into the room, and partially closed the door so that Max and Toyon could still see in.

"If you sit on the bunk there," Addy said, placing her kit on the narrow desk, "I can just angle this light over like this." She drew closer a halogen desk lamp with a swing arm. Tana took a seat.

"How are you holding up otherwise?" She had a kind face. Soft eyes—a pretty hazel color. Tana felt edgy. Trapped. Her pulse began to race.

"Good," she said.

Addy glanced at her face, then her attention shifted to the makeshift bandage Tana had bound around her palm. "Let me look at that first."

Tana held out her hand, and Addy unwrapped it. She cleaned the wound with sharp-scented disinfectant that stung. Using forceps she pulled out a small shard of glass.

"This one's not bad at all. The challenge will be in keeping it clean and dry," she said as she re-bandaged it.

Drawing the lamp even closer, she said, "Move up a little, yes, that's it." She grinned. "I've been wanting to practice my plastic surgery skills for a while now."

"Great," said Tana.

Addy laughed. "It's going to leave a bit of a scar—I'll do my best—but you can always get it cleaned up later by a surgeon." She got to work cleaning and stitching Tana's cheek. "Four. That should do it. The stitches will dissolve. Want to see my handiwork in the mirror?" She sat back, a questioning look in her eyes.

"God, no. But thank you."

She continued to hold Tana's gaze. Tana started to go hot all over her body as she took her own measure of Addy Armstrong in return. The woman was blonde, pretty. Late forties, Tana guessed. She knew that Addy was single, and she wondered what had brought this woman north. And why she stayed. Whether she could trust her with her own personal and medical issues. But she'd been pushed up to the edge now. She *had* to start somewhere. Normal people did this all the time, so why was she so afraid? It was voicing it, telling it to the world, that made her scared. It was the shame it would bring. The questions that would come. She'd wanted to hold off as long as she could until she felt her new job out here was a bit more stable.

It was everything but.

"Any word from Yellowknife on backup?" Addy said.

"Not yet. I'll be putting in another call tomorrow."

"You sure you're holding up okay?" she said, again.

"Yeah. Yeah, fine."

"How about that punch to the stomach? You hurt anywhere else?"

"I'm pregnant."

Addy blinked.

"I . . . yeah, I took a blow to my stomach. It was more on the side, though. I think it mostly got my duty belt. I . . . I'm worried about . . . about . . ."

"The baby. Of course you are."

Tana's eyes burned.

"Come, let's get that vest and weapons belt off you, and lie you down."

Tana removed her gear. She set her gun belt on the desk. "You want my shirt off?"

"Just unbuttoned is fine, and you can pull up your thermals. If you can undo your pants, lower them around your hips."

Tana did as instructed, lay back on the bunk, closed her eyes. Her heart thumped. Addy washed her hands again in the small basin in the room, warmed them, then palpated Tana's belly, working slowly, her face a study of concentration. Tana closed her eyes, unsure what to allow herself to feel. Relief that she was finally in the capable hands of someone? Anxiety about Addy's silence, and what the nurse might be detecting with her hands? Clearly this mother thing was not going to be a cakewalk—she couldn't even handle the pregnancy like a grownup.

"How far along?" Addy said, feeling Tana's pulse, watching her watch.

"About nineteen weeks. I haven't told anyone from work," she said. "Yet." She cleared her throat.

"You had any checkups so far?"

Tana cleared her throat again. "Just . . . at the hospital when . . . when I was going to get the abortion."

Addy's eyes met hers. Silence swelled in the room.

"I was going to get rid of it. And then I chickened out, changed my mind. Changed everything and came here. I want to start over."

Addy's eyes started to glisten. She nodded, her mouth going tight. She held Tana's hand for a moment, then said, "Let me help you, okay?"

Tana stared at her.

You can't do everything alone, Tana, my child. You need to let people help you. Man is not strong without tribe . . .

For a moment Tana couldn't talk. Then she nodded, and whispered, "Thanks."

Turning to her medical bag, Addy removed a narrow, wooden trumpet-like instrument. "Pinard stethoscope," she said. "To hear the baby's heart. I've got a few pregnant women in the area at the moment, so I travel prepared. Traditional midwives actually prefer this to a scan," she said, placing her hand on Tana's belly, and feeling the baby's location again. "It means the baby is not exposed to long periods of ultrasound." She placed one side of the stethoscope against Tana's taut skin and lowered her ear to the other end of the scope. "The wood gives good acoustics, too," Addy said softly. "I find it better than the metal or plastic ones."

She listened intently, then repositioned the stethoscope, and listened again. Nerves crackled through Tana.

"Is it okay?" Her voice came out thick.

Addy sat up. She grinned. "That's a happy baby."

Tana couldn't breathe, or swallow. Moisture swam into her eyes and blurred her vision. Her baby. It was real. It had a heartbeat. It was *happy*.

She managed to swallow. "Thanks."

"You can get dressed now."

Tana sat up and dropped her feet over the side of the bed. She started buttoning up her shirt.

"Rate of growth seems good for twenty weeks, judging by fundal height—the fact your uterus has reached your umbilicus, and the lie is normal. One fetus," she said as she packed up her bag. "You felt baby move yet?"

Tana's hands stilled on her buttons. "I . . . I don't think so," she said.

"You should be able to detect your baby's first movements, called 'quickening,' between weeks sixteen and twenty-five of your pregnancy. But if this is your first, you might not feel anything until closer to twenty-five weeks. Sometimes it can feel like butterflies," she said with a soft smile that made her eyes look oddly sad. "Or it can be like nervous muscle twitches, or a rolling, tumbling motion, not unlike an upset tummy."

Tana snorted. "That I've had. Bad nausea. Trouble keeping food down. "

"It should pass. That, and feeling like you're on an emotional roller coaster."

Tana waited for Addy to ask about the dad. To her credit, she did not. She asked nothing more. And the relief was profound. She liked this woman. She liked that Addy had made clear the fine line she walked in this community, and that she did not cross that boundary.

"You don't have kids?" Tana said, reaching for her gun belt.

Addy's hands stilled for a second, so briefly Tana might have missed it if she hadn't been watching for it from the moment she'd noticed the sadness in the nurse's eyes.

"No." Addy zipped up her bag, paused, then met Tana's gaze directly. "I was like you once. I went to that abortion clinic in Yellowknife. Except, unlike you, I didn't walk out." She took a deep breath. "I'm glad you did. I live in regret of my decision. I'd hate that for anyone else."

Tana blinked. She opened her mouth to say something but no words formed.

"You should come see me at the clinic, as soon as you feel ready. We can arrange for a proper ultrasound, if you like. And later we can talk about where and how you want to have your baby. Most women fly to the hospital in Yellowknife. Some prefer a local midwife. But if you go that route, the health authority prefers if you sign some paperwork, but we can talk about all that when the time draws closer." Addy gathered up her gear, hesitated once more. "You said you hadn't told anyone."

"Not yet."

"So, you haven't put in for maternity leave."

"No. I . . . need to prove I can handle this job first. I *need* this job."

"Take it easy out there, Tana," she said softly. "Fights at the Red Moose . . . *you* might be compelled to take a kick, or a bullet, but you've got another life to think about now. A little civilian life. The sooner you put in for maternity leave, the sooner you can get—"

"On to desk duty?"

Addy inhaled. "That's not what I—"

"It *is* what you meant."

"You need backup. That's what. You need a full complement of staff here, so that you don't have to be the one running in to physically break up a brawl at the Red Moose. Or be camping out all night at a wolf mauling." She held Tana's eyes. "It's not easy on a woman—anyone—at the best of times. I know what I'm talking about. My mom was a cop. She died in the line of duty when I was ten." She paused. "Be there for your baby, Tana."

Crash entered the office with two cartons of hot soup and freshly baked bannock.

Service at the diner had been slow. Half the Red Moose patrons had ended up there after Viktor, the saloon owner, had come around and cleared them all out. They were huddled around tables drinking coffee, eating bowls of chili, and doing a postmortem of the whole fight.

The station office was empty, the door to the passage open. Crash heard voices coming from there. He entered the passage. Tana's dogs were lying outside the little spare bunk room. He was about to call out that he had takeout, when he heard Addy's voice.

"You haven't put in for maternity leave."

Crash stilled in his tracks, a carton in each hand, wanting to leave but suddenly unable to tear himself away from the conversation that followed.

". . . My mom was a cop. She died in the line of duty when I was ten. Be there for your baby, Tana."

A memory noosed him. He felt hot. Her dogs looked up at him, thumped their tails. Panic kicked through Crash. He mouthed, "Shhh," to the dogs, and backed out of the passage carefully, his pulse racing.

He scanned quickly around the office for a place to set down the takeout. Spare desk. He left both cartons there. His appetite was gone. Maybe Addy was hungry—she could have his soup.

He exited quickly through the main door, shut it quietly behind him. He paused a moment, breathing the cold air in deep. What in the hell was wrong with him?

He dug his hands into his pockets, trotted down the stairs, and headed down the snowy street under the green glow of the sky.

But a voice whispered in his head, *It's too late, O'Halloran. You crossed the threshold already . . . you gave a shit . . . and now look what she's doing to you . . .*

Had he even had a choice? From the moment she'd come knocking?

From shadows across the street the Watcher huddles deep inside a jacket. Cold increases. So does the wind. Crash O'Halloran suddenly exits the police station. For a moment O'Halloran stands outside the building, as if indecisive about something. The Watcher studies him, thinking. Then O'Halloran suddenly seems to shuck whatever is worrying him, digs hands deep into his pockets, and strides with purpose down the street.

The Watcher saw him take the food cartons inside, but he was out too quickly to have eaten any himself. Which means it was a gift. For the cop woman.

The new Mountie who has come to town to mess with the natural order of things.

The lights inside the station shine warm squares onto the snow outside. The nurse is still in there. Curiosity twists through the Watcher. What's going on inside? Is the Mountie hurt? Is it her prisoner who needs the nurse?

A sentence comes to mind:

. . . as Cromwell regarded Moreau, he witnessed the moment the man knew he was prey . . .

Prey.

It's always more deliciously thrilling when a creature becomes cognizant of the fact it's being tracked, followed, hunted by something dark and unseen in the shadows. Something carnivorous, intent, and punishing.

The hairs on the Watcher's arms rise at this thought. Arousal stirs low and hot in the groin. Hunger, the heat of desire, burns into the belly. The anticipation of blood tingles upon the tongue . . . *No! Too soon, too soon, not supposed to feel it again so soon* . . . A slice of panic across the throat. Tightness in the brain. A buzzing. Closing in. Need air, need space, can't feel this now . . . no no no . . .

Only one way to stop it, only one way . . . punish, punish, punish . . .

CHAPTER 15

As Tana entered the office area with Addy she was struck by the aroma of food. Almost immediately she noticed the take-out cartons balanced precariously near the edge of the spare desk. *O'Halloran.*

He'd been in here.

Her gaze shot to the passage door. She'd left it ajar. The door to the small bunk room as well. For her dogs. Had he heard them talking? About her baby?

Why sneak out without yelling his presence, or something? He'd been so quiet. Her dogs hadn't even barked.

Unease curled through her.

"Looks like he left one for you," she said to Addy as she peeled the lid off a container. Her stomach tightened in hunger at the fragrant scent. Soup. Chock-full of vegetables. "Would you like some?"

"Thanks, but no," Addy said. "I need sleep. Got early appointments tomorrow." She took her coat from the row of hooks near the door, shrugged into it, and pulled on her mitts.

"Come see me for an ultrasound next week. I can let you know the sex of the baby, if you want."

Something in Tana went cold. Did she want to know yet? It made things even more real. She nodded. "Thanks. For . . . everything."

"Anytime. You know where to find me." Addy reached for the door handle.

"Tell me something," Tana said quickly. "How long have you been in town?"

"In Twin Rivers? Too long. Seven years total now."

"So you remember when the cop Elliot Novak's daughter was mauled to death? And when the student was mauled at the culture camp the year after?"

Addy's gaze locked with Tana's. She was silent for several beats. The color of her complexion seemed to change. "You . . . don't think—"

"That they could be connected? How could they? The animals were shot in both cases, right?"

The look in Addy's features darkened. Curiosity, unease, deepened in Tana.

"Does he ever come into town?" she said.

"Elliot? Once or twice, maybe two years ago. Then not again, as far as I've heard." Wind gusted outside, casting bits of ice from the trees against the windowpanes.

"But he's still out there, still alive?"

"He was hardly alive when he first went into the bush, Tana. A hollowed-out husk, a cadaverous shadow of himself, suffering from a severe form of post-traumatic stress disorder. Made worse for the isolation and bad nutrition. He looks terrible, too. He lost some of his extremities to frostbite—part of his nose, ends of several fingers and toes. That day he was brought back into town with the savaged body of his daughter, he . . . he was blackened by frozen flesh and of unsound mind. If he's surviving out there, he's not a normal man. He can't be."

Wind gusted louder, the sound of ice ticking against the windows like little rodent nails seeking a way in.

"Why do you want to know?" Addy said.

"I thought I might talk to him."

"But you said these attacks cannot possibly be connected."

"I was also told that Elliot wasn't convinced it *was* wolves."

Addy stared. Wind rose to a pitched whistle outside. Flames in the stove flickered. "Sometimes," Addy said quietly, "when the pain of grief is too great, the human mind seeks other avenues. Denial. Blame. A need to punish something external. Especially if there is guilt involved. I think that might have been why Elliot wanted so badly to believe there might be someone he could punish for what happened."

"Why was there guilt involved?"

"For not having been able to protect his child." She paused. "It drove him mad, Tana, looking to blame a monster." She turned the door handle, opened the door. Icy air washed in. "This place has a way of doing that—driving people mad, if you're not careful."

"You've been out here long enough and you're fine."

Addy held her eyes. "Am I?"

She stepped out and closed the door behind her.

Tana went over and locked it behind the nurse. She moved to the window. Through the crystals of frost forming over the glass, she watched Addy pulling up her fur-ruffed hood, and stepping into the snow. Her hooded figure moved down the street. Under the faint, eerie, green-and-yellow light that waved above the treetops, the image brought a fairy-tale figure to mind. A red riding hood. A wizard or witch.

A midwife crone.

Tana thought of what Addy had said. About being a mother. Her mind went to the dead wolf with swollen teats, and she imagined the pups crying in their den tonight. She wondered if they'd be alive come morning, or if some carnivore would be drawn by their plaintive, hungry calls, and kill them under the haunting light of the aurora borealis.

She thought of Apodaca's and Sanjit's mothers. They would have received word of the attack and deaths of their children by now. Tana rubbed her arms. Life wasn't fair.

As she was about to turn away from the window, a shadow moved across the street. Tana leaned quickly forward, rubbed off the frost.

Nothing.

She watched the empty street a while, a strange cold feathering into her bones.

Tuesday, November 6. Day length: 7:43:25 hours.

"Morning, Jamie," Tana said as she carried a tray of breakfast into the cell wing.

He was seated on the edge of the bunk, his big feet planted square on the floor. Slowly, he turned his head and faced her. But he didn't seem to see her. His eyes were empty black pools. An uneasiness filled Tana as she regarded his features.

"Want some breakfast? I'm going to unlock the door and come in, okay?"

Silence.

Tana unlocked the cell door, entered with a tray that contained hot cereal and a mug of coffee. She set the tray on the bottom end of the bunk. Dragging over a chair, she seated herself opposite him. Her dogs lay watchful at the threshold of the open cell door.

"The oatmeal will make you feel better," she said.

But he remained silent, seemingly disconnected from the world, and she wondered if this was an aftereffect of whatever narcotic was in the mushroom tea he'd allegedly consumed.

Tana had risen around 5:00 a.m. The wind had died and the air had gone so still that the sudden and heavy sense of silence had woken her—like the pressurized calm that came before a storm. She'd let her dogs out, showered, and downloaded her photographs from the wolf-mauling scene. After printing out an image of the silver and jade cuff that Apodaca had been wearing, Tana fed Max and Toyon while listening to the weather report on the radio and making oatmeal on the small stove upstairs. A series of massive storm fronts were on their way—huge amounts of snowfall and fog expected within the next forty-eight hours. An alert had been issued for their area.

Before going to bed last night, she'd checked the station database and found that while TwoDove had spent nights in the drunk tank before, and he'd been arrested after becoming belligerent at a protest to blockade the work of the ice road surveyors last spring, he'd not been charged. He had no criminal record on file. What had piqued her interest, however, were the police photos on file taken at the blockade. They showed that Selena Apodaca and Caleb Peters were present with Jamie TwoDove that day. Then again, half the village, it seemed, had also been at the blockade, if not protesting, just there to watch and warm themselves beside barrels roaring with flames.

She'd also searched the office database for Cameron "Crash" O'Halloran, and found zip on him, in spite of his obvious connections to local bootlegging. She'd Googled him, too, curious about where he was from, what he was doing here. She suspected he was going to be a thorn in her law-enforcement side. But she'd found nothing at all on him apart from a small mention on a hunting blog written by a guy who'd been a member of a group that had stayed at Tchliko Lodge last winter. O'Halloran appeared to be a cipher, which deepened her intrigue. And her suspicion.

From her pocket, Tana produced the print of Apodaca's cuff. She held it out to Jamie.

"Looks like one of your designs," she said.

Jamie's eyes lifted slowly, and fixed on the image of the cuff. A shadow seemed to pass under his skin. The temperature inside the cell fell a few degrees. He dropped his head, looked down at his hands resting on his knees. Big hands. Cut and bruised from the fight, and stained red where Addy had applied disinfectant and antibacterial medication.

"You gave Selena this bracelet, didn't you, Jamie? There's an inscription along the inside. See here? It says, *To Selena, with love, JT.* That's you, Jamie TwoDove, isn't it?"

He swallowed and a tightness overcame his face. "That her blood?" His voice was raw.

Tana inhaled. "I'm sorry for your loss, Jamie."

His eyes glistened. He looked up at the tiny window above the bunk. Behind the bars the day was dawning bleak and cold and gray.

"I was going to come and talk to you, to let you know. But you were already at the Red Moose. You'd already heard what happened."

He nodded.

"Had you and Selena been seeing each other for long?"

Silence.

Tana cleared her throat. "What happened at the Red Moose, Jamie?"

His mouth flattened.

"Did you start the fight?"

Silence.

"Look, you need to give me something here, because I need to file a report, and I'd prefer not to have to charge you, given the circumstances with Selena."

"I don't remember what happened."

"You attacked Caleb Peters—why?"

He shook his head. "Don't remember."

She shifted in her chair, damn vest pinching her thickening midriff again. She wondered when the new, larger one that she'd ordered would arrive. Better come before the storms or she'd be stuck in this straight-jacket for a while. Addy's words filtered through her brain.

. . . you might be compelled to take a kick, or a bullet, but you've got another life to think about now. A little civilian life . . .

She cleared her throat. "Tell me about bones, Jamie. What do you know about old bones?"

His eyes flashed up. Life burned suddenly into his dark face. The pulse at his smooth-skinned neck fluttered like a little mouse heart.

"I don't know nothing about bones."

"Last night you said some things about bones, Jamie. You said Selena had sinned. That she'd messed with the 'lonely ones,' or 'lovely bones.' You said that you told Caleb it was 'bad shit.'"

Silence.

"What did you mean when you said 'they' took Selena away to the 'dark side'?"

He glanced away, his skin beginning to show a sheen of perspiration.

"You and Caleb close friends?"

Nothing.

"I saw photos of you and him together, with Selena at that blockade. You looked like a close group."

He swallowed hard and scratched slightly at the knee of his jeans with his right thumb.

Tana scrubbed her brow. "You see, Jamie, here's what's puzzling me—and we'll know more once the forensics guys have looked at things, because that's what happens next. With any unusual death, there is a postmortem, and various scientific experts weigh in to try and understand what happened. But I found bones out there with Selena's body. And they looked like old bones. I was thinking maybe the attack just happened to occur where bones lay, but then you go ranting about bones and Selena last night." She paused and let that hang in the silence.

People underestimated the power of silence, and how it could compel someone to speak, to fill it.

But while TwoDove's pupils shrank inside his dark irises, he gave nothing.

"The forensics guys will be able to say exactly how old those bones are. DNA in the bones could even tell who they belonged to, whether they're related to someone in town." She leaned forward. "I think you know something about those bones, Jamie."

"I don't remember nothing, okay?" he said. "Had too much to drink. I was upset."

She came to her feet. "Caleb Peters might know something about bones, eh? I'll ask him."

He would no longer meet her eyes.

"Maybe Marcie Della or Chief Peters knows something—maybe some people went missing many years ago, and died at the north tip of Ice Lake. Maybe there's an old burial site out there."

He paled. A muscle flickered along his jaw. Marcie and Chief Peters moved a little higher up Tana's agenda.

"Eat up," she said. "Get something warm into you. I'm going to write you up, then you'll be free to go. I'll have a word with Viktor who owns the Red Moose, see if he's okay with you working off some of the damages. I'd prefer to issue you a warning this time, okay, but Viktor Baroshkov has to agree not to press charges."

He sat there. Unmoving. A statue.

But as she reached the cell door, he muttered something.

She turned. "What was that?"

He raised his eyes. "Wasn't wolves."

Her pulse quickened. "What do you mean?"

"Wasn't the wolves that killed her."

"What was it, then?"

"The soul eaters. The spirits of wild places. They scrape the soul— your heart—right out of your chest. Take your eyes so you can't see in the afterlife."

The image of Apodaca's body slammed through her. The gleaming rib cage in wet, red flesh. The missing heart. Eyes. She swallowed.

CHAPTER 16

Tana put down the phone and scrubbed her hands hard over her face, making her skin raw. Anger stabbed at her brain.

She'd just called her superior in Yellowknife, Sergeant Leon Keelan, to press upon him the immediate need for replacement staff and a new pilot. Reception had been cool. Sarge Keelan was a close friend of Staff Sergeant Garth Cutter. Married with three kids, Cutter was highly placed in the federal force, his policing career on a fast track. He'd set his sights high and was after a commissioned post, and beyond that, possibly a role with CSIS, the Canadian Security Intelligence Service. Tana knew all of this because she'd let him fuck her. Not just once, but several times, when they were both drunk. On each occasion Tana had been so wasted she could barely stand. Or think. And that's the way she'd wanted it, because when she was sober, all she could think of was Jim. And how he'd taken his life. And why. And how she hadn't seen it coming, and had done nothing to stop him. And he'd used her gun.

And now Cutter was the father of her baby.

A baby Jim had wanted. A baby she'd told Jim she *didn't* want. Not yet. She was too young. Only twenty-four. She'd wanted to make detective first—that had been her goal. Cutter's words swam into her head.

*Don't the fuck embarrass me with this shit. Get rid of it. Promise me
you'll get rid of it, and get your aboriginal ass the hell out of town. Because
you're mud on this force now, if I have anything to do with it . . . like mother
like daughter, eh . . . the apple doesn't fall far from the tree . . .*

Shame prickled her skin. Remorse. Fury. Frustration. A need to
hurt herself, punish herself, *do* something exploded inside her. Tana
pressed both palms flat on the metal desk, and inhaled deeply, slowly.
Tentatively she moved her right hand, and placed it over her belly.

*Screw them, happy baby. It's you and me now. Screw them all, because
we're going to do this . . . We're going to turn history around. I'm going to
be a good mom.*

And she'd do it in private—wouldn't reveal who the father was,
because as much as she'd like to nail Cutter's ass to a wall, she had no
intention of hurting Winnie Cutter, his wife, or their kids. This was not
their fault. This was her own fault. This was *her* shame. She'd slept with
a married man. A man she had fucking zero respect for, because he'd
shown himself to be a racist, adulterous, misogynistic prick, and he'd
used her. Just like all the men who'd used her mother, and Tana before
this. And she couldn't blame anyone but herself for that. She'd allowed
it—maybe she'd even wanted it as a form of self-hatred. But she knew
Garth Cutter for the man he really was. She knew the face he hid from
the public, and she'd bet her life that she was not his first affair, as sick
and sordid as it had been.

Leon Keelan knew, too.

And this was why—she was certain of it—they'd been so keen to
send her up here to nearly the Arctic Circle, to the Canadian policing
equivalent of the Siberian salt mines, under the pretense that it was
because she was part Dogrib, and that the Twin Rivers settlement area
needed someone of the north, who understood the culture. And she
figured that whatever went wrong out here now, or continued to go
wrong, they were going to let her wallow. They were going to hold off
sending resources as long as they reasonably could. They were going to

set her up to fail. Cutter would like that. In fact he'd probably like her dead. She rubbed her face again.

She would prove them wrong.

She got up, poured a mug of tea from the pot she'd left warming atop the cast iron stove, added honey. She'd also phoned the coroner's office, mentioning her specific interest in the extra bones, and had been told a full report following the autopsies and other forensic investigations would be forthcoming. She was the beat cop, the first responder who had simply secured the scene, and they were treating her as such.

She reseated herself at her desk and retied her hair. It was just after 9:00 a.m. She'd released Jamie, and Rosalie would be arriving soon. Police station office hours were 10:00 a.m. to 6:00 p.m. While she waited for Rosalie she'd transcribe her recording from the mauling, and get busy on that report. When Rosalie arrived, she could leave the station and go interview those K9 biologists before they left town. After that, she'd follow up with Viktor at the Red Moose, and speak to Caleb Peters about the fight. And bones.

Tana took a sip of her tea, put on headphones, connected her digital recorder, and began typing up a transcript of the recorded observations she'd made at the scene.

As she typed her own words, the images of the massacre shimmered up to the surface of her mind. She felt the horror rise again inside her belly as she was taken back to the scene . . .

. . . *the back of the head has been partially scalped, and there is a significant concave depression at the base of the skull. The long hair is matted with blood and clumped with what appears to be viscera. The color of the hair is strawberry blonde, very curly. Down the side of the face are four deep symmetric gouges, or rips . . .*

She heard emotion in her voice, a thickness she hadn't quite realized had been there. She heard the rapidity of her own shallow breathing in her words. She could see it all again. Smell the coppery, meaty scent.

Feel the cold. The light seemed to dim. Tana glanced up sharply, almost expecting to see a presence, a figure darkening the doorway.

But it was the fire in the stove. She'd neglected to refuel it, allowing it to burn too low, and it was dying, taking the warm glow in the room with it. She cursed softly and got up to add wood. The town relied in large part on electrical heat generated by the diesel plant for warmth, but most supplemented this with wood fires. And the electrical heating in this building was faulty. Yet another thing to address.

Van Bleek's words circled her mind as she stoked the flames back to life.

I take it that you've seen enough animal kills over your lifespan, at least—what's your read here. Something a bit . . . off about this one?

Her thoughts turned to Jamie TwoDove.

Wasn't the wolves that killed her . . . the soul eaters . . . they scrape the soul—your heart—right out of your chest. Take your eyes so you can't see in the afterlife.

Tana shut and secured the stove door. Toyon rolled onto his back in front of the stove with a sigh, exposing his belly to the warmth. She absently scratched his tummy, her mind turning to Big Indian.

*See, now, that is where Elliot went truly mad. He believed some*one *had killed his kid . . .*

Returning to her desk, Tana resumed transcribing. She reached the part where she'd noted the symmetrical gouges down the side of Selena Apodaca's ravaged face. She hit pause, and pulled up the corresponding thumbnails of the images she'd downloaded last night, enlarged them. Backlit on her monitor they came to brutal life—the torn-off soft tissue, the raked-out eyes. Nose in ribbons, exposing nasal cavity and cartilage. A bear had more than four claws.

Perhaps not all of the claws would catch skin in a swipe?

Tana worried her bottom lip with her teeth as she regarded the images. Quickly, she scrolled through the rest of the photos and enlarged the ones that showed the four distinct parallel rips on both Apodaca's and Sanjit's bodies. The same slashes appeared on the Jerry cans.

This is something Charlie Nakehk'o could help with, far more than any so-called large-carnivore experts the coroner's office might consult. Many of those experts were sent reports and photographs and examined things from afar. Charlie was on-site. One of the most experienced trackers around. And he knew local fauna and flora specifically. He'd be able to tell her whether this was a normal predation pattern for wolves, too. And he might know something about those past attacks.

She hit Print, and the office printer kicked into noisy life as it began pushing out images of the slashes, the bodies, the paw prints. As Tana gathered the printouts, something caught her eye in one of the photos that she hadn't noticed before. A left boot print with what appeared to be a jagged mark through the lugs. Frowning at the image, she went back to her monitor and pulled up her series of boot prints. While the coroner had been conducting her own investigation, Tana had matched Apodaca's and Sanjit's boot soles to various sets of prints, and recorded them. Apodaca had been wearing a size six Tundra-XC boot. Sanjit, size nine Exterras.

Both Van Bleek and Kino wore WestMin-issue Baffin Arctics. Van Bleek was a size twelve, Kino a ten. This print with the slash through the lug bore the same distinctive tread pattern as a Baffin Arctic. It looked to be a size ten, too. Or maybe a nine. But neither Van Bleek's nor Kino's left boot sole bore that jagged slash. It was as if the wearer of the boot had slipped on something sharp, cutting the sole. Tana tapped her pen on the desk, thinking.

The print was atop snow, and had been protected from further snowfall in the deep lee of a rock, so the markings were quite clear. Because it was on top of snow it had obviously been made after the weather had blown in on Friday. It could conceivably have been made before Apodaca and Sanjit had arrived. Or, it could have come after.

Who else had been there? Or was this lug mark an anomaly—something stuck temporarily under the sole of either Van Bleek's or Kino's boots that had caused the odd-looking slash in the tread pattern? Tana was also well aware of the vagaries of weather, and how melt-freeze temps, or hoarfrost, or wind could mess with tracks, giving weird results.

She scrolled carefully through all the other images of boot prints. Her heart kicked. There was another. Left Baffin Arctic. Same jagged slash. Although this one was less clear.

I saw you out there on Friday, Crash. Saw your bird parked just on the other side of the cliff from where those kids were working. Round lunchtime when I was flying another crew . . .

Tana printed the second image of the boot print with the slashed lug, as well as some images of the bones. Once the body retrieval guys had lifted Apodaca's torso, she'd found more bones down between a little rocky crevice over which Apodaca had been lying.

Again, her thoughts turned to Big Indian's words.

It's like with those other two girls who were killed. Bad shit, that. Happening all over again . . .

She shut down her files, opened the local RCMP database, and began searching for the reports that would have been filed on the Regan Novak and Dakota Smithers attacks three and four years ago.

She found nothing, not only on those cases, but no reports at all had been electronically entered pre-two-and-a-half years ago. *What the?* Had this station not been computerized, or what? Perhaps they were all on paper.

Tana got the keys out of her desk drawer, and pushed back her chair. She went down the hall, unlocked the small filing room beside the weapons locker room. She clicked on the light, entered. Banker's boxes of files lined shelves. Tana scanned the dates on the labels, finding the boxes for November, three and four years ago—the months Big Indian had told her the two previous maulings had occurred.

She hauled these boxes out, cleared off the second desk in the office, and began pulling out folders, searching for the reports.

Her body grew hot as she rummaged through the entire lot, finding nothing, then starting again in case the reports had gotten stuck between others. In frustration she pushed her flyaway hair back off her face. Perhaps they'd been misfiled. She returned to the file room, got more boxes, and began flipping through the contents.

The station door opened with a sudden blast of cold air, ruffling papers off the desk.

She glanced up.

"Tana—what are you *doing*?" Rosalie said in the very slow, singsong cadence that was indigenous to the region. She shut the heavy wood door behind her. "The place is a mess."

"You're late," Tana said, flipping open another file. Her dogs got up to greet the admin clerk.

Rosalie set her purse on her desk—a big fake leather affair with a gold chain for a strap and feathers affixed to the sides. "Diana's baby girl had colic last night. Diana was tired. She needed sleep." Rosalie peeled out of her down coat, and hung it up. "I had to feed the other kids breakfast, and get them off to school."

Tana looked up. "Diana?"

"My niece."

As if it was the most normal thing in the world for your niece and her kids to take precedence over work. Tana was about to say something, when Addy's words bounced back to haunt her.

It's not easy on a woman—anyone—at the best of times. I know what I'm talking about. My mom was a cop . . . be there for your baby, Tana . . .

She stilled, staring at Rosalie, and it struck her. How in the hell was she going to manage?

"What are you looking for?" Rosalie said, slowly unwinding the scarf bound around her neck. "You look like you seen a ghost, or something." She paused. "You okay?"

"Reports from three and four years ago. November—where would I find them?"

"The dates are on the boxes."

"Yeah, I can see that, but the paperwork for the two cases that I'm searching for is not in here. This place is a mess of disorganization, what in the hell? Those cases must have associated paperwork—there's nothing at all digital from prior to thirty months ago."

"You feeling okay, Tana?"

"Christ, Rosalie, I'm *fine*. Why does everyone keep asking me that?"

"Well, you've been out there with those man-eating wolves," Rosalie said as she palmed off her hat, and seated herself to remove her fur boots. "No sleep. And there was the fight at the Red Moose. Heard about that from Clive, Diana's boyfriend. He's a nice guy. I hope Diana keeps him." She stood, smoothed down her shirt, then her pants, pulled the chair out from her desk. "Just a normal question, you know. After good morning, people say, how are you. Jamie still in lockup?"

Tana stared, files still clutched tightly in her hands. It was this town. This weird Twin-fucking-Peaks town, and this case—it was off.

"Maybe I can make you some tea, Tana. You look all tight. Look at your hands."

She glanced down, swallowed, and released her death grip on the files. She laid them on the desk, took a deep breath. "I'm sorry. You're right—long nights. Jamie's gone. I released him with a warning and a promise to work off the damages at the Red Moose if Viktor agrees."

"Oh, he will. He'll agree."

"So," Tana began more slowly, "I'm looking for two reports that I can't find. One from November three years ago, and one from November four years ago. And there's nothing digital that has been filed from that period."

"We had a big system crash about two and a half years back. Before the new dish and the new satcom system. Ate all the electronic files.

And then we got the new computers. But we have the paper backups. Which cases are you looking for?"

"The mauling deaths of Regan Novak and Dakota Smithers."

A stillness befell Rosalie.

"What?" Tana said.

"Why do you want those?"

"What *is* it with everyone? I just want to see them. We've had a terrible wolf attack in this jurisdiction, and—"

"Those wolves were shot dead long ago. They had nothing to do with this new attack."

"Rosalie," she said quietly, "do you know where those missing files are? Why are they the only ones missing?"

She angled her head, a furrow eating across her brow. "It made him mad, you know? Elliot Novak. Stark raving lunatic mad. Wasn't good to keep looking like that, searching to blame some person, some evil, when there was none. Nothing but the way of the wild."

"The files, Rosalie?"

She heaved out a sigh and shook her head. "Come. I'll show you." She unhooked a key from the rack that hung near her desk. "They're down in the crawl space—he didn't want those two with the others."

"Who's 'he'?" Tana said, following Rosalie.

"The station commander who replaced Sergeant Novak, Corporal Barry Buccholz."

"Just *those* two reports? Why?"

Rosalie bent down to unlock the small crawl space door near the gun room. She creaked it open. A rickety set of wooden stairs led into a black hole. "Down there," she said. "In back. Light doesn't work—it needs a new bulb."

"You have *got* to be kidding me," Tana said, taking her flashlight from her belt. She bent double, panned her beam in. Cold breathed out from the underground space. It wasn't properly insulated down there. She coughed as she caught the scent of mold, dank soil, at the back of her throat. This would explain the constant cold in the building. It was creeping out from here.

"I don't see any file boxes."

"Near the back," said Rosalie.

Tana had to crouch down to half her height to enter. She peered deeper into the bowels with her flashlight, saw a shelf, and on it, a banker's box. Cobwebs wafted as she moved into the crawl space, and a broken strand floated out, curling around her wrist, as if pulling her in, gently, insistently.

"What on earth did Buccholz put them all the way back there for?"

Silence.

She looked over her shoulder, bumped her head, cursed, then bit the bullet and crept in a low crouch to the rear of the crawl space to retrieve the box. As she poked her head back out, the look on Rosalie's face chilled her. She scowled at her assistant, and lugged the box into the warm office. Rosalie locked the tiny door behind her.

Tana set the box on the desk, removed the lid. As Rosalie entered, Tana said, "Why, Rosalie, why did Buccholz stick these papers down there?"

"He was worried Elliot Novak would try and break in again, and get them."

She glanced up. *"What?"*

"Sergeant Elliot Novak broke into the station just over two years ago. He came out of the bush, broke the window, got the keys out of Buccholz's desk, and was going through the files in the storeroom when Buccholz found him."

Tana's jaw dropped. "What was Novak looking for?"

"I don't know. He's mad, Tana. He was just babbling and raving, and . . . he's not sane. He's dangerous."

"So Buccholz *hid* the reports?"

"Yup."

Jesus.

She dusted off the first file, coughed.

"Be careful, Tana." Rosalie said, her voice low, different. "Those cases messed up a lot of lives."

As Crash brought his Beaver in to land at the Twin Rivers strip after his early morning run to the lodge, he saw Heather pacing outside the hangar, smoking. Her long blonde hair blew loose in the mounting wind. Impatient and continually moving as usual—he didn't think he'd ever seen Heather truly still. Beautiful, too. The kind of strong-willed, capable, commitment-averse woman he tended to like, and bed. He grinned. It had been a while since he'd slept with her. He could handle some nookie. Get his mind off Tana Larsson, and whatever else was messing with his head when it came to that cop. He touched his Beaver down, bounced, then bumped and rattled down the runway. He slowed, taxied toward Heather, bringing his props almost up to her. She didn't move, nor flinch. Just stood there grinning, cigarette in her fingers at her side, hair flying back from her face as he came to a halt.

Game of chicken.

The blades slowed and stopped just sort of slicing her open. Crash chuckled, threw her a salute.

She came around to his side as he removed his headset. He opened his door, hopped down. Behind her, the windsock atop the hangar quavered at an erect ninety degrees—wind coming directly from the north, those big storm fronts announcing their imminent arrival.

"And to what do I owe this pleasure?" he said, removing his World War II goggles.

"You got any?"

He caught sight of Mindy watching from the kitchen window of his house next to the strip. He waved. Mindy did not respond, just kept staring, and an odd feeling trickled through him.

"Let's go into the hangar," he said to Heather, his eyes still on Mindy. Selling dope was one thing. Having the kid watch him do so was another.

Heather dropped her cigarette butt to the ice, ground it out with her foot, and followed him into the hangar and out of the wind.

Crash opened the lapel of his jacket, removing a smaller version of the baggie he'd delivered to Alan Sturmann-Taylor yesterday.

"Same price as last time," he said. "And it's going to go up if that cop starts on my case."

Heather took the bag of BC bud from him and handed him cash.

He counted it.

"Was it because of her listening—that cop—that you denied your AeroStar was parked out there, behind that ridge on Friday afternoon?" she said as she opened the baggie and sniffed for good measure.

He looked into her blue eyes. "I didn't lie."

Her gaze locked with his in silence for several beats, mistrust narrowing her pupils.

"Seriously?" she said. "You want Larsson to believe that there's, like, what . . . several little red AeroStars buzzing about near the WestMin camp? Because I know there's sure as hell not, and she doesn't strike me as stupid."

"Where, exactly, did you see this bird?"

"Right on the other side of the cliff where that team was attacked."

"That team had names, Heather. Selena and Raj. We've both had drinks with them at the Red Moose."

She fell silent, stuffed her baggie in her pocket, looked away. Wind gusted a flurry of crystals into the doorway of the hangar. "I know," she said finally, quietly. "It's just . . ."

"That naming them, personalizing them, makes it harder."

"Yeah."

"Brings back memories—military shit?"

She nodded.

"Still the military gal, just trying to block it all out." He punched her lightly on the arm.

Her mouth flattened. Something in her eyes told him that he'd pushed over the line this time, and she didn't like it.

"Hey," he said, in an effort to lighten her up, "I'm done with my morning run. I've got some hours to spare. I'll take a look at that sprag clutch if you want."

CHAPTER 17

Tana pulled up outside the Broken Pine Motel on her ATV. The K9 team would be flying out of town in just over an hour. She needed to interview them before they left—the Regan and Dakota files would have to wait. She turned her machine off, and removed her helmet. Her dogs ran into the trees to investigate while she approached the small motel office.

The Broken Pine was a standard strip of clapboard rooms, one story, doors opening out onto a raised, covered porch that ran along the front. Everything was raised here to accommodate the winter snowpack. A jagged pine speared into the sky beside the building—a landmark and the motel's namesake, she presumed. Viktor Baroshkov not only owned the Red Moose, the motel was his, too. He also owned the General Store and Diner, although he played a backseat role there, letting Marcie run the place.

She pushed open the office door. A bell jangled, and a balding man came out from the back.

"Hey, Viktor."

"Constable," he said. "I've been expecting you. Word is you want Jamie to work back damages."

She set her helmet down on the counter. "You good with that? You think you can come to some arrangement with him?"

"Hmm. I don't know, I—"

"Viktor, he was hurting. I'll get to the bottom of why he went for Caleb Peters, but my brief from headquarters in Yellowknife, and from the local band council, is that we need to work toward a system of restorative justice, wherever possible, especially with the local youth. Punish them, fine them, send them to prison, and we're just going to be making criminals long-term. My sense—" She held up her hand as he opened his mouth to protest. "My sense is that Jamie is not a bad person. You let him help you at the Red Moose, and you get some free labor into the bargain, how about that?"

He ran his hand over his pate.

"We'll need to bring everyone together," she said. "You, Jamie, Caleb, the band council, whoever else was affected by the fight, have a bit of a powwow, and we can go from there, okay?"

"Yeah, sure. I can give it a shot, but I tell you—"

"Are Dean Kaminsky and Veronique Garnier still here?" she said. "I need to see them."

"Checked out already, but still packing, I think. Rooms six and seven."

Tana thanked Viktor and made her way along the porch that fronted the motel rooms. She found number six, removed her gloves, knocked on the door. A dog barked inside and a female voice hushed it.

The door opened a crack.

"Veronique Garnier?" Tana said.

A slight, dark-haired woman with red, puffy eyes nodded. Her complexion was pale and her hair damp, as if she'd just stepped out of the shower.

Tana explained who she was, and why she was here. "Can I come in?"

Veronique stepped back. Tana scuffed her boots and entered. An Australian shepherd lay on the bed, eyeing her warily. Tana got the sense if she made one wrong move, the animal would be on her.

"Selena and I have been sharing this room since spring," Veronique said. "Dean—my teammate on the wolverine project—bunked next door with Raj." She blew her nose on a soggy piece of tissue. "I can't believe this happened. It was our last week. I . . ." Her voice caught. "We almost got out. Almost all got home . . . I . . . Christmas, New Year. She'll never make it. I can't believe they're gone."

Tana scanned the interior. It was basic. Two cot beds. A desk under the window. Walls painted a dirty cream. Old-style light fixture. The window looked out onto a vacant lot that was covered at the moment with a thin layer of snow.

"I've already checked out," Veronique explained, ruffling the head of her dog. "Just finishing packing. There's a North Air flight coming in shortly. I'll be leaving on that one."

"I won't keep you long," Tana said. "I just need a few questions answered for a routine report. This was Selena's bed?" Tana gestured to a neatly made cot with an open suitcase on top, clothes neatly folded inside.

Veronique sagged down onto her bed suddenly, as if someone had taken her out at the back of the knees. She hunched forward and dragged her hands over her face. "I'm still trying to process it," she said quietly. "I wasn't sure what to do with Selena's stuff, but I . . . I called her mother—I got the number from EnviroTech." She glanced at Selena's packed case. "She often spoke of her mother. They were close. Her mom's also a biologist—teaches at the University of Alberta. She asked me to bring Selena's things—everything. I'll be flying to Edmonton, where Selena's and Raj's parents have gone to ID the bodies, where they'll do the autopsies . . ."

Tana winced inside. No parent should have to see their child torn apart, gutted, eaten like that.

"You should see a critical incident stress counselor when you get back, will you do that?" Tana said. "I can get some names for you. What you saw, experienced, was traumatic."

"You saw it, too."

Tana nodded.

Veronique fiddled with her nails. "So, how do you get used to stuff like that, as a cop?"

"You don't," Tana said.

"You just buck up and deal with it, then?"

Tana thought of Jim. "Some try. But it comes out in ways in the end." She cleared her throat. She missed him so much it hurt like a hole in her stomach.

"Do you have any current photos of Selena and Raj?"

"Yeah. On my phone." Veronique reached over, opened a bag, took out her phone. As she searched through it for photos, the door opened and a guy entered. Average to short in height, powerful build. Pale, ash-blond hair and trimmed beard.

"Everything okay?" His attention went to the phone in Veronique's hand. He then looked at Tana.

"Constable Larsson," she said, holding his eyes, direct.

"Dean Kaminsky."

"I'm sorry for your loss."

His mouth tightened, hands going into his pockets. "Yeah. Thanks."

"I'll need a statement from you, if that's okay?"

"Sure." Dean made as if to sit on the bed beside Veronique.

"I mean, after I'm done here with Veronique," Tana said. "I'd like to talk to you separately."

"Why separate?"

"It helps," Tana said kindly. "Down the road, if there are questions about what actually happened."

"As in . . . if it *wasn't* an accident?"

"As in, how things might have played out, that's all. The goal is for the coroner's office to figure out how to mitigate the chances of something similar happening in the future."

"I don't want to get anyone into trouble—this was no one's fault," Dean said. "We've worked with really good people out here. The other teams, supervisor, pilots—this was just a terrible accident."

"Those wolves were human habituated, Dean," Veronique blurted out, her face tightening, her eyes lighting with sudden anger. "And you know it. *You* don't have to apologize for anyone. Those guys at the WestMin camp were feeding those same animals that we saw along the beach. And Selena *told* us that she felt as though she was being followed, stalked out there, these last few weeks. You guys laughed her off, like you always did. *We* did nothing about it. But she and Raj—they *were* being stalked, *hunted*, and no, it's not okay." Her eyes glimmered.

Dean glowered at her.

"Which is why I need to chat with you individually," said Tana quietly. "Separate opinions can be valuable."

"I'm next door," Dean said curtly. He made for the door. "And knock when you come. I have a dog. He doesn't like surprises."

He slammed the door in his wake.

"He's upset," Veronique said. "He . . . he had a thing for Selena, has had for the last two years, but it wasn't mutual."

Tana seated herself on Selena's bed, opposite Veronique. She took out her notebook, and flipped it open. "Why don't you start with the morning you left Twin Rivers, Friday, November second."

Veronique closed her eyes, inhaled deeply. And she gave pretty much the same story MacAllistair had from the time they were picked up, the route they flew out, how they saw wolves along the lakeshore, how MacAllistair noted the bad weather coming in fast and asked Apodaca and Sanjit if they were prepped for an overnighter.

"You saw nothing else on your flight in—no other sign of life? Just wolves?"

"Well, caribou. And the men in the camp . . . oh, wait. Selena thought she saw a man wearing furs on the ridge above the wolves."

"Did she?"

"I—we—no one else saw him. Raj figured it could have been a bear, or just a shadow from the chopper. The sun was at a very low angle, and blinding off the ice on the rock face. "

"Can you recall what Selena said?"

"Well, Raj pointed out that there were no vehicles in sight, so if it was a man that Selena had seen, he had no means of transport. Selena said he could have been dropped off by chopper, and expecting a pickup."

"So no one saw any other vehicles out there?"

"No."

"No other planes, or a chopper? Over the ridge, anywhere?"

"To tell you the truth, if there was a chopper on the other side of the ridge, I could have missed it. I was looking out the opposite window. I only saw to the southwest."

Tana scribbled a notation in the margin. *O'Halloran. Ask re: AeroStar.*

"What happened on Sunday afternoon, after Heather MacAllistair picked you, Dean, and the dogs up?"

"Heather was really worried because the fog and cloud was closing in again fast, and it was almost dark. We tried to reach Selena and Raj on radio, and on their satellite text device, but there was no reply. And there was no sign of them at the pickup location. Heather said she had maybe minutes before the fog shut us down, and she'd try looking for them along the route they were supposed to have been working. Then, as we popped through some mist . . ." She stilled, stared at her hands. Tana waited.

"I . . . I'm sorry, I . . ." She reached for another tissue, blew her nose.

"Take your time."

Moistening her lips, Veronique continued. "I didn't register at first what I was seeing—it was . . . a large animal kill. I immediately thought, caribou. But . . . it was them . . . their backpacks. And wolves . . . Feeding." She wiped her nose. "Heather swore and came in fast, trying to buzz them off. Some retreated." She paused, trying to scrape together her composure. "Dean was screaming for Heather to put the chopper down. He had his rifle ready. His eyes were mad. He wanted to kill the wolves. But if Heather *had* landed, yes, we might've killed those wolves, but there was nothing we could've done that would have saved Selena and Raj, and the mist was choking back in so fast . . . if we'd landed we wouldn't have been able to get out, or call for help, either." Tears streamed suddenly down her cheeks. "The way they'd been ripped apart, it felt . . . *evil*."

A memory slithered through Tana's brain—the loud scream of violence in the silence, as she'd looked over the valley that dawn, the sweet, foul, coppery smell of the kill.

"What did you mean when you said to Dean that Selena felt stalked out there?"

"It wasn't just out there. It sounds dumb, and it was probably just being in the north so long that was playing with Selena's mind—at least that's what I thought."

"Go on."

"She said she felt followed around the village. Watched. As if someone was stalking her."

"Some*one*?"

Veronique nodded. "About a week ago, I woke up one night. It was a full moon. Selena was out of bed, standing at the window in her sleep shirt. Shivering. I asked her what on earth she was doing, and she said there was something out there. Watching our window, watching us sleep. She said she was woken by a ticking noise against the pane."

Tana glanced at the window, then up at the drape rail. No drapes. No blinds.

"I know. We complained, but Viktor whoever said he'd get it fixed. He never did. And there were no other rooms available. I told Selena to get back into bed, and that's when she told me she was being stalked, watched around town, out in the field."

"And did *you* see anything? Outside the window?"

"No. My guess at the time was that it was night animals. Coyote. Fox. Bear. That vacant lot leads to the rear of the diner where the garbage is kept."

"So you didn't believe her—that she had a stalker?"

Veronique hesitated. "No. I . . . I didn't know what to make of her sometimes. She could be a dreamer. An idealist. A little bit weird."

"Was Selena romantically involved?"

"With Jamie TwoDove, a local, yes. He makes jewelry and lives on his dad's spread upriver. His father does taxidermy for the Tchliko Lodge guys."

"Had Selena and Jamie been going out for long?"

"They hooked up pretty early in the spring. They'd have these big philosophical conversations at the Red Moose, or around fires we'd build by the river. He used to take her to listen to old Marcie Della's stories about the elders, and she joined him when he protested the ice road."

"You mentioned Dean was romantically interested in Selena as well."

"Yeah, but that was a one-way thing."

"Dean or Jamie ever show signs of jealousy?"

Her eyes flashed up. "God, no. It wasn't one of *them* stalking her, if that's what you mean."

Tana closed her notebook and came to her feet. "Thanks, Veronique. I—"

"Wait, there was something . . . a bit freaky." She reached over and from under an item of Selena's clothing she took a scrap of paper with some words printed on it. "I found this when I was packing her things."

Tana read the hand-scrawled words.

> . . . *Where a midnight caribou mutilation*
> *awakens a howl of emptiness with ice*
> *where once there was heart.*

And it comes with hunger
for blood in its mouth.
For, in the Barrens of the soul
monsters take toll . . .

Tana looked up. "Any idea what this means?"

"None. I have no idea where Selena got it, either."

The piece of paper had a pinprick hole at the top, as if it might have been pinned to something.

. . . ice, where once there was heart . . .

A chill washed over Tana's skin. She felt a sense of distant drums, of stories told around campfires in the camp where her grandmother had lived. Stories her father had related out in the wilds—myths he said he'd learned from native elders.

"Can I keep this?" Tana asked.

"I guess."

Tana said, gently. "And the photo of Raj and Selena?"

Veronique pulled one up on her phone and showed Tana a pretty, freckled young woman with long, wavy, strawberry-blonde hair. Striking green eyes. With her was a lean, tawny-complexioned male. Tall. Glistening black hair. Liquid black gaze.

"Raj and Selena," said Veronique.

There was no resemblance in these faces to the mess of blood and gore Tana had seen at the north end of Ice Lake, apart from skin tone and hair color.

"I'd like a copy of this."

"I'll forward it to you. What address?"

CHAPTER 18

"No one was to blame," Dean Kaminsky said as he scratched his Lab behind the ear. His dog leaned into his touch.

"Those wolves . . ." He struggled, to his credit. "It's a wild act. Nature. We forget that we humans are encroaching into their space. I heard some guys at the Red Moose last night saying that it was evil. It wasn't. We shouldn't make value judgments."

Tana glanced up from her notebook. "You were at the Moose last night?"

"After the fight. For a bit, before Viktor came and cleared us all out."

"Veronique was there, too?"

"Just me. I needed a beer. I . . . I just needed—"

"To ease those sorrows, eh?"

His mouth tightened.

"You wanted to shoot them at the time—those wolves."

Heat rose into his face above the beard. He shuffled, ever so slightly, on the bunk where he was seated.

Then, as if having decided to draw his student philosophical line in the snow and test the strength of it, he came to his feet, shoved his hands deep into his pockets, and squared his shoulders. "If you're done with the questions?"

She stood, too, in order not to be at a spatial disadvantage. On her feet, Tana was maybe an inch or two taller than Dean Kaminsky, but what he lacked in height he made up in understated muscular power and breadth of shoulder. Long, strong arms. Prominent brow, pale eyes sunken deep and safely protected in hard bone caves. Low center of gravity. The kind of guy built to take a punch, and give one.

"Two more questions," she said.

He kept his hands in his pockets, his gaze locked on hers.

"The lure that Raj and Selena worked with, what was it made of, and where did they get it?"

"Mixed it themselves. On Crow TwoDove's property—the father of the guy Selena was banging. Crow supplied the guts and blood and stuff from his taxidermy business. Tchliko Lodge brings him the kills from their hunts, if clients want an animal stuffed. He scrapes out the insides, keeps it in barrels in a shed on his farm for Selena and Raj."

"So they mixed the lure primarily from animal guts and blood."

"Rotted blood. Fish, too. Added some vanilla."

"It wasn't easier to use a commercial hunting lure?"

"Expensive, and chemical. This stuff was available. It's not uncommon to make bear lure from what's around."

"It was kept in a secured shed?"

"Sealed drums. Corrugated, galvanized steel shed. Locked. They did their best to ensure it wasn't attracting animals out there."

Tana closed her notebook, and took in the state of Dean's room—his unpacked clothes littering the beds, rifle propped against the wall, boxes of ammo, a hunting bow. Paperback novel lying on the end of his bed.

"You were okay with Selena 'banging' Jamie TwoDove?"

His eyes widened momentarily. Heat burned red across his cheekbones. "Selena's sex life was not my business."

"Yet you raised it."

Silence.

Tana paused, thinking it was irrelevant to the wildlife attack, but, curious, she tested Dean anyway. "What did you feel about Selena's claims that she was being stalked?"

He glanced away for a moment. Then said, "She could be imaginative. Liked to see drama where there was none. Attention seeker."

Tana nodded, noting the cover of the paperback on his bed—looked like a horror novel—blood on snow, big prints leading into dark woods. It was titled *The Hunger*.

"Reading for your trip home?" She tilted her chin toward the book.

"Not going back right away."

"I thought you'd checked out of the motel."

Defiance crackled in his eyes, in his posture. "I'm not going to let this beat me. I'm not running home. I'm not due back for classes for another two weeks."

"What about Raj's and Selena's parents? Veronique said you guys were going to meet them in Edmonton."

"Veronique is going. She was closer to both Selena and Raj. I'm packing Raj's things for her to take. Then I'm going to stay a fortnight with a friend up at Wolverine Falls, do some hunting. And once I've completed my doctorate, I'm coming back out here."

"As in, to live?"

"I like it up north. I'd like to make my life here, yes."

Tana weighed him for a moment—a guy with issues. Defensive. "So, if I need you, I'll find you up at Wolverine Falls. Who are you staying with there?"

"That's none of your business."

"The fact that you're reluctant to cooperate inclines me to make it my business."

"Guy's name is Harvey Black Dog."

Tana noted the name, thanked Dean, and took her leave. As she came down the stairs and reached her ATV, she whistled for her dogs, who came bounding up through hoarfrosted stalks of deciduous scrub. She donned her helmet, careful not to pull at the stitches and bruising along her cheekbone. Firing up her quad, she made for the trail along the river that would take her to O'Halloran's place. She needed an official statement from him about the red AeroStar helicopter seen near the attack site on Friday afternoon.

It was that in-between time when the snow was too sparse for snowmobiles, yet still navigable with an ATV. She'd chosen the four-wheeler this morning so that her dogs could run behind her, and she picked up speed along the water. The morning sun sparkled on ice crystals and painted the river pearlescent pinks and orange. Her dogs chased in her wake, tongues lolling, doggie breath smoking in the cold.

Now those—thought Tana as ice crystals sparked tiny rainbows everywhere—those were the true gems of the north. Diamonds of weather. Precious and rare as the fleeting rays of the sun. There for all, but no one could own them.

She gave her machine juice, sliding and bumping and bashing upriver alongside the chuckling water, and glee filled her heart.

This, baby, this *is why we came here . . . we're going to get more of this. Open skies, natural jewels, a place where the dogs can run free . . . we're going to make this work . . .*

O'Halloran's yellow-and-burgundy plane was parked near the hangar.

Tana drew up outside his house next door to the airstrip, and banged on the door. A sheer in the window shifted. Then the door opened. Tana's heart took a plunge.

Mindy. Sleep-mussed. Swollen-looking lips and bleary eyes. She wore an oversize men's flannel pajama top, nothing else from what Tana could see. And she stank of booze. Christ. Memories slammed through Tana's brain. Guilt. Shame. Remorse. Rage. It boiled into a complex, fucking black cloud she seemed forever unable to outrun. Even here. How many rides along the river with her dogs would it take until she felt free?

The kid eyed Tana in silent hostility.

"Is O'Halloran in?"

"No."

Irritation snapped through her. "Do you know where I can find him?"

"What do you want him for?"

"I need to ask him some questions."

"About me?"

"No."

The look in Mindy's eyes was almost disappointment, then they hardened. "He went with that pilot slut he likes to screw, Heather MacAllistair, to Freak Farm. Bet they're banging away like rabbits right now."

Tana's pulse kicked. She hadn't seen that coming.

"What's 'Freak Farm'?" she said.

Mindy rolled her eyes, as if to say, "loser cop." "That's what everyone calls the taxidermist place," she said.

"Crow TwoDove's?"

Mindy shrugged, started to close the door.

"Wait." Tana halted the door with a gloved hand. "Mindy, if you ever need to talk—"

"I sure wouldn't talk to you."

"Look, I've been where you are. I know—"

"You know *dickshit*!" she said. Tana blinked.

"I'll tell you what I *do* know, Mindy. You're fourteen—"

"Fifteen next month."

"And you're living with a man old enough to be your father. And if he's sleeping with you—"

"Like I said, you know *fuck jackshit.* Loser." She shoved the door closed in Tana's face.

Tana stood there, hands fisting at her sides. Her heart pounded. Anger roiled in her blood, heating her cheeks. Anger at so much more than just what was here in front of her now. Choices. Mistakes. People who'd never helped her when they could have. She wanted to bash down that damn door, haul Mindy Koe out of there, take her somewhere safe, get her into a program. Obliterate her own past. She wanted to physically *hurt* the men who took advantage of women, and children. And in this instant she hated O'Halloran more than she could say. She stomped to her quad where her dogs waited.

Bastard. You sick-shit bastard. Who in this town have you not *screwed? Older meat not fresh enough for you that you must seduce underage teens with booze and God knows what other narcotics you feed the people in this lost and forgotten town . . . your illegal liquor nearly killed a nine-year-old boy, you bastard . . .*

She straddled and gunned her machine, riding too fast along the forest road that would take her to Crow TwoDove's spread, slipping dangerously on ice, adrenaline powering her blood. Her dogs raced to keep up, falling farther and farther behind.

Several blood-pumping miles later, Tana drew up outside the entrance to TwoDove's, breathing heavily. She killed her engine, and studied the place as she waited for her hounds to catch up.

Rough-hewn poles formed a square arch over a long, rutted, snow-covered driveway that led down to a squat log cabin under a listing roof. At the top of the arch, bang in the center, hung the heavy skull of a bison. Beside it on either side wind chimes crafted with what looked like bleached hyoid bones swirled slowly in the ice breeze.

A covered porch filled with junk skirted the log cabin. At the base of the stairs leading up to the porch, a thin husky-type dog lunged and barked against a rope. Smoke curled from the chimney. No vehicles out front. Off to the right-hand side, on land that led down to the river, several barns and outbuildings canted in varying stages of disrepair along with abandoned-looking trucks and an old tractor.

Tana used the moment to simmer her anger down. Her temper was an issue—they'd told her that when she'd started training at Depot Division in Saskatchewan to become a Mountie—something she'd need to work on. She forced herself to breathe deep, and to focus on why she was here: to find O'Halloran, ask him about the red chopper. And since she'd come this way, she'd check out where and how Apodaca and Sanjit had mixed their lure. The attractant likely played a key role in drawing in carnivores, and in leading to the attack. And if Jamie was on-site, she'd tell him that she'd spoken to Viktor, and that they needed to arrange a gathering of the community affected by his actions at the Red Moose.

The Mindy Koe–O'Halloran issue . . . she'd find a way to bite into that later.

Her dogs caught up to her, panting and happy. She dismounted her quad, took their leads from a box on the back. She clipped the leashes to Max's and Toyon's collars.

"You guys need to wait here," she told her dogs as she secured their leads to her quad. "I don't want you coming after me, because that mean-looking ol' husky-wolf down there—this is his place." Poor bastard. "We don't want to mess in his sandbox, okay?"

Dogs secured, Tana walked slowly down the driveway, or what passed for one. The husky yipped and yapped and growled, choking itself against the rope. As she neared the house, the dog fell suddenly silent and slinked under the deck. Awareness prickled down the back of her neck. She slowed, her right hand going instinctively toward her sidearm. She was being watched. Felt it. Tana took in her surroundings carefully. Wraiths of mist sifted up from the river, snaking around the old barn to her right, curling and caressing the derelict, rusting vehicles.

A bent willow rocker stood silent near the front door, which was behind a weather screen. Crows beaded the arms of a totem pole that had been constructed to the left of the cabin.

If this was the place of a great taxidermist, she'd bet her life that the Tchliko Lodge owner never actually brought his clients out here. Tana moved closer, caught sight of a little inukshuk garden in the snow in front of the porch. Her pulse quickened. She told herself it meant nothing. Garden gnomes, northern style. She was being unnaturally jumpy.

Wind chimes tinkled suddenly, and a gunshot blasted the air. Birds scattered off the roof of the barn, filling the sky like swirling black harpies.

Tana froze. Her heart thudded.

A man became distinct from the shadows on the porch. Another shot boomed.

The slug whirred past her face. Tana sucked in air sharply. Heart racing. Her baby rolled in her stomach—*she felt her baby.* She swallowed, eyes burning.

You might be compelled to take a kick, or a bullet, but you've got another life to think about . . .

Slowly she raised her hands out from her sides.

"It's okay," she yelled. "I mean no harm."

The porch creaked. A man with long black hair streaked with gray emerged into her line of vision. He reloaded his shotgun, put stock to shoulder, and aimed the muzzle straight at her heart.

"Trespassers ain't welcome here, Constable. Back off nice and slow, and get the fuck off my land."

Tana's face went hot.

"Just a moment—"

He fired.

CHAPTER 19

Heather's head snapped up. "Gunshots," she whispered.

Crash froze, spanner in hand.

Another crack. Followed by the sound of crows fluttering and dogs yelping. Crash set down his tools, came quickly out from behind the small chopper. He reached for his rifle propped against the wall of the creaking old structure that Heather rented from Crow TwoDove. She was already at the barn entrance.

"Shit," she said, looking out of the door. "It's old man Crow in a standoff with that Mountie. He's going to kill her."

Crash's heart gave a small kick, and a sharp spurt of adrenaline flooded his blood. He hated it the instant he felt it—that old, fucking protective surge. That give-a-shit. Irritability bit into his chest as he came up to Heather's side.

Tana stood in the snow-covered field in front of Crow's house. Crow stood on the porch, shotgun aimed at the Mountie. She held both hands out to her sides to show that they were empty.

What in the hell . . . what did she want here?

"Put that gun down, Mr. TwoDove. I just want to talk to you." She moved closer as she spoke, voice clear, strident.

"Jamie ain't got nothing to do with what happened to those biologists!" Crow's voice carried in the cold air. "White man's police not welcome on my land. I don't got to listen to your law. Your badge, uniform mean nothing to me."

"Sir, please—"

"One step closer and I blow a hole right through your belly, feed you to those scavengers." Up high, two raptors circled, either sensing a kill, or attracted by something else already dead on the property.

She took another step toward the house.

Shit.

Crash stepped out of the barn, loaded rifle in hand. "You're being an ass, Crow! Give the lady a chance—"

"Mounties had their chance three years ago. And look what happened—what they did to *me*, my family. Not on my life am I going to let that shit happen again."

"She's half Dogrib for Chrissakes, if *that* means anything to you." Crash marched out into the field, coming between Tana and the old trapper-taxidermist. "She's northern blood. Like you."

Crow had enough Froot Loops short of a cereal bowl that he'd do it—he'd kill the cop. Or Crash would now take the slug, being in the direct line of fire, so what in the hell was he doing this for? But he knew. Deep down, he knew why he was standing here right now between a half-crazy man and a cop. Even though he didn't want to go there, or articulate it. But if he let Crow kill this woman with an unborn child in her belly, an innocent little thing yet to be screwed over by life, he wouldn't be able to live with himself. Not the second time around.

"She arrested Jamie," yelled Crow. "She's here about Jamie and the wolves and those biologists." He spat into the snow off the deck.

"I'm not here for Jamie," Tana called out. "I came for him, Crash O'Halloran. Mindy told me he was here. And I want to see where those biologists mixed their bear lure. Their teammates said they made it here.

No blame. Just part of a routine report. It's not a criminal investigation, okay?"

Christ, she was taking a step closer. Did she have a fucking death wish?

"Tana," he growled, voice low. "Get your ass over here."

She ignored him.

He surged forward, grabbed her by the arm. "Shut the fuck up about the lure," he hissed. "Let me do the talking."

"Get your hands off me."

"I swear, he'll kill you and leave you on his front lawn for those crows."

She kept her eyes on TwoDove and his shotgun. He could feel her muscles wire-tight under her jacket sleeve, her body humming. Her energy flowed into him like an electrical current. She was setting him to her frequency, and he fought it, fought to keep his hard-won Zen. His devil-may-care, but he was losing.

"See, Crow?" Crash yelled. "I've got her. Now you go put that gun down, nice and slow. And I'll take her from here, okay? I'll take her into the barn. She can ask me whatever she needs. I'll show her where Selena and Raj made the lure, then I'll escort her off the property. All on me, okay?"

Her dogs were going crazy, yelping, barking, and jerking against leashes that had been secured to the ATV she'd parked at the entrance to the farm. Crow's dog watched from under the deck, at the end of his rope, where the animal had dug itself a den to sleep both winter and summer.

TwoDove lowered his weapon. Spat again over the deck railing.

"Come with me," Crash said, his voice low, mouth close to her ear. "Stay near. And just keep your mouth shut."

She shot him a hard look. Her cheeks were pinked. Her dark eyes sparked. He could scent her soap, shampoo. Something trickier, dangerous, braided hot into his already pulsing adrenaline.

"You need to trust me, Tana," he said quietly. Her eyes narrowed sharply at his use of her first name. "I don't want this any more than you do. Just come into the barn. We can talk there."

"Wouldn't trust you if my life depended on it—"

"It does."

Her brow crooked up in interest. "What's his problem with the RCMP?"

"Just walk."

CHAPTER 20

Tana fell grudgingly in step with O'Halloran as he steered her toward the old barn, her dogs still howling and straining against their leads. Her pulse raced. Her mouth was dry. She was shaking. In front of the barn door, snow had been trampled. She saw his truck now, parked around the side, alongside a quad.

"Crow once worked as a guide and wilderness skills teacher for the Twin Rivers culture camp," O'Halloran said as they neared the old building. "He was instructing a course in the trapping and the dressing of small game the year a fifteen-year-old student went missing—"

Tana stopped in her tracks. "Dakota Smithers?"

Something flickered in his eyes. "Keep moving—barn," he said. "Crow's still got his weapon trained on you." She clenched her jaw, allowing him to manhandle her toward safety. His body was up close against hers. She could feel the warmth of his breath. In this light his eyes were the palest green.

"A severe snowstorm hampered the search," he continued. "Dakota was found dead two days later, mauled by animals. Elliot Novak was the cop in town at the time. His own kid had been killed by animals the previous year. He was looking to blame something other than wolves, so he started with Crow. Made it personal."

"What do you mean, 'personal'?"

They neared the barn entrance. Heather MacAllistair was leaning against the door, watching them approach. She wore a pale blue down jacket, jeans. One boot crossed over the other. Casual. Confident in her own body. Tana thought of what Mindy had said about them being sexual partners.

"Dakota's mother, Jennie, told Elliot that Crow used to look at her daughter 'funny,' and she claimed Dakota had felt she was being stalked. That gave Elliot all the ammunition he needed to gun for Crow as a sexual pervert of some kind."

Tana's pulse quickened.

"Other kids then started coming forward at Elliot's urging, and told him that Crow had looked at them funny, too. Long story short, nothing was proved. No signs of sexual abuse on what was left of Dakota's body, which wasn't much. But Crow lost his job and all respect that he might have had in this community. And Elliot was replaced. By that point it was clear he'd long lost the plot. After that, his wife left him, and he went into the bush."

They entered the barn.

Inside was a small red helicopter, tiny thing, the bubble just taller than a man of average height, and just big enough to wedge two people in behind the controls, rotors pretty much right above their heads. Tana stared at it, MacAllistair's words replaying in her mind.

I saw you out there on Friday, Crash. Saw your bird parked just on the other side of the cliff from where those kids were working . . .

At the back of the barn a ladder led up to a walled-off loft that overlooked the floor area. Flight suits and grease-stained coveralls hung from hooks along the wall near the base of the ladder, along with an assortment of farm implements and several large dry bags—the kind used for river rafting trips.

"Hey," MacAllistair said from her position against the door, a glint of amusement in her big blue eyes. "See you got a shiner of your own." She tilted her chin toward Tana's bruised and stitched cheek.

Tana gave her a cursory nod, but the heat of her attention remained fixed on O'Halloran and what he was saying about Crow TwoDove. MacAllistair pushed herself off the doorjamb and followed them into the barn.

"Go on," Tana insisted. "Why did Dakota's mother press this angle?"

O'Halloran inhaled deeply and blew a cloud of white breath out into the cold. "She had a hard time processing her daughter's death, too. She didn't *want* to believe it was an accident. Which fed into Elliot's obsession. They enabled each other. But, bottom line, Dakota's COD was equivocal."

"COD," she repeated, her gaze tunneling into him. "Equivocal?"

"Death—cause of death," he said quickly. "It wasn't clear what killed her. Only that bears, wolves, and other scavengers had picked her pretty much clean after the fact."

"I know what COD means," she said, eyes remaining locked on his. He swallowed. She saw the tattoo on his neck move. "You watch too much crime television, or did I just miss when using 'COD' and 'equivocal' in the same sentence became common lay speak?"

"What are you looking for, Constable, what are you really driving at? What's firing *your* crusade?"

MacAllistair watched them with keen interest while she pretended to busy herself with tools behind the chopper. Irritation flared through Tana's adrenaline.

"Heather," she said quietly, "could you please give me a moment alone with Crash?"

MacAllistair raised her brows, glanced at O'Halloran. "Well, maybe you should take a ticket and stand in line, Constable. Crash was just showing me—"

"I've got it, Heather. I'll finish off later." O'Halloran jerked his head toward a door at the rear of the barn. "Let's take a walk around the back, shall we, officer?" His voice was even cooler now. "I'll show you where those eco-kids mixed their lure, then you can get back to your nice warm—safe—office."

Her jaw tightened. Her eyes held his. Something hot crackled unspoken between them. "Show the way, then," she said, her tone equally cool.

They exited through the rear door, and O'Halloran led her past a paddock in which two skinny horses chewed hay under the cover of a shelter. The scent of them was strong. But then Tana realized the pungent odor was more likely coming from the pigpen they passed next. Snow squeaked under their boots. Eagles wheeled up high.

He took her down to a clearing near the river. "Over there, upriver, is where Jamie lives." He jerked his chin toward a little log cabin nestled under conifers. "And down that way," he tipped his head in the opposite direction, "is the lure shed."

Tana started toward the shed. He followed, still carrying his rifle. The shed was indeed reinforced with galvanized steel, and padlocked. She snapped a few photos with her phone. On a peg outside the shed hung what looked like stained fisherman's waders. In front of the shed was a metal drum, and a fire pit.

"They mixed the lure sludge in that drum there, poured it into containers, and kept those locked in the shed," he said. "In these temperatures it's like keeping it in a freezer. But there is a generator-powered chest freezer inside the shed, and that's where they stored the jerry cans during summer. They only used fresh stuff from Crow. He gets extremely regular business from the lodge, and always has a supply. It's not as weird as it seems."

She jiggled the padlock. "Where's the key?"

"I wouldn't go asking Crow for keys right now."

She inhaled, tamping her frustration down. If need be, she could find a way to return.

Tana took a few more photos, one of the padlock, others of the drum and fire pit. Cold temperatures or not, the place stank.

"Did Selena Apodaca meet Jamie TwoDove here?"

"I guess. What difference does it make?"

She didn't answer. She walked a short way down to the river, getting her bearings.

"So, what did you want with me?" he called down to her. "You told Crow you came here for me."

She walked back up to him. "You own a red AeroStar like that one in the barn?"

"Yeah."

"Did you land it on the northeast side of the cliff at the north end of Ice Lake on Friday, November second?"

His face darkened. "Heather suggest this?"

"Were you there, or not?"

"I was not."

"Who else has a red two-seater AeroStar craft like the one back in that barn?"

"Apart from Heather—I don't personally know of anyone else. Could have come from anywhere. A chopper can cover vast distances, officer. People use helicopters and planes out here like urban dwellers use cars. Only way to get around most of the time."

His patronizing tone rankled.

"Where were you, then, on the afternoon of Friday, November second?"

"What's this got to do with a wildlife attack? It's not a criminal investigation."

"Should it be?"

His eyes slanted to an angry angle. The energy crackling off him became tangible.

"I was doing a supply run."

"For who?"

A muscle started to pulse along his jawline. "For Alan Sturmann-Taylor at Tchliko Lodge. It's a regular gig. Couple of times a week when the weather is good."

"Supplies from where?"

"Depends on his requirements."

"Whole day Friday?"

"Whole afternoon."

"Sturmann-Taylor can vouch for you?"

"Flight logs, too. Speak to him. Fill your boots, Constable. Are we done here?"

She looked away, her mental wheels turning. The wind shifted suddenly, kicking up a fine, white dervish of ice crystals. It whirled over the land toward the forest boundary. And Tana just could not help what came out of her mouth next.

"I saw Mindy," she said. "In your house. Dressed in what was probably your pajama shirt. Stank of alcohol." Her eyes bored into his. "I want you to know, O'Halloran, I find out you're hurting that girl, I swear I'm going to nail you for this. Hard. You're going to go down, no matter how long it takes me."

His shoulders squared, and his gaze locked with hers. His eyes narrowed further and his jaw went tight.

"I don't do PJs," he said, very quietly. "I sleep naked." He paused, letting that visual sink in. "I'd suggest you come around one night and check it out for yourself, because for a while there I reckoned you'd make a pretty decent lay, and I figured I was going to try, but right now I'm getting kinda pissed off with your angle here. So get this straight. First, the liquor. I don't sell to kids, got that? And if it's not me flying illegal booze in, it's gonna be someone else. A demand will always be met. But there's also a system out here, and this system doesn't sell to minors. Whoever crossed that line with little Charlie, you have at him. Or her. And I'll help you fuck the bastard up. But don't make a mistake here, officer, by making enemies of the wrong people." He held her eyes. "Because you're going to need allies."

Fire burned in Tana's throat. Her hands fisted in her gloves.

"And, second, I don't fornicate with minors. Got it?"

She blinked. Anger bled into her cheeks. Wind gusted. Cold. Her eyes started to water.

"So, is there anything else left that you'd like to cover before I show you safely off this property?"

Words eluded her.

"Fine, then let's go." He started to walk away. She remained stationary. He turned, irritated. "I'm not kidding. Crow *will* kill you."

"Why?" she said. "Why even bother with the 'safe escort' bravado shit? Why not just let him shoot me and be done?"

"This a trick question?"

She weighed him, trying to measure, understand him.

He took a step back toward her. "Let me guess something," he said, coming too close, looking down into her face, his voice low, soft. It made her swallow, and this appeared to please him by the glimmer she detected in his eyes. "You know girls like Mindy, and you know them very, very well, don't you, Tana? Because I think you've been there. You were a girl just like Mindy. Men didn't treat you very nicely, and now it's payback time, right? Maybe you even did some of your own time at the deep, dark bottom of a bottle of liquor when you were far too young. And *that* is where this burr under your saddle comes from. *That's* why you're gunning for me."

Heat burned high on her cheeks. Her heart began to gallop all over again.

"Am I right, Constable?"

"Fuck you, O'Halloran," she whispered, her body trembling with outrage. "I'm going to speak to Mindy, her parents—"

"Yeah, good luck with that. Because it's her father who's abusing her and her mother refuses to admit this to herself. And that's why the kid's at my house. And before you go thinking of flying in some social worker for backup, know this—no one is going to voice any complaint to a government outsider. Not Mindy, nor her parents. No one in this community. No complaint—no proof of abuse."

She stared.

"Be careful," he said. "Very careful. You might think you know the game out here, but like I told you, this place has its own rules."

A kestrel screamed up high.

"And before you come accusing me of abusing children again, you think about that one you're carrying."

Shock ripped through Tana. Her eyes burned. "You heard," she whispered. "Last night, you heard me and Addy when you brought the soup."

"Yeah. And maybe *that's* why I bother with the 'safe escort shit,'" he said, taking her arm. "Crow can shoot you for all I care, but you're being an ass about your kid, and I'm not going to stand by watching some innocent baby die."

He steered her back toward the barn. She jerked out of his hold. "Fuck you. I can do this myself."

"Tana, Crow will—"

"Just don't the fuck touch me, okay." She marched back to the barn ahead of him, her whole body shaking inside. This man had just stripped her butt-naked with his words. He saw right into her, and through her. Tana wanted to throw up. She hated him more than anything in this world right now for being right, and being a fucking jackass about it. But deeper down, she knew the real source of her vitriol was her hatred for herself.

160

Heather glanced up as Crash returned to the barn after seeing Tana Larsson off the property. Energy—dark, electric—rolled off him in waves. She'd never seen the crazy dude like this before, without an easy smile, a twinkle in his eyes.

"What did she want with you?" she said, wiping the grease off her hands with a rag.

"To follow up on what you told her—asked if the AeroStar that you saw was mine."

She cocked her head.

"Jesus, I said it wasn't *me* out there, MacAllistair."

"Yeah? Well, I didn't tell her that it was *yours*. I just described the chopper. Said it could have been anyone's."

He started packing up his tools in simmering silence.

"Hey, I don't give a damn whether it was you out there, or not."

He slammed his toolbox shut, not responding.

"Why is it even such a big goddamn issue anyway? It's not like she's hunting some criminal—just information."

He looked up, held her eyes.

"She's not, right?" Heather cursed, looked away, then back. "What? She thinks it's a homicide now? What in the fuck for?"

He came to his feet, and hefted up his toolbox. "That clutch should work fine now." He started for the door where he'd propped his rifle.

"Great," she said. "Another crazy-ass lunatic cop in development. I don't know why you let her get up your nose like that."

He said nothing, grabbed his gun, stepped outside.

Heather hurried after him. "Hey." She touched his arm, stopping him. "Thanks for doing this. The clutch."

"Sure."

"I mean it, thanks."

He held her gaze, then looked down at her hand on his jacket. She withdrew it. Rejection sparked through her, along with hurt. No, not just hurt—it rankled. She hadn't thought it would, not coming from him. She didn't think she'd care if he showed overt interest in another woman, and while he came off angry as a bull, she could tell there was something far deeper and more complicated simmering between him and that Constable Larsson.

"What are you not telling me, Crash?" she said softly. "Why are you letting her get to you like this? What else did that cop woman say?"

"Nothing that's your business."

He left her standing there as he made for his truck parked around the side. Slamming his door, he fired his engine. Heather watched him drive off, her brain churning over the ripples of change the new RCMP officer had brought to town.

CHAPTER 21

Tana opened the file box. A dank, musky scent rose from the papers inside, pervading her nostrils, branching down into her lungs, as if something dead and cold and awful was entering her body. She found the coroner's report on Regan Amelia Novak's death, dusted it off, coughed, and seated herself at her desk.

Rosalie was in the kitchenette, making cocoa. "Can you put some more wood on, crank up the heat?" Tana said, opening the file.

"Are you sure? It's really hot in here." Rosalie said, plugging in the kettle and reaching for the tin of cocoa. "Maybe you're coming down with a chill or something."

Maybe she was, after her frigid night in the wilderness, general lack of sleep, hot-cold hormone flushes, having the stuffing knocked out of her during the fight at the Red Moose. TwoDove nearly shooting her brains out this morning.

O'Halloran's comments . . .

You know girls like Mindy, and you know them very, very well, don't you, Tana? Because I think you've been there. You were a girl just like Mindy . . .

Tana shut her eyes as self-recrimination knifed through her. She'd misread, or rather, not anticipated the situation with Crow TwoDove.

On the back of her self-chastisement came raw anger. At Cutter and Keelan for having turned blind eyes toward this remote, fly-in aboriginal community for so long that it had culminated in a situation that had left her alone, a rookie, to police the town. Because if she'd had a partner—someone who would have known and briefed her on Crow's state of mind and his history and relationship with the RCMP—she'd never have gone onto his land solo like that.

She wouldn't have put her baby in danger.

What ate her from the inside out, though, was the fact that it was O'Halloran who'd saved her ass. And she despised how easily he saw inside her. He saw her shame. Her lack of self-worth. He knew her for what she really was. But what was *he*? What gave him such acute profiling powers? What in hell gave him such self confidence in his assessment?

A confidence that crossed the line into rude.

Crow can shoot you for all I care, but you're being an ass about your kid . . .

She swore out loud. Rosalie, and Max and Toyon all cast a wary eye in her direction.

"You okay?" Rosalie said.

"Peachy." She started to read the Chief Coroner's Office report on the death of Regan Amelia Novak, age fifteen. Only daughter of Sergeant Elliot Novak and Mary Louise Novak.

Four years ago, Twin Rivers RCMP station commander Sergeant Elliot Novak booked off the first weekend in November to take his daughter, Regan, ice fishing and camping. There'd been an early and severe cold snap in late October, and good fishing was to be found on a lake about five miles northwest of the Sleevo Creek tributary that fed into the Wolverine. About six inches of snow covered the ground. Temperatures were in the minus six to ten range, light snow in the forecast. A more serious front was predicted to hit later, but not until after their trip was due to be over.

Some time during the early morning hours of November 4, Regan vacated the tent in which she'd been sleeping with her father.

According to the report, Novak noticed his daughter was missing when he woke around 8:30 a.m. and saw that her sleeping bag was empty. Her boots and jacket were gone, and the tent flap was unzipped. He thought Regan had gone to the bathroom.

But when Novak exited the tent, he saw no fresh tracks leading from the tent. The brunt of the storm was moving in earlier than anticipated, and several inches of new snow had fallen during the early morning hours. This snow had filled in what appeared to be an older depression of Regan's prints, leading away from the tent toward the river. From the amount of snow in his daughter's tracks, Novak deduced that she had left their tent several hours earlier, on her own volition, probably to go to the bathroom, but for some reason, she'd not returned. That was when he began to worry. He called out for her, and quickly began to search the immediate area.

Tana's gaze shot back up to the top of the page. *The early morning hours of November 4 . . .*

Her conversation with Big Indian sifted into her mind:

"You said there was another one."

"Following year. Also just at the start of the snows—first week of November. Dakota Smithers. She was only fourteen years old . . . part of the culture camp that the Twin Rivers School used to hold every year out at Porcupine Lake, to help the kids stay in touch with their indigenous roots. She and some others went out with their dogsleds one afternoon. Dakota got separated from the group when fog rolled in . . .

"November," she said out loud. "Early November."

Rosalie, pouring cream into her mug of cocoa, looked up and said. "What?"

"Regan Novak, Dakota Smithers, Selena Apodaca, and Raj Sanjit were all mauled to death in the first week of November."

Rosalie took a sip from her mug, leaving a chocolaty-cream mustache on her upper lip. She set the mug down. "November is a hungry time for wolves and bears," she said, pouring boiling water into a second cup. She stirred in the cocoa as she poured. "Often a lot of animal activity just before the first really big winter snows. It's like they can smell the storms coming and need to fatten up. And the animals do come closer to town as the cold closes in. Ask Charlie. He'll tell you. Especially the bears. They need to bulk up to full hibernation weight before that snow hits really bad, or they could die over winter. Or the cubs they have in the winter dens wouldn't make it to spring."

Outside a shutter started to bang. Tana looked out the window. Wind was mounting, lifting a fine layer of snow and whirling it in clouds down the street. It was growing darker, too, black clouds boiling in low.

"First of the storms coming," Rosalie said with a nod to the window as she brought a mug of cocoa over. She set it on Tana's desk.

"Where's Porcupine Lake?" Tana said.

"About ten miles south of town. Pretty place, especially in the summer. Nice trout. Traditional fishing place."

"And that's where they used to hold the school culture camp?"

"Each winter. But they stopped after Dakota died. Wasn't an appetite for it any more. Maybe that will change with more time," Rosalie said.

Tana reached for the mug, took a sip, and resumed reading.

According to the report, Novak claimed he had not heard any unusual sounds during the night, apart from an eerie howling in the wind. He explained that sometimes if wind blew in a certain direction, at a certain velocity, through a nearby rocky outcrop, it made that noise—like a human moaning. He also stated that he noticed no drag marks, or scuffles around the tent, no blood, only the depression of snow that led to the river. Novak took his loaded rifle and spare ammunition, and followed the trail up the riverbank. About fifty meters upriver, he noticed what he thought was a second set of snowed-in tracks. That's where snow began to appear "scuffed up" and became tinged with pink, but he said it was difficult to read what might have happened there, because this section of the riverbank was littered with small rocks and stones. He believed the pink to be blood. From there the trail left the river and made a direct line to the woods.

Sergeant Novak became convinced that he was following one set of human prints, and deeper indentations, which he figured were drag marks, possibly made by his daughter's feet.

Novak admitted that he was not a tracker, nor hunter, and he was not experienced in reading spoor. But he insisted it was not animal tracks with the drag marks, but rather a second set of footprints.

Novak followed the tracks to the forest fringe. It began to snow heavily at that point.

Tana reached for her mug, turned the page. Sipped.

At the edge of the forest, Novak came across Regan's flashlight sticking out of the snow. He found this troubling. It was dark under the treed canopy, even during the day. She'd have needed her flashlight, and would have been using it if she'd gone into the forest on her own volition. He entered the woods, and immediately saw signs of a violent scuffle, copious quantities of blood. He noted a piece of a branch in the snow, about the length of a baseball bat, or club. It was heavy, sticky with blood that contained long strands of blonde hair, like his daughter's.

He testified that the area resembled a large animal kill site.

Novak screamed for his daughter. But he said at that point he knew she was dead. "I just knew."

Tana inhaled deeply.

Novak had made these statements from his hospital bed in Yellowknife. He'd made them to Corporal Bo Hague, who'd been brought in to handle the investigation, and to temporarily fill in as the Twin Rivers station commander while Novak recuperated.

She scanned through Hague's notebook pages, which were also in the file box. Tana noted that Hague had asked Novak if he'd had any alcohol to drink before going to sleep in the tent that night.

Novak claimed to have had some brandy, but not much. He said he needed it to sleep. Tana chewed the inside of her cheek, thinking. Perhaps this is why he'd heard nothing—had Elliot Novak been sleeping the sleep of a drunk?

She returned to the coroner's report.

Novak stated that he'd found his daughter's body a short way deeper into the trees, being pulled at by three gray wolves. There were wolf tracks all around. He shot the animals, but there was little left of his daughter. Her body had been badly scavenged—eviscerated. Entrails had been dragged over the snow. Organs eaten. Clothes ripped off. Her head had been torn from her body. Part of her face had been chewed and her eyes ripped out.

A chill trickled down Tana's spine as she thought of Selena Apodaca's decapitated head. The similarities.

Novak did not clearly remember the sequence of events from that point on. He also appeared to have lost all sense of time, because he couldn't say how long he'd sat in the snow with his daughter's remains.

A trapper running his lines on a dogsled found Novak a day later, cradling his daughter's hollowed-out, headless corpse. According to the trapper, Novak was howling like an animal. It was this inhuman, yet not quite animal sound that had drawn the trapper deeper into the woods to investigate.

The trapper's name was Cameron O'Halloran.

Tana froze. Her gaze shot up.

"It was Crash O'Halloran who found Elliot Novak and his daughter?"

"Yes," said Rosalie.

CHAPTER 22

Tana's pulse raced as her mind looped back to what O'Halloran had told her at the barn about TwoDove and the Dakota Smithers case. But not once had he mentioned he himself was also intimately acquainted with the Regan Novak case. *Why?*

Mistrust snaked into her.

He'd been around town in both cases. It could also have been his chopper on the other side of the cliff where Apodaca and Sanjit were killed. This was starting to look weird.

"Were you here, Rosalie, when O'Halloran brought Novak and his daughter's body back into Twin Rivers?"

"Yes. Crash wrapped that poor girl's remains up in his tent, and brought her and her dad into town on his dogsled."

"Did you see them when they came in?"

Rosalie nodded as she fiddled to reset the answering machine. Tana glanced at the clock on the wall. It was late afternoon already. Darkness had fallen outside.

"How were they?"

"What do you mean?"

"How were they behaving? What did they look like?"

"Elliot was badly hypothermic. His mind had gone—he was blathering nonsense about monsters in the forest. He looked terrible. Frostbitten nose, lips, ears. Fingers like blackened talons. You couldn't recognize him as the same man who went out there."

"And O'Halloran? How did he appear?"

"Crash? Like he always is. Can never tell with Crash."

A dark feeling about him filled her.

"So he just happened to be out there in the wilderness, right where Regan was attacked?"

"Nearby. He was helping K'neekap Eddie with his dogs and trap lines. Eddie was sick that season, couldn't get out to check what had been snared in his traps. Crash ran the lines for him that winter."

"Out of the goodness of his heart, I suppose."

She glanced up. "Well, yes. Elliot was lucky. Without Crash out there, he would have died, too."

"How long has he—Crash—been here in Twin Rivers?"

Rosalie pursed her lips. "That winter was his second, I think, when he ran the trap line for old Eddie."

"And he's been in town ever since?"

"On and off. The following summer, I think, he went to fly contract for some mining outfit up near Nunavut, but he came back the next fall. That's when he brought his own plane, that de Havilland Beaver, and started flying supply runs. His first big local contract was for Alan Sturmann-Taylor at Tchliko Lodge. Sturmann-Taylor had bought the lodge the year before Crash arrived, and had started doing big renovations. He needed all sorts of things all the time. Then Crash began some flights for Harry Blundt's crew." Rosalie stopped to listen to a voice mail. She jotted down a number, and said. "Elliot came back, too, you know. As soon as he was able."

"Back here, to the station, to work?"

"Yes. Corporal Bo Hague only filled in for a while. But it was not a good thing that Elliot returned to work. He became increasingly obsessed by what had happened to his daughter. Although the autopsy couldn't show without a doubt *how* she died it was clear that wolves and bears ate her body. But which animal—or what—killed her, nobody could tell for sure. Elliot, he got to thinking it was some person who'd murdered Regan and left her out there."

"Because of the tracks? Because he saw what he thought were human prints with bloodied drag marks?"

Rosalie nodded. "But those tracks—it was only Elliot's word. By the time the other cop and a coroner got out there, there'd been heavy snow, then freezing rain. They couldn't find the tracks."

"What about O'Halloran, did he see the tracks when he found Novak?"

"Crash's priority was to get Elliot back to Twin Rivers for medical attention. Bundled him and Regan's body up. And came right in." She paused, her face changing, eyes going distant at some memory. She shook her head. "It was like guilt drove Elliot's obsession to find and blame someone."

"Guilt?"

She nodded. "Like with Jankoski, he'd started drinking a bit."

"So, you think he was inebriated that night, sleeping like a drunk while his daughter was attacked?"

"That kid had to have screamed, Tana, *something*. Maybe if Elliot had been sober, he'd have woken, and been able to help her."

Tana stared at Rosalie.

"I think that's why Elliot's wife left in the end. She blamed him, too."

"So, when did Buccholz arrive to take over?"

"The next winter, after Dakota Smithers was mauled. That's when Elliot had started to go really crazy, drinking very heavily. Having blackouts. Not remembering where he'd been, and for how long. So they had to let him go. They brought Buccholz in. But Elliot kept coming around to the station, pestering him on the Dakota case. And then he broke in."

"And that's when these files ended up in that crawl space?"

"Yup."

Tana muttered a curse. They were all nuts. This place was nuts. And this wolf stuff was downright weird. What were the odds of all three attacks occurring the first week in November, different animals—same pattern of predation? She definitely needed to talk to Charlie.

"What really got Elliot in the end," Rosalie said, "was when Corporal Bo Hague hinted that maybe he'd hurt his own daughter, then left her out there where the wolves could get her and cover things up. And Bo was kind of wondering if maybe Elliot could have hurt Dakota, too."

The shutter banged louder, temperatures dropping as wind sought ways in through the cracks.

"You mind if I leave early today, Tana?" Rosalie said, glancing out the window. "Snow will be here soon, and I want to check on Diana with her sick baby."

"Sure. It's fine. Go."

Tana returned her attention to the pathologist's report on Regan Novak while Rosalie fussed about, getting her gear on.

The cause of death was equivocal—it could have been a bear, or wolves. There was clear evidence both animals had fed on her.

Regan likely succumbed to exsanguination—catastrophic blood loss. There was blunt-force trauma to the base of her skull, along with symmetrical tearing, and partial scalping. One carnivore expert said this was consistent with a grizzly attack. A five-hundred- to six-hundred-pound bear could wield phenomenal force. Similar claw marks showed on parts of her body. Four parallel rips.

Like Tana had seen on both Selena and Raj.

"See you tomorrow, Tana," Rosalie said.

"Yeah. Have a good night," Tana said without looking up. The door opened with a blast of cold, and then Rosalie was gone.

Tana studied the photos of Regan's torso closely. The hollowed-out stomach, and chest. No heart. She shivered, and looked up. The fire was still burning fiercely, her dogs lying contentedly in front of it. She got up, checked the windows. They were all tightly closed and locked. She turned the heating thermostat up, making a mental note to get someone in to insulate that crawl space.

Reseating herself at her desk, she pulled out the black-and-whites of Regan's head. Tana swallowed. The flesh at the neck stump was torn and chewed-looking. Just like Apodaca's.

The similarities, the power and violence in the violation of these bodies, was both sinister and undeniable. Her brain wanted to go there, but reality, logic, resistance was saying no: it *couldn't* have been a person who'd done this, and then left the bodies for the scavengers.

Could it?

The implications would be shocking—the kind of thing you might get away with on a weekly TV show that featured a gruesome serial killer case for thirty-five minutes each week, where viewers clicked their television sets on and sat there all ready to just throw disbelief away to the wind, and watch the horror porn. Because, in reality, this sort of thing was rare. Very rare.

Or was this getting to her, was she going places that Elliot Novak went in his mind? Or . . . had Novak actually been onto something?

Could it have been Novak himself?

She needed to find him. She needed to talk to him.

THE HUNGER

Moreau was taciturn at best, prone to bouts of dark solitude should he spend too long a span away from the northern wilds. He could carry, paddle, walk and sing as well as any Voyageur Cromwell did see. The small man would rise early, often around two, or three, setting off without breakfast, eating only a piece of pemmican along the day, but always stopping a few minutes each hour to suck upon his pipe. Not in all the while that Cromwell had traveled the fur route with his man had he seen raw fear in the Voyageur's eyes. But on this night along the fringe of the Barrens, the territory of the Copper Indians, as Cromwell regarded Moreau, he witnessed the moment the man knew he was prey . . .

The Reader rams a spike down into the page. Frustration fires along the periphery of the Reader's mind. It's changed. All changed. The pleasure, the privacy is no longer there. The Hunger is coming again, too soon.

It's the Mountie. Circling closer, closer. Like a hunting carnivore herself . . .

CHAPTER 23

Tana fed her dogs, stoked up the fire, and returned to the pile of papers on her desk. Outside the wind howled down the street and rattled at the police cabin windows. It had started to snow. She could see the white stuff being plastered against the dark panes.

She opened the report on Dakota Smithers, fourteen years old.

The account matched what she'd been told. Dakota had been attending the Twin Rivers School annual wilderness culture camp at Porcupine Lake over the last days of October into November. The camp was held over the same period each year. On the morning of November 3 she'd participated in a fish smoking demonstration, and a tallow candle-making workshop.

Tana's heart quickened—November 2, 3, 4—a sequence? Or just close dates because this was usually when the really big winter storms started? She flipped over the page.

After lunch Dakota was part of a group that went out on dog-sleds with headlamps. Fog had blown in thick along the river late that afternoon, and it had started to snow. In the darkness and fog, Dakota became separated from the group.

The rest of the group returned to camp, and a small search party was launched, but severe weather and fog hampered efforts. That night the dogs returned with the sled. No Dakota.

She was found two days later, down the riverbank in a ravine. Her body had been severely scavenged by predators.

Tana studied the autopsy photos, and the chill deepened into her bones.

Ripped-off head. Evidence of four parallel claw marks on parts of her body and clothes. Concave depression at the base of her skull and partial scalping. Missing internal organs, including heart. Eyes ripped out and part of her face eaten. The pathologist found no evidence of sexual assault, but her pubic and bowel area had been eaten.

On Dakota's body were trace amounts of fish blood, and . . . vanilla.

Her breathing quickened, tension crackling through her limbs as Dean Kaminsky's words came to mind.

. . . *Rotted blood. Fish, too. Added some vanilla . . .*

The coroner's report suggested the blood and vanilla found on Dakota had come from the fish smoking and candle-making workshops, respectively.

Tana lurched up from her chair and began stuffing all the papers back into the file box. She lugged the box through to the small interview room, clicked on the light. The room contained a table, and a whiteboard that ran the length of the back wall. She dumped the box onto the table and fetched a black marker. She drew four stark parallel lines down the whiteboard, dividing it into five wide columns.

Alerted by her change in energy, her dogs came into the room to see what she was doing. They settled under the table while Tana spread photographs out on the table and sifted through them. She returned to her desk, retrieved the Apodaca-Sanjit scene photos that she'd printed to show Charlie. She also printed out the image of Apodaca and Sanjit that Veronique Garnier had forwarded to her.

At the top of the third column she stuck Regan Novak's photo. Dakota Smithers's headshot went at the top of the fourth column, and in the fifth column, she placed the photograph of Selena Apodaca and Raj Sanjit.

She stood back a moment. Three young women. One guy. The bodies of the women all showed remarkable similarities in pattern of predation. The male body had suffered far less indignity. Was there a reason for this?

With her marker, under the image of Smithers, and under the one of Apodaca and Sanjit, she wrote: *Vanilla?*

The upcoming autopsies would show if there was indeed evidence of vanilla on the bodies of Apodaca and Sanjit, but Tana had seen traces of blackened sludge on them. It looked the same as the dark contents she'd seen in the jerry cans. And Dean Kaminsky had said the biologists had added vanilla to their lure mix, so she was guessing.

There was no mention of vanilla or any kind of lure in the Regan Novak case, however.

Under Smithers's photo, Tana wrote: *Stalked?* She did the same under the image of Apodaca where she also pasted the scrap of paper with the hand-printed poem that Veronique had found among Selena's things.

For, in the Barrens of the soul
monsters take toll . . .

Wind howled under the eaves, and something *thucked* against the wall outside, making Tana jump. Max growled. Tana paused, marker in hand, listening. But no more bumps came in the night, just the sound of the wind.

She stood back and studied the words, frowning. What did they mean? Where had they come from? Why had Selena had this? She turned and carefully sifted again through the images in the Dakota Smithers case, and then she came across one that made her blood run cold.

The team that had finally gone in to investigate the area where Dakota's body had been found had photographed the surrounding terrain. And at the top of the ravine an inukshuk had been captured on film. Quickly, Tana rummaged through her own printouts, found the one she'd taken of the inukshuk at the Apodaca-Sanjit scene.

Dryness balled in her throat. It was almost identical in its construction, the longer of the two stone arms pointing toward the scene of death. A wayfinder of the north. Tana told herself many inukshuks looked the same—how many different ways could one build a stone man, anyway, with the flat rocks available out here? And these things were everywhere. Her mind went to the inukshuk garden in front of Crow TwoDove's house.

She pinned up both images. The one in the Smithers column. The other that she'd taken in the Apodaca-Sanjit column.

Then at the top of the first column she wrote: *Persons of Interest.*

In that column she wrote:

Cameron "Crash" O'Halloran—*Owns red AeroStar. Heather MacAllistair saw a red AeroStar near scene around possible time of deaths. Sturmann-Taylor alibi? O'Halloran was in the woods near Regan Novak mauling site—first on scene. In a position to compromise evidence. Where was he when Smithers was killed?*

Beneath that she wrote:

Crow TwoDove—*Investigated for possible stalking and sexual interest in school kids. Lost job. Resentment. Violently anti-cops.*

That was one thing about these deaths, Tana thought as she went back to the photos spread out on the table. Violence. Bloody chaos. Power. Raw strength.

She found the photo she was searching for—a head shot of Sergeant Elliot Novak looking dark haired, square jawed and handsome in his official red serge and Stetson. She stuck that image up in the *Persons of Interest* column as well. Beside it she placed the photograph that had been taken for the coroner's report after Novak had been rescued by

O'Halloran. The contrast was shocking. In the "after" photo Novak was missing part of his nose, and two wide nasal cavities gaped at the camera. His eyes had sunken into hollows beneath the bone of his brow, his cheeks had been sucked in. Part of his lip was missing, also due to frostbite.

There was a sense of "otherness" about him. As if he'd gone out there into the wild and returned a hollowed-out husk of the human he once was, as if he'd been changed into some kind of cadaverous monster.

Wind gusted again, and hair prickled up the back of Tana's neck. She didn't want to fully articulate to herself yet the patterns she was seeing on this board. She felt surreal, as if she'd entered some strange landscape, and to admit what she was thinking would forever suck her down into that world with no avenue for return.

She rubbed her arms, trying to get some warmth back into her body, then she reached again for her marker.

Under Novak's photos she wrote: *Alcoholic? Blackouts? Memory issues? Mentally unstable? Possibly hurt his own daughter? Where was he when Smithers went missing? Where is he now? Where was he when Apodaca and Sanjit were killed? Could he be the man in fur that Selena Apodaca thought she'd seen from MacAllistair's chopper on the morning of Friday, November 2?*

In the second column, Tana wrote: *First week of November, consecutive dates—significance? Inukshuks—relevant?* In the same column she stuck up the mystery Baffin-Arctic size-nine boot print with the rip in the lug. Just about everyone in the north owned a pair of Baffins. And size nine was common. But that ripped pattern in the tread was unique. Or a temporary anomaly caused by something stuck under the boot.

To the first column she added: **Jamie TwoDove**—*involved with Apodaca. Knows something about bones found with Apodaca's body? Attacked Caleb Peters in connection with bones?* Tana stuck up several photos of the old, porous bones.

She added a few more names that had piqued her curiosity in connection with the attacks.

Caleb Peters—*what does he know about old bones? Where was he at times of attacks? Had connection to Apodaca through Jamie TwoDove. Any connection to other victims?*

Beneath his name she wrote: **Marcus Van Bleek, Teevak Kino, Big Indian, Harry Blundt. Other mine crew?**

Apodaca thought she'd seen a man. He could have been any one of the above given the proximity of the camp to the attack site.

She added the name **Dean Kaminsky**—*Unrequited romantic interest in Selena Apodaca. Jealous? Possible stalker and threats?*

But Kaminsky was likely not around three and four years back. Still, she needed to keep an open mind. Apodaca's stalking might have no relevance at all to the attack on her and Sanjit. Or to the possibly manufactured account of Dakota Smithers being stalked.

And the attacks might just be wolves, or bear. It was entirely possible. And it was believable that most people had been able to accept this outcome . . . until now. Until Selena Apodaca and Raj Sanjit's case, which was throwing some stark parallels into focus.

She stood back, examining her board.

Irrespective of how all four had actually died, the patterns of wildlife predation on the bodies of Regan Novak, Dakota Smithers, and Selena Apodaca were starkly, hauntingly, undeniably similar. The hollowed-out rib cages. Missing hearts. Ripped-out eyes. Parallel clawlike gouges. The concave depressions at the base of the skulls. Heads torn from bodies. Evisceration.

Jamie's words slithered back into her consciousness.

. . . They scrape the soul—your heart—right out of your chest. Take your eyes so you can't see in the afterlife . . .

Tana stepped up to the board and beneath Raj Sanjit's photo she wrote: *Different predation pattern on male. Left with heart and parts of other organs. Head and eyes intact. Why? Females prime target? Male = collateral damage?*

Tana walked to the window, thinking of the two inukshuks, the vanilla—why? To lure scavengers after death, to cover something up? Frost feathered the panes, and snow stuck to the outside surface of the glass. She listened to the moaning wind. She could see it. How the isolation and darkness of this place, the sense of otherworldliness, could allow obsession—madness—to take hold. And she hadn't even begun to face the winter yet. It was only November.

Early November. When the clocks changed for winter. Her father used to say it was at this time that the veil between seasons—between the living and the spirit world—grew thin, at least according to his childhood Scandinavian tales. It was when the dark things began to creep out of the woods.

Toyon came to his feet and pressed his warm body against her leg. She smiled, bent down, and scratched his furry neck. She glanced at her watch. It was after 9:00 p.m. already, and she was famished.

"Time to get some food, boys," she said to her dogs as she exited the room. They followed, and she closed the door to the interview room behind her. She reached for her jacket, gloves, hat, and bundled up to face the storm on the way to the diner just down the street. She could use the company she might find there.

CHAPTER 24

Tana stomped snow off her boots, dusted off her jacket, and pushed open the door to the Twin Rivers General Store and Diner. A bell chinkled and warmth embraced her, along with the scent of fried food, coffee, freshly baked bread. The aura inside was convivial, the chatter loud, the tables almost all occupied. Most of the patrons looked up as she entered.

Tana identified a huddle of old-timers seated near the counter, hands cradled around steaming mugs. She was surprised to see Van Bleek at one table, his back to her, but unmistakably him. He was talking to a round-faced, balding man with red-rimmed glasses in his late fifties, she guessed—someone she'd not seen in town before.

A bunch of teens occupied two tables down the room to the right, Mindy among them. They conversed over glasses of pop and plates heaped with fries, and were partially cut off from the main diner area by a shelving partition stocked with chips, chocolate bars, peanuts, and other snacks. At the far back was the general store area, and a tiny section with pharmaceutical goods, as well as a small shelf of books, DVDs, and old-style videocassettes.

Tana removed her snow-caked hat and mitts, thinking Mindy was the same age as Regan Novak and Dakota Smithers when they'd died.

She placed her mitts on one of the few unoccupied tables—a small two-seater next to the door and under a window from where she could watch her dogs out on the deck.

Mindy glanced up, stared. Tana nodded. Mindy flipped her the finger, then put her head down and laughed with the others. A bad taste filled Tana's mouth, and an ache swelled in her chest. For Mindy. For her old self, which she recognized in the kid.

. . . *You were a girl just like Mindy. Men didn't treat you very nicely, and now it's payback time, right? Maybe you even did some of your own time at the deep, dark bottom of a bottle of liquor when you were far too young. And* that *is where this burr under your saddle comes from. That's why you're gunning for me . . .*

Heat burned into her face and she hated O'Halloran all over again. For reading her. For whatever he was doing with Mindy. She didn't believe a word the bastard had said about the kid. She didn't trust him as far as she could throw him.

She shrugged off her jacket, hung it over the back of the chair, and made her way to the counter.

Van Bleek looked up as she passed his table.

"Officer," he said, his eyes expressionless.

"Markus," she answered. "Harry gave his mine security the night off, then?"

He didn't smile. "Pretty much," he said, rolling his *R*s in his thick Afrikaans accent. "Some of the other guys are back from Yellowknife. Even us badasses get time off. This is Henry Spatt." The round, baby-faced man nodded. "He's a writer visiting Tchliko Lodge."

"Pleased to meet you," Tana said, offering her hand.

The man half got up, and shook her hand. His skin was warm, fleshy, his grasp limp like a woman's. She noticed a novel on the table at his side. It faced cover down.

"First time out at the lodge?" she asked.

"Been coming for the last five years, and will keep doing so as long as Charlie Nakehk'o can, or will, guide us." He smiled. His incisors hung lower than the rest of his teeth and were small and pointed. "He's the draw—one helluva tracker, that guy, best guide I've ever had the pleasure of hunting with. I met Markus here on our second trip four years back."

"Hadn't realized you'd been in town for so long," Tana said to Van Bleek.

"Back and forth for the last four plus years," he said. "Since Harry found the first kimberlite pipes. He brought me on board that same year, to check out the lay of the land, start planning."

"Well, enjoy your meal." She hesitated, then said to Van Bleek, "Thanks for your help Sunday."

He gave a nod. But again, his eyes remained dark and unreadable.

She made her way to the counter where Marcie worked with remarkable stamina for her seventy-eight years.

"Good evening, Tana, how are you tonight—what can I get for you?" Marcie said in her halting, singsong voice. That she was a native North Slavey speaker was clear by her accent and cadence, the slow formalities of culture.

Tana smiled—Marcie had that effect on one. With her wizened old face, smooth brown cheeks, deep-set tiny brown eyes, and the way she wore her colored head scarves tied under her neck, she seriously reminded Tana of her gran who'd passed right after Jim shot his brains out in her white-tiled bathroom.

"I'm good, thanks, Marcie." Tana studied the whiteboard menu behind Marcie. "I'll have the chili with the bannock."

"Good choice. I just baked a fresh batch of the bannock," she said.

"And all's well with you?" Tana said.

She gave a slight bow of her head. "It's been a good day." She leaned up to the hatch that opened to the kitchen at the back, and asked the chef for one chili special. Tana figured it was going to be moose mince. In Tex-Mex disguise.

"I'll bring it over to your table," Marcie said, ringing Tana's purchase in and noting it on her tab, old style, in a ledger. Tana signed for it and made her way back to her table. She seated herself with her back to the wall so that she could observe the room, as well as her dogs outside. They lay in the snow on the porch, waiting for her. Fat flakes swirled in the wind around them. They didn't mind. They loved the cold—were born to it with their thick coats. Her heart warmed whenever she looked at Toyon and Maximus—her true friends. Never any judgment as long as she was there with food and water for them, and plenty of exercise. Both had had a rough start in life, and she'd given them a second chance, and second chances resonated with Tana.

It's what she was striving for out here herself.

Marcie brought the bowl of chili and a hunk of bannock over.

"Terrible thing," she said as she set the simple supper down in front of Tana along with a spoon. "Those biologists and the wolves."

"It is." Tana reached for the bannock and tore off a chunk. Steam exploded with the fragrance of freshly baked bread. Hunger cramped her stomach. She delivered the bread to her mouth, closed her eyes, savoring the taste for a second. She grinned. "Reminds me of my gran," she said.

"She makes bannock?"

"Used to. On the fire, outside. I lived with her a while."

While my mother was too drunk . . . and my dad did one of his disappearing tricks . . .

"You did a good job, you know, with Charlie's little nephew, and taking that alcohol away from Damien and those boys. It's a good thing that you are here," Marcie said in her soft, slow voice.

Tana paused midchew, met Marcie's eyes. "You have no idea how much that means to me—thank you."

"Is Jamie going to work off the damage at the Red Moose now?" she said.

"I think so." Tana hesitated, glancing at the other tables. All occupants were engrossed in conversation. She lowered her voice and said, "Marcie, do you know of anyone who might have gone missing, many years ago, at the north end of Ice Lake, or if there could be an old burial site out there?"

Marcie's body went still. Her eyes changed. Tana could literally feel the walls go up.

"Why?" she said.

"Just curious."

"The names of old burial places belong to the families of those buried," she said. "They are not to be asked about."

Tana nodded, and brought a spoonful of chili to her mouth. "What about missing people? Not just locals, but are there any old stories of missing outsiders in that area."

"I don't think so."

"This is good, Marcie," Tana said, pointing her spoon at the chili bowl. "Tell chef."

"Moose," Marcie said.

"I guessed." Tana smiled.

"Well, I will go and tell chef. Let me know if I can get you anything else, Constable?"

Tana hesitated. "There is one thing—do you know anyone who'd take me out to find Elliot Novak?"

The whole diner seemed to suddenly go still. Faces turned to look at her. Marcie made a small sign of a cross—the visible legacy of the Catholic colonization out here decades ago. Like the small church down the street. This place was a mix of myth and religion and aboriginal tradition unique to the area.

Crystals ticked against the windows. A gust of wind lifted a whirlwind of flakes, momentarily obliterating the porch light.

"You want to be careful, Tana," Marcie said, very quietly. "I don't know why you are asking all these questions, but you should stop. Let the natural order of things—the way of nature—take its course. It has a way of doing what is right. It was this kind of thing that drove Elliot mad. Too many questions."

"I just want to meet him. I need a guide to help me find him."

"He's in a dark place. Badlands. Not safe. You will not find a local guide who will go in there."

"Not even Charlie?"

"Not Charlie."

The door swung open with a gust of cold. Crash O'Halloran entered, dwarfing the space, sucking the air out of it like a vacuum, right out of Tana's chest. He froze at the sight of her.

Shit.

"Oh," Marcie said. "Someone like Crash. He might take you. She will be safe with you, won't she, Crash?"

Safe was the last thing Tana felt when she thought about Cameron "Crash" O'Halloran.

He palmed off his hat, bits of snow falling off him. "What are you talking about?" He didn't look at Tana. He addressed Marcie.

Marcie wavered. Her gaze darted to the group of old-timers who were now all openly listening, faces turned toward them. Among them Tana noted two ice road engineers she'd been seeing in town recently. A sense of tension tightened into the warm, food-scented air.

"To see Elliot Novak." Marcie walked back to the counter. "What can I get for you, Crash?"

He stood there, looking at Tana. Then Marcie. Mindy got up, started coming over. Tana tensed. He did, too.

"Why do you want to see Elliot?" he said, green eyes sparking into hers.

Tana's jaw tightened. "To talk to him."

Mindy reached them. "Hey, Crash." She placed her hand on Crash's arm, and he did not push her away. He kept his eyes locked with Tana's.

Animosity spewed through Tana. Mindy angled her head and gave a sickly sweet smile. "This lady cop is trying to tell me who I can sleep with, Crash."

He said nothing.

Tana shoved her bowl aside, slapped her napkin on the table, pushed back her chair, and came to her feet. She grabbed her hat, jacket, gloves, and brushed past him as she made for the door.

"No need to leave on my account," he said.

"Lost my appetite." She yanked open the door, and let it swing shut behind her, slicing off warmth, light, the scent of food, sound of chatter. Him. Outside the air was sharp and awhirl with snow. She tugged on her gear as her dogs wiggled over. She crouched down to pet them.

Everyone needs a tribe, Tana . . .

She was trying, by God she was trying, but she seemed to be alienating herself at every turn.

She inhaled deep, drinking in the cold, cold air, drawing comfort from her dogs. "Hey, guys," she said softly, ruffling their fur with her mitts. "At least I got you two—" She stilled. Blood covered their muzzles.

There was blood on her gloves.

Fear, shock slammed through her. She glanced up, saw meat bones on the deck, near the stairs. Great, big, raw and bloody ones, pinking the snow where her dogs had been eating them.

"Who gave you those?" She held Toyon's head between her mitts. He was salivating, strings of drool hanging from his mouth. His body was trembling. Max's, too.

Oh, my, God.

A screaming noise began inside her brain. Her heart began to pelt in her chest.

"Come on." She took them by the collars, and led them down the steps. Tana hurried with her animals through the blizzard toward the lights of the police station, panic rising, suffocating her chest. She took her dogs inside, brought them in front of the fire where she could examine them properly in the light. Her hands were shaking. Tears blurred her eyes.

Max flopped onto his mat, his legs quivering. Toyon sat, listless, blood-stained saliva foaming at his mouth. As she peeled back his lips to check the color of his gums, glass tinkled behind her. A small windowpane shattered as a rock hit Rosalie's desk and bounced onto the floor. Cold wind tunneled in through the broken window. Shadows darted in front of the light coming from the satellite-and-cell-tower communications enclosure outside.

Her heart thumped. Fear kicked her. Triage. Dogs first. No vet in town. She had to do this herself, make them throw up. If she was lucky, it might get rid of whatever was poisoning them. But if it was rat poison, or something like that . . . they wouldn't stand a chance. They could die a slow and horrible death over days.

It had to have been in those bones. She needed to know what the poison was. Someone coming into the diner, or leaving the diner, could have poisoned her dogs.

"Wait here!"

She flung open the door and ran, head bent into the driving snow. She clumped up the stairs to the diner. The bones were gone. Just bloody spots remained. She bashed through the door in a flurry of flakes and wind. Everyone spun around. The place fell silent.

"Who!" she yelled. "Who poisoned my dogs? Who gave them those bones!?" Her voice shook. Her arm trembled as she pointed to the window. Her eyes blurred with tears.

"What's on them? Marcie? Bones—*who* gave my dogs bones, I need to know what they ate, dammit!"

Everyone just stared. Marcie looked frightened. Crash came to his feet. He gripped her arm hard.

"Tana. *Tana! Look at me. Focus.*"

Yes . . . Yes, focus.

"Max and Toyon have been poisoned," she said. "I . . . I don't know with what."

"Go back to them. *Now.* Be with them."

He strode to the pharmacy section at the back of the building. "Peroxide, Marcie, you got hydrogen peroxide? I know you have charcoal. Tana—*go!* I'm coming."

She swore under her breath, face hot, and she raced out.

CHAPTER 25

Crash sat near the warm stove. At his feet Tana lay asleep on the dog mats with her arm over Max and Toyon as they slept.

It was near midnight. The wind howled and outside the window snow shapes lurched and ducked and danced like spirits—bumping and ripping against the plastic that Crash had taped over the broken window.

He wiped his brow, and realized his hand was trembling, just slightly. He held it out at arm's length, stared at it, willing it still, reminded of the terrible heroin withdrawal. The methadone treatment. The rehab center.

His past.

It was leaking like a dark ink through the cracks—hairline fissures that this woman at his boots was feathering through him. He inhaled deeply as he studied her in repose, liking how the glowing embers behind the little smudged window in the iron stove cast a reddish glow on her dark-brown gloss of hair. It spilled around her now. She'd taken the hair tie out. Her gun belt and bullet-suppression vest had been removed and her top buttons undone. It made her look vulnerable. So young. Softly feminine.

He'd found peroxide in the store, but had been forced to go wake Addy upstairs at the clinic for activated charcoal. He knew she used it for the not-so-occasional emergency overdoses in town. He'd helped Tana administer the peroxide to her dogs, showing her how much. They'd made them vomit on the porch outside the police station, and she'd sat there in the snow with them, tears streaming down her face and she'd repeated again, and again, "You can't leave me . . . not now. Max . . . Toyon . . . Not now."

Crash had then administered the activated charcoal as per Addy's hurried suggestions.

Now they waited.

If it was strychnine, or something in that vein, their efforts could prove useless. Her pets might yet succumb, and die, and the thought killed him. He could see how she needed these dogs.

But their muscle tremors had quieted. The extreme salivation had stopped. They'd started drinking water. And now they slept.

He watched the heave and exhale of the canine stomachs as they breathed, Tana's hand rising and falling with the movement. No ring on her finger.

No man in her life.

His gaze moved down to her waist. A single mother-to-be. A cop on her own in more ways than the obvious. She had more spunk than most, too. He respected her, the way she'd handled him and demanded a flight out to WestMin on Sunday night. The way she'd stormed into the fray at the Red Moose, and how she'd tackled Jamie, shoving him to the ground, and cuffing him, but with compassion at the same time. She was strong, no question. Stubborn. But she'd been rattled, badly, by the assault on her animals. And yeah, he'd seen the rawness of fear in her eyes, in her face. He knew that kind of fear, too, that came when you were going to lose someone or something you loved, and were powerless against the forces coming to claim those lives from you.

Unless this was an accident—unlikely, given the broken window, and the meat bones that had gone missing—whoever had done this to her had hit a home run. Tana Larsson had made enemies. Who, he wondered, hated her enough to do this? Damien and the gang from Wolverine Falls, because she'd confiscated their shipment of liquor?

Guilt, unwanted and familiar, washed over Crash. He was behind the liquor shipment that could have put her in this position.

Crow?

Maybe, but Crow was more inclined to defend his home than come out on the attack.

Not Jamie, although he'd seen Maximus latch onto Jamie's leg outside the Red Moose. Perhaps someone else at the Red Moose had seen it, too, and taken offense?

As he studied her features, the way her mouth was open slightly as she breathed, his chest crunched, and a tendril of anger snaked around his heart. With the conflicting emotions came all sorts of complicated shit. He got up, paced, edgy again. Increasingly so. He needed to leave. He was desperate to leave, yet unable to abandon her like this.

"Has anything like this happened in town before?"

He jumped at the sound of her voice, spun around.

"Pet poisonings," she said. She was up on her elbow, hair falling in a soft and distractingly feminine frame around her face. Her eyes were large, fathomless hollows in this light. A strange kind of longing filled him, something quite apart from desire, yet totally a part of it. He shook his head.

"Not that I know."

She weighed him. "How did you know?" she said. "How did you know how to treat my dogs?"

"I had one—a dog," he said, before he could catch himself from wading in further. "He was a Lab who ate everything, and one day he got into some toxic shit."

Her gaze locked with his. "When?"

"Another life," he said quietly. "When I was married."

Asshole. What in the hell do you think you are doing . . .

Her eyes narrowed slightly. She was profiling him, trying to understand whether she could trust him—he could read it all in her face. And he wondered just how rounded a picture of him she now held in her mind. How true, or how false. And did he care? To her credit, she decided not to push him, sensing, perhaps, that this was a big revelation for him. And that a more gentle cracking of his balls might yield better results. She was a good cop. She had the instincts. She could have a long career road ahead if she didn't get too jaded, or if this place and the oddity of her situation here didn't break her first. And there was the baby thing.

He'd do best to distance himself from her, but it was too late for that now.

She turned and ruffled Toyon's ear softly, her eyes filling again, and he wanted to touch her, hold her, kind of bury himself in the puppy pile on the dog beds in front of the fire. Cuddle her and the dogs, all together, close, which was just insane. He dragged his hand over his hair, tension crackling under his skin.

A memory, sharp and hurtful, knifed through him—him lying with Leah, baby Gracie and the new pup between them, the smile on Leah's face.

And as if reading his mind, she said, quietly, "Kids?"

He walked to the window, examined the plastic he'd affixed to the pane with duct tape, his heart beating a sudden tattoo in his chest. He heard her opening the stove door, clunking logs into the fire, stoking it, closing the door.

"Yeah," he said finally. "A daughter." *And an unborn child. Also a baby girl.*

"How old?"

"She's twelve now." *The other one is dead. I could have saved her.*

Silence.

He turned to judge her reaction. A strange intensity crackled in her eyes. He knew she had to be thinking of what he'd said to her at Crow's ranch. She had to be thinking of her own baby. Crash returned to the fire, reseated himself, bent down to stroke Max.

"Where is she now—your daughter?" Tana said.

"Estranged. She and her mother moved to New York, last I knew."

"What happened?"

Shit, Crash, how'd you get here—this place you never wanted to be again, talking about it? Caring what this young woman with a whole future in front of her thinks of you and your wrecked past?

Wind howled, sifting between the houses, rattling at windows and locks, sneaking into any unattended gap, curling into the warmth of homes and touching those who slept.

Eaves moaned. The whole building seemed to creak.

He gave a snort and grinned suddenly. His fallback—his mask going up. He was good at masks. Too good. And he *liked* them. He'd made a living wearing them. It had cost him his old family, and at the time he hadn't been able to dig deep enough to care before they were gone.

"I could do with a cup of joe," he said. "Want some coffee?" He surged to his feet, made for the small kitchenette.

"Nice try, O'Halloran."

He stopped, turned. "Look, I don't do past. Don't talk about it, don't like to think about it. A lot of folk come north to get away, leave it all behind, start new. I don't know, maybe you did, too."

"I didn't *come* north, I'm *from* the north. I was born in Yellowknife. And if you're referring to that . . . incident on TwoDove's farm, what you said, you're wrong. But I'm guessing you don't do sorry, either."

"Am I? Wrong?"

Her gaze locked with his. She was fighting herself. He could see that—he was an acute and trained reader of the psyche. Body language, nuances, micro tells, things others didn't even notice were all tricks of his past trade. It's why he'd been so good, why he'd gone so deep, into the dark world of crime. Why he'd gotten so tangled between the rights and wrongs and the gray areas of justice. Why he wasn't dead right now.

And if he was a betting man—hell, he *was* a betting man—he'd bet his de Havilland Beaver she'd once been a kid like Mindy. Abused. Addicted.

"It's none of your business." She got up, tucked in her shirt. "Thanks for your help here."

"And about Mindy and me—you're the one who's wrong there, Tana." Why was he even bothering to explain—reiterate?

She stilled tucking her shirt into her pants, continued to hold his gaze, wholly, fully, absorbing, sucking him down and deep and spiraling into places he did not want to go.

"I found her frozen and barely conscious, blind drunk," he said. "Late last spring, sleeping in that old shed on the river. Parents didn't give a shit. So, I took her home, thawed her out, sobered her up. Fed her. And she told me she often slept there, had been doing it since she was eight years old." He paused. "She tried to go home a few times. Or to a boyfriend, or others. And then I would find her again at the shed, because I knew to look. Others in town tried to help her but she has a screw-you attitude toward them that she doesn't have with me." He paused. "I'm simply giving her a place to stay. Read into it what you will, or what Mindy wills you to read into it. But that's the truth of it. She has nowhere to go that's safe."

She stared at him, things shifting in her features, a frown creasing into her brow. Both question and doubt in her eyes. She glanced at her sleeping dogs. Alive, for now. Her gaze went to the charcoal packet and bottle of peroxide on her desk, the dropper, the spoon, then to the plastic he'd taped over the shattered window.

"A rescuer of women," she said slowly. "And kids. And dogs."

He did not reply.

"Yet you seem to hate it. So why do you do it?"

He fought the answer, running a hundred lies through his brain, before being sucked back to that look in her eyes. And the truth.

"Because," he said quietly. "I fucked up my own life." *I lost an unborn child of my own. I got the baby and mother into the line of fire, and did nothing to stop them from being killed.* "I don't want to give a shit, and usually I get by pretty well."

"But then someone comes along carrying a baby and you feel you've just got to interfere and tell them how to do their job? What are you *not* telling me, O'Halloran? What's giving *you* such guilt?"

He snorted. Yeah—she was profiling him alright, putting the jigsaw pieces together, getting close. Life in Twin Rivers was over for him the way he'd known it before she blew into town.

"The name's Cam," he said.

She blinked, then said, "Maybe I'll just try 'Crash' for now."

He smiled.

Her mouth curved in response. And it was a slam to his gut. The most sensual, provocative, personal thing he'd felt. And it scared the shit out of him. So he did the thing that came naturally—deflected, avoided, grinned. "So, want that coffee? Or tea, cocoa, something?" He moved toward the small kitchenette, turning his back to her as he spoke.

"Tea," she said. "Bags are in that cupboard above the coffeemaker."

He plugged in the kettle, got mugs down from the cabinet, relieved to have something physical to do with his hands.

But by the time he'd made her tea, she was asleep again, curled up with her dogs. Passed out from stress, fatigue. Her condition, probably. Slowly he set her mug down on her desk, and sipped from his own.

Leave, Crash, sneak out while you still can . . .

But she lay there defenseless. In more ways than one. He *couldn't* leave her like this—he was in to the hilt. And he wasn't so sure he was sorry about that. Now *that* was the most scary thing of all.

He took his complex soup of emotions, and walked slowly around the detachment office. It was warm inside now, the fire crackling at full capacity in the stove. With the storm howling outside, Tana and dogs curled in front of the flames, it made him think of his old life. Home and hearth as he'd once known it.

He shucked his flannel shirt, hung it over the back of a chair, paced, looking around. It was primitive in here. Old computers, old phones. Old desks. The stove itself was quaint. This little police cabin in a remote fly-in town, it cut to the heart of policing, Mountie style. It reminded him of history, of the stories he'd read as a kid about the North-West Mounted Police fighting off the American whiskey traders, of why he'd wanted to become a cop himself, since he was about ten. Kind of ironic considering what he was doing now.

As he opened the door to the interview room he wondered about Tana, why she'd become one.

He stilled.

A whiteboard ran the back length of the wall. It was covered in autopsy photos, head shots, names, arrows, lines. Details of the wolf maulings. His pulse quickened. She was linking the attacks. *What the?* He stepped inside, made slowly for the board, a cold, inky feeling sinking through him.

There, top left, was his own name under "Persons of Interest."

CHAPTER 26

Wednesday, November 7. Day length: 7:37:40 hours.

Tana woke with a start. Hot. Wind was wailing, snow thickening against the window. The plastic taped over the broken pane made a *tic tic tic* sound. Disoriented, she sat up. She was on the floor . . . *her dogs?*

"Max? Toyon?" she whispered, shaking them. Both her pooches opened their eyes. Max lifted his head, and Toyon thumped the tip of his tail. Tears of relief burned into her eyes as she stroked them. Their muscle tremors had quieted, no more drool. She lifted their lips. Their gums looked brighter. Oh, God, they were going to be okay. "You are," she whispered to them. "You *will* be fine. You'll see—you'll feel even stronger tomorrow."

Crash?

She looked around. The room glowed a soft orange from the fire. A light came from the interview room. *The door to the room was open.* Quickly, she pushed herself to her feet. Stiff and still hurting from the fight at the Red Moose, she made her way to the door on socked feet, entered.

She stilled.

He stood in front of her whiteboard, up close, examining the lines she'd made linking photos, what she'd written, his own name up there. He'd removed his flannel shirt and wore a white tee, jeans. A big-ass hunting knife was sheathed at his hip. The form-fitting fabric of his shirt accentuated his musculature, his simmering, latent strength. The small room underscored his height. But her focus was drawn to the tattoos down his arms. On his left bicep dark ink depicted a big fist holding a trident that speared three small skulls. On his right arm a pair of handcuffs was tattooed.

Her heart started to race.

Prison tats. Gang ink.

He tensed. Sensing her, he turned slowly.

His face looked different. Something in his eyes had darkened, and the look in them made her fight taking a step backward.

The RCMP had run a course for all the cops back in Yellowknife when the Devil's Angels started to infiltrate the diamond industry there. Diamonds were the cleanest currency for organized crime, terrorism. The emblem of the Devil's Angels was the speared trident. A fist grasping a trident with skulls upon the tips had to be earned. It was like a patch. It meant access had been granted to the highest levels of a chapter, and to gain entry, a DA member had to kill someone, or hurt them very seriously. Handcuffs often signified time served.

Fear fingered into her chest.

"Get out," she said.

"What is this?" he said.

"You shouldn't be in here."

He eyed her, unsmiling. Her gaze flickered to his name on the board, what she'd written under it.

Owns red AeroStar. Heather MacAllistair saw a red AeroStar near scene around possible time of deaths. Sturmann-Taylor alibi? O'Halloran was in the woods near Regan Novak mauling site—first on scene. In a position to compromise evidence. Where was he when Smithers was killed? She could now add, *member of organized crime chapter? Killer? Ex-con?*

"You're conducting a homicide investigation." He went to the table where the other glossy photos were scattered, the autopsy reports. He picked up the pathologist report on the Dakota Smithers case, started to read. Nerves whispered through Tana.

"O'Halloran," she said, "put that down, and get out of this room."

"Vanilla." He looked up. "I didn't know there were minute traces of vanilla and fish blood on Dakota Smithers's body."

She swallowed, her hand automatically going to position near her sidearm, even as she realized it wasn't there. She'd taken off her duty belt and vest. No gun. He had a knife.

"They'd been cleaning fish that morning," she said. "And making vanilla-scented tallow candles."

"Vanilla and fish blood is what Raj and Selena added to their lure." He pointed to images of their ravaged bodies. "In these photos that you took here, what's this dark stuff on the bodies?"

"They were carrying lure, working with it. Could have gotten it onto their bodies during the attack."

He turned back to the whiteboard. "And bones," he said quietly, as if to himself. "Old bones. And those claw marks, the patterns of predation, the blunt force trauma at the base of the skulls—"

"It could just be coincidence," she said. "Smithers could have fallen off her sled and rolled down that ravine. The fall could have killed her, or she might have been severely injured, and then the animals got to her. Apodaca and Sanjit were working with large-carnivore attractant. There were human-habituated wolves in the area. It could—"

He spun around. "I never saw, or knew any of this about Dakota. I was on the outside. I just knew that the kid had been mauled by wolves or a bear. It happens. I only saw Regan's body. That was a weird case. But now . . . coupled with this—" He gestured to the images of Apodaca and Sanjit. "The similarities on these remains, the dates of deaths, all during the first days of November, all on the cusp of bad weather that would seriously hamper an early search, giving time for scavengers to destroy evidence. The regularity of those *four* claw marks, the missing eyes, heart, vanilla, fish blood."

Tana stared at him. He consumed space, air. A vibrating intensity hummed around what he'd just voiced. His words had breathed life into what she didn't even want to articulate, making it more real. More stark. More terrifying.

Her gaze warred with his. "I need you to get out of here, O'Halloran."

"This could be the work of a madman, Tana. A bizarre, ritualistic serial murderer working in remote locations and using wild animals to cover his work."

"It *could* also be coincidence."

"One thing you don't have up there is the inukshuk I saw where Regan died. No one took a photo of that. But I was *there*. I saw it. It was constructed in the same fashion as these other two." He tapped the photos on her board. "And the long arm of the inukshuk pointed to the copse where I found Elliot Novak cradling the headless, gutted corpse of his daughter."

She swallowed, her attention returning to his tats. He was a criminal. A dangerous one who'd done time. She had to find a calm way to remove him from this room, and this police station.

"And those words," he said quietly, holding her eyes. "That poem, *For, in the Barrens of the soul, monsters take toll* . . . I've seen that line before."

"Where?"

"A book."

"What book?"

"At Tchliko Lodge. In Alan Sturmann-Taylor's library. Words on one page, an ink drawing of a monster on the other. It was written by a man who hunts each year with Sturmann-Taylor's outfit. He stays there part of each year to edit his novels. He sets them here, in the Barrens." He paused. "Horror novels."

Her mouth turned dry.

"Have you informed major crimes?" he said. "Are they sending people out?"

His intensity, his keen interest, his degree of comfort while faced with these gruesome autopsy photos of real people, his tats, the rumors in town that he'd killed a man, his pattern of thinking, terminology—it all set warning bells clanging. He'd had opportunity in each of those deaths on the board. He'd been there—with Regan and Elliot Novak, in the woods. It was possibly his chopper that had been parked on the other side of the cliff from where Apodaca and Sanjit were slain. He had access to carnivore lure on TwoDove's ranch. He knew the work patterns of the biologists. He knew that poem. He could be sleeping with Mindy.

For all she knew O'Halloran could have poisoned her dogs, given them the tainted bones on his way into the diner, setting it up just so that he could save them, gain her trust. He'd already nailed her past. He was reading her like a book, and could be playing her, too. A cat with a little rookie mouse. Some psychopath getting off on inserting himself into the investigation. She'd read stories of killers who'd actually applied to become officers in order to get an up-close insider police view of their own crimes.

Psychopaths are brilliant liars, Tana, charmers. Like Ted Bundy . . .

She cleared her throat. "Who is the author of this book, and what is the title?"

"*The Hunger* by Drakon Sinovski. A pseudonym for a guy named Henry Spatt."

Her brain raced. That name. She'd heard it, just recently—the diner. The man eating with Markus Van Bleek.

. . . Been coming for the last five years, and will keep doing so as long as Charlie Nakehk'o can, or will, guide us . . .

"What does the ink-drawing image look like?"

"A wendigo thing. A cannibalistic, mythical 'soul stealer,' part man, part wolf." He paused. "It was depicted with bloody teeth, squatting, holding up a woman's head by the hair, the neck a ripped and bloodied stump. The woman's eyes had been gouged out."

Mistrust and fear curdled into her stomach.

"O'Halloran," she said quietly, firmly. "You need to get out of this room. I want you to leave this station."

He took a step toward her, and again Tana fought the urge to step back. His raw masculinity, his size over hers, the hot fervor in his eyes scared her. Her gaze went again to his tats. She needed to run a criminal record check—O'Halloran might not even be his real name, which is why he'd come across a cipher on her earlier, cursory Internet search.

"When will you get the autopsy reports?" he said.

"I'm going to tell you one more time, step out of this room."

"Or what? You'll call for backup?"

She forced herself not to glance toward the phone on the table. She was on her own. Totally on her own. Just her, and her sick dogs.

"You're going to need help with this, Tana."

"Not your help."

He looked at her long and hard. Inhaled, then nodded slowly. He brushed past her and reached for his jacket. He shrugged into it.

"Be careful," he said. And he left.

Tana affixed her headlamp, and stepped outside with Toyon and Max on leads. It was just after 7:00 a.m. The world was a dark snow globe.

She'd hardly slept since the early hours of the morning after O'Halloran had left.

She trudged into the big, soft drifts, a silent maelstrom of snow-flakes dancing around her. She let her dogs do their business before taking them back inside.

"You're going to be fine, boys," she said as she unhooked and hung up their leads. "I know it—you look much better, already. And we're not going to take eyes off you guys for one minute, me or Rosalie. You're going to stay here, inside the detachment and only walk on leash. For your own good, okay? Until I can figure out who did this."

She stoked up the fire and fed Max and Toyon, then sat down to call Yellowknife. It was far too early for Keelan or Cutter to be in the office, but that's what she was counting on. She wanted to sideline them, to reach some detective coming off night duty who could alert major crimes to the startling similarities between four apparent wolf-bear attacks over a period of four years.

She picked up the receiver, and stilled.

Dead silence.

She tapped the bar on the phone. Nothing.

Tana got up and went to the phone on Rosalie's desk. Also dead. So was the one in the interview room.

The satellite dish probably needed to be swept of heavy snow.

Tana re-donned her heavy gear, and tromped outside feeling like the cop woman from that movie *Fargo*.

She waded through the drifts to the RCMP garage that housed the truck, two snowmobiles, and two ATVs. In the garage she found a long-handled broom and a snow shovel. She headed for the fenced-in sat dish and telecommunications enclosure adjacent to the station. The area was lit by a tall and useless security light that cast a pale halo into the darkness and swirling snow.

In the beam of her headlamp she noticed what looked like a soft depression in the new snow. It led to the fence. She thought of the stone that came through her window last night, the shadows she'd seen outside. She followed the depression. Her heart gave a slight kick as she saw that the track led right up to the telcom area fence. And picked up on the other side, *inside* the enclosure.

She worked up a sweat, hurriedly digging snow away from the wire gate, and while she dug, it continued to come down, caking her hat, flakes melting on her lashes. She pulled open the gate, waded in through the drifts, and when she reached the satellite dish, the toe of her boot kicked something hard under the powder. She bent down and felt through the soft snow until she grasped it. Tana pulled it up out of the drift—an aggressive pair of bolt cutters. Her gaze shot to the dish, and she gaped as her flashlight beam hit on the cables. Cut. *All* of them. Clean through. Her gaze shot up higher. Even the cables that led up the length of their little cell tower that broadcast to their small village cellular network had been severed.

Twin Rivers had just been cut off from the rest of the world. No satellite signals. No cellular. No Internet, nothing.

"Constable?"

She jumped, spun. Through the whirling white darkness came a Cyclops with his headlamp. "It's me," he said. "Bob Swiftriver. The maintenance guy. I sweep the dish when it snows."

"Bob. Yeah, hi, right. I was just going to do it myself. I needed to get a call out."

He neared, and she saw his familiar craggy face. He was studying the path she'd dug out with her shovel. "We have a snow blower in the garage, you know?"

"Look—" she said, pointing the broom up at the tower cables. "Cut. All of it. The whole system is down. Internet, everything. How long will it take to get this fixed—who in town can fix it?"

He stared, eyes going wide. Then he whistled slowly. "Holy jumping steelhead. Who would do this? *Why?*" he said.

Fucking vandals, that's who. That's what they'd been doing last night while her dogs lay dying. Her money was on those kids—Damien and his gang. The ones she'd busted for the booze. Payback—Damien had threatened it when she'd put him into the cell for a couple of nights. Probably them who'd tried to hurt her dogs, too. A raw, red ferocity burned into her chest. She was going to find them. At first light. No fucking way was she going to let these bastards win. She'd show them who was boss.

She also had to inform Chief Peters and the band council about this sabotage—the whole town, business, was going to suffer until they could get this fixed.

"I've still got a portable sat phone," she said, as much to herself as to Bob as she stared up at the tower. I can call NorthTel—I should be able to get a signal out as soon as this weather lifts."

Because right now they were socked in. Cloud cover was dense, and the snow was like wet concrete.

"The NorthTel repair guys will have to fly in," Bob said in his lazy singsong voice. "And bring spare parts." He looked at the sky. "That's not going to happen for a few weeks with this weather. Still more storms coming in. Lots of snow. More fog."

Tana put her head back, letting the flakes settle cold on her cheeks, her eyes. And she breathed in deep and slow through her nose.

You can do this.

Just keep doing your job. Finish your report, your investigation. Keep trying to contact Yellowknife.

She would not let the Twin Peaks-Fargo weirdness of this remote, dark place get to her.

Like it had gotten to Sergeant Elliot Novak, and Corporal Hank Skerritt, and even Corporal Barry Buccholz, it seemed.

O'Halloran's words circled her mind . . .

You're going to need help with this, Tana . . .

Yeah. And she'd get it. On her terms. Her first order was to sort out whoever did this, and to inform the town via the chief.

She asked Bob to clear the snow around the garage area, and she stomped up the steps to the police station, but at the entrance she froze in her tracks.

Something had been pinned into the wooden door by a metal tool about the length of a pencil. She stepped closer with her headlamp. And her breath caught.

Bile lurched to her throat. Her heart stuttered and then raced.

An eyeball.

Skewered to her door.

She swallowed slowly, forcing calm. It was too big for a human eye, thank God—almost an inch in diameter. More like a deer eye. Tana removed her heavy mitts, and took several close-up photos with her phone.

She ferreted for the latex gloves she kept in her inside pocket, snapped them on. Tentatively, she touched the eye. It was frozen. It had been out here a while. And the metal tool skewering it, she did not recognize. It reminded her of something that might be found in a dentist's office.

She glanced over her shoulder, heart thumping. Everywhere snow shadows seemed to swirl and duck into the darkness.

CHAPTER 27

"Who did it?" said Chief Dupp Peters.

"Don't know yet," Tana said. "I was hoping you might have some idea. Do you think Damien and his crowd are capable of sabotaging town communications and poisoning my dogs like that?"

"Damien?" said Dupp, taking a sip of his coffee. "I dunno. The kid on his own is not all bad, but that pack of guys from Wolverine Falls that he runs with? Some bad eggs in that bunch."

Tana was seated with the chief and his wife Alexa at a small table in their kitchen. After walking and feeding her dogs, and leaving instructions for Rosalie, Tana had stopped by the chief's house on her way to find Damien. She was duty bound to brief him on something as serious as the satcom sabotage. She also wanted to ask his son, Caleb, about the fight with Jamie TwoDove at the Red Moose.

Alexa was feeding their grandson Tootoo, who burbled in his high chair at her side. Tootoo's mother had died shortly after giving birth. Cancer. And watching Tootoo playing with his cereal, Tana wondered how she was going to do it—be a single mom and a cop. She'd need a sitter. And she still hadn't put in for maternity leave.

"What about Jamie?" Tana said, struggling to tear her gaze away from chubby little Tootoo. "D'you think he's capable of sabotage and poisoning?"

"You mean as revenge, because you put him in jail?" said Alexa.

"Maybe. And my dog did go for his leg when I arrested him."

"Nah, not Jamie," Dupp said. "He's too upset about Selena. That's all. He's not a bad boy. He's a real sensitive kid, and he loves animals. It's why he never really took to the taxidermy."

"What about Jamie's father—what's your read on Crow TwoDove?"

"Crow has big issues with police, for sure," Dupp said, reaching for the coffeepot. "It goes way back to that time when the cops went looking at him as a pedophile, or stalker, of some sort." He held the pot out toward Tana's mug. She shook her head. He poured himself a refill and set the pot down.

"Dakota's mother thought it was possible that her daughter was being stalked," Tana said, playing devil's advocate.

"It was a bad time for everyone." Alexa spooned more porridge into her grandson's mouth. The kid ogled Tana with huge dark eyes as he gummed his food, and she felt an odd little pang in her chest. "Elliot Novak might have pushed that idea into Jennie Smithers's head," Alexa added. "And Crow keeps to himself if no one bothers him. He doesn't come out looking for trouble."

From her pocket Tana removed a baggie containing the silver tool she'd extracted from the frozen deer eyeball. She set it on the table. "Ever seen one of these?"

"Why?" said Dupp, picking it up, turning it over.

"I found it pinning a deer eyeball to the police station door."

Dupp's and Alexa's gazes shot to Tana's. They both stared at her in silence. Dupp cleared his throat. "Who would do that? Why?"

"Revenge, maybe. To spook me. Whatever the motive, I'm going to find out," Tana said.

"It's a taxidermy tool," Dupp said.

"Who does taxidermy around town, apart from Crow TwoDove?" Tana asked.

"Well, Crow does teach people. And Jamie tried it for a while, but like I said, he doesn't really have the feel, or stomach, for it. He's better with his jewelry."

Tana repocketed the bagged tool. "Have either of you heard of any other wildlife attacks like Dakota's, or Regan Novak's, or this latest one? Farther afield, perhaps? Or are you aware of people who went missing, maybe even several years ago, and were later found scavenged?"

Dupp took a long sip from his mug, thinking. "Well, thing is, if you go missing out in these parts, any number of things will get you. Terrain and weather for one. If you fall and break your leg, hypothermia will set in. It's remote. No cell phone reception. Two-way radios have limited range. And if you're not carrying some kind of personal safety satellite beacon, you're going to die out there on your own. And if you die, by the time they find you weeks, months, maybe even years later, you will have been scavenged. Nature's recyclers. It's just the way of the wild. In old times tribes would just leave their dying members for the wolverine. Eaters of the dead."

"There was that one geologist," Alexa said. "Remember, Dupp? She was from Kelowna in BC. She got separated from her party in bad weather, and they think she fell down a ridge. They couldn't find her before the snows came that year. But they did locate her remains the following spring. She'd been eaten by grizzlies and wolves and whatever else. Broken leg bones, like she had fallen."

"When was this?" said Tana.

Alexa made a moue. "About two years ago, I think. But it was quite a lot farther north of here. In the Nehako Valley."

Tana made a note to check it out when she could get online access again. It fit a pattern: bad weather coming in, a search delayed because of it, remote area, extensive animal predation before the victim was found.

Tana finished the last of her coffee, relieved that she was finally able to stomach it again. At least in small amounts.

"Before I go," she said, "I was hoping to have a word with Caleb about the fight at the Red Moose. Is he home?"

"That boy is still sleeping," said Dupp, pushing his chair back. "I'll get him. Caleb!" he yelled down the small passage. "Someone here to talk to you."

"Coming," called a bleary voice.

While they waited, Tana said, "I was wondering if I could pick your brain, Dupp—I'd like to start the ball rolling on an auxiliary-type policing program for Twin Rivers. Bringing together a few volunteers to be on call for emergencies, or for search and rescue. Do you think the band council would be interested in getting something like this going?"

He grinned. "It's been long overdue. We'd *love* to see some of the local youth involved, especially. Alexa and I have been talking about it. And with you guys so short-staffed—"

"Hey," Caleb said as he entered the kitchen. But he stalled at the sight of Tana in her uniform at the table. Slowly, he seated himself, features guarded.

She smiled. "How are you, Caleb? Recovered from the dustup?"

"Yeah." He rubbed his arm, a nervous tic. "Did you charge him—Jamie?"

She shook her head. "We're going to see if Jamie can work off the damages." She leaned forward. "But I wanted to ask you what you know about bones. Old bones. Jamie was yelling at you about bones that night in the Red Moose."

He paled under his dusky skin. "I don't know nothing about bones."

His parents fell quiet. Tension in the room thickened. Even Tootoo's gurgling stopped as the baby sensed the change.

"See, Caleb, we did find bones where Selena Apodaca and Raj Sanjit died. Old bones. Forensics experts will tell us a lot about those bones. How old they are. Cause of death, maybe. Sex. Cultural background."

She paused. "I'm just wondering why you and Jamie were fighting about bones, given the find."

He looked down at the table, scratched at something imaginary on the melamine surface. "I don't know anything."

Tana placed on the table the picture that she'd taken from the police files after she'd booked Jamie. She slid it toward him. It showed Caleb Peters, Jamie TwoDove, and Selena Apodaca at the blockade held last spring to protest the ice road and the development of the WestMin mine.

"Some people in town really don't want that mine, Caleb. And Harry Blundt from WestMin was telling me that if old bones or burial sites were found, it could stop him from getting approval. You were there that day, at that protest." She tapped the photo. "Jamie, and Selena, too."

"Half the town was there," his mother said.

"The anthropological study will start next spring," Tana said. "Following on the back of the wildlife studies that Selena and Raj were a part of." She paused, waiting for him to meet her eyes. "Just *if* someone planted bones, where would those bones have come from, Caleb? Because this could be a crime. Or, what Jamie was calling . . . a sin, maybe, in the eyes of your community?"

Sweat gleamed on his brow. "This is bullshit." He shoved the photo back at her.

"*Something* is going on here, Caleb, and it's more than just wolves. Keeping information from the police could get you in deep trouble, because those forensics experts are going to tell us a lot, and will raise even more questions. If you remember something, or if Jamie does, you guys come talk to me, okay?"

She got up, thanked the family for the coffee, and as Tana left, she heard the men inside the house arguing. Loudly.

Tana drew up on her snowmobile outside the tiny cabin on the river where Damien lived. She removed her helmet and goggles. Trees grew dense on either side of the cabin, and behind it the river, silver-gray, chuckled around rocks mounded with snow. Flakes were still coming down heavily.

Her mind went to her dogs, how they'd almost died, to the vandalism of the cell tower, to the eyeball skewered to the police station door. Anger began to thud in her veins. If someone was trying to spook her, they were messing with the wrong person. She killed her engine.

Hand near her weapon, her gaze flicking around, hyperaware, she made for the door through gusting snow. She banged hard with the base of her fist.

No answer.

She tried again before going around the back. She rubbed ice from a rear window, and peered inside.

Cabin was a mess. Empty bottles. Dirty glasses. Bong. Old food cartons. If it wasn't for the below-freezing temperatures, the interior would be covered in mold. It looked like no one had been back here for a while. No prints outside, snow piling in drifts against the door.

She returned to the front of the cabin and stood on the porch, thinking, her breath misting. She'd heard from young Timmy Nakehk'o that these guys had a hide somewhere in the woods across the river where they stashed the booze and dope.

But in order to locate that bootleggers' hide, she needed info. O'Halloran knew where that hide was—she was certain of it.

Shit.

Baby steps, Tana . . . you can do this. You need to handle this gang and the illegal liquor sales one way or another. And you need to arrest and charge whoever sabotaged the satcom system and poisoned your dogs . . .

She remounted her snow machine and punched through the drifts, making for O'Halloran's place.

She parked her machine outside, and clumped up the steps. She could see his Beaver in the hangar on the other side of the airport fence, and she wondered where he kept his red AeroStar.

She knocked on his door. It opened almost at once. Mindy stood there smirking. "You're sure hot for him, aren't you, Constable? Can't stop yourself from coming around now, can you?"

"Where is he?"

"Out back. In the meat shed."

Tana made her way back down the stairs and started round the rear of the tiny clapboard house.

"What?" Mindy called after her. "No lecture for me this time?"

Tana ignored her. She wasn't going to get the truth of Mindy from Mindy herself. She knew that much now. Triage. First things first.

Snow was several feet deep out back, but a beaten path led down to what looked like two garages joined together. The door on the left side was shut, but the one on the right was open. Music emanated from the interior—sounds from the late eighties. She stopped in the entrance.

Inside, a dead buck hung from a meat hook in the ceiling. O'Halloran had his back to her and was busy slicing hunks of dark-red flesh from the carcass, dropping them into a metal bucket. The music and snow had quieted her approach, so he was not aware that she was standing there. There was a power and practice in his strokes with the sharp blade. He wore a quilted lumberjack shirt over bloodstained Carhartt pants. Baffin-Arctic boots.

Tana glanced back over her shoulder, toward the trail leading from the house. There was no distinct sole imprint immediately apparent in that trail—it was too tracked out. But as she looked, she noticed Mindy at a window in the house, watching from behind sheers. A strange chill washed over Tana. She drew in a deep breath, marshaling herself, and she turned and entered the shed. "O'Halloran," she said.

He stilled, slowly turned, met her eyes, bloody knife in hand.

She eyed the blade.

"Didn't think I'd be seeing you so soon, Constable." He turned back to cutting. Plopping hunks of meat in the bucket. Tana felt sick again, memories of those biologists' remains, the smell, suddenly fresh in her mind again.

"Dogs okay?" he said.

"Yeah. We need to talk."

"Talk away." He didn't stop what he was doing, and she wanted to look in his eyes.

"I need to find Damien," she said.

His hand slowed. "I'm not his keeper, Larsson. You know where he lives."

"He's not there. Doesn't look like he's been there in a while. Where can I find his hide?"

"So, *now* you need my help?"

"Not only were my dogs poisoned, O'Halloran, but the town's satcom system was sabotaged while my dogs lay dying and I was trying to save their lives. This is not just about booze any longer. This is about the whole community being cut off. A serious crime."

His body tensed, but he still didn't look at her. "Sabotage?"

"Cables, all of them, severed from the satellite dish to the broadcast tower. It could take weeks to repair if NorthTel can't fly parts and techs in these storms. You said I had enemies, but this is not just about me now—I want who did this."

Still not looking at her, he sliced off another wad of flesh. "What makes you think it's them?" She heard a slight tension in his voice now and it gave her a punch of satisfaction.

"It's my first line of investigation," she said.

He swiveled the carcass on the hook so that he could access the uncut side of the buck. The animal's head spun round to face her—open mouth, tongue. Tana's pulse quickened. *The animal had no eyes.*

"Where are the deer's eyeballs?" she said.

"Someone took them, while the meat was hanging." He sliced off another slab.

Tana stared at the empty sockets, her pulse starting to gallop.

He cast her a sideways glance. His green eyes were watchful, reading her. Gone was the crackling mirth, the quick, easy grin that she'd encountered the first few times she'd met him. A dark, hot energy radiated off him now. The place smelled of sweet meat, tinged with metallic copper. She needed air suddenly. "What do you mean, someone took the eyes?" she said.

"Just that. They're a delicacy for some people out here."

Tana dug into her pocket and removed the bagged tool she'd shown Chief Dupp and Alexa Peters earlier. "You seen this before?" She held it out to him.

"Where'd you get that?"

"It was pinning a frozen deer eyeball to my police station door."

His hands stilled. And what she saw in his features worried her.

"When?" he said.

"It was there this morning."

"That's not Damien's style, Tana—to knock out the whole town. Or hurt pets. Or screw around with eyeballs from *my* buck. He knows where his bread is buttered."

"Then whose style is it?"

Silence. His gaze locked with hers.

The words from that poem snaked through her mind.

For here is bitter and cold where the sun hangs low. Where a midnight caribou mutilation awakens a howl of emptiness with ice where once there was heart . . .

A darker thought followed as her attention returned to the gutted dear—its heart and other organs gone—and she thought of Selena Apodaca's heartless torso lying in ice and snow. What if this wasn't about illegal liquor, and revenge? What if the poisonings and the sabotage and the eyeball were all linked to what was up on her white-board, and the fact that *she* was asking questions around town, linking old attacks?

"I can tell you one thing," she said. "Maybe this isn't Damien's style when he's alone, but stick a guy into a gang and a weird pack mentality can take hold." She paused. "But you know all about gang psychology, don't you, O'Halloran, and what it can make people do?"

He turned away, shoulders tight. He stared at the deer carcass. Wind gusted into the shed, swiveling the deer. The meat hook creaked on its hinge.

"So, you going to tell me where his hide is?" she said.

"Fuck," he said quietly.

"You got a problem?"

"I got a problem taking a cop into his hide, yeah."

"I didn't ask you to *take* me, I just asked you to tell me where it is."

"And what are you going to do when you get there?" he snapped.

"Question them. They're my top suspects, my first line of inves-tigation in the sabotage. Depending on what I hear, or see, I'll act accordingly."

"They won't cooperate with you. All you'll be doing is putting your-self in a dangerous situation."

"I can't *not* address this—or them. What kind of statement would that be making of me as a law enforcement presence in this town?"

"Well, you're not going alone. You're right about his mates from Wolverine Falls—they can get trigger-happy, especially if they've been drinking. I don't know what they're capable of. Place is also booby-trapped."

"And *you* can get in?"

"Yup." He wiped his blade on a cloth, slid the knife into the sheath at his hip.

"Because you supply them with booze?" she said.

"Yup. You got it."

"No, I don't get it. I don't get why you want to escort me into Damien's hide. Because if this is about my pregnancy—"

"What if it is?"

She stared at him, his words from last night echoing through her mind. *I fucked up my own life. I don't want to give a shit, and usually I get by pretty well.* Conflict twisted through Tana. She couldn't trust this guy. Yet she also knew that barging into Damien's hide to confront his armed gang on her own was a dumbass move.

. . . you might be compelled to take a kick, or a bullet, but you've got another life to think about now. A little civilian life . . .

Tana swallowed. Either it was waiting for backup from Yellowknife, which might never come. Or it was Crash O'Halloran. Or it was doing nothing to assert her police presence in town, and letting a bunch of kids run her, and Twin Rivers. And possibly worse.

"Look, you want my help or not? Because the only way you're going out to that hide is on the back of *my* snow machine."

"I have my own machine—"

"With RCMP written all over it. No, we go on my equipment, my gear, my terms. Because I sure as hell am not going to be responsible for getting you killed." He shucked off his lumberjack shirt as he spoke. He followed this by removing his T-shirt.

His torso was ripped, tanned, and sported more ink. His shoulder was badly scarred. His abs, too, as if a knife blade had been scored across his belly several times. Like torture marks. He was all sinew and muscle and fluidlike movement as he turned his naked back to her, and ran water into a sink at the back of the shed. The heat from the water steamed into the cold air.

"Give me a minute while I clean up." He began soaping his arms.

Tana stared at the back of him. The way his jeans were slung low on his hips made her hot inside. Uncomfortable. Old tensions twisted painfully through her. She'd gotten into way too much trouble trying to drown her pain—herself—in lust, in fierce, mind-numbing, risqué sex.

Coupled with alcohol it had become a crutch, a way to blot it all out. Then an addiction—a mixed-up Russian roulette that she'd played with herself after Jim's death. A form of saying "fuck you, world." A kind of self-hatred, self-flagellation even, that all tied back to her deep lack of self-worth. And now she was pregnant. And here she stood, trying to start over, watching this ex-con covered in serious organized crime tats, soaping blood off himself before taking her out to a gang hide in the woods. A person of interest in what could possibly be a bizarre serial murder case.

She shouldn't trust him.

He glanced over his shoulder, as though he'd felt her watching, assessing. As though he could read her thoughts about his body. Heat washed into her face as his gaze held hers. And his eyes darkened.

She cleared her throat. "You need to come clean with me first. About those Devil's Angels tats. About who you really are, what you did to land in prison, what you're doing here. Or it's no deal."

His eyes narrowed. A defiance set into his stubbled jaw.

"Right," she said. "Forget it." She turned and exited the shed, moving fast into the snow and cool air.

CHAPTER 28

Crash splashed cold water over his face, and braced his hands on the crude basin in his work shed. He stared into the rust-pocked mirror above the sink. He knew what Tana was seeing. She was seeing what he wanted people to see—a badass, jaded, washed-up shit. Fuck. It's what he *was. What he'd become.* Not a good man. A man who'd lived too long in a world of extreme violence and corruption, where good guys and bad guys changed places in a heartbeat. Where justice was not black, nor white, and sometimes was written in blood.

And he'd been good at that life.

He swore bitterly.

Now he was being forced to make a decision. Help her, and maybe screw up five or six years of waiting. Watching. But waiting for what, exactly? His taste for blood revenge had dulled. Oh, he wanted retribution alright, but maybe not in quite the same sharp, deadly way he'd first come for it. But he still wanted it.

He could let her go, stick with the order of things, carry on with his plan. But if she and that unborn child of hers got hurt—it made no sense. It cut right back to the heart of why he'd come out here in the first place. To avenge the deaths of a mother and unborn child.

He grabbed a towel, scrubbed his face dry, tossed the towel over a bench, and unhooked a fresh shirt he'd left hanging beside the basin. He pulled it on, snagged his jacket, gloves. Shoving his arms into his jacket, he went after her.

"Tana!" he yelled as he saw her disappearing around the side of his house. He broke into a run, caught her by the arm.

She swung around, eyes sparking. Her mouth was close. She was breathing heavily, their breaths clouding together. Snow settled like confetti on her fur hat. He wanted to kiss her. By God, he just wanted to kiss that full mouth, bury himself in her freshness and youth, cover himself in it. His eyes burned, heat seared his chest. And suddenly he ached—to start again, a second chance, just to try. But he didn't dare. He could not do that to her. She was young, idealistic. He was far too jaded, carried too much dangerous baggage. She was going to be a mother, and there was no way in hell he could realistically be there for her, or a kid, so why in hell was his head even going there?

"Information," he said slowly. "A way to pass under the radar."

"Excuse me?"

"It's what I'm doing here, with the bootlegging, the dope running, because I want underground information. I want bigger jobs from the lodge. And they're starting to come. Bigger jobs equals more, better information."

She blinked. Wind gusted, sending flakes dancing and laughing about them. "I don't know what you're talking about." She shook his hand free, turned and walked away.

He watched her go.

Just let her go . . . let her go, let her go . . .

She was stubborn. She'd do it—find that hide on her own, confront Damien and his gang. He thought of her whiteboard, the dog poisonings, the sabotage, the isolation of the town—her. The deer eye skewered to her door, very possibly stolen from *his* deer . . .

Fuck!

"Tana!"

He caught up to her again under his bedroom window. "Stop, just listen—hear me out. I was UC."

She blinked. "Excuse me?"

"Until five years ago."

"*You* . . . were an undercover *cop?*"

"For almost four years I was part of a joint FBI, RCMP, Interpol, and Canadian Security Intelligence Service task force—Project Protea—formed to track laundered diamonds that were being used to finance organized crime, drugs, human trafficking, prostitution, terrorism. I was seconded to the joint team from major crimes in Edmonton, because I was uniquely positioned at the time to move deep undercover—I had particular experience in diamond trafficking and the infiltration of Asian organized crime into the local diamond industry."

She swallowed. Her gazed dipped over him, as if she was taking him in anew, weighing the odds of him lying.

"The tats—"

"I infiltrated a chapter of the Devil's Angels in Vancouver. They held control of the port. They were the intermediary, and we needed to crack them first."

"The scars?"

He gave a soft snort. "I was shot. Knifed. Tortured at one point. Left for dead in a bust that went sideways. Got addicted to heroin as part of a test to gain entry to the Angels' inner sanctum." He hesitated. "My UC gig, my policing career, ended when the Vancouver city police force—unaware of the international deep-cover Project Protea operation—moved in on a major deal I had going down with a human trafficker. I was shot in the head while attempting to flee with the conflict stones that I was trying to get into the system for laundering. It left me in a coma for almost a fortnight. I went in for over a year of extensive rehab—for the heroin, brain damage. I had to learn to walk again. To feed myself again. I was put out to pasture on disability."

Something changed in her features as she regarded him. And he knew what she was thinking: *Is he sane now? How is that gray matter functioning now?* And yeah, he sometimes asked himself those same questions.

"What you said about your wife, your daughter—"

"I lost them because of the job. Whenever I went home for a break I was like a K9 who was not happy until he was back on the scent. It became like crack. I was in too long, too deep. I . . ." Crash dragged his hand over his wet hair. "My family was collateral damage, Tana. And I regret it."

Her eyes tunneled into his, an intensity crackling around her. "And you're here, looking for information, because?"

"Because that deal that went bust was supposed to help net us the international syndicate that controlled the illegal diamond trade—the laundering of conflict stones—among other sophisticated criminal enterprises. We had to cut our losses after the bust. We never got to finding out who comprised the syndicate, and who controlled it. But while I was going through that year of rehab, it became an obsession for me. I didn't stop looking. I *couldn't* stop trying to piece together every little thing I'd learned over those four years undercover that cost me everything, including my career. I think I know who runs it now. And I think he's here, Tana."

"Who?"

A noise sounded above them. Both Crash and Tana glanced up. Nothing. Just a small gap open in the bedroom window, the breeze billowing a drape.

"Come," he said, watching the drape for a moment. "Let's go finish this in my workshop."

Mindy scurried around to another window from where she could watch Crash and Tana returning through the snow to his outbuildings. He was a *cop?* Fuck. Men were such liars. All of them. She'd thought he was super cool with his plane and his liquor runs, and the dope. He was nothing but a fucking liar, duping them all.

She saw Crash place his hand on the back of the constable's jacket, guiding her into the doorway of the workshop attached to his shed where he dressed game. Like they were now fucking soulmates-in-blue, or something equally pathetic. Her eyes blurred.

Her chest hurt. Really hurt. He'd even had a wife and a *daughter*. Fucking, fucking, fucking liar. She swung her heel, and kicked hard at the base of the bed. Pain screamed through her toes. And she didn't care. She hobbled to the kitchen, and dug through the drawer for the meat thermometer. She found it, yanked up her shirt, and began stabbing the sharp tip of the thermometer into the fat flesh of her stomach. *Stabbity, stabbity, stabbity. Stab.* Blood swelled in shiny red beads from the small holes. It started to dribble down into the waistband of her pants. She loved him. She hated him. Hated Tana for coming here. She wanted to kill Tana Larsson. *Kill, kill, kill.*

Crash had been the only one there for her in a way that she'd needed. He'd saved her from that shed in which she'd been sleeping, and he'd sobered her up. Mindy figured she'd have him some day. He'd have made love to her eventually, if not for Tana coming into town. Mindy had believed that the only reason she and Crash hadn't had sex yet was because he *cared*, and he was waiting for her. Until she was older. *Mindy, you're too young. You need to find a good man your own age. You need to go to school . . .* Tears streamed down her face.

CHAPTER 29

They sat in Crash's workshop on two small stools, facing each other. It was where he kept his little red AeroStar, adjacent to his meat shed. He'd closed the garage door behind them, and put on a bar heater. It glowed orange and warm near their feet. Outside, snow thudded as it slid off the roof.

"My wife's name was Leah," he said, then smiled in a way that looked sad. "Still is. Ex-wife. My daughter's Gracie. I imagine she prefers Grace now. She's twelve. Like I said, we're estranged." He dragged his hand through his wet hair, making it stick up, which lent him an oddly vulnerable air. He flashed a deeper grin, a glimmer of the old Crash in his eyes. The one who wore a crazy World War II flight suit, and whose plane was probably just as old. And as Tana listened, she was learning him. He hid behind that smile and all that bravado-badassery, but she understood broken men, and this man was that, too.

"Because of the complexity, the breadth of the operation, the links to international terrorism, rules were bent. I was allowed to go in deeper and for far longer than usual. And the deeper I infiltrated, the more my isolation increased, because the more there was to lose if I was pegged as a cop. My trips home grew less frequent by necessity. The line between my identities began to blur. I grew my hair, acquired the tats, met the tests. I learned how to survive in that other world, formed relationships there."

"Is Cam O'Halloran your real name?"

His eyes tunneled into hers and he was silent a moment.

"Partly."

Shit. Tana got up, paced in front of the small chopper, turned to face him. "You're still playing the game, aren't you? You still think you're undercover, but you've gone rogue. That's why you're messing with illegal liquor, and dope and whatever else." That's why she could find nothing when she searched the Internet for him. "What's your real name?"

He swallowed. "Dave O'Halloran. Sergeant Dave O'Halloran—you'll find a record."

She stared at him, brain spinning.

"You don't look like a Dave."

The one side of his mouth twisted up in a rueful grin. "Use Crash. I've been called Crash since I was a kid. Bit of a wild child."

Slowly, she reseated herself opposite him, leaned forward, resting her forearms on her knees, her eyes boring into his. "So, when you were shot by the VPD cops, you went into the hospital with a coma as who?"

"Sten Bauer, member of the Devil's Angels."

"And what did everyone on the street think happened to you?"

"It was leaked out that I'd become a vegetable. That I was being moved into an institution where I'd probably live out the rest of my life drooling in a wheelchair and sucking food through a straw."

"How did you earn the Devil's Angels' trident tattoo—I was told you need to kill someone to wear one of those?"

"It was a setup. A low-level drug dealer who'd been messing on the Angels' turf had been shot dead by UC cops involved in another operation around 2:00 a.m. that day, no next of kin. He was placed in an alley where I shot him again before 4:00 a.m., took the credit."

Tana rubbed her chin, trying to process.

"By that time Leah was having an affair with a banker named Kev Simms. When I found out, she gave me an ultimatum—quit the UC work and go into rehab for the heroin, and she'd leave Kev. We'd try and start over from scratch. I couldn't. Rehab had to wait—I was managing the heroin addiction, or so I thought, and the big deal was about to go down. I had a haul of rough blood diamonds from West Africa that had been secured by the FBI and Interpol—stones that had been chemically marked by the FBI lab with a brand-new technology. I was to meet with a guy from Europe, and pay with these diamonds for a shipment of women and weapons. He said he had a way of laundering the rough stones. I'd been infiltrating this group for four years, Tana, and if I didn't show with the stones, they'd smell a ruse. People would die. The whole fucking operation would fall apart. So I asked Leah to wait. She said no go. Gracie needed a father, and Kev was offering relocation to New York where he had a new job. She was going to take Gracie and start a new life."

Tana held his gaze. She saw sincerity in his eyes. She heard it in his voice. Pain, too. It cut her. She felt for him, and his wife and daughter. If there was one thing she'd learned from her own messed-up life it was that bad shit happened to good people. They became things they didn't want to be.

She broke his gaze, looked at her hands, because suddenly the connection with him was too intimate. "So . . . those blood diamonds from the FBI were going to be tracked, via the chemical trace, once they went into the system?"

"Yeah. Somehow the rough stones out of Africa were coming north, here to the territories, and going into the system. They were coming out the other end cut and polished with nice little polar bears or maple leaves lasered onto them."

"Plus a certificate that stated they were conflict free—pure Canadian diamonds."

"Correct. With far more value on the international market compared to stones coming out of conflict zones in Africa and other places around the world. And clean Canadian diamonds are infinitely more attractive to the world of high-end organized crime and terrorism."

"What happened? What went wrong with the deal?"

"A jurisdictional clusterfuck is what happened. A Vancouver PD officer was told by a small-level snitch that some big gang deal was about to go down. I was on my own. That had been made clear to me from the start. The VPD was not aware of our joint op, or that I was undercover, and they organized a raid."

"Your task force wasn't watching?"

"Nearby, but not so close as to give wind to the European dealers. It was a supersensitive operation at that point. And the idea was to *not* bust them, but to let the deal go through, get the marked stones into the system from where they could be tracked far beyond these guys. We knew who *they* were. We wanted to get in even deeper, all the way back to the syndicate running the show. Bottom line is, the VPD Emergency Response Team moved in as I was handing over the gems. The joint force was alerted to the fuckup, and moved in on top of them, trying to contain the fallout at the last moment. A gun battle ensued. I fled, as per my cover, with the haul of stones. I was shot by VPD cops waiting in the back alley. One bullet to the shoulder. One in the head. I went into surgery, and was in a coma for almost two weeks. Then I was moved back to Edmonton where I went into all kinds of rehab and was put on long-term disability leave."

He rubbed his brow. It was warm in the little shed. They were cocooned from the world in here. "The Vancouver chapter of the Devil's Angels went down—we managed to secure convictions on numerous charges including human trafficking. The two European dealers were killed in the gunfight. But beyond that, after all those years, all that effort, we got nowhere close to the syndicate, and who was behind it. The syndicate cut ties with their Vancouver connections, and pulled up the drawbridges, going under again. We also never found the connection to whoever was running the conflict stones through the production system in the Northwest Territories."

"How did this low-level snitch in Vancouver know there was a deal going down?"

"Don't know. He was found floating in the Burrard. The leak could have come from a weak link in the Angels, or even via a dirty cop. As a guy in the Angels once told me, one of the most valuable assets to their organized crime operation was a turned policeman. He said undercover works both ways. At the time I thought he was testing me, fishing. But he might have been referring to someone high up in the RCMP. It would make sense if there was a dirty cop or two in the system. It could explain how a blind eye might have been turned to blood stones entering the production system in the Northwest Territories."

Tana studied O'Halloran's face carefully, and she believed him. Yeah, maybe he was a sociopath, a brilliant liar—you'd have to be a little bit of both, perhaps, to go deep cover like he had, and to live a lie by your wits. No backup.

"And because of all this, because you said you fucked up *your* life, you felt you had a right to lay into me about my pregnancy and my own past?"

He inhaled deeply and looked away for a moment, and Tana knew then he was still keeping something big from her.

"What is it?" she said. "What are you not telling me?"

He turned back to face her. "After Leah and Gracie left, I got involved with a young hooker who'd first introduced me to members of the Devil's Angels. We were both doing heroin at the time." He swallowed. "Her name was Lara. She was a good person, Tana. She'd had a rough start in life, like so many others who end up on the street. And it's a one-way track from there. That's the thing about UC. You get to know these people as human beings. Yeah, these guys are operating on the wrong side of the law, but how they get there . . . it's gray. No little boy sits on his dad's lap and says, 'I want to be a drug dealer when I grow up. I want to get addicted and hurt people.' No three-year-old daughter tells her mom, 'I want to be a sex trade worker.'"

Tana swallowed.

"I don't know," he said. "Maybe I thought I could keep her safe from herself. Or from the Angels, by making her mine . . ." His voice caught. He cleared his throat. "But there came that ultimate test, before I could 'earn' the trident and skulls, when the chapter leader took me to meet a member who'd two-timed him. Lara was with me. On the spot, he handed me his gun, told me to shoot the guy in the skull. I was a cop. I tried quick-talking my way around it. He didn't give me half a chance. He took another gun from his holster, and blew Lara's brains out all over me."

Wind gusted and the shed creaked. Crash's eyes gleamed. His features were twisted into something tight, and Tana's chest hurt.

"What . . . what happened then?" she whispered.

"He turned his weapon on me, and said, 'What are you, a cop?' I said, 'Whoa, no fucking way. You want me to kill someone, I will.' And I brought him that dead low-level dealer who'd been messing on his turf—the setup."

"But . . . Lara."

He scrubbed the stubble on his jaw. "Yeah. Lara. I actually loved her—I cared. And then I found out she'd been five months pregnant with our baby daughter."

Tana blanched. Her breathing became light. She lurched up from her stool and went to the tiny shed window that was plastered with snow. She stared blankly at the frosted panes. "That's why," she whispered. "That's why you flipped at TwoDove's place. That's why you dumped the take-out soup on my desk and fled when you heard Addy and me talking. That's why you came down on me, for being like Mindy when I was a kid." She hesitated. "Because you know. You know what can go wrong. And does."

Silence.

She turned. And the look on his face cracked her heart. It made her think of Jim. And how she wished Jim had spoken to her. How she'd told Jim she didn't want his kid, not yet. And then it was too late and now she was carrying some asshole's kid. And here was this man, this broken man, trying to save her where he'd not been able to save Lara and his own unborn child from being shot to death.

When she spoke, her voice was thick. "What happened to that Devil's Angels chapter leader?"

"I killed him."

She held his eyes.

"How?"

"In that shootout. In the confusion. I shot him dead before I fled. The delay cost me. If I'd tried to get out right away, I might not have gotten shot in the head myself."

"And you were never charged."

"Justice can be gray."

"And what brought you *here*?"

"Alan Sturmann-Taylor and his world-class hunting lodge."

A buzz started in Tana's brain. "You think *Sturmann-Taylor*, the lodge owner, is behind the syndicate?" She watched Crash's face, his eyes, trying to find signs of madness, obsession, instability.

"I think he could *be* the syndicate, Tana. He bought that lodge just over five years ago, around the same time Harry Blundt found the kimberlite pipes beneath Ice Lake and laid claim to the area. And he started with his high-end renovations, hunting trips—flying in international clients, low key, to this remote and private location from around the world. Big businessmen. Connected people. Entertainment and drugs and toys for them. Then I read an industry article about Blundt hiring a man named Markus Van Bleek. I knew from the UC work I'd done that Van Bleek had managed security—basically private armies—for

African diamond outfits, and that he was considered something of a shady, international hit man."

"And you came out here to check the links for yourself?"

He gave a half shrug. "Those raw stones out of Africa will need another place to enter the system. This is something Van Bleek is capable of orchestrating, especially if he's involved from ground-level planning in a brand new and potentially massive diamond op. I know," he said, "I could be chasing shadows. I know what you're thinking. You're wondering if I am nuts—if the bullet and heroin have rewired my brain. Maybe they have. But sometimes, when you've been through hell, when you've made bad decisions about life and people, and you feel like shit, and you don't know how to go on, you just mechanically do something because you know how to do it, and you do it, putting one foot in front of the other as a way of moving forward. It becomes something that gets you out of bed each day. So I kept looking. Maybe I'm still just that old dog who won't give up on that scent." He hesitated. "Yeah, maybe I *am* that conspiracy-theory dude hunkered in his room with papers all over his wall and red lines linking everything. But I think Sturmann-Taylor is the genuine article. And both Van Bleek and Blundt hunt with him, spend time at Tchliko. And one of his subsidiaries has put serious financing into WestMin."

"What will you do if you find proof?"

He pushed to his feet, turned up the bar heater. "The original plan was to hear him confess, and then kill him. Payback. For Lara. Our kid."

She stared up at him, cleared her throat. "And the plan now?"

"Not sure."

"You wanted to die—you wanted to wait long enough just to find him, force him to confess, then commit a kind of suicide."

"Astute."

She thought again of Jim. Of his easy smile. How he lived on the edge in order to *feel*—how he *needed* the rush of EMT work, being a medevac paramedic. Like Crash with his UC work. But it cost him.

She thought of how he'd hidden his depression, and what a black dog it could be. Addiction. Self-medication. Her feelings for this man standing in his shed in front of her, naked in a sense, were suddenly complex. He'd just demonstrated his absolute trust in her. He'd put everything into her hands, even telling her, a cop, that he'd murdered a man out of revenge, and had been planning to do so again. She believed him. She got him. And she needed to stay away from him.

"And now?" she said.

"And now that you know, Constable, what are you going to do about it?"

She sucked air deep into her lungs and sat silent, listening to snow thud from the roof. "I'm going to let you show me Damien's hide."

CHAPTER 30

Crash cut his snowmobile engine. Up ahead, through a dense copse, a low cabin was covered almost to the roof in soft piles of snow, and the flakes were still falling. Faint yellow light sliced through boarded-up windows. All around, snow plopped and thudded off trees as the weight of it on boughs grew too heavy. And as the snow released, branches bounced back in glee, arms waving in the lengthening shadows. It felt as though the trees were alive, moving, shifting. The late-afternoon twilight was low, an eerie blue.

They'd crossed the river, and traveled for almost half an hour into boreal forest before Crash had slowed and turned down into a hidden valley.

He'd made Tana wear a different jacket, one without her RCMP logo and stripes. And he'd insisted on her leaving her RCMP snowmobile behind at his house.

"Wait here," he said, as he strapped on his snowshoes. He started into the woods, circumventing the main and obvious trail that led through the trees into the copse. He'd told her that the snow hid a trap that had been dug deep into the ground on the main trail, and covered with branches.

Through binoculars Tana watched him disappearing into the shadowy forest. And as Crash vanished, a sense of the vast, lonely wilderness pressed down on her, a silent weight, a sentient presence.

She checked her watch. It would be full dark soon.

A few minutes later Crash came into view again. He'd reached the cabin. The door opened and light spilled out. A silhouetted figure stood in the doorway. She refocused her scopes. Damien. He had a long gun. Other figures moved behind him, inside. They'd been watching, waiting. They'd known it was Crash coming.

She had mixed feelings about not interrogating the teens herself, but Crash had said he'd get more out of them without her present. She'd weigh whatever information he retrieved, and decide her own course of action from there. The fact he was a trained cop had shifted perspective in her mind. And this was better than doing nothing about those kids.

"Are you sure you want to do this?" she'd said to him.

"Do what?"

"Help me. With my job." *Considering your rogue cover in town, your wildcat investigation into Sturmann-Taylor . . .*

He'd looked her deep in the eyes, and smiled. "Are you sure you want me to help, considering it's your job?" Then he'd chuckled and said with that grin of his that hid everything that was broken inside, "Besides, I'm not going in there and announcing that I was a police officer. I'm going in to ask them if they hurt your dogs, and if they cut off the town's communications, because even us 'bad guys' have lines that are not crossed. I want to drive that home. They'll listen—they'll talk if they think it'll cost their booze and dope shipments. But only if I go in alone. Now, give me that bag with the taxidermy tool—I want to ask what they know about that, and if they took my buck's eyes."

Unspoken between them lurked the more sinister question: *Was this gang of guys capable of behaving like a pack of blood-thirsty wolves . . . could they have ritualistically slashed and beaten Apodaca and Sanjit, leaving their remains for scavengers?*

As the cabin door closed with Crash inside, Tana panned her scopes across the building to study the shadows that moved in the gaps between the boarded-up windows. She'd play it step by step, see what he returned with. But she had to admit, it was a relief to feel part of a team after struggling on her own out here. Her other growing feelings for Crash were trickier. More dangerous.

The door opened suddenly. Crash came out. There was a moment of more discussion between him and the guys, then he began to make his way back through the trees. He popped out of the shadows a few minutes later, breathing heavily from the exertion of tramping through the deep drifts.

"What did they say?" she said.

"They don't know who cut the cables, or poisoned your dogs."

She eyed him in the waning light. "Is it the truth?"

"I think so." He removed his snowshoes. "They want to keep their liquor flowing. I made it clear that I'm only helping you with this because lines were crossed with the dogs and telcom sabotage. I made it clear I need those lines open for my business, and theirs."

"You *sure*? About the Wolverine Falls guys, too?"

"I've been reading bad guys, con artists, tricksters for years, Tana. I've needed to make split-second life decisions depending on my read, my gut. I wouldn't have survived deep UC if I didn't have a quick tell on people."

She thought of how quickly he'd seen through her anger around Mindy, how he'd read her own past.

"But would you have a read on a sociopath?" she said. "Would you be able to tell if these guys were psychologically capable of murder as a group, perhaps?"

"I don't think that's what we're dealing with here—yeah, Damien and his gang are low-level, social animals. But they're all about making a few bucks, and generally rebelling. I'm not reading any signs of ritualistic behavior, or blood lust, or any need for extreme violence for the sake of it."

"What about the eyeball, and the tool?"

He secured his snowshoes to the back of the machine. Light was fading fast and snow was coming down heavier again.

"Only one of the guys—a hunter from Wolverine Falls—knew what the tool is for. He's also a friend of Jamie's, and he said he's seen several like it in a shed on TwoDove's land—said it's used to scrape and poke out brains from small animals and birds."

"We need to go back to TwoDove's ranch. Those kids were top of my list for the vandalism and poisonings. If they didn't do this—"

"Then someone else did," he said. "And the question becomes, *why*? Why you? Why your dogs? Why the eye and that particular tool on your station door? And was the satcom sabotage designed to cut you— the lone cop—off specifically? What other enemies have you made out here, Tana?"

She dusted snow off her brow, turned, looked into the bleak woods. "And it's *your* buck, in *your* garage, that is missing eyes." She met his gaze in the haunting light. "How vindictive is Mindy? She's made no secret she hates me, and likes you. The deer eyes are a link between you and me. Could she have done this—be trying to say something?"

"I don't think so. I'll talk to her." He mounted the machine in front of Tana. "I don't know what to do with her. There's a special course designed to help kids finish school and get jobs that she wants to take, starting in Yellowknife in January, but until then, she just needs a roof over her head. But while she might meddle with deer eyes, she's not going to have the wherewithal, or motive, to go cutting satcom cables."

"You sure?" Tana tucked herself tightly in behind Crash, wrapping her legs around him.

"And she loves dogs. I don't see her poisoning pets."

He fired the engine. Blue smoke coughed into the dusk as the machine rumbled to life beneath them.

He drove fast, trying to outrun the dwindling light, his headlights dancing and glancing off the snowy landscape as they crashed through the soft drifts. Tana hugged her arms firmly around him for balance as they lurched and swayed through the forest. She liked the feeling of him against her body. It was just the humanness of the connection, she told herself. Warmth. Strength. In an otherwise lonely environment.

How long had it been since someone'd held her in their arms? Loved her? Tenderly, with empathy, and compassion, and care? Not just fucked her. The pain of loss was suddenly acute, unbearable. She missed Jim like a hole in her heart. It was making her vulnerable. She needed to put some distance between herself and Crash, because she couldn't resort to her old coping mechanisms. She did not need new problems. Not now—not with her baby, this new job, this fresh start she was striving for. And Crash was the definition of "problem." Tana knew guys like him, who lived on the edge just to feel alive. She knew his kind too well.

And they were bad for her.

. . . you've got another life to think about now . . .

Mindy lugged her old suitcase through the snow, tears streaming down her face. She'd packed all her shit and was moving out of Crash's place, heading for town but unsure where to go once she got there. She had no money for the motel. She couldn't bear the idea of returning to the old shed by the river. She walked in the middle of the road because it had been sort of plowed. Bob, who did the maintenance in town, mounted blades on his truck at the beginning of each winter. He tried to keep up with the heavy dumps of snow in the early season, maintaining a rough track between town and the airstrip, and up along the river on the road that led past Crow TwoDove's ranch toward the Wolverine Falls settlement.

Headlights and the sound of a truck grinding through snow came up behind her.

She hurriedly moved out of the road and into the drifts on the side.

A dark-gray vehicle drew up alongside her, and stopped, engine running, exhaust fumes chugging into the twilight. The passenger window wound down. An interior light went on.

"Where are you going?" said a man's voice.

Mindy peered inside the truck. It was that man she'd seen in the diner from time to time. The one with the accent. He worked at the WestMin camp.

"I don't know," she said. "To town. Maybe."

"I know you," he said. "You're the young lady who comes into the diner. You live with that pilot—O'Halloran."

"I moved out."

"You got a place to stay?"

"No," she said.

"Why don't you hop in?" He leaned over, opened the passenger door for her. "My name's Markus. I'm heading up to Wolverine Falls. Got a friend with a house there. He's got plenty of room for another." He smiled. It was a warm smile. But Mindy hesitated. She glanced up and down the road. It would be fully dark soon, and getting colder.

She started to put her bag into the front of the truck cab, and Markus moved aside a book that lay on the seat. It looked like a horror novel with the image of a wolf-man with a head like a skull and horns, and long teeth dripping with blood. She wavered again, suddenly unsure. Markus had dark stains on his pants and black dirt under his nails.

"What's that book?" she said.

"Friend of mine wrote it. I brought him my copy to sign the other day. I think you saw him at the diner? Balding guy, round face."

She remembered now. She had seen the round guy in the diner, the night Tana's dogs had been poisoned. She started to climb in. As she did, headlights illuminated them. Another truck was coming up the road.

It pulled up alongside, and the window came down. It was Heather.

"Hey Mindy, Markus," she said. "Where are you guys going?"

"Giving her a ride, a place to stay for the night," Markus said.

Heather studied him for a long moment, her eyes narrowing, then she said, "Mindy, why don't you come with me? I've got an extra bed." She got out of her truck, came around, and took Mindy's suitcase. "Here, let me take that."

Heather hefted it out of Markus's truck and hauled it around to her own. She dumped it into the snow-filled bed of her vehicle, and opened the passenger door for Mindy.

"Thanks," Heather said to Markus with a fake smile. "I've got it."

He eyed her, something going dark in his face, then he gave Heather a small salute, and wound up his window. He drove on.

"You okay?" Heather said once they were inside her warm truck cab. Heather was pretty. Her eyes super blue in this cold, hair like gold. Snow sparkled on her fur ruff. Mindy was jealous of Heather, because she knew she'd slept with Crash. But it was just fucking, because they weren't having a relationship or anything. She'd watched them once, going at it in that barn last summer, after the Festival of Light where everyone had too much to drink under the midnight sun.

Mindy started to cry again.

"What happened with Crash, honey?" Heather said.

"Don't know. Just not staying with him anymore."

"Where were you going?"

"Don't know."

"You can't go sleeping in that shed again."

"Nowhere else." She sobbed, and it was stupid, because Crash was like forty or something and she was almost fifteen, and he'd never feel for her the way she felt for him.

"I'm taking you to my place," Heather said gently. "You can stay there as long as you need to, okay?"

Mindy nodded, wiping her eyes.

Heather put her truck in gear. "Buckle up." As she drove, she kept casting Mindy glances. "So what did happen with Crash? Why're you leaving?"

Mindy looked out the window.

"Hey, you can tell me."

"He's a liar."

"What do you mean?"

"And he's trying to get into that new cop's pants. Should have seen him touching her on the way to his workshop. They were inside there, like forever. Door closed."

"Tana Larsson?"

Mindy nodded.

"His name probably isn't even Crash anyway."

"Well, yeah, that's his nickname. Cameron is his name."

"It's a lie. All of it. I thought he was badass. But he was a cop."

"What?"

"Yeah, and he had a wife, and a daughter. I heard them talking. He was an undercover cop before he came here. Some shit to do with diamonds, and he's helping Tana with something, because after they were in the shed they went off on his snowmobile, and she wasn't wearing her uniform jacket. She was wearing one of his."

Heather frowned. "Are you *sure*? A *cop*?"

"I heard them under the bedroom window. I swear on my life. Fucking men. All liars."

Heather drove in silence for a while. "Mindy, are you sure you're not making this up, to get at him or something, because of Constable Larsson?"

"No."

Another few beats of silence, then she said, "Well, you shouldn't go off with men like Markus Van Bleek. Men like him use women. I've seen him bring young women into the camp." She shot her a glance. "You're worth more, okay? You don't want to go down that road."

Mindy looked out the window into the snowy dusk. She wanted to feel smug, because now Heather wouldn't trust Crash, either. But all she felt was like trash. What else could she feel? It's what she was. There'd be no way out of this shithole for her now. The words she'd had with Tana crawled into her brain.

"Mindy, if you ever need to talk—"

"I sure wouldn't talk to you."

"Look, I've been where you are. I know—"

Mindy blinked back tears.

CHAPTER 31

"Oh, this is *heaven*," Tana said, taking another bite into a slice of piping hot take-out pizza from the diner. Crash grinned as he watched her eat. Seeing her happy made him feel good.

Her cheeks were pinked by the warmth of food after their day out in the cold, and her eyes smiled. Gorgeous, lucid, dark-brown eyes. Like rich chocolate. It was the first time he'd seen her really smile.

They were seated at the table in the station interview room looking up at her whiteboard of autopsy photographs and head shots. In front of them on the table were spread more photos and the coroner's reports. He remembered life like this—working major crimes. Long nights. Eating while brainstorming the crime. The strange kind of camaraderie detectives could feel. He could get used to this again.

Her dogs lay at their feet. They'd been fed and walked, and although subdued, showed signs of getting better. Rosalie had taken good care of them. She'd left a note for Tana, saying that Jamie and Caleb had come by the station with Chief Dupp Peters.

They'd wanted to confess about the bones. Jamie had learned from Marcie where some of the old burial sites were, and he and Selena and Caleb had gone out to plunder the sites for remains. Apparently they thought it was worth the sacrilege to get Selena to take the bones out to the north end of Ice Lake where the anthropological study team would find them the following spring. Their naive goal was to halt mine development. Jamie felt that Selena's death was retribution from the spirits for having sinned by meddling with remains of the forefathers. Furious at Caleb for having pushed him into robbing the grave sites with him, Jamie had gone for Caleb at the Red Moose.

Chief Dupp Peters had told Rosalie the boys wanted to set the record straight with the RCMP, and that the band council would handle it. There would be a sweat lodge for the boys, a spirit quest of sorts to ask forgiveness, and a roundhouse gathering to discuss remediation. The community would need to get those bones back from the coroner's office so that they could be reburied with proper ceremony.

"At least we've made progress on the old bones side of the investigation," Tana said, reaching for a second slice dripping with cheese. Crash liked the way she said "we." He liked it more than he should.

She chomped another bite into her pizza and closed her eyes as she chewed. "Preferable to moose stew any day," she said around her mouthful.

"I make good venison." He didn't know why he said that. It just came out.

She stilled chewing, met his eyes. Something swelled between them—a question about where things would go from here, once they'd gotten to the bottom of this case, whether there would be a dinner of venison made by Crash. She swallowed, and quickly returned her attention to the whiteboard.

"So, what do we have? Let's hash this out. There's no concrete evidence that this was *not* an act of nature. However, we have three separate apparent wolf-bear attacks that show undeniable similarities in the pattern of advanced predation and organ loss on the female victims, right?" She reached for her glass of juice, sipped, looking at the whiteboard, avoiding his eyes.

"Yeah." Crash swallowed his pizza, and wiped his mouth with a napkin. "And we have the inukshuks in all three cases, the same symmetrical gouges in all three attacks, fish blood and vanilla for sure in two of the incidents. We have remote locations with Twin Rivers as an epicenter, and the attacks all occurred at the same time of month—first week of November—each time on the cusp of a severe snowstorm that hampered search efforts, allowing animals time to scavenge the bodies. One death occurred four years ago, one three years ago, and one this year."

"Plus there's the possibility that the geologist from Kelowna who went missing in the Nehako Valley last November, and whose body was found the following spring, could be linked. Damn," she said. "We need Internet. I need to access missing persons files. There could be more incidents out there with the same pattern. I mean, *if* there is a monster out there doing this, he could be getting around in a chopper. Which means he could travel for miles. And nobody just gets up one day and starts with something this violent and depraved. These killings required planning. Whoever did this does not want to get caught, and went to great lengths to ensure animals covered his tracks and other evidence. Surely he must have escalated slowly, over time? He could have been doing this somewhere else before he arrived here."

"That would be my guess," Crash said, picking up a photo of the Baffin-Arctic boot print with a rip in the tread pattern. He'd voluntarily shown Tana the soles of his own shoes before they'd sat down to eat pizza, and there was no anomaly in his lugs. Besides, he wore a men's eleven. This print, judging by her forensic ruler positioned next to another print in the same photo, was about a men's nine. If they could match this, they'd have a solid suspect.

"And there's obviously some cultural, wilderness, or mythological significance around the motive, given the clawlike gouges, and the possibility that animals are being purposefully brought in with lure, plus the inukshuks." He got up, and read again the words of the poem he'd seen in the horror novel.

"I need to get out to Tchliko Lodge," she said.

"We." He held her gaze, reminding her. "We do this together, Tana, until you can get your satcom system connected again, until you get backup. Because if the dog poisonings and the eyeball warning and the sabotage are connected with *this*"—he tapped the whiteboard—"whoever might have killed these four could be targeting you directly now because you're nosing into their business. And you're vulnerable right now, stuck out here alone in the thick of a series of rolling snowstorms."

She swallowed. "Fine," she said quietly. "*We* go to the lodge. Tomorrow. We talk to Henry Spatt, find out more about this novel of his. I want a copy."

"We'll have to travel on snowmobile. There's no flying until the weather lets up again."

She regarded him in silence for several beats. "What about Sturmann-Taylor and what you're trying to do at the lodge—if you show up with a cop?"

Crash knew what she was asking. She wanted to know if helping her was going to blow everything he'd been trying to do here for the last five-plus years. And yeah, maybe it would. But he couldn't *not* do this now. It was like she'd been put in his path to save him from himself, trip him up en route to his own destruction. He didn't know yet if he was sorry, or grateful, but if he could keep her and that unborn baby safe until this was over, then maybe the universe could forgive him for getting Lara and his own baby killed.

Maybe there was such a thing as a second chance.

"Let me worry about that," he said.

"Tell me about finding Novak with his daughter's body," she said.

Crash rubbed the stubble on his jaw. "I was working old K'neekap Eddie's trap lines for him. He was sick that year and wouldn't come into the clinic. He'd probably have died out there with his dogs, besides, I wanted to get in tune with this whole winter-north thing, get known and accepted among the locals."

"Part of the cover."

He snorted softly. "In a manner of speaking. I was running Eddie's dogs downriver that morning, still twilight. Snowing pretty heavily. And I heard this weird, inhuman howling. The dogs went off." He glanced at the "after" head shot of Elliot Novak that Tana had stuck on her board. "It was pretty brutal. Novak was hunkered in a grove of trees, in the middle of a bloody slaughter scene, cradling what was left of Regan, covered in blood himself. Hypothermic. Moaning like an animal, babbling stuff about wolves and bears getting her in the night. I absorbed what there was of the scene, which was fast becoming covered in snow. Regan's head had been ripped off. There was an inukshuk at the edge of the clearing, which struck me as vaguely unusual, but nothing hugely out of the ordinary. And I was worried about losing Elliot. So, I wrapped what was left of Regan in my tent fabric, and bundled them both onto my sled. Took a few hours to get into town. Addy stabilized him while a medevac flew in. Investigators only managed to get out to the attack site several days later."

She eyed him. "Could he have done it—Novak—hurt his own kid?"

Crash chewed the inside of his cheek. "Possibly. He might have been going loony a lot earlier than most realized. It could explain a few things."

"And these others? Dakota Smithers, Apodaca, Sanjit? He's still out there. Is he mad enough to have attacked them all?"

"Hell knows. It's difficult enough to think of *anyone* doing something as depraved as this. But it happens."

"Can you show me where he is—will you take me there?"

He eyed her, then nodded his head slowly. "It's at least a day out on snowmobile. We'd need to overnight in the bush. Are you sure you—"

"I'm sure."

"If we got going at dawn tomorrow, we could hit the lodge first," he said. "It's en route. We could either overnight at the lodge, if we get an invite, or carry on from there, and overnight in the wilds, reach Novak's lair the next morning."

"And Jennie Smithers, I want to talk to her, too. Maybe I can set it up to see her first thing tomorrow before we hit the trail. We can prep tonight, be ready before dawn."

A soft, hot rush of adrenaline washed through Crash, the feeling of being back on a job. But with it came anxiety. Was he helping, or enabling her? Was he going to get her into deeper water?

"Are you going to call this in, Tana?"

"I did," she snapped, and suddenly pushed back her chair. She grabbed the paper plates, left the room. He heard her angrily tossing the leftovers and plates in the garbage in the kitchen. She returned with more juice.

"What happened when you called it in?"

Her eyes flashed hotly to his, irritated that he was pushing. "I told my immediate superior that I'd found significant similarities between the three apparent animal attacks. He suggested we wait for autopsy results, something concrete. I . . ." She hesitated, then inhaled deeply. "It's a long story, Crash. I've got a bad record with brass."

"Want to tell me?"

"Not particularly. Just that . . . there's some personal bad blood. And I figure they're setting me up to fail here, to see me leave the force for good. Just go away. I'm just another Elliot Novak or Hank Skerritt they're waiting to see happen. I . . . I kinda lost it before, you see. I think that's partly why I got this post. And they're not going to send a homicide team out here until I can give them some irrefutable evidence that these attacks might in fact be murders. That's why I must go to the lodge, speak to Spatt, see Novak, talk to Jennie Smithers." She pointed to the Baffin-Arctic boot print. "I need to find the owner of that boot.

And the red AeroStar chopper. Match handwriting to the poem found in Apodaca's things. I need *something*."

The words he'd overheard ran through his mind.

. . . I need to prove I can handle this job first. I need this job.

He moistened his lips, taking a deeper measure of Tana Larsson, thinking that this woman had more than a little bad baggage. Maybe that's why she got him, bought into his history.

"You sleep with one of the bosses, Tana?"

She blanched. Wind howled. Her mouth tightened. She was fighting herself.

She sat again suddenly, dropped her face into her hands, and scrubbed her skin hard. "I slept with a lot of men, Crash." She looked up slowly, and swallowed. Her eyes glistened, and his heart crunched. "I have made so many bad mistakes."

"Whose baby is it?"

"Someone high up at head office. He's an asshole, and he's tight with my immediate superior." She paused. "I was drunk." She got up fast again, paced, stopped. "See, here's the thing, I can try and justify it every which way, but I'm a shit person—"

"Tana—"

She held up her hand. "No. Don't. It's just a fact."

"You came here to start over, to prove yourself?"

"Yeah, and like you said, sometimes there's nowhere else to go, so you go do something that puts one foot in front of the other in the hope that one morning the light will shine again. And"—she shrugged— "Twin Rivers seemed like the end of the world, a last little fly-in town on the fringe of civilization, far enough away to hide from past mistakes and start over." She gave a half laugh. "And you know what? It really *is* the middle of nowhere."

He wanted to touch. Hold. Comfort.

"How did you become a cop?" he said.

"How? That's an odd way of putting it. You think it's surprising? That I was some half-breed not good enough for—"

"Don't. Don't you dare go putting words into my mouth."

She sank back onto her chair, and he could see her debating whether to open up to him, or how far. "So here's the deal," she said quietly. "Maybe I *was* too fucked up to become a cop. I had an . . . interesting childhood, like Mindy. So kudos to you, Sergeant O'Halloran, on your mean profiling skills. You could sniff me out a mile away. A good beat cop picked me up off the streets when I was eighteen. I was a mess, and it was a turning point. He believed in second chances. Because of him, I became a cop, okay? He was just a nice guy. Maybe like you picked Mindy up. He sobered me up, got me into some programs, and I came around. I started volunteering at the food bank, and at the women's center. I got to see girls, women, like me, struggling, and sometimes they just needed a strong helping hand. And compassion. I went back to school, and I decided I wanted to be exactly like that beat cop who turned my life around. I wanted to join the RCMP. I figured if I could help other kids, women like me one day, that was a good enough reason to live. It gave me a way of rationalizing my past. I applied. I was finally accepted. I went down to Depot Division. Did the basic training. And I got posted to Yellowknife as a rookie. That's when I met this guy, Jim Sheridan. He was a paramedic, flew the runs up north to Nunavut, remote parts of the Northwest Territories. He lived for adrenaline, the rush of being on call. And he saw bad stuff on a regular basis. But he was a happy guy, and he loved me, and he was good for me. We moved in together, and—" Her voice hitched. She looked away, struggling to hold it together.

"And life was good . . . for nearly two years. He bought me a small diamond, and we were going to get married. And then one day, after work, I came home, ditched my uniform, and told Jim I was going for groceries. When I returned, it was quiet. Too quiet. That kind of

silence that screams something is wrong . . . He'd taken my Smith &
Wesson—I'd neglected to lock it in the safe—and blown his brains out
in our bathroom."

Silence, just the sound of the wind ripping away at the plastic Crash
had taped over the broken pane in the adjacent office. Under the table
Max groaned, and rolled onto his side.

"And you slid off the rails?" he said, quietly.

"Big time. Hit the bottle, and . . . slept with men, serially, until . . ."
She blew out a huge breath.

"Until the baby."

She nodded. And she looked small and vulnerable suddenly.

"He—the father—told me to get rid of it, that I was shameful,
would ruin his name, destroy his wife and older kids, his family. His
career. And I almost did get rid of it. I came so close. I made the
appointment, had the ultrasound and counseling. Was given a time
to come in. And I did. But in that waiting room, when I was about to
dissolve that misoprostol medication in my cheek before going into
surgery, the nurse reminded me that once I'd taken it, there could be
no turning back. So I sat there awhile, just kind of frozen. And on the
wall in front of me there was a poster. A group of firefighters, cops,
civil workers, men and women both, standing in the snow holding
placards that said: 'You are not alone. You are of the north. You are
strong. You will not be broken.'" She cleared her throat, and Crash
could see she was struggling.

"It was a mental health awareness message. And there was a song
that had been written to go with the campaign, sung in all the languages
of the north. French, English, the indigenous languages, throat singing.
I'd heard that song on the radio that very morning. *You are not alone.*
And as I was sitting there, looking into the eyes of those diverse people,
I suddenly saw the eyes of the cop who'd picked me out of the gutter
and told me that I was worth more. I saw him looking at me out of
all those eyes in that poster. I heard that song in my head. I heard my

grandmother's voice. And suddenly I was *not* alone." Her voice hitched, and she fell silent.

"I think you're a lot stronger than I am, Tana Larsson," he said quietly.

Her eyes flashed up to his. Shock rippled across her face. And then she was fighting tears.

He did what he did best—deflected. He reached for a photo on the table and got up to pin it on the board, giving her space, and his heart ached. For so many reasons.

Redemption.

Second chances.

He cleared his throat, and still studying the board, he said, "So, I think we can rule the old bones out. We can plot the trip tonight, start gearing up, and leave at first light tomorrow, go to the lodge, go talk to Elliot."

"And Jennie Smithers."

He turned. Her eyes had been rubbed red, and she was pale.

"Do you think it could be more than one?" she said. "Acting in a group, a pack? Some sort of cult thing?"

"Well, there's a lot of violence in those images. Strength. Rage, maybe. We should keep it on the table as a possibility."

"I'll get the maps and compass. You can show me the route to the lodge and badlands." She pushed her chair back, and Crash watched her go to fetch the old-school topography maps because satellite navigation out here right now was tricky, and relying on it alone could prove deadly. And he thought he might just be falling for her in all the wrong ways.

Through the late evening and into the night they planned, and packed survival gear, and rations from the storeroom. The rest they could pick up from the diner and his place tomorrow along the way.

It was close on midnight when Tana said she needed to sleep.

"I bunk here tonight," he said.

She was about to protest.

"Until we figure out if the poisonings and sabotage and the warning on your door are related to the killings, you're not safe alone. I'll take the cot in the little room down the hall."

Her eyes held his. She was tired, and she nodded. Crash took Max and Toyon out for a pee as she locked the place down. When he came inside, she'd removed her flak vest, and untied her bun. Their arms brushed as she made for the stairs up to her apartment. He caught her scent. Their lips were close. He touched her face and she went stone-still. Time stretched and hummed between them, as did an undeniable, surging awareness that there was a mutual physical attraction between them, something dangerous and powerful and unstoppable that made no sense, and all sense.

Slowly, he bent his head to kiss her, but she clamped her hand tightly over his wrist, her dark eyes holding his. She swallowed. "No," she whispered, voice thick. "This is not a good idea."

"No," he said quietly. "It's not." Then, "Goodnight, Detective."

"I'm not a detective."

"Not yet," he said quietly. "But you'll make a damn fine one when the time comes."

The wind howls and snow billows in gigantic curtains down the street.

Once more, from a familiar "hunting" blind in shadows across the street, a figure huddles in the cold and watches the police station, feet going numb in the snow.

It's past midnight when the lights inside finally go out one by one. O'Halloran has walked the cop's dogs. His snowmobile is parked outside. He's sleeping over tonight. They've become a team, and now everything must change. Because it can never be the same again, not while the Mountie hunts for a killer. She has to go. They both do now.

A blinding, suffocating vitriol swells inside the chest of the Watcher, and out from the dark wilderness and whirling storm comes a howl of rage. It carries on the wind, and takes shape in the twisting veils of snow. It's the Hunger, the retribution of the wild and lonely places. It's coming closer than ever before, right into town, and it wails and twists down the streets, hitting windows as people sleep, poking down chimneys, and testing under doors.

The Watcher waits a while longer. Cold sinks deeper. A plan is formed.

Then the figure slips out of shadow and is sucked away by the monsters of night . . .

CHAPTER 32

Thursday, November 8. Day length: 7:31:57 hours.

"My marriage broke up, like Elliot's," Jennie Smithers said as she set mugs of coffee onto the low table in front of Tana and Crash. Tana watched the woman carefully as she seated herself on the worn sofa opposite them. Jennie's frame was bent, skeletal, as if grief had consumed her from the inside out, leaving a dry husk of a human who was once a robust mother and wife full of life and laughter. Tana could see from old photos on the mantel what Jennie Smithers had looked like before the wolves got her daughter.

She and Crash had come past the Smithers' tiny clapboard house early, and had seen the lights on inside. Jennie had welcomed them in despite the hour. Her story was a tragic one and she rubbed her arm nervously as she spoke.

"It was Elliot who pushed the idea about Dakota maybe being stalked by some sort of sexual predator. I was mad with grief. I so badly wanted something to hold on to, to *do*. A way to make things right again. But it was a mistake, listening to Elliot—that whole Crow TwoDove thing, targeting him. Look what happened to his life. So much pain all around. So much. I'm so sorry for my part in it."

Tana leaned forward. "But why, in your opinion, was Elliot so gung-ho on the fact that it *wasn't* wolves? What convinced him that Dakota might have been hurt by a person, and then left out there for the animals? Why did he think it wasn't an accident—that she didn't fall off her sled, hurt herself?"

Jennie rubbed her knees. "Guilt," she said finally. "Elliot was driven by guilt, remorse, anger that he'd not been able to protect his daughter, that he hadn't kept her safe inside the tent that night. You see . . . he was drinking."

"So you think he might have been passed out in the tent that night, which is why he didn't hear screams?" Tana said. And she appreciated that Crash was sitting back, just observing and letting her do her job.

"I started to hear talk around town that Elliot had been going on worse and worse liquor binges, after which he'd pass out. And he was suffering from memory blackouts. Looking back, I think he needed to pin blame on something in order to absolve himself." She wavered. "I . . . I finally saw a mental health worker myself," she said. "And it was her who suggested this about Elliot. She thought I might be trying to do the same sort of thing, find blame, by pointing fingers at Crow, perhaps. And that I shouldn't beat myself up over it. She said grief was tricky, not linear, not the same for everyone, and we all went through denial, and had our own coping mechanisms."

"When did he start drinking heavily?"

A big orange tabby cat jumped up into Jennie's lap, and she began to stroke it like a lifeline.

"Word around town was Elliot had had an extramarital affair, and when it ended, that's when he really upped his intake."

Tana and Crash exchanged a fast glance. "With who?" Tana said.

"I don't know."

"How do *you* know?"

Jennie inhaled deeply, looked away for a moment. "The therapist, the health worker that I was seeing, she became my friend. She was the one who told me. She said Elliot's wife came to her about it, but never said who the other woman was. She said the daughter, Regan, knew about the affair, too, and that after Elliot had broken it off he took Regan ice fishing because he was trying to make amends with his family, be a dad again."

Tana's mind shot to Addy, how she'd explained the fine line that needed to be drawn between friendship and professional distance and patient confidentiality when working in a closely knit and small community like Twin Rivers. Jennie's therapist had crossed that line. "Is this health worker still in town?"

Jennie shook her head. "She works in Whitehorse now."

"Can you give me her name?"

"I . . . no, I can't. I shouldn't have said anything. I can't, please understand."

Tana nodded. She could check records, find out herself. She'd also call Elliot's wife if need be.

They thanked Jennie, and as she showed them to the door, Tana said, "So, there was really no evidence at all of stalking? No strange . . . drawings, or quotes from a book, maybe?"

Jennie's gaze shot to Tana's. "What?"

"Dakota never received words from a poem, or something unusual like that?"

"Wait . . . wait right here." She hurried down the hall, and returned with a piece of paper.

On it was an ink drawing of a wendigo-like beast like the one Crash had described seeing in Drakon Sinovski's *The Hunger*. In the sketch the cadaverous creature held a dripping female head. Beneath the image were scrawled the words: *In the barren grounds of the soul, monsters we breed, with heart of ice and eyes that roll in blood.*

The handwriting was similar to the writing on the note Veronique Garnier had found among Selena Apodaca's things.

Tana felt Crash tense beside her.

"When did you find this?" Tana said.

"When I finally cleared out Dakota's room, two years after she was gone."

"She hadn't mentioned it to you before?"

"No. Is . . . is it important?"

Tana forced a smile. "It's probably nothing. But why, if I might ask, did you keep this one thing when you cleared out the rest of her belongings?"

"By accident, really. I'd set it aside in my dresser to ask my husband if he knew what it was, because it was just so . . . strange. Then . . ." She coughed. "Then my marriage started falling apart, and I forgot about it."

"Can I keep this?" Tana said.

"Sure. I . . . why are you looking into all this now? Is it because of that wolf attack on those two biologists? It's not linked, is it? It can't be."

"We're just covering all bases. Thank you so much for your help, Mrs. Smithers."

"Jennie, please."

As they walked back to their snowmobiles, which were already being covered in a layer of freshly falling snow, Crash said, "It's a copy of the same drawing I saw in that book. Similar wording in the text."

"This is weird," Tana said, reaching for her helmet.

Crash dusted off their machines. "So, Elliot was having blackouts," he said as he worked. "And guilt from his affair. After he's broken it off, he takes Regan out on an ice fishing trip to make amends, but he couldn't leave the bottle behind. He slips that night, overindulges. Goes to sleep blind drunk. And some time in the night, Regan dies, and he hears not even a scream. His guilt, remorse, self-flagellation deepens tenfold. He starts drinking harder, looking for blame. His wife takes it out on him, and the Novak marriage finally folds. And he starts losing the plot completely."

"That, or he did it. He killed his daughter. Maybe even in a black-out, and he knows he did something, but can't remember."

"And who was the woman he'd had an affair with? If we could find her—"

"We'll ask him directly," Tana said, pulling on her balaclava and then her helmet. She swung her leg over her machine, and fired the engine. She was kitted out in full foul-weather gear—padded with down midlayers and covered with waterproof shells. It was still dark, and it would probably remain so because of the heavy fog and thick snowfall. Crash revved his own engine.

They were using two machines for the trip. For safety, and because Tana had no need to hide her RCMP logo this time. And because they also had to carry a fair bit of gear and extra gas as the journey would require an overnight stay, possibly in the bush. They'd risen early enough to finish packing survival gear, and Tana had left a note for Rosalie, asking her once again to watch over Max and Toyon, and to stay overnight at the station if she could. She was going to owe Rosalie big time.

Crash took off at a clip ahead of her. They needed to travel fast to make the distance. Tana tucked in close behind him. Releasing the throttle, she picked up speed, and felt the g-forces gathering low and delicious in her gut.

CHAPTER 33

"Why did you bring *her* here?" Sturmann-Taylor said, voice low.

"Is it a problem?" Crash held the lodge owner's penetrating blue gaze without a blink. It was early evening—he and Tana had ridden hard all day to reach Tchliko Lodge before nightfall, and Sturmann-Taylor had not even tried to hide his surprise—and irritation—at seeing Crash and Tana rolling up like two snow-covered yetis on their snowmobiles in the storm.

"It was just unexpected," Sturmann-Taylor said, keeping Crash back in the hallway as his butler led Tana into the library ahead of them. "Seeing you with that cop—I thought she was on your ass for bootlegging."

Crash had known *this* would be the risk of escorting Tana into the Tchliko lair. Because nothing, no possibility, escaped the shrewd and calculating brain of Alan Sturmann-Taylor, especially when he'd made clear that he was considering working with Crash on shipments of a more sensitive nature, and most likely highly illegal.

Having brought Tana here could derail everything. Would Crash make the decision again if he was given a second run? Yes. Things had changed, were changing. But what worried him now was not so much what might happen to his cover with Sturmann-Taylor as what could happen to Tana. He might be endangering her, because if he was correct about Sturmann-Taylor, the reach of the man's power was limitless, and his desire to hold on to that power knew few bounds. And now that Tana was in Sturmann-Taylor's sights, he was going to be watching her keenly.

"She's a paying client, that's all," Crash countered quietly. "She came bashing on my door, asking for a flight out to Tchliko. I said 'no-way-hosay,' not in this shit. But she knows I'm familiar with the route out here, so when she could find no one else, she returned asking for a snowmobile guide. I wasn't going to draw attention to myself by refusing." He continued to meet Sturmann-Taylor's quietly assessing stare. "Besides, I like to know what I'm up against."

"What does she want with Spatt?"

"I don't know. Let's go in and find out, shall we?"

Tension whispered through Tana as she was shown into the library ahead of Crash. Sturmann-Taylor had held him back, and they were conversing quietly in the passage. She figured it was about Crash bringing her here. If Crash was correct about Sturmann-Taylor, and if Crash's "cover" was now slipping because of his alignment with her, they could both be in serious trouble in this isolated lair.

"It's good to see you again, Constable," Henry Spatt said as she entered. He pushed himself up out of the deep, burgundy leather chair in which he'd been seated beside his evening cocktail. He proffered his hand. Tana shook it, and found his grip no less limp and fleshy than the last time around in the diner.

"James here"—Spatt nodded toward the butler—"tells me that you came all this way in this terrible storm to see *me*, of all people." He chuckled, and it caught phlegm in his throat, which made him cough. "S'cuse me." He dabbed at his lips with his hankie. "Years of tobacco."

He chuckled again. "And it's not really 'James,' by the way. However, Alan likes to keep his manservant obscure, or mysterious perhaps. So I call him James, as in James the Butler, from that British show that was so popular in the seventies. You know the show?"

"Uh, no, sir, I don't."

"Well, of course you don't, would you?" He tucked his hankie back into his breast pocket. "You're far too young, and too . . . local. Please, do take a seat. And thank you, James, you may leave now."

The manservant did not leave. He simply stepped back into shadows.

"Local?" Tana asked. She remained standing.

"Oh, and call me Henry. Much nicer to be on first-name terms. Was it . . . Tana?"

"Larsson," she said. "Constable Larsson."

His small round eyes met hers in silence for a few minutes, then his equally round face cracked into a smile that showed his sharp little incisors. "Of course. You're on a job. Professional reasons are what must have brought you here." He reseated himself in the leather chair. "Now, I am most intrigued, what can I do for you?" He reached for his cocktail.

Crash and Alan Sturmann-Taylor entered the room. It was warm inside. Fire burned in the hearth. Shelves of books covered the walls. And where there were gaps between the shelves, the heads of dead things had been mounted. Animal pelts were draped over the backs of chairs and had been fashioned into pillows as well—bear skins, leopard, zebra, antelope. The chandeliers were crafted from antlers, the side-table lampshades, she guessed, were real animal hide, too. Sumptuous and macabre, a hunter's trophies of the murdered.

Crash did not meet her eyes as he made his way to stand beside the fire. She knew his game would be this, and she kept her distance.

"Can I get you a drink, Constable?" their host said.

"Water would be great. Been a long ride."

"Of course." He nodded to his butler, and the man sifted like a specter from the room.

"So, to what do we owe this honor, Constable? What is so urgent that brings the Mountie out on her mechanical steed in this foul weather?" said Sturmann-Taylor.

From her pocket she produced the drawing that Jennie Smithers had given her this morning. "I believe there is an image like this in one of Mr. Spatt's books." She turned to Spatt. "I'd like to ask you some questions about the story, and to see a copy of the novel."

Spatt reached out for the drawing, forcing Tana to lean forward and hand it to him.

The man frowned and pursed his lips as he studied it. "It's not a fantastic rendering, but yes, there is a drawing like this in *The Hunger*." He looked up. "Where did it come from? Why the questions?"

The butler appeared with a glass of water on a tray, and she took it, sipping deeply—the ride had been long, and she was not only thirsty, she was ravenous. "It came to light in connection with a cold case," she said, wishing Sturmann-Taylor's shadowy manservant had brought snacks as well. "One that might be relevant to a current investigation."

"Is it a *homicide*? It must be something serious like *murder* that forces you out on such a long ride?"

"It could possibly tie into a death investigation."

"Oh, this *is* exciting. Who was killed?"

"I'm not at liberty to divulge much more than I have at this point."

Sturmann-Taylor glanced at Crash. Crash's features remained indifferent.

"Yes, yes of course. I see," said Spatt, getting a little fidgety in his chair. "*The Hunger* is one of my earlier works, about a cannibalistic beast—a wolflike creature crossed with a man that craves human flesh once a year, just as the world turns toward winter. It has a heart of ice, and it can never satisfy its hunger. And it particularly loves maidens. The story is based on ancient local lore, and it's set right in this area of the Northwest Territories, but in the past. Mid-1800s. It features an intrepid gentleman-adventurer hero with a taste for the Canadian wilderness and a curiosity for the supernatural—Cromwell is his name. It was my biggest seller—haven't made it as big since." He launched out of his chair, and waddled toward the shelves. "You do have a copy of *The Hunger* here somewhere, Alan, don't you? Where is it, which shelf?"

The butler stepped forward and slid a hardback out from one of the library shelves. He handed the book to Spatt.

"This." He reverently presented the book to Tana with both hands and a slight bow, as if an offering. His eyes glittered. "This is it. My blockbuster."

She opened the cover. The sketch was right there, just as Crash had described it, and there was no doubt that the drawing in Jennie's possession was a copy of this same image—a skeletal human-beast, with a head that was part wolf, part human skull. Bared, bloodied fangs. In its blackened talons it clutched the dripping head of a woman. Four parallel gouges like claw marks ripped open half her face, and she was missing eyes. Tana breathed in slowly as she read the words on the opposite page.

> *In the Barren ground of the soul*
> *nothing can grow.*
> *For here is bitter and cold where*
> *the sun hangs low.*
> *Where a midnight caribou mutilation*
> *awakens a howl of emptiness with ice*
> *where once there was heart.*
> *And it comes with hunger*
> *for blood in its mouth.*
> *For, in the Barrens of the soul,*
> *monsters take toll . . .*

Her heart began to slam against her ribcage as she turned the page and started the first lines of the first chapter.

And there carried upon the night wind an odor that was both fetid and fragrant. So subtle was this scent, that had Cromwell not noticed the queer change that came suddenly upon his Voyageur guide as the draft stirred the flames to brightness, he'd not have noticed it himself. But his man, Moreau, who was squatting in his furs before the campfire smoking his pipe, abruptly snapped his eyes toward the dark forest. It was then that Cromwell became aware of the gentle but malodorous scent. Moreau's nostrils flared, as though he might be a creature of the woods catching the carrion stink of a predator upwind. And as the flames settled back to embers, Cromwell saw a look in the Voyageur's dark face that deeply disquieted him. His man was scared, to the very quick of his soul . . .

She flicked through pages, reading random passages, her body going hotter and hotter.

. . . Above the gorge in which the ravaged and decapitated body lay, stood a man of tundra stone common to the north that Cromwell knew to be called an inukshuk . . .

She checked the publication date. *The Hunger* had first been released in hardcover five years ago. Tana flicked quickly to the acknowledgments at the back.

Thank you to Charlie Nakehk'o, our native guide, a Twin Rivers elder, who told us the story of the hungry spirits of the wild around a campfire one hunt. And a deep debt of gratitude must also be extended to Alan Sturmann-Taylor for his gracious hospitality at his new lodge . . .

Tana cleared her throat, and said quietly, without looking up, "Is Charlie Nakehk'o here at the moment?"

"He is," replied Sturmann-Taylor. "He'll be with us all winter."

"Can I speak with him?"

"I'll have him brought in—"

"In private," she said, glancing up and meeting Sturmann-Taylor's gaze. Her blood was racing. Someone was acting out, bringing to life, the things in this book, word for word, and had been doing so for at least four years.

"I'll have my butler bring him to the sunroom." Sturmann-Taylor nodded to his man, who slipped out at his command.

"Why—what is it?" Spatt said, his grin fading, consternation creasing his brow. Crash watched in silence from near the fire, his face giving nothing.

"I'd like a copy of this book," she said. "I'd like to read it."

"I can gift you a signed paperback, I have several copies in my—"

"A signed copy shall be delivered to your room, Constable," Sturmann-Taylor said calmly. "You will of course be staying for dinner, and for the night. All right with you, O'Halloran?"

"Whatever the officer wants, or needs."

"We have a trip to make farther north, at first light," Tana said.

"No problem. Whatever time you need to leave, my staff will see you out with sustenance and any other supplies that you might require."

She turned to Spatt, who was now pacing the room. "Where would people generally find copies of this book—are there any available locally? In the Territories?"

"Well, of course there are," he said. "I got great coverage in the Yellowknife media when it was first released. And I delivered a whole box of complimentary copies to the Twin Rivers library, as small as it is. Copies were on sale in the diner store, as well, and still might be. *The Hunger* is available to anyone who visits the lodge. It's sold all over the US, Canada. Germany—translated. I do very well in the Scandinavian countries. England. And you can get it online, in digital format."

"And where were you in early November, four winters ago?"

He stalled his pacing. "I've been coming here to overwinter every year for the last five years, arriving just before Halloween. I was one of Alan's first guests after he bought the place, and that year was the best hunt I'd had of my life. I've seen this lodge grow from a rundown old outfit into one of the most discreet high-end, luxury wilderness experiences around the globe. And I will only hunt with Charlie as my guide, like many others who come here."

"And this past Friday, November second, where were you?"

Worry darted through his beady little eyes. "Where is this going, Constable?"

She forced a smile. "Just covering bases."

"I . . ." He exchanged a glance with Sturmann-Taylor. "It was a hunt day, right, Alan? Friday?"

"Correct." Sturmann-Taylor's demeanor, like Crash's, belied nothing, but Tana could feel tension humming off him.

"Where did you hunt?" she said.

"North of Headless Man."

"How did you get there?"

"Chopper. Like that one there." He pointed to a photograph on an antique-looking, black wood dresser. "We use a local pilot."

She walked over to the set of photographs, leaned closer. "What kind of helicopter is this?" she said.

"AS355 Eurocopter Twin Squirrel," said Sturmann-Taylor. "Six seater. One of Boreal Air's."

Tana studied the other photos—groups of hunters on excursions. Sturmann-Taylor with various women. Another picture showed a laughing group in camo gear with guns, arms around each other's shoulders. At their feet sprawled a dead grizzly. Sturmann-Taylor's boot rested on the grizz's head. With him was Henry Spatt, Markus Van Bleek, Harry Blundt, and Heather MacAllistair, who must have been their Boreal Air pilot.

"And where was this one taken?" she asked, gesturing to the picture.

"That one?" Sturmann-Taylor said, coming to her side. "Nehako Valley. Grizzly bear hunt."

Tana's pulse gave a kick.

Nehako—where Alexa Peters had said the body of a Kelowna geologist had been found scavenged.

"Oh, that was just a fabulous trip," Spatt said, coming over. "I have an even better photograph than that one." He whipped out his wallet, and flipped through it. "Here," he said proudly. "One with the brown bear that I bagged with a bow, moreover."

Tana took the image from him, and her heart slowed to an erratic beat. There was an extra member of the hunting party in this photo. Trying to keep her voice level, and without looking up, she said, "Impressive. Did you hunt often with this particular group, Mr. Spatt?" Her voice came out tight, and she heard it. In her peripheral vision she saw Crash glance her way suddenly. He'd heard it, too. Which meant Sturmann-Taylor and Spatt had probably noticed as well.

Be careful what you say now, Tana . . .

"On more than one occasion, yes. That particular hunt was November three years ago, wasn't it, Alan?"

The geologist went missing three years ago . . .

She glanced up. Sturmann-Taylor's features had gone hard. His eyes were narrowed, sharp, assessing, like a predator. And she knew she was not supposed to have seen this photo. With this extra man in it.

The library door opened, saving her. "Charlie is awaiting you in the sunroom, ma'am. I'll show you the way," said the manservant.

CHAPTER 34

On a table in the sunroom, Tana laid out the photographs of the Apodaca-Sanjit attack aftermath that she'd brought for Charlie. "What I'm interested in, is does this look like a wolf or bear kill to you—is this pattern of animal predation something you've seen before in the wild?"

Charlie's long braids swung forward as he bent to study the photos. He smelled of sage and wood smoke. Tana had apologized for the subject matter, but he'd said he was okay to examine the photos she'd taken at the scene. She'd also brought for him images from the Dakota Smithers and Regan Novak autopsies.

His face went dark. The air around him seemed to grow thick. He took his time. Then his hand went slowly up to the jade talisman he always wore on a thong around his neck. It was to ward off evil, he'd once told Tana. The evil of lonely places. And his brown, gnarled hand curled around it.

"Not wolves," he said in his husky voice. "Not bear. Maybe they come later, but something was there before."

A chill ran down Tana's back.

"What makes you say this?" she said.

"They don't do it like this."

"But they *could* have?"

He shook his head.

"Has anyone asked for your input on the Dakota Smithers and Regan Novak attacks before?"

"No one. I never saw the sites where these kids were killed, either. I never saw *this*." He was silent for a long while as he studied the glossy black-and-whites. Then his old, rheumy eyes looked up and met hers— eyes that had witnessed many things over many years. Eyes that had absorbed the wisdom and mysteries of the wild. "You saved my nephew, Tana. Now I must save you." He paused. "Leave this alone."

She weighed him for a moment, unease growing in her chest.

"That author, Henry Spatt, said it was you, Charlie, who told him about the legends of a spirit-beast who kills and rips apart women, and who takes their hearts and their eyes."

His face blackened to thunder. His eyes changed. An energy surged about him that she'd not experienced in his usually calm presence. Lights almost seemed to dim inside the room. "It is the way of our culture to tell the old stories. I did not know he would put it in a book."

"It angers you?"

"It is for oral history. It is to be spoken around fires in the night. It is to be interpreted by the listener—a conversation between the story-teller and the listener. The stories are to stay out here in the north, in the wild, where the spirits of our forefathers can hear, also, and so can the wind." He shook his head in disgust, and walked toward the door, fringes of his brown leather coat swinging.

"Charlie," she called after him.

He stopped, turned.

"It's possible that someone could be trying to act out this legend, or the story, as it's told in Henry's book. You are out there in the bush all the time—do you have any idea who it might be?"

"There are things out in the bush that do not make sense in books," he said. "But they are real." He paused. "Do not anger this spirit, Tana.

Do not let it inside you." He formed a fist and beat it once, hard, against his chest. "It turns the heart to ice."

Dinner was held in a room named Wolf Hall. Or, the word "staged" might be more appropriate, thought Tana as she glanced up at the words engraved on a plaque above the door. Sturmann-Taylor followed her gaze.

"Each room in the lodge is named after a wild animal," he explained with a sharp smile. "This one is for the noble wolf. And I do like the historical allusions to Wolfhall, or Wulfhall, the name of the manor from whence came the third wife of Henry the Eighth, Jane Seymour. It's also the title of a fabulous fictionalized account of the time. Please, enter." He held out his hand, showing them in. "And of course, the psychology of the king himself is riveting."

The room was paneled with dark wood, and a long, narrow table ran down the middle. The table was adorned with crystal goblets, sparkling silver cutlery, white china, linen napkins. Candles in several pewter candelabras provided most of the light in the room, and the glow quavered and shimmered and danced off the silverware, the crystal, and it flickered in the glass eyes of the beast heads mounted on the walls. A fire also burned softly in a stone hearth at the far end of the table.

Who in their right mind wanted dead animals watching them eat?

"Some of Crow TwoDove's work, I presume," Tana said, nodding to the stuffed heads.

"Yes," Sturmann-Taylor said. He pulled out a high-backed chair for her, seating her beside fat Henry Spatt. "Crow is by far the finest taxidermist I've ever had the pleasure of working with. A true artiste. We had him out to the lodge earlier in the season to do a demonstration and workshop for some of our guests. It went very well. We've started bringing in equipment, and have set up a facility for him here. We'd love to have him on site permanently, or at least for a good part of each year. Henry was among our first taxidermy workshop guinea pigs. Went well, didn't it, Henry?"

"Delightful!" Henry reached across the table and clasped a bottle of red wine. He began glugging its contents into his goblet. "Markus thought so, too." He took an immediate swig from his glass, and sighed with pleasure.

"Equipment?" Tana said, "As in taxidermy tools?" She thought about the tool skewering the deer eyeball to her door, and how Spatt had been in town with Van Bleek at the time.

Crash was shown the seat across the table from her. His eyes caught hers for an instant. His face was tight. It was clearly eating him to know what she'd seen in Spatt's wallet photo. Eating her, too. She needed to get through dinner and find some time on her own to process it.

"Yes," Sturmann-Taylor said, seating himself at the head of the table, and flicking out his linen napkin. He placed it on his lap and nodded for the server standing quietly at his side to pour wine into the remaining empty glasses. "We had a special outbuilding built to Crow's specs. Far superior-looking to that beastly place he has in Twin Rivers. And much better suited to meeting the taxidermy needs of my clients out here. And while he is on site, we can . . . how shall we say . . . massage his style a little." Again, a fast flash of that wolfish grin.

An array of appetizers was brought in by silent staff. More wine was poured. Cutlery chinked as they ate, and Spatt drank copiously, becoming more loquacious with each goblet full of fine Burgundy.

"Must be fascinating to be a Mountie," he breathed onto Tana. "An investigator of homicide and all that."

She eyed him, wondering if he could be capable of the murders, the bloody violence. He'd been in town for each one. He had opportunity. He knew the scenarios in his book intimately—he'd created them. Could he be trying to bring them alive? To relive that rush of success he'd had with that first Cromwell book, and had not managed to replicate since? Was *this* why he came out here annually—for a human hunt?

Was she dining arm to arm with a demented killer?

Crash spoke very little throughout the meal. He was posing simply as her guide.

Sturmann-Taylor was intently observant, assessing them all in turn. Tana was besieged by the sense they were his minions, his toys in a psychological game, and that he'd brought them into this room to eat dead meat while the dead heads of animals watched them as some sort of test.

"I mean—" Spatt leaned toward her, his meaty, alcohol breath washing hot over her face. Her stomach recoiled, and she concentrated fiercely on breathing shallowly. She did not need to embarrass herself by fleeing for the bathroom right now. Spatt continued, "Murder, and the legal process that follows, it's a kind of theatre, don't you think? A theatre of the macabre."

Like this room. This lodge. This opulent malevolence.

Outside, the storm howled as it intensified. Wind gusted down the chimney, and the flames darted while candles shivered.

"It's no wonder we are all drawn to murder in so many ways," said Spatt. "It throws under a spotlight the pathologies of our communities. It forces us to examine elements of our society, and in ourselves, that we try to ignore: deviance, violence, anger, hatred, frustration, malevolence, greed, mental illness, cruelty. It's why we write about it, I think. We create fictional monsters, so that we can examine these abhorrences as something quite apart from ourselves. Because if we didn't have this outlet, we'd be forced to look into the mirror, and see the eyes of a beast looking back."

Tana glanced at Crash. He was staring hard at Spatt. Her mind returned to the photographs of Spatt on the mantel in the library. Like so many outdoor enthusiasts in the north, he'd been wearing Baffin-Arctic boots in those photos. She'd judged his feet to be around a size nine. When she and Crash had arrived at the lodge, the butler had taken their wet gear into a mudroom off the entrance hall. Perhaps Spatt's boots were drying in the mudroom with the others.

Plates were removed and main courses were arranged in front of them. More drinks were poured. Tana declined the wine each time, but exhaustion was beginning to weigh a heavy mantle over her nevertheless. She needed to persevere for one more course, and then she could respectably excuse herself and head for her room, possibly via the mudroom to check out Spatt's boot soles. And she wanted to read more of his novel, and think about the implications of what she'd seen in his wallet photo. Plus they had a very early start planned for tomorrow, and a challenging ride ahead into the badlands.

"And the way we police our crimes," Spatt was saying, "reveals the true authority of a government. It demonstrates the ultimate power it holds over the lives of its citizens. It's why the early Canadian governments sent mounted police proudly riding into the wild, wild west—to stake a sense of ownership and control over the untamed land, and subdue the natives."

Tana's mind went to Crow TwoDove, and his hatred for cops. Her gran had once told her that the old Dene word for police meant "the takers away of people." She made a personal vow. She was going to change that deep-seated cultural view in her own small way, right there in Twin Rivers. Cooperative policing. Communication. She'd already started by convincing Viktor Baroshkov to work with Jamie TwoDove on reparation for the damage at the Red Moose. And she'd broached Chief Dupp Peters on the subject of auxiliaries. She knew this philosophy was already well touted by her federal force. But whether she'd personally get cooperation from brass at a micro level was another matter.

"Why a wendigo creature in your book?" Crash said suddenly.

"Hah!" said Spatt. "Because it cuts to the true 'heart of darkness' trope—the idea that if a traveler ventures into wilderness, and if he goes too deep, too dark, for too long, he will be touched by that which is uncivilized, untamable. And he will return a profoundly changed man with some of the wild inside him. He has, in effect, become 'The Beast' himself. It's a common enough metaphor that is retold in many ways. You even see echoes of it in vampire lore. The creature bites you, and you become a vampire. The zombie infects you, and you become a zombie. It's essentially a trip down into the wild Jungian basement of the human soul, for down there is where the dark jungle really thrives, and where your own monsters are buried."

Tana set her glass down, thinking of Crash, how he'd ventured undercover into the dark world of organized crime and returned a changed man, with perhaps a touch of the underworld beast himself. "It's been a fascinating conversation, and delicious meal, thank you," she said as she folded her napkin and laid it beside her plate. "If you don't mind, I need to call it a day." She got to her feet, feeling dizzy suddenly, and she braced for balance on the back of her chair.

Sturmann-Taylor came instantly to his feet. "And thank *you* for the company, Constable. My butler will show you to your room." He eyed Crash. "I've placed you two side by side."

Crash met Sturmann-Taylor's gaze coolly. He was being tested. He simply nodded.

Nerves and a tentacle of tension followed Tana out of the room and down the corridor. The butler led the way, a silent shadow through the stone-tiled halls. She wasn't going to get a chance to slip into the mudroom without him.

If she wanted to see Spatt's boots, she was going to have to ask Spatt directly.

CHAPTER 35

It was just after 2:00 a.m. when Crash entered his room, his head slightly fuzzy from drink. He closed the door behind him, clicked on the light, and jumped to see Tana standing there in socked feet, long johns, her down jacket over top. Her hair hung glossy to her shoulders and her face was ghost white.

"What in the—"

"You look remarkably sober for someone who's been drinking all night with the boys," she said.

He shucked off his flannel shirt, tossed it over a chair. "Want to tell me what's eating you? What did you see in that photo from Spatt's wallet?" He sat on the bed, started removing his boots. He was beat. He'd had to work hard to keep appearances with Sturmann-Taylor, matching him drink for drink.

She sidestepped the question. "I skimmed Spatt's novel, entire thing. Someone is reenacting the murders in his story. Everything. Talon marks, the ripped-out heart. Eyes. Torn-off head. Someone has been doing this for at least four years. And it might be Spatt himself. He was wearing Baffin Arctics in that one photo. I need to see his soles, what size he wears."

"He looks a nine to me. What did Charlie say?"

She hesitated. "He said it wasn't wild animals that killed Apodaca, Sanjit, Smithers, and Novak."

Crash glanced up.

"He reckoned the animals came afterward. He said 'something' else was there before them."

"Some *thing*?"

She dragged her hand over her hair. "He's inclined to believe there's a real spirit-beast-monster thing out there. He's angry that Spatt stole an indigenous oral story and put it into print."

Crash dumped his boots on the floor. "You think Charlie could be capable of murder?"

"I have no idea. He's an enigma."

"You think Spatt has it in him?" he said.

"I've never dealt with anything like this before, so I've got nothing to go by. He's odd. He gets excited by violence, by the idea that I am looking at his novel in connection with a possible homicide—it might be exactly what he wants. Attention. A thrill. To relive the excitement of that bestseller. He had opportunity in each case. You saw the way he practically ejaculated when he heard that we—I—might be looking into a murder."

He put his finger to his lips, reminding her to be quiet. To not be heard in his room with him.

She heaved a sigh of exasperation.

"Come sit here," he said quietly, patting the bed beside him. She hesitated.

"Hey, I'm not going to bite, I just—"

"Want to keep it down. I know." She acquiesced, seating herself close to him, and he caught the scent of her shampoo. She smelled good. He glanced at her legs—the shape of them revealed by her slim-fitting long johns. Her jacket hung open and he could see the swell of her belly. Heat washed into his chest, and his pulse quickened. He'd had a bit too much to drink and it had edged the lid off his control, and his need for her right now was sudden and basic. He avoided her eyes for a moment, getting a grip on himself. Then he said, quietly, "Spatt has access to taxidermy tools here at the lodge, given what Sturmann-Taylor said about the new workshop, and he was in town with Van Bleek, in the diner, the night your dogs were poisoned, and when that eyeball was pinned to your door, and the satcom system sabotaged. But there's something else that's worrying you, Tana. You saw something in that wallet photo of his. You went sheet white. Your voice changed. What was it?"

She stared at her hands for a moment, debating what to tell him.

Inhaling deeply, she said, "The father of my baby. He was in one of the photos taken in the Nehako Valley with Sturmann-Taylor, Spatt, Van Bleek, Blundt, and MacAllistair."

Surprise washed through Crash. He studied her profile because she wouldn't meet his eyes.

"Who is he, Tana?"

She glanced up, and his heart crunched at the conflict, the confusion he saw in her face. "Cutter," she said. "Staff Sergeant Garth Cutter."

Crash stared at her. "Christ," he said. "Your staff sergeant? You sure know how to pick 'em, girl."

She lurched off the bed and paced to the other end of the room.

"Tana, I didn't mean—"

She spun around. "What *did* you mean?"

"He . . . I know the name, that's all. And he's high up in G-Division." Crash could see it all now—why she'd needed to get out of Yellowknife. Why she was worried about her job. Why she figured people might be trying to make her just "go away." She and her growing belly were a time bomb for a married, respected, and ambitious staff sergeant like Cutter. Crash knew of the man because he'd made it his business to watch what was going on in Yellowknife, the diamond business, the associated crime. Cutter had been instrumental in creating an arm of the RCMP to specifically police the diamond trade in the territories. He was also a political animal with his sights set on a commissioned post. His blood suddenly cooled as it hit him—Staff Sergeant Garth Cutter, with a diamond background, was in some way connected to Sturmann-Taylor. And the WestMin guys.

He sat forward. "Tana," he said slowly, quietly. "You might just have found the missing piece."

"What?"

"Remember what I told you? About the Devil's Angels guy who said the next most valuable thing to the Angels after clean diamonds was a turned cop, the higher the better?"

She stared at him.

Silence swelled.

He could hear the storm outside, sense the snow piling thick against the lodge windows, smothering them in.

"What? You think it's *Cutter*?"

He got up, and went over to her. He took her face in his hands. "I think you just gave me a key, Tana. I think the other puzzle pieces might all start to fit now."

"*If* Sturmann-Taylor is who you think he is, and *if* Cutter is connected to this illegal enterprise, why would he go posing for a photo with him?"

"Maybe he didn't. Maybe it was snapped in the moment by someone, and Spatt just happened to end up carrying around a copy of that particular image in his wallet—I mean, Cutter wasn't in the one on display in the library, was he?"

She blew out a heavy breath.

"Think about it, Tana. If someone with Cutter's profile was dirty, and became aware that a UC sting was going down in Vancouver, and if he felt that those chemically marked blood stones entering the laundering chain might lead Project Protea back to him, who better to leak word of the deal and scuttle it in order to save his own ass?" Crash's blood began to heat as he spoke. "He—Cutter—could be responsible for the bust that went sideways, for me getting shot in the head."

"Tell me one thing," she said. "If Sturmann-Taylor is behind this blood diamond syndicate, why doesn't he recognize you as the UC cop?"

"Like I told you, everything in this syndicate is removed from operations on the ground. It's all managed in tightly controlled cells, on a need-to-know basis only, for everyone's protection. Sturmann-Taylor might have learned through Cutter that a UC operation was going to go down in Vancouver, but not *which* cops were undercover. I was deep under. Many years. I *was* a Devil's Angels gang member for all intents and purposes. Not even Cutter would have known my identity. Only my immediate handlers had that information. And so far as anyone else knows, Sten Bauer is now either dead, or a vegetable in some institution somewhere."

"This isn't proof that he's the bad link."

"Face it, it's a very solid lead. If Sturmann-Taylor heads the illegal diamond syndicate, his personal friendship with a top diamond cop from Yellowknife is potentially explosive."

She plopped herself back down onto the bed and rubbed her hands hard over her face.

"If we hadn't started working together, Tana, I might never have found that link."

She looked up, and her eyes gleamed. "He's the fucking father of my baby, Crash."

He sat beside her, took her hands in his. "I'm sorry."

She shook her head. "I don't know what to say, what to think. Other than I don't care if you nail his ass to the wall, but . . . but what's eating at me now, is why *I* was sent out here." She met his eyes.

"There's the father of my child standing next to Van Bleek, who you claim is a hit man—a merc who managed small armies in Africa. And with them is Sturmann-Taylor, possible head of a huge, secretive international syndicate running blood stones through Northwest Territory mines, and Blundt who is about to open one of the biggest mines in the territories, and there's Spatt, a potentially psychotic author who could be a thrill killer. Maybe Cutter wanted me posted out here because he thinks I'll either never sniff out what WestMin and Sturmann-Taylor might be up to. Or . . . I might be heading for a planned little accident out here in the wilderness before my baby is born—because, in all honesty, how can Cutter trust that I'm never going to use this against him one day? He's politically minded. Ambitious. He wants to go places where the revelation of an affair with a subordinate employee, and an illegitimate child, are going to hurt him. I could be fatal to his career. His family."

She extracted her hands from his hold. "It sure would explain why they're not in a rush to send me some backup right now. They'd more likely prefer to see me and my baby dead. Maybe they'll get Van Bleek to do it."

The implications of her words, cold and sinister, leaked down into him. And now he'd brought her here, where Sturmann-Taylor had witnessed her reaction to seeing Cutter, to seeing the link between a top cop and himself. Fuck. He really had brought her into the beast's den.

He needed to get her out. They had to get on top of this before it got on top of them. These men were more than dangerous.

His eyes went to her belly. "You okay?"

She gave a half laugh, the rest of which sounded like an odd sob. "Yeah. I'm fine."

"You are fine, Tana."

She glanced at him. Her gaze went to his mouth, and his cock stirred. She swallowed at something she saw in his face, and got up.

"I need to sleep," she said crisply.

He nodded. He didn't trust his voice right now. He watched her ass in those long johns as she made for the door. She reached for the handle, and just before she opened the door, he managed to say, "I've arranged with Sturmann-Taylor's butler for us to leave by 5:00 a.m."

She paused, turned slowly, and the dark look in her eyes was a sexual punch to his gut. He cleared his throat. "We must be gone before Sturmann-Taylor and everyone else wakes up."

"I wanted to look at Spatt's boots," she said.

"I already asked the butler which boots in the mudroom were Spatt's. He told me Spatt just started wearing a new pair of Exterras."

"Where are the old ones?"

Crash shrugged. Her gaze held his. There was defiance, stubbornness in her posture.

"Tana, it's best we clear out of here. Soon. Let's go see what we can get out of Novak," he said. "Then if you need to, if you have enough, you can always come back here with a warrant. And a team."

She snorted softly, and left, shutting the door behind her. He put his head back and swore.

For the rest of that night Crash lay staring at the ceiling, listening to the wind, knowing that the drifts were piling higher and higher. His hand rested on his hard groin. The ache in his belly was hot and sweet. He wanted her. He liked her. Too much, on too many levels. She'd been burned by men like him. Sex was something off the cards for him and Tana. At least at this point. Forging a relationship with her would require going very slow on that front.

Besides, he was too old for her.

She was too young for him. She was going to be a mother and that wasn't even in the realm of his future plans right now. Her life lay ahead of her yet—her career, trying to build a family. She'd make it, if he helped get her over this big hump. He believed in her. She possessed a formidable strength in character, and she just had to learn to recognize it, to find pride—see her self-worth—shuck the shame of her past. Yeah, fine thoughts coming from *him*.

He'd burned all those bridges long ago. Would he even want to try, start over?

How in the hell would he then justify his previous marriage, the estrangement of his daughter? The loss of Lara and his baby?

Irritable, hot, he rolled over and punched his pillow into shape. *You're wrong for her, O'Halloran. And she's wrong for you. All fucking wrong, on every count. Best you can do for her, if you really feel something, is keep her safe. Get her through this next haul, escort her safely into the badlands—into the heart of darkness, as Spatt had called it—and when you get back, you're going to find a way to nail Sturmann-Taylor and Garth Cutter.*

His gut told him he was on to something. And he needed to take them down before they took her down, especially now that he'd gone and put Tana Larsson squarely in their sights.

He wasn't going to do the lone ranger thing, either, not any more. This had changed. He'd take all the information he'd gathered over the years, and he'd go see his old contact in the FBI, out of country, where things were less likely to leak out and come back and bite Tana when the shit started hitting the fan.

CHAPTER 36

Friday, November 9. Day length: 7:29:16 hours.

The ride into the badlands had taken longer than anticipated due to driving snow, deep drifts, several detours. After nearly getting their heads shot off by Novak, who'd been watching their approach from a lookout up on the cliff above his camp, Tana and Crash managed to talk him down, explain why they'd come, and secure an invite into his primitive home.

It was now just after 3:00 p.m., and she and Crash were huddled with Novak around a smoking fire in the cave dwelling that he'd dug into the black earth of the cliff face. An awning of log beams had been extended beyond the cave mouth from which Novak had draped animal skins to cut the cold. The skins flapped in the wind, and an occasional flurry of snowflakes darted in. It was already growing dark outside.

The place was thick with wood smoke and the smell of fetid furs, old meat bones. By the fire in front of them a pair of scarred husky-wolf crosses slept. Five pups gamboled over the adult animals and gnawed on bones. Outside the cave, down a small rise, several other shelters had been constructed using rough-hewn logs, bits of plastic, and animal skins. Cracks between the logs had been sealed with a paste of mud and moss that had baked hard beneath the summer sun. Near the shelters several more dogs were tethered by stakes in the ground littered with bones. There was also a homemade dogsled outside.

From pegs that had been hammered into the cave wall hung a large pair of old gut snowshoes along with metal leghold traps and snares. At the rear of the dwelling, above a fur bed area, long strips of lean meat hung from a line, drying into what Tana presumed would be pounded and mixed with animal fat into a kind of pemmican—balls of which Novak was currently heating in a pot of melted snow over the fire. He was making them stew after he'd finally decided to invite them in to sit down and talk. It was a traditional meal, he'd said, containing chokeberries.

"The berries grow wild in the muskeg swamps around here," Novak explained. "And the meat in the balls is caribou. Once it's dried, you grind it down to a powder and mix it in a one-to-one ratio with rendered animal fat. You form this into balls, and it stays good all winter. A high-energy source the natives used to use, and the old Voyageurs of the fur trade."

Tana had read the same information in Henry Spatt's horror novel. Spatt's fictional Voyageur guide, Moreau, ate pemmican. Moreau met his fate at the talons of the wendigo beast. He'd had his head ripped off and his heart torn out.

"Why were you so convinced that Regan and Dakota were murdered, as opposed to killed by animals?" Tana asked, trying to draw him back to the focus of their meeting.

It was a struggle to maintain composure while talking to Elliot Novak—he did not look fully human, and it was distracting. His hair slicked in oily, gray strands past his shoulders, and his mouth was set in a permanent, peeled-back sneer due to parts of his lips missing. His skeleton-like grimace reminded Tana of Selena Apodaca's decapitated head with the soft tissue missing.

His cadaverous frame was swathed in heavy furs that had not been properly cured. Combined with old sweat, it gave him a rank odor. Part of his nose was gone, his nostrils dark, gaping caves. In his truncated fingers, which were stained black with dirt, he clamped a cigarette, and he dragged on it using the intact part of his mouth as he considered her question, blowing the smoke out his cavernous nostrils like a dragon creature.

That he was mentally unstable was not even a question. His eyes darted around as though constantly searching for things in shadows that were waiting to spring at him, and his thought processes appeared illogical. He jumped from topic to topic. He carried a machete in a sheath at his waist, under his fur cape. On his feet he wore homemade mukluks.

Questions tumbled through Tana's mind as she waited for him to answer: Had it been him in his furs that Selena Apodaca had witnessed along the ridge? Could he have gotten there via dogsled without snow cover? How did he get around in summer? Had he read about pemmican in Spatt's book?

"The tracks," Novak said suddenly, pointing his cigarette at her. "It was the human tracks that ran alongside the drag marks made by my daughter's boots that told me. Someone lured Regan away from our tent, then maybe hit her unconscious, and dragged her into the woods."

Tana leaned forward, trying to engage his eyes, but he would not maintain contact at all. "Are you certain that—"

"Yes, by goddammit, I'm certain! Don't *you* start with me, too! The prints were made by two boots, not paws!" His dogs glanced up at the sudden aggression in his tone. One growled softly. Tana did not trust those wolf-animals any more than she trusted fidgety Novak and his machete. She glanced at Crash, who was seated on a log stump next to her. His hand hovered near his own knife. He nodded for her to continue, letting her know he was alert to both the dogs and Novak's machete.

"Besides, what would have made Regan go upriver alone in the dark like that?" Novak snapped. "She wasn't a brave kid. It was someone out there. Someone she *knew* and *trusted* who lured her. Had to have been. Someone who hit her with that bloodied log I found. It had Regan's hair on it."

"No one else saw those human tracks, Elliot," Tana said gently. "I'm just following up on all bases. As a fellow officer I'm sure you can understand this. Besides, I'm not certain it was animals, either."

That got him. He angled his head and studied her in silence while the fire crackled and popped and the skins flapped in the wind. "So . . . is that why you're here? To help me solve this?"

"Yes. We all want to solve this. And *any* information you can give us will be helpful."

He nodded and tapped his knee rapidly with his free hand while he inhaled deeply again on his cigarette. He nodded his head again as smoke billowed out his cavernous nostrils. "Go on. Go on. Ask me questions, then."

"What was it about Dakota's case that made you so certain she'd also been murdered?"

"I don't know why they thought it was me. Fucking bastards. They thought it was me, you know, who could have done it?"

She nodded. "I know. But you believe Dakota was being stalked. Did you have any reason to think your daughter might have been stalked as well, prior to her death?"

He rubbed his brow. "In the Barrens of the soul, monsters take toll, they come with hunger and ice in their heart."

"Excuse me?"

He repeated the line. She shot a glance at Crash. He was watching Novak intently.

Clearing her throat, she said, "Elliot, where does that come from?"

His eyes lit briefly on hers, then his gaze darted off to the shadows at the back of the cave. "Words. Words. They were written on a piece of paper and stuck to Regan's locker at school."

Tana's pulse quickened. "And you remember these words?"

He nodded. "She showed the piece of paper to me. It was odd. Very odd. Of course I remembered them. I read them over and over, trying to figure them out. She told me that someone had followed her home from school, in the dark, the day before she found that note stuck to her locker. She was scared. I thought it was some prank, one of the boys at school. So I took her camping, to lighten things up."

"Was that the only reason you took her camping?"

He stopped talking and turned his body away.

"Elliot," she said gently. "I need to ask you some personal questions, do you mind? It will help—it could help clear you of suspicion once and for all."

He tossed his cigarette butt into the fire, grabbed a stick off the ground, and stabbed it into his pot. He stirred his pemmican stew, which had started to bubble and roil steam into the air. The motion released a rancid, meaty smell that hit Tana in the stomach like a punch. She almost gagged.

Clearing her throat, she said, "There was another reason you took Regan camping that weekend, wasn't there? It was to make up for an affair. You wanted to rebuild family relations."

He got up so fast that Tana reeled back, almost toppling off the wobbly wood stump on which she sat. Novak began pacing up and down, up and down, jabbing his hands at his thighs. Crash tensed. So did the dogs.

"Who was she, Elliot?"

He swirled around to face her. "It's none of your business."

"Did you break it off, or did she?"

"None of your business! She's gone, left town years ago. Irrelevant." The larger wolf-husky came to his feet, and walked slowly around the fire to Novak's side from where he eyed Tana warily. Novak dug irritably into a leather pouch that hung from his belt and pulled out a bent packet of Marlboro cigarettes with shaking hands. With his cropped fingers he managed to extract a cigarette and wedge it between his teeth. He lit a stick in the fire, ignited the end of his smoke, and inhaled deeply. It seemed to calm him. Tana thought of the health care worker that Jennie Smithers had mentioned—the woman who'd left town, and who'd told Jennie about the affair. She wondered if it could actually have been her who Novak had been involved with. She scanned the cave again as her mental wheels turned. Most of Novak's belongings had been fashioned from the wilds, apart from some tools, his knife and axe and machete, plus basic materials like plastic, which he could have brought out with him when he first moved here. She wondered how much contact he had with outsiders on the whole.

"Where do you get those cigarettes?" Tana asked, changing her tack.

"Friend brings them."

"What friend?"

Silence.

"Can't be a Native friend," she said. "Or at least not a Twin Rivers local. Most won't come into the badlands from what I hear."

"Cursed place. Yes, it is. I live in a cursed place. In summer it's all buggy swamp dotted with tussock for mile after mile. You need to know where the channels lie, which way to go, or it will suck you down. They won't come here. I'm safe here."

"Do you have any books to read out here?"

"No. Lost my glasses. Need glasses."

"When you did have glasses, did you ever read a book called *The Hunger*?"

He began to pace irritably again, the jerky movements releasing the odor of his furs, and his unwashed body. "It was written by that man,"

Novak said. "The one who stays at the lodge every year. He had a book signing at the diner when it first came out."

"Did you read it?"

"I don't remember. Maybe. Yes. Perhaps."

She moistened her lips. "So, do you know about the recent wolf-bear mauling? Two biologists?"

"I heard."

"How did you hear?"

"I get visitors sometimes."

"Your friend?"

"Maybe. But it wasn't wolves or bear that killed those two biologists," he said. "The animals came after."

"How do you know?"

"I just know. It was the same with Regan and Dakota. The animals came after. Someone else was there first."

"Do you have any idea of who might have been there first, then?"

He drew hard on his cigarette. "Someone from around here. Around Twin Rivers. Someone bad. Very bad. Evil. Someone who is still here."

"Do you consider yourself 'bad' or 'evil,' Elliot?"

He shot her a brief glance. "Everyone's got some bad. Evil is relative to who is judging."

"Were you drunk the night Regan left the tent?"

He went stock-still. Tension swelled inside the cave. The fire cracked and the stew bubbled noisily into the quiet. He crumpled suddenly onto his log stump. Tears began to glisten on his cheeks above his beard. He nodded.

"Is that why you might not have heard her screaming?"

He nodded.

"You couldn't have hurt Regan yourself, could you? In a blackout? Maybe by mistake, even?"

He shook his head, and his body bowed forward.

Tana cleared her throat. "You sure you can't tell me who your friend is, Elliot?"

He shook his head again.

Crash took a piece of jerky from his pocket. He reached down, and using the dried meat he coaxed one of the pups over. The adult dog observed with hostile eyes as the puppy wiggled closer and closer to Crash's fingers. As the pup snapped at the jerky, Crash grabbed the animal, flipped it quickly onto its back. A small reddish-brown mark had been branded onto its belly.

"It's trapper Eddie," Crash said quietly. "It's him who's been coming to see you, isn't it, Elliot? That's where you got your sled dogs. This is how Eddie brands his pups. This is one of his. He recently brought you a new supply of dogs."

Novak scuffed his mukluked feet.

"And I think it was Eddie who showed you how to run trap lines, and how to feed yourself out here. He gave you some dogs and helped you build that sled you've got outside. Because Eddie would do that, help others. It's in his nature. Eddie isn't from these parts, either. He believes in different myths, not the ones about these badlands. It wouldn't worry him to come here."

Novak grunted.

"But here's the thing," Crash said, leaning forward, resting his forearms on his thighs. "Eddie hardly ever comes into town, maybe once or twice a year, so I don't think it's him who brings you those Marlboro cigarettes. Is there another friend who brings those?"

"Maybe."

But no matter how Crash and Tana tried, this was the only information they managed to elicit from the ex-cop who'd gone bush.

Tana felt a sadness for him as they made their way back down past the other shelters to where they'd parked their snowmobiles. It was still snowing heavily, and full dark, and they'd needed to don their headlamps in order to find their way. The dogs outside lunged against ropes and snarled at them, steam coming from their hot breaths. She was sure the animals would tear them apart if they got free. Her mind went again to the wolves that had ripped Apodaca and Sanjit into pieces, and she felt sick.

Crash stopped at one of the sheds, and poked his head inside. His body stiffened. "Hey, Tana," he said. "Come here, look at this."

She came into the doorway beside him. On the shed wall hung tools. One of the tools was a claw-shaped, plow-like thing with four sharp, curved prongs, and a long handle. It looked as though it was made from heavy metal. She went inside to take a closer look. Under the beam of her headlight she could discern no blood on it, or at least none that was immediately apparent. She removed her gloves and took some photos with her phone, plus a few more of the other tools in the shelter. Then her attention turned to the mud floor. And there, frozen in mud, was a print with a familiar tread pattern. Baffin Arctic.

She crouched down, her flak vest once again pinching her stomach. "Shit," she whispered. "See here?" She pointed where her beam lit up a ragged mark through the lugs of a left boot print. "It's the same pattern."

Crash crouched down beside her. "There's another one there. Also the left foot. Same tear mark in the sole."

Hurriedly, she snapped more photos, using her glove as a comparative measure because she didn't have her forensic ruler with her.

"They're not Novak's," Crash said, pushing back up to his feet, staring at the prints. "Novak was wearing mukluks, like Eddie always wears, and he has some seriously big feet—bigger than a twelve, I'd venture."

"So, you don't think these prints could be Eddie's?"

He shook his head. "Unless things have changed, Eddie is convinced all modern footwear is bad for you. He has this harebrained notion that the reason he's pigeon-toed is because his mother forced him to wear regular shoes as a kid. He told me ages ago that as soon as he could, he started making his own mukluks, and has worn them since."

"That means Novak does get another visitor out here. But who?"

"Same person who brings him cigarettes, maybe."

"Who do you know who smokes Marlboro?" she said.

"Several of the crew at WestMin do. Viktor Baroshkov—I've seen his pack on the counter of the bar at the Red Moose. A couple of Damien's friends from Wolverine Falls. It's one of the three most common brands in North America. But just because Novak smokes that brand doesn't mean he smokes it all the time, or that the person who brought him the cigarettes does, too. They might not even smoke at all."

"What do they want from him, then, coming out here? It can't be friendship—the guy's cracked."

"Yeah," he said, glancing up as wind suddenly gusted through the shed. "We should get going, Tana. It looks like we'll need to find a safe place to hunker down tonight if this storm gets any worse, and I sure as hell don't want to stay here."

CHAPTER 37

Tana cradled her steaming mug in both hands and sipped her soup. It had been made from a packet on a small gas burner using melted snow, and she and Crash snuggled in thermal gear and sleeping bags in a tiny orange dome of a tent as the wind plucked and tugged and pushed at them from the darkness outside, and snow continued to pile in drifts. A small battery-powered lantern swung from the apex of the tent dome, casting an intimate halo of yellow light.

They'd managed to set up camp before the full brunt of the storm had hit, pitching their tent on a level area in the lee of a rise. Their snowmobiles were parked behind the tent and fast becoming buried in snow.

"Do you think it could be Novak who's been doing this?" Tana said, taking another tentative sip. Her lips were so cold that even the lukewarm soup scalded them.

Crash considered her question for a moment, and she watched the shadows on his face. She liked looking at his face. His eyes were beautiful, and the lines around them told stories. She wondered about the things he'd seen and done, and her heart squeezed.

"He's psychotic—clearly he's lost touch with reality," Crash said. "Plus he's mobile with his dogs."

"A dog sled wouldn't have gotten up over the cliff behind which Apodaca and Sanjit were killed."

"He could have left it and hiked over on foot. According to your notes from the scene, Heather said Selena had mentioned seeing a man in fur. Elliot wears furs."

She sipped again, listening to the wind, thinking of the endless, barren land all the way up to the arctic. "There wasn't enough snow for a sled yet when Apodaca and Sanjit were attacked."

"So maybe he hiked the whole way. It would have taken a long time, but he could have been camping out there already, hunting, perhaps even watching the kids working day after day, planning."

"What about the red chopper?"

He shook his head. "I don't know. Coincidence?"

"I'm not feeling big on coincidence with this. And trapper Eddie? He's always out there."

"I don't see him for this. And the boot print is not his—I'd stake a lot on that. There's also a possibility that the print has nothing to do with the actual murder."

"What about Crow TwoDove, and his taxidermy tools? He's accustomed to taking out hearts and guts. Could he have stepped over some line and started working on humans, copying from the book?"

"Crow can't read," Crash said.

"He doesn't need to read. This cannibal beast thing is a local myth, an old story that any local could have heard told around a fire."

"Yeah, but someone actually *wrote* down those lines from the book, and copied the drawing. This definitely ties into that book, and someone who can read."

"True." Tana's mind went to the author, Henry Spatt, and the other names she'd listed on her whiteboard.

"I need to go out to WestMin again," she said. "I need to interview the rest of the winter crew at the camp, check their boots, their histories. If Harry Blundt and Markus Van Bleek were already staking this area and mapping out a mine four years ago, they would have had teammates, and those same mates could be at the camp now. They'd potentially have had opportunity in all cases."

"Would be a lengthy expedition out there on snowmobile," Crash said. "Might have to wait for a break in the weather so that I can fly you in."

She met his eyes. He held her gaze. And something surged between them—a bond, tangible. Plus something darker, a little more sly. It made Tana feel scared. Vulnerable. And in the whisper and tick and rush of the wind, she heard her gran's voice.

Vulnerability isn't good or bad, Tana. It's not a dark emotion, nor a light one. It's not a weakness. It's the birthplace of all feelings. If you run away from it, if you fear it, and shut it out, you will be shutting out all that gives purpose and meaning to life . . .

She couldn't go there. She could *not* rely on anyone but herself right now—she had to do this motherhood thing, her job, on her own. She had to prove she could. She'd made far too many mistakes with sex, and men. She needed to separate that out from what was important now, get on track. And Crash was so wrong. He had heavy issues he was still trying to resolve. He lived like Jim—on the edge, daring the universe to take him, maybe even *wanting* to be taken. She couldn't bear caring, and losing, again. It would just kill her. She inhaled deeply.

"It's hard to see anyone for this, you know?" she said. "Doing this depraved, incredibly raw, and violent thing, and still living, functioning normally among a community. Must take so much energy to hide it. To plan it, clean up. Look normal."

"Normal is relative, Tana."

He was right. She'd thought Jim was normal. You never really knew what hid behind the eyes of others.

Crash took her mug, and unzipped the vestibule. He emptied out the dregs and cleaned the mugs with snow, stashed them back in the pack. "You should get some sleep if you can. The worst of this weather should let up by morning, and if the forecast holds, there'll be a slight lull before the next big one rolls in. We should manage to reach Twin Rivers before that socks us in again."

Tana pulled her wool hat down over her ears and cuddled into her sleeping bag. Crash did the same, and they pressed together in the small tent. He reached up and clicked off the lantern. Their orange globe went out and the dark wilderness seemed suddenly, impossibly vast. Just them together with a skein of orange fabric between them and the universe out there. Tana's mind went to the shredded bits of orange tent she'd seen at the Apodaca-Sanjit massacre. She thought of Crash wrapping Regan Novak's remains into his tent fabric four years ago, and she shivered.

"Cold?" he said in the dark.

"I'm fine."

"You going to call this in now, Tana?"

"Yeah," she said. "I don't have answers, but I have enough questions to force Yellowknife to send in a homicide team. I have Spatt's book, and it's clearly a blueprint for murder. Someone out here is stalking and hunting humans, using Spatt's words as a map, and to instill fear before he strikes. Maybe it's Spatt himself. We need forensics out here, fingerprints taken, DNA analysis, a fast track on those autopsy results. I'll get it now."

"Will you deal with Cutter?"

Tana heard the layers in his question.

"No," she said quietly. "Sergeant Leon Keelan. But I don't care who I deal with . . . I have enough evidence now. I'll go through central dispatch, make sure other people hear about this—the coroner's office, pathologists, Apodaca's and Sanjit's parents. It'll embarrass Cutter and Keelan into fast action, if nothing else. They won't be able to ignore this, or me. Not this time."

He fell silent, and she wondered if he was sleeping. She listened for a while to the storm and the cold crept in, right into her bones. Her body gave an involuntary shudder, and Crash put his arm over her.

"Come closer," he whispered, his breath warm against her neck. Her body went ramrod rigid. Her heart began to stutter.

"Don't fight it. Survival value. Body warmth."

Reluctantly, she tried to relax into his arms as he spooned her.

"What about you?" she whispered. "What are you going to do about Cutter, Sturmann-Taylor?"

She heard him inhale deeply.

"You still want to kill him?"

"No, Tana. Not any more."

Relief rushed through her. "What changed?'

"You," he whispered.

Fear rose again, tension twisting in her stomach, her mouth going dry. She wanted his touch, his mouth to press firmly against her neck. She ached for his body, warm and naked in her arms. To feel him between her legs. Her eyes burned. And on the back of it all came another worry—Cutter and Sturmann-Taylor, Van Bleek, what they could do to her and her baby in this wild and isolated place, and no one would know.

"So what are you going to do, then?" she whispered.

"FBI," he said. "Interpol. I'm going to take everything I've gathered over the years to one of the old guys who was on the joint ops task force. Give it to him, let them look at Sturmann-Taylor and Cutter from the outside. Combined with the intel accumulated by the task force over those four years, plus the information I've gathered about Sturmann-Taylor, the lodge, the people he flies in, Cutter's role—it should show them where to look. I think they'll find the rest of the pieces now."

Wind blew, and snow brushed and rustled against the tent fabric.

"So, thank you, Tana," he whispered, resting his lips ever so slightly against the skin under her hair at the nape of her neck, the weight of his arm over her body heavy and warm. Heat washed into her belly and her nipples tightened with an exquisite ache. "I think it was destiny," he said, and she heard the old smile in his voice. "That brought you to me, and gave me the missing pieces. Maybe, finally all those years will have been worthwhile."

He was talking about more than just his UC operation. He was talking about the personal losses he'd incurred through it, the choices he'd made years ago to stick with the job while losing his family. He was talking about Lara and his dead baby, and how he felt he hadn't protected her from having her brains blown out all over him. She swallowed and held dead still for fear of arousing him, or herself, further, and eventually she heard Crash's breathing deepen and grow more rhythmic as he fell asleep.

Only then did she allow her muscles to fully relax. But just as she was drifting off, she gasped.

He came awake instantly.

"What is it?"

She felt it again, a rolling motion in her tummy, a little punch from the inside. Emotion filled her eyes.

"My baby. It moved. Here, feel it." She opened her sleeping bag and guided his hand under her thermal underwear. His palm was rough and warm on the tight skin of her stomach. Her baby rolled over again, kicked. A little thump.

"Did you feel it?"

He made no reply. She rolled over and turned her face toward his, and she saw the gleam of wetness on his cheeks. "Yes," he whispered, voice thick. "Yes, I felt it."

He kept his hand there on her tummy, and they lay like that for a long while, just connecting with the precious little human life in her womb. And Tana no longer felt alone. This was real, this little creature growing determinedly inside her. This man holding her.

"Do you know if it's a boy or a girl?" he said.

"No," she said softly. She hadn't wanted to find out. She'd been hoping for a boy, because in her experience girls had it tough. But right now, she didn't care. It was hers. Her baby. And for just this nanosecond in time, she thought it might all work out okay.

A little tribe, Gran, I'm building my own little tribe . . .

Tana finally drifted slowly toward sleep with Crash holding her like that, his hand on her belly, warm against the storm. To be held like this, not judged, not used, no pressure for sex . . . to feel no shame at all in this rugged man's arms, to feel the raw bond of friendship . . . the feeling was indescribably profound. And intimate.

CHAPTER 38

Saturday, November 10. Day length: 7:20:37 hours.

It was 3:24 p.m. when Crash drew up outside his house on his snow-mobile. He and Tana had finally made it back into Twin Rivers around 2:30 p.m. The snow had stopped falling and wind was now pushing through the valley, briefly clearing away some of the cloud cover. He'd escorted her to the police station where her dogs had gone insane with happiness to see her. Both animals looked as though they were going to be fine, and it had lifted his heart to see her with them.

Rosalie would still be at the station for a while, and Bob the mainte-nance guy had been up on the roof. He'd cleared the small antenna that fed through to the mobile satellite phone dock inside the office, enabling Tana to use her portable phone inside. And now, in this small window before the next storm rolled in, she'd be able to contact Yellowknife and call in a major crimes team. How soon detectives might be able to fly into Twin Rivers was another question, but at least backup would be on standby. Crash had told Tana he was going home to shower, change, see that the airstrip was being plowed before the next dump arrived, and to check on his business. He also wanted to see that Mindy was okay.

He killed his engine and the sound of a scraping plow filled the air. The contract guy was busy running his blades over the strip. Crash removed his helmet, waved. The man waved back from inside his truck.

Gathering his gear, Crash trotted up the porch stairs. His house was in darkness despite the twilight. Snowdrifts had blown up across his front door. He frowned. Mindy must not have left the building since the snow had started falling. But why so dark?

He tried the door. It was unlocked. He pushed it open, stepped over the snow piles, and entered his house. The interior was cold, all the heat off.

"Mindy?" He dumped his stuff in the mudroom, clicked on the lights, and removed his boots. "Mindy—you here?" No answer came.

He made his way through to the living room, flicking on the lights and turning up the heat. The baseboard heaters ticked and creaked as they came to life. Empty booze bottles and beer cans littered the coffee table. He cursed.

"Mindy!"

Silence.

Crash marched down the hall and flung open the door to the spare room. The bed was mussed up, the closet open, empty. He swore again. She must have had a relapse, got drunk, and boomeranged right back to that old boyfriend of hers. She hadn't done that for almost two months. He'd hoped she'd kicked that bad habit.

Feeling uneasy, he made for the bathroom, stripped down, and stepped into a steaming shower. A cocktail of adrenaline and anxiety churned through his gut as he soaped himself and thought of Tana. And her case. Of Mindy. Of his next steps in contacting the FBI, Interpol, the choices he was making that would put him out there again.

He dried off, dressed in clean gear, and made his way into the kitchen to grab a beer or two. Or at least see if Mindy had left him any to grab. He'd told Tana he would bring takeout from the diner, and he was in the mood for a brew with his food tonight. His plan was to spend nights at the station until Tana's backup arrived. In the meanwhile, Rosalie and her dogs were with her, and people were out and about in the village, making full use of the break in the weather. Whoever might have killed those four, and who'd been trying to spook Tana, was not someone who wanted to get caught. That much was evident from the remote locations chosen for the killings, and the considerable efforts made to cover up the crimes. This was some sick son of a bitch who skulked in darkness and shadow. He'd wait until nighttime to strike, when and if Tana was alone. If he was going to strike near home at all.

The blood caught his attention the moment he entered the kitchen—smears of it on the white stove and across the counter. His pulse kicked. He lowered his gaze to the floor. There were drops on the linoleum. He crouched down, gently touching the tip of a finger to one of the dark beads. Tacky. Old. His heart beat faster as he came to his feet. Then he saw it—the meat thermometer lying on the countertop behind a bowl of mandarins. Slowly, a dark sensation leaked into him. Crash picked up the thermometer. Traces of blood smeared the silver shaft designed for spiking into raw meat.

Shit.

Mindy had done this once before in his house, that he knew of, hurt herself. He'd found her cutting her arm with a razor blade after she'd discovered that her jackass of an ex-boyfriend was screwing someone else. Tana's words filtered suddenly into his mind.

. . . How vindictive is Mindy? She's made no secret she hates me, and likes you. The deer eyes are a link between you and me. Could she have done this—be trying to say something?

Crash headed fast for the mudroom, punched his arms into his jacket, pulled on his snow boots. He grabbed his hat and gloves and stepped out into the cold. The noise of an approaching chopper

pounded the air, and out of the clouds emerged a bright-yellow bird—
Twin Squirrel. Heather.

As Crash descended the stairs, the Squirrel landed gently in a swirling blizzard of a downdraft and swishing conifers. He stopped to watch
the doors open and three guys hop out as the rotors slowed. Contract
workers for the ice road, judging by their gear. They ran from the chopper in a crouch, making for a truck idling down near the end of the
runway, waiting to pick them up.

The rotors stopped, and the pilot door opened. Crash made his
way over as Heather removed her headset, and jumped down in her
winter flight suit.

"Hey," she said with a smile, her blue eyes mirroring the color in
the gaps of cloud behind her. "Took a run in the weather window." She
nodded to the men climbing into the truck, which was puffing white
exhaust clouds into the air. "Those poor bastards were stuck out at their
job site in the storm for two nights." She laughed, closing her door
behind her. She made for the hangar. "Never seen anyone so happy to
get a ride back to civilization," she called over her shoulder.

"Have you seen Mindy?" he asked, following her into the hangar.

She stopped, turned, looked into his eyes, and must have seen the
worry in his face, because she said, "No, why? What's wrong?"

He exhaled in frustration. "I don't know where she is. Last time
I saw her was . . . shit, I think it was Tuesday or Thursday morning."

"I saw her Tuesday afternoon," she said. "I thought you meant had
I seen her today."

"Where?"

"She was walking along the road to the village. I drove by in time
to see her getting into a dark Ford truck."

"Whose truck?"

"I don't know. Gray. It had a logo-sticker thing across the tailgate—
a red ram's head."

"Markus Van Bleek? Shit." *Suspected assassin. Trafficker of women, diamonds . . .*

"You didn't try to stop her?"

"Crash, I'm not Mindy's keeper. I don't know where she was going."

"Which way did the truck go?"

"Northeast. The road to Wolverine Falls."

Van Bleek had a friend with a cabin up there. Crash had made it his business to know where Van Bleek went, the company he kept. And if the South African merc hadn't left town in this small gap of weather, chances are he'd still be here, because returning to the WestMin exploration camp via land in this new layer of deep powder would be a full-on expedition that could take all day and longer. Crash spun around and made for his machine.

"Hey," Heather called after him. "Where are you going?"

"To find Mindy."

Before mounting his sled, he dialed Tana's sat number with his own portable sat phone. He glanced up at the sky, checking the weather as the phone rang. Would be full dark in minutes. And already a fresh bank of black clouds was broiling in from the north. His call kicked to an automated voice mail system. Clearly, Tana was still busy on the phone to Yellowknife. He left her a message saying he was heading out to find Markus Van Bleek because Mindy had gone with him to Wolverine Falls two days ago, and he believed she could be in serious trouble.

"Markus might even be our guy. If I'm not back before Rosalie leaves tonight, *please* get someone to come stay with you." He killed the call, pocketed his device, pulled on his helmet, and straddled his machine. He gunned the engine, revved, and roared around the back of his house, punching through drifts, taking a shortcut toward the road that led upriver to Wolverine Falls.

CHAPTER 39

Tana paced in front of her whiteboard. It was 5:14 p.m. and black outside. She'd phoned Yellowknife as soon as they'd returned from the wilderness, and had been relieved to not only get a satellite signal through, but to learn that neither Leon Keelan nor Garth Cutter were in the building. Her call had gone to a young detective in major crimes—Corporal Mack Marshall—to whom she'd relayed her information. He'd jumped all over it and secured a green light to form a team that was on standby for the first possible flight out of Yellowknife.

Now they waited for weather.

Meanwhile Cpl. Marshall had appointed a 24/7 point person at HQ to take Tana's calls, and answer questions. Databases were also being scoured for similar "attacks" or missing persons/predation cases throughout the Northwest Territories, Yukon, and the more remote regions of the provinces across Canada. The autopsy reports and forensics in the Apodaca-Sanjit case had also been put on fast track, and the Regan Novak and Dakota Smithers cases had been officially reopened. Rosalie had done her part by securing the cleaner from the band office to ready the small RCMP cabin by the river for an influx of law enforcement personnel. Viktor at the Broken Pine Motel had also been put on notice that they might need rooms.

Tana's room with the whiteboard would become the incident room. She was totally amped that she'd pulled this off without Cutter or Keelan. No more stonewalling, because they'd look like asses if they tried to mess with the snowball she'd gotten rolling now. But nerves nipped at her, too. Her backup was not here. Yet.

She stopped pacing, and reread the names she'd written in the first column. She reached up to rub out Crash's name, but stopped just short. Conflict twisted. She believed in him, she really did. But a new team coming in here would see the statement she'd taken from Heather, read the comments about the red AeroStar chopper, learn that Crash owned one of the only two in this area, and the only one that had done any flying time—because MacAllistair's was still barely out of the box— and they'd want to know why his name was *not* up there.

Tana ran through the other persons of interest: Elliot Novak, Markus Van Bleek, Crow TwoDove, Jamie TwoDove, Caleb Peters, Teevak Kino, Big Indian, Harry Blundt. Other mine crew? Dean Kaminsky. She grabbed her black marker and to the list she added Henry Spatt, Alan Sturmann-Taylor, Damien Sallis, and his gang. She rubbed her brow. It was half the bloody town, and she still hadn't really narrowed anything down.

Don't beat yourself up. You dug up enough evidence to bring in a team. You're not a homicide detective. You're a twenty-four-year-old pregnant beat cop who's in way over her head with a potential serial killer loose in your jurisdiction that covers 17,500 square miles and you're socked in with a series of rolling blizzards.

You need to let people help you, Tana, my child. Everyone needs a tribe. Man is not strong without tribe . . .

Yeah, well, she had asked for help. Big first step, Gran. And she'd made another friend out here now, apart from Charlie—Crash. Whatever happened now, her gut told her Crash would have her back. Another big step. Trust.

She chewed on the inside of her cheek, debating it, then added Charlie Nakehk'o's name. She felt uncomfortable doing so. Charlie was old, and whether he had the sheer physical power to hurt someone the way Apodaca and Sanjit had been bashed and ripped apart, she didn't know. However, while she guessed that all four victims had been dealt violent blows to the bases of their skulls, and had been ripped open with a clawlike tool, she couldn't be certain until the latest autopsy results. And even then, questions might remain about what actually killed them, and what the animals did after, given the time the bodies were out there.

Her mind went again to their visit with Novak. The boot print in his shed. It linked him to the killings, even peripherally. Who was his visitor?

Who brought him cigarettes?

The only place to officially buy cigarettes locally would be the diner shop. She could check purchase records with Marcie. But she'd bet her life they were also being sold illegally, probably by Damien and his mates. Or, Novak's smokes could have come from someone outside the community. Someone who flew a small red chopper.

She kept coming back to that AeroStar. And the one in Crash's backyard.

"Tana?" Rosalie's voice came from the office. "I'm going now, is that okay?"

Tana's gaze shot to the dark window. She wondered where Crash was. "Fine, Rosalie, yeah. Thanks."

Rosalie came to the door. "Want me to go by Chief Dupp's place, get him to find someone to come stay with you? Crash said not to leave you alone."

"I, uh, no, I'm fine. I'm sure he'll be here any minute. Just lock the door on your way out, will you?"

"Alright then. Good night."

"Night, Rosalie."

Tana sifted through the papers on the table and found MacAllistair's statement. She read her notes—MacAllistair had claimed the AeroStar was not O'Halloran's, because O'Halloran had told her it was not his. Tana pursed her lips, recalling the sense she'd gotten that MacAllistair was trying to cover for O'Halloran, protect him. Her mind went to Mindy, and how Mindy had noted that MacAllistair and O'Halloran had had intimate relations.

Tana cursed and pushed the report aside. She was referring to Crash by his last name again, going all official, allowing doubt to creep in, and it was making her twitchy.

Was she being blind? Could he really be a seductive sociopath leading them down the forest path?

Tana cast her mind back to when she'd first arrived at the WestMin camp, and she'd overheard MacAllistair asking Crash about the AeroStar. She could picture them there, in the mist, talking.

That red damn chopper.

No one else had seen it, either. Just MacAllistair. It was like a little red . . . herring. Tana froze. Red herring. The term came from hunting—the act of dragging a smelly fish across a trail to send tracking dogs off course. A ruse. Misdirection. A lie.

Jesus. She began to pace. No . . . *couldn't* be.

But MacAllistair *was* the only witness of the AeroStar. The K9 biologists hadn't seen it. According to Veronique Garnier and Dean Kaminsky, neither had Apodaca nor Sanjit. No one from the camp had reported seeing it. Could MacAllistair have been lying? And why *would* she lie? To throw a cop off. And how better to do so, but to then make it appear that she was covering, protecting, the person she'd stuck into the line of fire.

If Tana believed Crash—and she *had* to, she'd come so far down this road with him—then he'd not been there in his AeroStar on the afternoon of Friday, November 2. Maybe there'd never been an AeroStar there at all.

Blood began to boom in Tana's ears as she pictured meeting MacAllistair that first night. The woman had been edgy, pacing, shivering. Pale. Inebriated. Eyes bloodshot. Tall—around five foot eleven. Strong handshake. Cold, rough hands that were hurt and chapped. Big-boned woman. Athletic. Tana grabbed the back of a chair with both hands, closed her eyes, taking herself right back to that night. Visualizing the fog, the cold, the swirling snowflakes. MacAllistair wearing a down jacket, no gloves . . .

You must be the new cop . . .

MacAllistair had dropped her cigarette butt to the snow, and ground it out with her boot. She'd reached forward to shake Tana's hand.

. . . Nice to meet you. Sorry about the circumstances.

Her boot. Grinding out the cigarette.

The leather had been dark reddish-brown. Came just above the ankle. Thick sole. Shearling-lined. Like a classic Baffin-Arctic work boot. MacAllistair was tall enough, big enough, to wear a men's size nine. Ex-military, she'd seen brutal action. At the time of meeting her and learning that she'd quit the US military to come north, Tana had wondered about the possibility of PTSD.

Her mind shot back to the interview at the yurt—MacAllistair laying her pack of cigarettes on the table before pouring herself a coffee.

Marlboro Lights.

She'd not considered a female. Was it possible? Could Heather MacAllistair be psychotic? Psychopathic? Could she be capable of PTSD-induced violence, rage? Was it something that went back a hell of a lot further? How long had she been doing this, and where?

Where had she come from in the States? What was her history? Why had she been discharged from the military?

Tana tapped her marker faster and faster against the palm of her hand as she paced, her brain racing, her pulse galloping, her skin heating with adrenaline.

Heather MacAllistair had been in town for more than four years. She was highly independent and mobile. She could travel vast distances. She'd had opportunity in every one of those cases. She potentially had the right boots to have made that print. She'd flown those kids all season, and knew their movements, and when the weather windows would close.

And according to that photo at Tchliko Lodge, she'd also been in the Nehako Valley the fall that geologist had disappeared and wound up dead and scavenged.

She lived on TwoDove's ranch. She had access to bear lure. Taxidermy tools. Other tools in the barn. Tana's mind went back to the stained-looking flight suits she'd seen hanging at the back of the barn. The dry bags, the kind used for river trips to keep the contents from getting wet. The stained waders hanging outside the lure shed. These were things that could be worn for a messy attack. Body parts—like a heart—and the dirty clothes could be transported in those bags without leaving blood all over the interior of a chopper.

Bile washed up the back of Tana's throat at the sick thoughts. *Why?* What would motivate someone to do this? What satisfaction did they get from it, or need from it?

A female serial killer? Female violence. Rage. A need for power—to dominate. Tana was not unfamiliar with female aggression. Her mother had beaten her nearly unconscious on more than one drunken occasion before the age of eight, after which she'd fought back, or managed to get away.

Her mind went to Novak. The boot print in his shed. Could it have been MacAllistair's? She'd have easy access to Novak's camp via her chopper. Lots of places to land.

But why visit him? Why bring him things? Why—

The affair.

No. Novak had said the woman he'd been involved with had left town. But he could have lied. He was mad—he could be speaking with double meaning. He might have meant that MacAllistair had gone, left him figuratively.

Tana reached for the sat phone that she was now wearing secured to her duty belt. She dialed the point person Marshall had given her in Yellowknife, and she cut right to the chase.

"Heather MacAllistair, a local helicopter pilot, flies for Boreal Air, she's ex-US Army—I need to know why she was discharged from the military, and when. Where she came from before enlisting. I also need to be connected with the public mental health worker who was appointed to Twin Rivers three and four years ago. There should be a government record."

Tana hung up, and tried Crash's number. It kicked straight to voice mail. She checked the time. Where in the hell was he? A soft spurt of worry went through her. She went into the office, checked the door locks, stoked the fire, and petted her dogs, who were sprawled out on their beds in front of the stove. "Where is he, boys?" Doubt, insecurity, a deepening unease corded through her. Was she on the wrong track? Crap, she had no idea what she was doing.

CHAPTER 40

Mindy came aware slowly. Everything was dark. A thick, dizzy, syrupy, swoony feeling roiled through her and she felt as though she was falling, but she wasn't. She was lying dead still. She hurt. Whole body. Badly. Felt like she was going to throw up. What happened? Where was she? She could hear fire crackling. Hot, very hot. Her body was sweaty. She could smell herself. She stank. As consciousness crawled back in, she realized she was lying in a weird, twisted position. She tried to move, but she was trapped. Fear spiked a stake into her heart.

Her wrists were tightly bound behind her back. Her ankles were tied together. Her knees, too. Pain crackled up and down her spine and her left leg. Her head pounded and burned at the back and felt wet. She tried to swallow, and gagged. Her mouth was blocked. Taped. She shook her head, trying to call for help, to awaken from the grogginess. She must be dreaming. Nightmare.

She managed to open her eyes a crack. Her lids were swollen thick and crusted.

Things in the darkness slowly came into focus. She was in some kind of cavern. Very hot. A reddish kind of quivering glow provided the only light. She tried to remember what happened. She'd left Crash's house . . . with her suitcase.

That man had come by with his truck. Pain sideswiped her again and vomit rose up her throat. Her stomach heaved. Panic screamed through her brain as vomit came up the back of her nose. *Couldn't breathe—mouth was taped shut.* She thrashed her body, writhing like a snake, and then swallowed her vomit. She lay there, sweating, shaking, terror a vise around her brain, struggling to breathe through her nostrils, which burned with gut acid.

Tears pooled in her eyes, and she could see nothing again. Heather.

Heather had saved her from that man, brought her to the barn on Crow TwoDove's ranch. The memory, like faint smoke, began to take shape.

Come this way, Mindy. It'll be safer down here.

Why not upstairs, in the loft, where you live?

No one will find you down here. No one will hear you. You can make as much noise as you like.

I'm not hiding. What do you mean?

Take a look. You can have the whole place.

Heather had grasped an iron ring and opened a big, wooden trapdoor set into the floor at the back of the barn.

Go on. See if you like it.

Mindy had taken the first few steps down the wooden stairs into a cavernous basement below the whole barn. That's when it came—a terrible, cracking blow to the base of her skull. Light had sparked through her brain, her vision going black and red. She'd started to fall down the stairs, but after that . . . it was blank.

Mindy edged her head carefully to the side. The wetness in her hair—was it blood? The back of her head had been split open. She struggled again to open her eyes. Gradually the room swam into some sort of shape. Long. Dark shadow at the far end. It was walled with those big concrete blocks, which had been painted shiny black. And on the walls, all around, was white paper with wild black-and-white paintings and drawings of creatures—like devils. Half man, half animal. Some of them were like skeletons with wolf heads, animal haunches, long hair on their backs. Talons for hands. They reminded her of the drawings in that old German fairy tale book in the library, where the wolves hunted children and ate Little Red Riding Hoods in snowy, dark, Scandinavian forests. The creatures in the drawings on the wall clutched heads and skulls that dripped with blood. One creature held what looked like a heart—high and dripping above an open human rib cage.

Slowly she moved her thumping head a little more to the right. Fierce flames burned red and orange in a stone stove thing at the end of the room. A chimney vented up to the roof. Near the kiln thing was a long, narrow table shoved up against the wall. Candles flickered at either end of the table. In the center was a big empty jar. Beside the jar was a hardcover book. Above the table was a shelf holding more jars. These were filled with liquid and . . . things. Parts. Organs. Like in the biology lab at school. Above the jars words had been painted in white across the black wall in big, mad-looking letters: *In the Barrens of the soul, Monsters we breed . . . retribution our creed.*

Raw terror braided into confusion.

I'm inside a horror novel . . . there's madness on these walls . . . insanity . . . Evil . . . wake up! Come out of this nightmare . . .

Her stomach heaved again, and Mindy held herself rigid, trying to control her body. If she threw up again she might suffocate and die.

Where's Heather? Why isn't Heather helping me?

Mindy listened carefully to see if she could discern anything beyond the crackle and pop and roar of the flames and wood in the stove. She could hear no wind. Sense no air. Just the pressing heat of this dungeon. She was underground. Down in that basement dug beneath the barn.

No one will find you down here. No one will hear you. You can make as much noise as you like.

Desperation rose like a tide in her chest. Then she stilled at a sound. Mindy moved her head to try to find the source.

Heather.

She was naked, apart from panties and a sports bra. Not an ounce of fat on her honed body. Her skin was white and gleamed with sweat. She was pulling on a flight suit. Her hair was drawn back in a tight French braid. Then came another noise.

Heather went motionless, listening. Mindy's heart kicked.

It came again. A voice. Coming closer. Calling.

"Heather! Are you there?"

A man's voice.

Mindy jerked her body, trying to scream. But her voice was stifled into a *mmmnh mnnnnh* sound.

Heather whipped around, glared at her.

Mindy froze. The look in Heather's eyes—it wasn't Heather in there. It was a mad thing. A creature. For a moment confusion seemed to chase over Heather's face, that scared Mindy more than anything. Then Heather slowly raised her finger to her mouth.

"Shhh," she said. "Or I'll cut your throat. Understand?"

Mindy didn't move.

"Understand?"

Mindy nodded.

The man's voice came again. "Heather? I heard a scream earlier. Are you okay?"

He was coming closer. He would see the trapdoor. He had to. He'd sense the warmth coming up from the floor, or smell the fire in the kiln. He would find her. He would help her.

Quickly Heather yanked up the zip of her flight suit and put on her boots. She reached up to where weird tools and a gun were mounted on the wall. She took down a long, fat-bladed knife—like the ones that homesteaders used in the bush for all sorts of things, including clearing brambles.

She moved slowly up the stairs in a kind of crouch. Like a stalking animal.

Her phone rang and Tana jumped. *Crash?* It was 9:05 p.m. and she was now anxious.

"Constable Larsson," she snapped into her phone.

It was Constable Fred Meriwether, the point person on duty in the Yellowknife incident room. Tana's blood ran cold as she listened to the information he was relaying to her via satellite. Heather MacAllistair had been dishonorably discharged in connection with several incidents of violence while on tours of duty. She'd been born in a remote area of northern Alaska. Her mother died in childbirth. She was raised by her father until the age of fourteen when her father was caught in one of his own brown bear traps. When he did not return home from checking his trap lines, MacAllistair's older brother went looking for him, but his efforts were hampered by a severe and sudden snowstorm. It appears that he found his father's remains four days later, savaged by animals who then attacked the son, killing him, too.

MacAllistair was taken in and raised by a German aunt on her mother's side who lived on a farm in northern Minnesota. The aunt was later found drowned in the farm reservoir. MacAllistair enlisted at eighteen, obtained her pilot's license through the army, and saw several tours of duty. After her discharge, she worked briefly as a contract pilot around the states, and for three years in Africa for the oil industry. She'd entered Canada and obtained a work permit seven years ago.

Meriwether then gave Tana the number of the health care worker posted to Twin Rivers four years ago. The woman's name was Vicky Zane. He then reported that fog was closing in around Yellowknife airport, but the major crimes team remained ready to fly as soon as they got the all-clear from air traffic control. ETA unknown.

Electricity crackled through Tana's body as she killed the call and dialed Zane immediately. Again, when the call connected, she wasted no time on preamble.

"This is Constable Larsson of Twin Rivers RCMP. I'm investigating a serious crime, and time is of the essence. I've been told that you know the name of the woman with whom Elliot Novak, ex-RCMP station commander, had an extramarital affair."

A pause. "*Who* did you say you were?"

"Constable Tana Larsson, Twin Rivers RCMP."

"That's a long time ago. I . . . I'm afraid I was told in a professional capacity, and I can't give out patient—"

"This is a criminal investigation, ma'am. Lives could be in jeopardy. I understand that you broke protocol in revealing the affair to another patient in the first place. It will make things a lot easier if you cooperate with me now."

A longer pause. Tension crackled through Tana. Wind was starting to whip outside—the next front moving in.

Zane cleared her throat. "How can I be certain that you are who you say you are?"

Tana gave the woman her badge number. "You can call Yellowknife RCMP to verify, however, things are going to look a lot better for you professionally if you cooperate with me right now. You could cost lives." And if the coming storm was as bad as the last one, Tana only had a narrow window in which she could be certain of communications.

The woman inhaled audibly on the other end of the line, then said, "Fine. Okay. Elliot's wife believed that her husband was having an affair with a local helicopter pilot. I don't even recall her name now, but—"

Tana didn't let her finish. She killed the call, dialed Crash immediately. She needed help.

No answer.

She glanced out the dark window. It was frosting over, temperatures dropping fast with the temporary clearing of skies. It was going to be a very,

very cold and windy night. Her gaze went to the dispatch setup on Rosalie's desk. The public couldn't call in, nor leave messages. Not until NorthTel came in to repair their satcom system. And it struck her suddenly—she'd been busy on the only phone available for hours with Yellowknife, replacing and recharging the batteries as she'd consumed juice. *If* Crash, or anyone else, had tried to call on this phone, it would have gone into some automated system. She checked the satellite phone, figured out how to get into the system. She dialed in, pressed the key, and there was one message.

Hurriedly, she connected with the message. Crash's recorded voice came through.

". . . Mindy went with Markus Van Bleek to Wolverine Falls two days ago. I think she's in serious trouble, Tana. I can't leave her out there. Markus might even be our guy. If I'm not back before Rosalie leaves, *please* get someone to come stay with you."

Tana killed the call, rushed through to the interview room, found the statement she'd taken from Van Bleek, along with his contact details. He'd given her a satellite phone number. She called it, perspiration breaking out on her body as it rang.

"Markus here."

"Van Bleek, it's Constable Tana Larsson. Is Crash O'Halloran with you?"

"Jesus. What is it with everyone today? He was here earlier looking for that local kid. But he's barking up the wrong tree. Heather took her."

"When?"

"The other night. Two days ago. I was trying to give the kid a ride, and Heather stepped in like some white shining knight and whipped the kid away with her, all sanctimonious. Then she apparently told Crash *I* had taken her."

"Where is Crash now?"

"Looking for the kid back at Heather's place, I presume."

CHAPTER 41

Crash spun into Crow TwoDove's driveway and brought his machine to a stop. The place was in darkness. No light glowed from Crow's house. No light showed through cracks in the barn. Unease whispered into him. He turned off his engine, and removed his helmet. Temperatures were plunging fast. The breeze cut like fine blades against his ears and face. Ice glistened. Everything was frozen. Heavy clouds scudded across the sky, revealing small glimpses of a yellow sickle moon. The storm was blowing in fast.

He'd found Markus Van Bleek at Wolverine Falls. The man had said he'd tried to give Mindy a ride, but that Heather had intervened and taken her instead. Crash had made it clear that he'd not believed Van Bleek, but Van Bleek had given him free rein to search his friend's house and see for himself. Crash had.

There'd been no sign that Mindy had ever been there.

Heather had looked dead into his eyes at the airstrip when she'd told him that Van Bleek had taken Mindy—so what was up with that? He had more reason to trust Heather than a shady diamond industry hit man. He took out his phone, called Tana again. Once more, his call clicked over to an automated message system. He killed the call. She was probably busy organizing things with major crimes.

Pocketing his phone, he unstrapped his rifle from his machine. This quiet was not normal. Not even the dog was barking. Crow could be out, but not with his dog. He never took that poor animal off the rope. It never left this place.

He dismounted, and slowly made his way down the rutted and frozen driveway. He headed for the barn. Mindy was his priority and something here was off. Tana's words followed him:

. . . *would you have a read on a sociopath?*

Van Bleek could well be exactly that.

He could have sent Crash on a wild goose chase back to Twin Rivers and this ranch. He could be doing Mindy harm right now. But there was no doubt things were wrong here, too. The closer he got to the house and barn, the more his sixth sense screamed and the hairs rose on his arms. He moved off the driveway and into the shadows on the snowfield that led to the barn. For a moment Crash stilled, and listened. Silence roared. He cocked his rifle, and resumed his cautious approach to the side of the barn, his mind acutely aware of the hunting knife at his hip. And he wished he had a smaller sidearm.

The barn door was ajar. Crash peered through the hinge gap on the side. A faint quavering glow came from the back. A gentle current of warmth touched his face, then it was gone. Entering the door, he moved slowly around the gleaming chopper, and froze.

His heart thudded.

His brain screamed as he tried to process the sight on the barn floor in front of him.

Crow.

His head had been partially severed, and he lay in thick, congealing puddles of dark blood. His eyes stared up, each impaled by a taxidermy tool. Blood leaked from his eyeballs like the black tears of a heavy metal rocker. Crash swallowed. His gaze tracked a line of bloody boot prints that led from Crow to the softly pulsating orange glow at the back of the barn. The glow seemed to be emanating from a hole in the floor—an open trapdoor that led down to a basement of some sort. The rear exit door at the very back of the barn stood wide open. Cold air breezed in.

No sound came from the open trapdoor.

Carefully, moving along the barn wall, he followed the footprints toward the trapdoor. Crouching down, closer to more light, he studied the bloody boot prints. His pulse kicked as he noticed the odd gap in the tread of the left boot prints.

The same as the print Tana had photographed at the Apodaca-Sanjit slaying. The same print they'd seen at Elliot Novak's camp.

Heather?

Fuck.

His brain wheeled in on itself, shards of information slicing into place like a mirror shattering in reverse, and as a picture emerged, it started making sense—insane, depraved horrific sense.

. . . would you have a read on a sociopath?

Not Van Bleek. Heather. A dangerous killer. A female psychopath. One he'd slept with. And he hadn't seen it. She was different—most people who came out here were, but this—he had not seen *this* coming.

A scream knifed the air outside. His head jerked up.

It came again—female, in pain. Raw terror. There was nothing like it, once you've heard a human scream like that. It cut to the quick of a human soul. Crash moved quickly to the open door at the rear of the barn. Pressing his back against the wall, he peered out through a crack between the wood slats. A small light bobbed in the darkness down by the lure shed. Another scream rent the icy air. The light went out.

Crash stepped out of the barn into night shadows. He stood motionless, watching, listening. Wind sifted through frozen branches, caressing ice crystals with a brittle, whispering sound. Moving at an oblique angle from the path, Crash edged slowly toward the lure shed down by the river. But it was impossible to move in silence. Ice crunched each time he carefully set his boot down. Every now and then, clouds would part and the moon would throw into relief a shadowy black-and-white scene. He came around the animal enclosure and a horse whinnied. He stilled, heart hammering. He could smell the manure and warmth of the animals. What in the hell was going on here? Where was Mindy?

Clouds parted again and moonlight fell on the shed. In the moment before darkness reclaimed the scene, he saw what appeared to be a snowmobile trailer with skis parked in front of the shed, next to the drum the dead biologists had used to mix their blood lure. A figure was lying motionless atop the trailer. Dead? Or alive, and hurt?

Mouth bone-dust dry, Crash watched for a few moments, assessing his surroundings, listening. Nothing but the brittle wind, the odd crack of ice freezing over the river. Time ticked, stretched.

Slowly, he moved forward again, first his left foot. Snow crunched. He paused, then carefully put his right foot forward. Another crunch. He cursed mentally. Waited. No movement came from the prone figure on the trailer. No movement anywhere at all apart from the breeze softly blowing across the frozen landscape. He put his left foot down, and a metallic snap sounded. Pain exploded through his shin and radiated up his leg as metal teeth rammed deep into his flesh, closing his leg in a vise. His brain roared as he swallowed a scream. His mind fought, even as he grappled in his pocket for his flashlight, but he knew before his beam hit the metal teeth and hinges what he'd stepped into.

An old grizzly bear spring trap.

Shaking with pain, shock, he panned his light over the monstrous thing. Rusted teeth speared through his Carhartts, through his thermals, into his skin, cutting deep into his leg. It had gotten him above his boot.

He crumpled to the ground in pain, quickly removing his gloves so that he could get a good grip on the metal. His fingers burned with cold as he closed his hands around the trap, and pulled, trying to pry it open. He heaved, shaking and sweating from the effort, from pain. He stopped to gather a breath. He knew his efforts would prove futile—he knew he needed to depress the spring release, and for a trap this size he needed a special tool to do that. As he tried again to relieve pressure from the teeth, a blow thudded his head from behind. Sharp claws raked across the back of his skull, ripping skin open. Blood was instant, copious, and hot down his collar. Head wounds . . . bled a lot. He tried to keep thinking, but his vision was going. Blood poured into his ear. With Herculean effort, he turned his head, looked up.

Heather.

A clawed plow tool in her hand, like the one in Novak's shed . . .

She was panting, eyes glittering in the dark, her body hulked over him like a wild beast.

Fire roared through Tana's veins as she tried one more time to call Crash. Still no answer. She needed to go out there. He could be hurt. Mindy could be hurt. Time could be of the essence.

She made for the gun locker. But as she passed the small room where Addy had stitched up the cut on her cheek, Tana heard Addy's words.

You need backup . . . You need a full complement of staff here, so that you don't have to be the one running in to physically break up a brawl at the Red Moose . . . I know what I'm talking about. My mom was a cop. She died in the line of duty when I was ten. . . . Be there for your baby, Tana.

She froze. Panic, fear, adrenaline—it all whipped through her like a downed and live electrical cable snapping along the ground.

You can't do everything alone, Tana, my child. You need to learn how to ask for help. You need to let people help you. Everyone needs a tribe. Man is not strong without tribe . . .

She unsheathed her sat phone and hurriedly dialed her point person in Yellowknife.

She gave him the details of what she faced—two civilian lives possibly in jeopardy on a remote ranch. A female suspect on the loose who could be responsible for multiple brutal murders. She was armed, dangerous. Mobile.

Tana was told to stand by. Keelan came on the line and her body snapped wire-tight at the sound of his voice. He asked her to repeat her information. She did.

There was silence for a long, unbearably tense moment.

"Larsson," he said coolly. "Find out if those two civilians *are* actually on that ranch, and whether they *are* actually endangered by this suspect, and *then* I will have authority to engage an ERT via military chopper at full expense. Understand?"

Fuck you, Keelan.

"Yes sir. Stand by."

She hung up. Heat seared her face. Her heart slammed against her rib cage as she unlocked the gun room. *You fucking asshole.* A military chopper flew IFA—instrument flight rules, not just visual flight rules. It could negotiate fog and snowstorms. But even once engaged, an Emergency Response Team would still be two hours out. People could be dead in a few hours. Yeah, so, it was super expensive to send a military chopper and ERT personnel, and brass would have to justify it down the line. And yeah, she wasn't one-hundred-percent legal-certain that Crash and Mindy were on that ranch and in trouble. But her gut screamed it was so.

She grabbed a shotgun, rifle, ammunition, thinking about all the reasons she'd come out here to this small and isolated fly-in town in the first place—to build a tribe, a community, a sense of family for her child. To be a good mom. To start over where people wouldn't judge her on her past mistakes. To be *respected.* To keep her baby safe, unlike her mother who'd hurt her own child. To save the vulnerable, like Mindy. To pay it forward like that beat cop who'd picked her up out of the gutter. And yet, here was her past, her old nemeses, still ruling her life.

She'd just have to go out there herself, check things out, call it in again.

. . . you might be compelled to take a kick, or a bullet, but you've got another life to think about now. A little civilian life.

She stilled. Her brain churned.

If MacAllistair was good for these murders—and Tana believed they were murders, and that MacAllistair was responsible for them—and if Crash had gone out there looking for Mindy and caught MacAllistair in her lie, she'd have been exposed. She'd likely have acted to protect herself. And if she'd somehow taken Crash by surprise, and now held him and Mindy hostage on that ranch, she'd be expecting Tana to come looking for them at some point. She'd be waiting, ready.

And the woman was lethally dangerous, a shrewd killer who did *not* want to get caught. Who went to extreme lengths to make her kills appear accidents of wilderness. A woman capable of depraved violence, one who'd survived this long, and gotten away with it.

Tana could ask for local help in going out there, but her number one priority of the job was protecting the lives of civilians. Engaging them in a police matter could cost her career.

Conflict warred inside her. *Maintiens le droit*—that was the motto of the Royal Canadian Mounted Police—maintain the law.

But it also meant "do the *right* thing." A tenet that Keelan and Cutter had lost a long time ago.

"Heather?" Crash's voice came out a hoarse whisper. He was losing consciousness, losing blood. Cold. Starting to shiver.

"Shut up. Shut up. Don't talk."

"Where . . . Mindy. Is sh—"

She swiped him again with her tool, across the side of his face. His flesh tore. Pain screamed through his brain.

"Don't talk. I need to save you. You need to stay alive awhile. For bait. Blood lure. She'll track us. Can't take the chopper or she won't find us. Need to be found. She *will* come for my blood lure. Human bait. You and Mindy. You. Her weak points. Tana Larsson has weak points. We all got weak points. They blind us, those weak points."

Tana . . . she was after Tana . . . it had been her all along, trying to terrorize Tana, poison her dogs . . .

"Why—"

She kicked his rifle aside. It clattered and skidded over ice. Fisting a handful of his hair, she yanked his head back and ripped his hunting knife from its sheath in one fluid movement. She was ex-military. Trained. Athletic. Physically powerful—the primal strength of insanity. She was out of touch with reality. But not all the time. Did she slide into these episodes? Become a different persona? How often? What triggered it? Could he negotiate with someone like this?

She pressed the cold edge of his own blade against his throat. He could feel it slicing into his skin, feel the dribble of blood. He heard the rip of duct tape. She plastered his mouth shut. Crash's nostrils flared with adrenaline, a raw need to breathe. He fought to remain conscious, but was failing.

"I want her. She's hunting *me*, the Hunter. The Reader. Watcher. Reader-Hunter. All a dialogue between me and the Storyteller. Her fault. She changed the Story. Wrong ending. Need different ending. She should have left me alone. I must hunt her now. Stop her. She's smart, but not that smart. She'll come. She'll fall into my trap. Hold on, and you can watch her die." As she spoke, she bound his hands tightly together behind his back with duct tape, and crouched down. Using a tool from her pocket, she depressed the spring on the bear trap, and heaved back one side of the metal jaw. Blood gushed back into his leg, stinging like all hell.

Crash rolled onto his side, and kicked at her. But she caught his boot, twisted hard, and he felt something pop in his knee. A tide of blackness and pain took him. Soft, rolling, cold, warm . . . he was sucked down. Was he bleeding out? Was it a concussion? He could no longer see. He fought to stay up on top of the black tide. Time stretched as he went in and out. Somewhere he heard a snowmobile starting up.

He felt his body being rolled, dragged, moved, and another wave of pain consumed him.

Hang on, O'Halloran, hang the fuck on. You have two things left to do in your life and that's save Mindy, if it's not too late. And save Tana and her baby. If you do that, then you can let the universe take you . . . then maybe you'll be forgiven and can die in peace . . .

But the black tide took him into its sea.

CHAPTER 42

Tana bombed her sled over hard-packed snow and ice along the track to Crow TwoDove's ranch, rifle and shotgun slung across her back. Fog roiled up from the river. Flecks of snow dotted her visor. She slowed to a crawl as she neared the entrance to the TwoDove property. A snowmobile was parked under the pine arch. Her throat turned dry—it was Crash's machine. She drew up to it, killed her engine.

The ranch was in darkness. All she could make out in the mist were the black shapes of the buildings. Even the dog had gone silent. A pervading sense of evil seemed to breathe out of the place with the mist.

Hair pricked up the back of her neck.

Crash was on the ranch somewhere, yet there was no sign of life. Why had he left his sled out here and gone in on foot? Nerves rustled through her.

Tana tried his satellite phone number again. It rang, then went straight to voice mail. She sat a moment, just listening, watching. No sound came out over the snow, either. Something was wrong.

Every instinct in her soul screamed to go in there and find out. Yet every nerve in her body also screeched her to a halt—don't be a fool. Don't be the asshole who goes into the basement when all the lights have gone out. Protect your baby. Be smart. Conflict roiled inside her.

She had to act, but in a way that mitigated danger, even if it cost a little time, because going in there alone and getting shot dead wasn't going to help Crash and Mindy, either. They had more chance if she moved carefully. She was learning this about life the hard way.

Tana gunned her machine and spun around in the road. She gave it juice and raced back into town. Fog thickened as she went. Snow was coming in heavily now, plastering her visor. Wind was kicking up.

She put on her siren as she entered Twin Rivers and made for the band office and community hall. It was Saturday night. There was always a potluck and bingo at the hall on Saturdays. The chief, council, all the elders would be there. She drew up outside the entrance, sirens still wailing, the lights flashing on her snowmobile. People came up to the lighted windows to see what was happening. Tana yanked off her helmet and ran up the stairs.

She bashed through the double doors into the hall. Heads turned. People stood up from their seats at the bingo tables. Marcie, dishing up food from a station at the back, stopped, stared. Tana scanned their faces, heart hammering. She saw Rosalie among them. Viktor was here, too. And old Bob Swiftriver, the maintenance guy. Chief Dupp Peters came forward.

"Tana? What's going on?"

"It's Heather MacAllistair," she said, breathing hard. "I think she did it—she killed Regan Novak, Dakota Smithers, Selena Apodaca, Raj Sanjit, and who knows who else. And I think she's got Mindy and Crash on TwoDove's ranch."

As she spoke, the community gathered closer around her, eyes wide.

"This woman is armed and dangerous, and she has killed one of your own daughters," Tana said. "She has destroyed lives in this town—"

"Heather? How can that be?" Marcie said. "She flies everyone so safely."

Murmurs started. Voices began to rise. "It was the wolves," said someone. "It wasn't a person who killed those kids."

"Elliot Novak started thinking like this," said another. "And look what happened to him. Look what happened to Crow, and Jennie Smithers and her marriage, because of this kind of thinking."

"It's the way of the wild," said another. "It's the animals' territory."

Tana held up her hands. "One step at a time. I believe Mindy and Crash are in trouble. I can't get the kind of backup I need from Yellowknife until I'm certain that Heather has them. I need help to find out, now."

She'd done it.

She'd asked for help.

And her career could be over for involving innocent civilians in an operation, but fuck the rule keepers, fuck Keelan and Cutter, because if being a cop meant playing by rules that didn't apply out in the remote field, and that could cost lives, she didn't want to be a cop any longer.

"There are risks," she said. "I need you to understand that. Whoever offers to help me has to obey my orders at all times, because I don't want anyone to get hurt. If we find out that Heather has Crash and Mindy at the ranch, we back out of there, and I call for an ERT team from Yellowknife. If I'm wrong, if Crash and Mindy are not in trouble, we can all go home."

"What if you can't get a call to Yellowknife?" said Chief Dupp Peters. "Fog and snow are getting thick as concrete out there right now. And even if you can get a signal out, how long would it take for an ERT team to get here?"

Maybe too long.

"One step at a time," said Tana, because she had no idea herself. "Is there anyone here who wants to help find out if Mindy and Crash are on that ranch?"

"If this is true what Tana says about Heather, then Heather has hurt all of us," Alexa Peters said to the crowd. "Mindy is one of ours. This is *our* community. Our problem."

"Agreed," Chief Dupp Peters said. "Everyone agrees, right?" He turned to address the members of the council, the elders, everyone present in that hall. "We would go and look for Mindy ourselves if there was no outside police presence here. We would have to."

Murmurs of agreement rose in crescendo.

"What do you need, Tana?" Dupp said.

She cleared her throat, her brain racing. "I . . . I'm going to need a central command, and that can happen right here, in this town hall. Chief, I need you to take control of the command, and to coordinate the gathering of some volunteers—fit, able-bodied people who are familiar with weapons, and who can take orders. I want Jankoski brought in, if he's sober. He's ex-military. While he is a civilian, he's contracted to the RCMP. He knows the risks. I also need those five volunteer firefighters that Twin Rivers has on standby. They've been trained to work as a team, and they know how to operate under a command structure. And anyone else who has had *any* kind of paramilitary type training—like wildfire fighting, search and rescue, emergency first aid—I need them to come in. I want Addy on call at the clinic. And snowmobiles and fuel. Bob, can you keep running the plow over the airstrip and be ready for when flights can get in again? Get some portable, generator-powered floodlight towers running out there. I saw some in the storage hangar that the ice road guys are using." She rubbed her brow. "The first step is to put together a team to come with me to the TwoDove ranch. Armed. Experienced with guns. I'm going back to the station, and I'll fetch whatever weapons I can find back here. Anyone else with weapons, please get them. And we could use more two-way radios, batteries. I'll return here with the radios we have at the station." She paused. "And no one—I mean *no one*—goes out to that ranch without my green light."

She was going overboard perhaps, preparing for the fact they *would* find Crash and Mindy there. Anxiety at involving civilians churned like acid through her gut. She'd try to mitigate risk. She'd call Keelan as soon as she knew . . .

"Is Crow on the ranch?" someone asked.

"I don't know," she said "The place is in darkness. Quiet. No dog."

"That dog is always there," came another voice.

"What about Jamie? Where is he?" said Marcie.

"I don't know," she said. "These are things we need to find out. You guys get busy here, and I'll be right back with guns, radios, and other equipment."

Tana left the hall and ran down the steps toward her idling machine, the red-and-blue lights still pulsing and bouncing off fog and snow-flakes. Her heart pelted in her chest. She was terrified. She had no idea what she was doing. But she was going with her gut. Tana just prayed that the delay she was incurring while she gathered forces wasn't going to kill Crash or Mindy. At the same time she also knew acting brashly and just barreling into the ranch alone, and getting herself killed, was not going to help them, either. It could cost their lives in the long run.

This, Tana, this is what you came here for. A crucible. You wanted to be tested, and to rise to the challenge. Now, girl, now is the time. Someone has to do something. Someone has to take control, be a leader. And if you take the fall for your actions, if people die, you can go down knowing that you tried your damnedest, and that you tried with heart, to do the right thing. To "maintiens le droit."

Heather secured her prisoner sausages tightly onto her snowmobile trailer with woven nylon straps. She'd rolled the bodies up in canvas, leaving their heads sticking out the tops, and trussed them with rope—like stuffed beef rouladen. Her aunt in Minnesota used to make those. Every fortnight, on a Sunday. It was their German heritage, she'd said. Strips of beef rolled around chopped-up smoky bacon and pickles, and simmered in a pot. Served with dumplings. Heather pictured the trussed beef sausages floating in their dark stew juice, and for a moment they looked like her aunt, whom she'd drowned and left floating in the farm reservoir . . . no more beef rouladen on Sundays . . .

Breathing hard, Heather stopped and stared suddenly at Crash's face. His complexion was ghost-white in the stark light of her headlamp. Snow was settling on his cold, torn-up features. She pulled off a glove and placed her fingers gently at his carotid. His pulse was weak, but he was still alive. He was losing blood, though. She'd bound up his leg, and pulled a tight hat down over the wounds on the back of his head, but the gashes across his cheek were split wide, and the hat was dark and sodden with blood. What had she done? For a moment she was hit with a sharp flash of lucidity. With it came fear.

What in the *hell* was she doing? What was she doing to Crash? She felt for Mindy's pulse. There was none. Panic whipped through her and she spun around, and screamed into the fog.

She stood there, panting, hands fisted at her sides, listening to the echo of her own scream bouncing downriver into the vast nothing. She was fighting it. It was messing with her brain. It was melding into one—Reader, Watcher, Heather, Reader. The monster inside was taking over, and she didn't know how to stop it, or if she even wanted to, but it scared the shit out of her. It had been under control, smooth going, until the Mountie flew into town. If Heather had to pinpoint the trigger, it was when Tana had taken her arm at the WestMin camp that night, and looked into her eyes, and told her she was too drunk to go out to the site and help. And then it had all started to hum inside Heather's brain when Tana Larsson had questioned her in the camp mess, and Heather had detected suspicion and cunning in the young cop's face. And the monster inside had stirred, and rolled, and become uncomfortable as the cop closed in.

What to do, what to do? She whipped around and studied Crash's face again.

Get rid of the cop—like a cancer, cut it out. That's what to do. Stop the monster. Sate the Hunger. Put it back in its hole.

It used to be okay. She could control it. She'd let it out once a year, and feed the Hunger, always around the time of her birthday during the first week of November, when her mother had died giving her life. Her first real kill had been a kid who lived on the neighboring farm in Minnesota—she'd left that young girl's body down a deep ravine, and returned over the following days to watch scavengers feeding on the remains. It made Heather feel strong, in control—the way she'd felt watching those wolves eat her father and brother. Killing that girl killed the female weaknesses in herself. And she liked the way animals were her friends, how they destroyed evidence.

A sharp memory, a flash of the wolf teeth ripping and tearing the wet flesh of her father, hit her. Suddenly she could hear again the sound of her dad's screams as he flailed against the bear trap holding him while the carnivores tore him to pieces, ate him alive. While she'd watched from the trees. And when her monster-dad fell silent, she'd finally felt strong. Turned on. Empowered. So alive. Those wolves had brought her justice. At last. She was not alone. The wildness, the Hunger had entered her.

No more visits in the night from her father . . .

And then she'd followed her brother out into the storm while he was searching for their missing dad, and she'd clubbed her brother on the back of the head, right there, as he stood in shock over their father's carcass lying bloodied in the snow. And she left him there, too, and the wolves returned to help clean her brother away.

No more tying her down and fucking her in the shed from her brother . . .

Then she'd done her aunt, whom she'd hated, and who'd whipped her with a belt.

No more beef rouladen.

No more dumplings.

Heather didn't like beef rouladen . . . Heather hated dumplings . . .

Later she'd refined things, planning carefully, as she began to take lives more out of pleasure, to *feel*. The blood. The violence. To taste the flesh. As a kind of sexual release. And to punish young women for their stupid weaknesses, or promiscuity, or for looking at men that Heather liked. The annual November kill was a way for her to keep her tendency toward violence in check over the remainder of the year, until the Hunger grew again. And always, she worked in remote locations when she could, using weather, terrain, and wildlife to cover her trace.

But it was only when she'd finally come north, and found that book, *The Hunger*, a story set right here in the Barrens, that things fully, beautifully, coalesced. The wolf-beast in the Story—it was *her*. It was as though the author was speaking directly *to* her. He understood her need, the art of what she did. And it gave her company, as if she had a partner. It made her feel brilliantly clever, acting out the scenes. It gave her a way to neatly compartmentalize this need in herself. And she became Reader.

It became her Story. Nature doing its justice.

In the Barrens of the soul, Monsters we breed . . . retribution our creed . . .

Focus, Heather!

She reached into her breast pocket and took out her hip flask. She swigged back half the contents. The whiskey burned on the way down, and heat branched like fire into her chest. *That's better*. She felt halfway normal again. *Focus. Put the Beast down. Focus. Sate the Hunger. Kill the cop.*

She hooked the trailer onto the back of her snowmobile, strapped on the cans of bear lure, rope, snowshoes, and guns, and swung her leg over the machine. She started the engine, and glanced over her shoulder. Crow was step one. Tana would find Crow. She'd come alone—because she was the only cop in town. She'd follow the blood trail from the barn down to the lure shed.

At the shed she'd discover more blood, and Crash's gun, and his knife. And Mindy's fluffy pink scarf, which she'd left lying near the lure drum.

Her snowmobile tracks would lead the Mountie on a trail across the river ice, and north toward the treeline at the badlands.

Yesterday, while the Mountie was gone with Crash, while Mindy was tied up in the basement, Heather had gone out there and started to prepare. She always prepared. And if the Mountie did not happen to come alone, the treeline at the badlands would ensure she did. People from town didn't cross into the badlands. It was taboo.

Revving her engine, Heather took off for the river, dragging her sled behind her.

CHAPTER 43

Tana pushed through the doors and dumped the guns on the table. Another nail in her career coffin—she'd be toast when headquarters found out she'd armed civilians with police-issue weapons. She shoved the thought out of her mind.

Others had placed two-way radios, batteries, and hunting knives on the table. Someone had brought a collection of odd-looking whistles on thongs.

"For those who don't have radios," a voice said behind her.

She turned around, and surprise washed through her.

"Jamie?"

"I made them." He selected a whistle, blew into it once. It produced the shrill shriek of a kestrel. He blew another. The call of a raven. "It's a good way to communicate if you don't want people to know you are there."

She met his dark gaze. "You weren't at the ranch?"

"I've been staying at Wolverine Falls," he said. "Too many memories of Selena at the ranch right now. But tonight I'm worried about my father. He was supposed to come for supper. I was setting out to find him, then I heard about Heather, and how you wanted no one to go to the farm." He paused. "I need to come with you."

Emotion surged into Tana's eyes. She nodded. "Do you know how to use a rifle?"

"We all do. We all hunt. I've used a rifle since I was three."

She handed him a police rifle and ammunition.

Jankoski pushed his way through the crowd. "Tana—are you all right?"

She studied his face. His eyes were clear. He was clean shaven. He looked better than she'd ever seen him looking. "I could use you," she said quietly.

"I'm sorry," he said near her ear. "For the other day. Let me know what I can do. I have my own hunting rifle."

"Thank you," she said.

Other young men and several young women entered the hall on gusts of cold wind, among them the volunteer firefighters, and Caleb Peters.

"Okay, listen up, everyone," she said. "I need a reconnaissance team to go with me onto the ranch, stat. Crow TwoDove might, or might not, be there. He also does not like police. This could become a problem—he could become a loose cannon."

There were more murmurs.

"So I need you, Jamie, to be a buffer between your father and me, okay? Jankoski, you're coming, too. Caleb, you know the ranch from visiting Jamie. Can I count on you?"

"Yeah, for sure."

"I'll come, too," Dupp Peters said.

"No, Chief, thank you. I need you to lead the community, man the command here. Any messages that need to go in, or out, can come through here, however we manage to send them in this storm."

"I can make coffee," Marcie said. "And soup and sandwiches."

Tana smiled in spite of the tension. "Thanks, Marcie."

The elder dipped her scarfed head.

"Jamie, you and Caleb will enter the ranch property from the front, going down the main driveway. If your father comes out of the house, talk him down, get up close to him, explain what's happening, and get him inside the house. Jankoski will cover you guys from the north side of the driveway, across the field, where there is shadow from a row of spruce.

I will go down the south side, along the buildings toward the barn. I'll cover you from there. Just in case. We'll use your whistles, Jamie. One sharp birdcall means all is clear. Three bursts means you need help. Two short bursts is a question: Are you all right, do you need help? Got it?"

All nodded, and started selecting whistles. Tana also handed out radios. "In case we need to talk, but use the whistles first until we know what we're dealing with. We don't want to blow our cover. Set the radios to channel four. Everyone else not involved in the operation, please stay off channel four."

They all set their radios to the same channel, and tested them.

"If Crow comes outside armed, Jankoski and I will wait until you've gotten him inside. One of you please remain with him inside, the other come out. Is there a back entrance to the house, Jamie?"

"Yeah—back door."

"Okay, the other person, either Jamie, or Caleb, comes out the back door, and approaches the barn from that rear angle on the river side. If Crow is not around, both come via that approach. The barn is where Heather lives in a loft, and that's where she might have taken Mindy, or could be holding Crash. Jankoski can approach the barn obliquely from the front. I'll come around to the back door at the rear of the barn. Whoever leaves Crow's house can come around the back side and join me." She paused. It was a crapshoot, but a start. "Proceed with caution, and only on my command. This is critical, understand? Only fire to stop deadly force. No other reason." Tana scanned the group. "And like a group hunt, you don't want to go shooting the other hunters. Be aware where everyone is at all times, and if there's doubt, use the question whistle call—two bursts. Above all, stay calm and focused. If there's one thing that will get someone killed, it's panic."

"And if they are in the barn?" Caleb said. "What then?"

Then it's the worst-case scenario, and I don't the hell know yet.

"Then you wait for my orders." Tana scanned the group. "I could use additional backup to cover from the road, and up and downriver on either side of the TwoDove ranch while we approach the barn. And I could use the best trackers on standby in case they've left the farm and we need to go after them."

"Me. I'll track."

Everyone turned to face the back of the room.

Near the door stood a lean, black-haired youth with crackling eyes and a leather jacket with chains. With him were five other guys in black leather, chains, braids with feathers. Tats. Huge hunting knives at their hips. Snowflakes flecked their hair.

"Damien?" she said.

"I heard Crash might be in trouble. I can track. I'm good—learned from Charlie when I was little. I want to help. So do these guys."

His bootlegging gang.

Emotion slammed Tana in the throat.

"We got some shit—guns," said the tallest of the young men. "These two guys here, from the Wolverine band, they've both done survival-man training—they know about indigenous man traps, counter-tracking. They know the land. What do you need?"

"Thank you," she whispered, then quickly cleared her throat and outlined the rest of their approach. "Depending on what we find at the ranch, we'll decide on the next steps." She paused, taking in the faces around her, the sense of community. And in their eyes she suddenly saw the eyes of that poster in the abortion clinic—those firefighters, cops, social and civil workers—men and women. She saw the eyes of the beat cop who'd turned her life around. She saw community. A tribe.

You are not alone. You are of the north. You are strong. You will not be broken.

"Let's do this," Chief Dupp said with a clap of his hands.

344

CHAPTER 44

Tana crouched down outside the rear door of the barn and examined the blood on the snow. A trail of it led down toward the water, and it was fast becoming covered by snow. Her mouth was dry. She got quietly to her feet and peered through the hinges of the barn door.

Jamie and Caleb had disappeared safely into the front of Crow's house. Jankoski was now in position at the entry of the barn. All was uncannily quiet. She could make out a faint, quavering light inside the building. It seemed to be coming from the back end, near MacAllistair's loft. The light glinted off the chrome of the small chopper. Something lay near the AeroStar's skids. It looked like a body, but Tana couldn't be certain in the dim light. They were not using headlamps. Damien and his guys were in position, keeping watch along the road for signs of anyone approaching, or trying to leave the ranch. The volunteer firefighters were stationed around the boundary, and up and down the river in case MacAllistair tried to come or go that way. Her truck was here, but no snowmobile. A crunch in the snow behind her made her spin around, heart galloping.

Caleb and Jamie's forms materialized from the gauzy darkness and snowflakes.

"My dad's not there," Jamie whispered as he came up to her. "And his dog is gone. Collar has been removed, been left attached to the rope. My dad wouldn't have done that."

A dark notion sank into Tana as her mind flipped back to the shape lying in front of the chopper.

"Jamie, you stand guard out here. Caleb and I will enter the barn from the back. Jankoski from the front."

He nodded. She sensed his fear. If that was Crow TwoDove's body lying in there, she didn't want him to be shocked, and spin out of control.

She blew her whistle. Two quick shrieks, like a night bird.

Jankoski blew the all clear.

Tana crept forward into the barn with Caleb at her side. Jankoski came in the front door. The faint orange light came from what appeared to be a hole in the barn floor near the base of the ladder that led up to MacAllistair's loft, but Tana moved quickly toward the prone shape in front of the chopper while Jankoski and Caleb swept the rest of the barn. Her heart spasmed at what she found.

Crow, almost decapitated. Blood puddled in huge pools around his body. His eyes were skewered with tools similar to the one that had stuck the eyeball to the station door. Blood leaked from them.

"Shit," Caleb hissed as he came to her side. Jankoski approached behind him.

"Stay back," Tana commanded in a whisper. "No one touch anything." Her skin was hot. Adrenaline screamed through her. "Caleb, go outside and tell Jamie. Ease him into it. Keep him calm. Tell him to leave quietly, go back up the road. I don't want him in here seeing this. Jankoski, clear the loft."

Jankoski made his way carefully up the ladder to the darkened loft, got in position, then flung open the door.

Tana moved toward the trapdoor in the floor.

"All clear," Jankoski called softly from the top of the ladder.

Tana motioned for him to come down. Quietly he descended the ladder and came to her side. They crouched at the open trapdoor, and listened.

All was silent. Tana made a move to start down the ladder but Jankoski's hand clamped onto her arm. He shook his head. "Let me go first," he whispered.

Conflict warred inside Tana.

"We need you in charge," he said. "I go." And he started down the stairs. Tana waited, wire-tense. He gave a whistle, and she followed him into the barn basement. Shock stopped her dead.

It was as though they'd stepped into a devil's dungeon. Tana turned in a slow circle, trying to absorb the scope—the horror—of what they'd found beneath the barn, the insanity in the wild drawings and sketches that plastered the black walls. It was hot down here, glowing, pulsing embers in a kiln-like oven. Someone had been here not too long ago, judging by the life still in the fire. She walked up to a long table against the wall. Candles burned at either end of the table, wax puddling onto the black cloth beneath them. It reminded her of an altar. A jar, empty, had been placed in the center of the table, as if waiting to be filled like those on the shelf above it. Tana leaned closer to examine the contents, and recoiled. A human heart floated in one. Human eyes in the others. A hardback book had been placed beside the jar, like a bible. Tana read the title. *The Hunger*. By Drakon Sinovski.

"Looks like Mindy could have been here," Jankoski said. He stood at the back of the basement beside a metal bed with chains and cuffs. "Long black hair," he said. "And this."

Tana came up to see what he pointed at. A silver chain with a little fish on it. She'd seen one like it around Mindy's neck.

"Don't touch a thing," she said. Her brain raced. She needed to try to call this in ASAP. She also had to secure the scene. But her priority was to find Crash and Mindy, and the blood trail outside was her starting point.

Four snowmobiles and eight people made their way through deep snow, following the trail that had led them down to the river, over the ice, and northeast into the forest.

The snowmobile at the rear towed a trailer in the event they had to transport someone who might be injured—a makeshift ambulance of sorts. Preston, one of the volunteer firefighters and a trained paramedic, drove the machine with the trailer. Straddled on the same machine behind him was Caleb.

Damien led the convoy. On his machine with him was his survivalist friend, Wayne Wolfblood, from the Wolverine Falls band. Tana and Jamie followed next. Jankoski piloted the snowmobile behind Tana. With him was Len Di'kap, also from Wolverine Falls.

They had with them weapons, snowshoes, ropes, first aid kits, spare fuel, and other survival gear.

Jamie had refused to return to the village. He was simmering with a quiet and potent rage, and supremely focused. Tana had relented, and allowed him to come. She'd left two of the firefighters stationed at the ranch along with the remainder of Damien's crew to guard the scene, and to watch in case MacAllistair tried to return. The other two firefighters she'd dispatched to the airstrip, to watch MacAllistair's Boreal Air chopper in the event she tried to escape that way. Tana had also sent someone back to Twin Rivers to update the chief, and to ask him to keep attempting at regular intervals to get an emergency sat signal out to RCMP central command.

She'd tried herself, but was not getting reception. If the chief kept trying, there was a chance he could sneak something through a small gap in the unusually dense fog and unrelenting snow—it was like being underground as far as getting a direct sightline to a satellite orbiting in space was concerned.

Weather and darkness made it challenging to follow the trail ahead. Their headlights kept reflecting off flakes and mist. Tana had removed her visor because it was being plastered over with snow, but blinking into the flakes and inhaling blue two-stroke engine smoke wasn't helping much, either. Their convoy entered dense woods and the going got more difficult.

Damien's machine came to a sudden stop. His hand shot up into the air, making a halt sign. Tana applied brakes but her heavy machine slid in to the back of Damien's.

"What is it?" she called out.

Damien pointed.

In his headlights, directly over their path ahead, swaying from a rope tied to the topmost branches of a tall conifer, was a large cocoon thing. It took a moment for Tana to register what it was.

Jesus.

A body.

Tied up in blood-soaked canvas, hanging from a tree.

She dived off her snowmobile and stumbled wildly through the snow toward the object swinging in the wind and snowflakes. Damien tackled her from behind, bringing her facedown into the drifts. "Stop!" he said, and pointed.

Tana blinked through the flakes. He was pointing at a tiny piece of blue sticking out of the snow just in front of her.

"It's a trap," he said. "There's a pit that's been dug under that snow and covered with blue tarp beneath that strung-up body. I'll bet there's a hole big enough to swallow a whole sled hidden under there."

"How?" she whispered, staring up at the cocoon twirling on the rope. "How did she get it up there? How did she dig a hole that big in frozen ground?"

"Explosives," said Wayne, coming up behind them. In his hand he held remnants of a stick of dynamite. "She blew it, not dug it." He looked up, studying the cocooned body and rope. "Stringing the bait up like that is not hard if you know how to use leverage and pulley mechanics."

Tana swallowed, getting to her feet. MacAllistair could have accessed explosives at the WestMin camp. Or any one of the other remote job sites to which she transported contract workers. "It's not bait," she said, staring at the trussed-up body. "It's a human." A head was partially sticking out the top. On it was a dark hat—no, not dark, blood-soaked in places. She got her hunting spotlight and shined it on the head. Hair spiked out from the front part of the hat. Her heart stalled, then kicked into a fast staccato beat.

"It's Crash," she whispered. Her stomach clenching. As she spoke, the sack wiggled.

"He's alive! We've got to get him down! Now."

CHAPTER 45

Damien and his guys located the edges of the blue tarp and pulled it backward toward their snowmobiles. Freshly fallen snow and cut branches avalanched into the exposed trap in a soft explosion of white powder.

"Fuck," Damien said, as they all stared down into the pit. Birch poles had been honed to sharp points and porcupined up from the bottom of the pit. They gleamed like bone in their headlamps. Whoever might have fallen into the trap would have been pierced by those deadly spikes.

"If someone climbs up there," Preston said, peering up into the tree, "and cuts that rope holding Crash, he's going to come right down onto those spikes. A single guy won't be able to hold the weight, and that branch is not going to support more than one guy."

"You got to set up another rope first," Wayne said. "From that branch in that other tree there, closer to us. Someone down here at the edge of the pit holds one end of the new rope. We get up there, loop it around that branch, then feed it up to the tree in which he's tied now. Then we secure his sack to the new rope. When you cut the old one, the body sack will swing this way, lower, and the person holding the end of the rope down here can belay him down to the ground."

They got to work. Len and Damien climbed into the trees with ropes. But as Jankoski positioned himself at the edge of the pit so he could be ready to halt the swing of Crash's bag should it come in low, a shot cracked the air. Everyone froze.

Jankoski made a small noise.

Tana spun to face him.

His eyes were wide, his gloved hand pressing against his neck. Blood oozed out between his fingers. He toppled, and before Tana could grab him, he tumbled down into the pit. He made a sickening grunt as stakes pierced through his jacket into his body. For a nanosecond they stood in shock, staring at Jankoski in the pit, his eyes wide, blood beginning to ooze black from his mouth, two spikes sticking up through his chest.

Tana dropped her gloves and lay flat on her stomach. "Hold my legs, somebody."

Len straddled her ankles as she reached down into the pit, struggling to feel Jankoski's neck for a pulse, knowing just by looking at his unseeing eyes and the way he'd been impaled that she was not likely to find one.

And there was none. She edged a little further forward, straining for a better feel, just to be certain, but another shot slammed a bullet into the snow near Tana's hip. She gasped and wiggled backward. Another bullet slammed into a tree trunk and bark shrapnel whizzed through the air.

"Lights out!" she yelled. They were sitting ducks—target practice with their headlamps in the dark forest. They put out all lights, and lay silent. Wayne and Damien were still up in the trees. Urgency nipped at Tana. They needed to get Crash down while he was still alive. She leopard-crawled toward Caleb, who was lying flat in the snow at the side of the trail.

"It sounds like the shots are coming from somewhere up there, to the east," she said, pointing. "High up. Must be a ridge up there. I think we're in a kind of gully, and she probably lured us in here for that reason. Can you and Preston try to find a way up to that ridge and get behind her while we work in the dark here? Use the whistles to give the all clear, or if you need help."

Caleb was silent a moment.

"You okay, Caleb? Can you do this?" Guilt bore down heavy on Tana. She'd done this. She'd put these guys in danger, and now they had no choice but to fight their way out or they'd all die.

"Fuck, yeah. I'm going to fucking kill that bitch."

"Easy, Caleb. Stay smart, okay? Stay focused. We're going to need you to replace your dad as chief one day. You got that? We've all got to get home alive."

"Jankoski's not alive."

A wave of nausea, remorse, slammed through Tana. So powerful she had to close her eyes for a second.

There's no time to look backward, Tana. Keep focused or you're going to get more people hurt . . .

"We got this, Constable," Caleb said. "We're going to get her." He took his weapon and slipped into shadows with Preston.

Another shot *thwocked* into a nearby tree as they worked carefully in the darkness to finish rigging the ropes to Crash's sack, the whiteness of snow providing limited visibility.

As Damien got Crash's sack secured with the new rope, they heard gunfire cracking back and forth along the ridge. Tana prayed her guys would be okay.

"You ready?" Damien called from the branch above Crash.

"Ready," Wayne responded from his tree.

"Ready down here," Len said, holding the rope.

As Damien cut through the old line holding Crash, another shot rang out on the ridge, and they heard the roar and whine of a snowmobile fading into the distance. One sharp bird whistle came from high on the ridge. Relief burned into Tana's eyes. It sounded like Damien and Preston were okay, but that MacAllistair had fled.

The sack dropped like a boulder, and swung toward them as the weight was caught by the backup branch. "Go for it, Len," Wayne yelled.

Len braced, getting down to his haunches as he took the weight, and he quickly belayed the sack down to where Tana caught it in her arms. Shaking, she eased Crash onto the ground, and clicked her headlamp back on. Shock pounded through her. His face looked like it had been clawed by a grizz—great big, gaping wounds that were now bloodless. The bottom of the sack was soaked with blood where his legs were.

"Crash?" she whispered, touching the cold skin of his face. "Crash?"

His eyes fluttered open. Her heart crunched. Oh, God. "You're going to be okay. We've got a paramedic. Here he is now." Preston emerged from the woods with Caleb.

"She got away," Caleb said. "She's heading east. Oh . . . Jesus," he said, catching sight of Crash's face.

"Tana—is that you?" Crash whispered.

"I got you," she said, her voice choking, her eyes blurring with emotion. "You're going to be fine." And the bastard even managed to smile, just for a second, before pain twisted his face. He tried to speak again.

"She . . . Heather . . . took Mindy into . . . bad . . . lands." His voice came out in a dry croak. His lips were cracked. "I came . . . around . . . as she . . . she was leaving Mindy in . . . boulder . . . garden . . . dangerous . . ."

"Is she alive—is Mindy alive?"

He shook his head slightly and her heart plummeted. "Don't know . . . she might . . . not be . . . careful, Tana . . . be care . . ." He moaned in pain and passed out again.

They got to work fast, cutting him free from the ropes and canvas. Tana caught her breath when she saw his leg.

"Looks like the work of a bear trap," Wayne said. And Tana's mind shot to what she'd been told about Heather's father, being killed by wolves while stuck in a bear trap.

Preston cut open Crash's pants and sock and removed the boot. He sprayed antiseptic and antibacterial medication into Crash's wounds, and bound them tightly. They wrapped him in a survival blanket, and then in a sleeping bag into which they'd inserted emergency chemical warmers. While Preston and Tana worked on Crash, Caleb used Tana's camera to photograph the trap, the spikes, and Jankoski's body impaled upon them. Len, Wayne, Jamie, and Damien then struggled to free Jankoski's body and roll it in the tarp they'd cut off Crash. They secured his body alongside Crash to the sled trailer. They worked fast and quietly, conscious of the fact MacAllistair was making headway, and that Mindy was still out there, dead or alive, possibly left in some "boulder garden" in the badlands, if they were to make any sense of Crash's words.

Preston mounted his sled, and fired the engine.

"Len," Tana said. "I need you to go back with them. Travel in twos—it's survival one-oh-one, especially in this weather. Help Preston with Crash. Get him . . ." Her voice caught. "Get him to Addy. Then you go make sure Chief knows what's happening, and that he keeps trying to get an emergency sat signal out. We need a medevac stat."

As Len climbed onto the back of the snowmobile behind Preston, Tana bent down, touched her hand to Crash's face. "You better stick around, you hear? I . . . I still need a pilot."

Sunday, November 11. Day length: 7:15:00 hours.

The forest grew sparse and soon there were no trees at all, just driving wind, and blinding snow. The five trackers that remained had been following MacAllistair's snowmobile tracks from the ridge for over an hour, heading slowly, steadily toward the badlands.

If Crash had been talking sense, MacAllistair had gone ahead and left Mindy in some boulder garden—which, to Tana's understanding, was a swath of giant, round boulders, the size of washing machines and televisions, rubbed smooth and gathered into a mass by the push of ancient glacier movement. It provided challenging—sometimes impossible—terrain to navigate in both summer and winter.

After leaving Mindy in the boulder garden, MacAllistair would have had to backtrack in order to string Crash up and use him as bait. Which meant she had a plan—*if* Tana had survived the pit trap, MacAllistair *wanted* her to come out here in search of Mindy. She was luring Tana into the badlands, and into the boulder garden. The woman wasn't fleeing at all—rather playing some kind of cat and mouse game.

The snowmobile in front of Tana stopped. So did the one behind. It was just after midnight.

"What is it?" Tana called out over the rumbling engines and wind.

Jamie, who was seated behind her, leaned forward and said over her shoulder, "Badlands."

Tana cursed inwardly. This had to have been part of MacAllistair's plan, to strip Tana of support, or backup. And Tana had pushed these civilians far enough. As desperate as she was to apprehend MacAllistair and save Mindy, her conscience would not allow her to force her teammates into territory that was taboo. Anything they did had to be of their own volition.

She wiped snow off her numb face. The decision loomed stark in front of her—go into the badlands after MacAllistair on her own, risking her life, and the life of her child. Or turn back, leaving Mindy to die—if she wasn't dead already.

A sense of defeat and fatigue suddenly swamped her.

"What will happen if she gets away?" Jamie said over her shoulder.

"If she survives out there, and escapes, she will hurt more people. Killers like Heather, they don't just stop. They can't. It's an addiction and it gets worse and worse. She's devolved. She's a loose cannon now."

Jamie sat silent. They all did, exhaust fumes and engines chugging into the cold and whirling flakes.

"Fuck," Jamie said suddenly. He stood up, straddling the machine behind Tana. "I'm going," he yelled over the engines, as if to bolster himself. "I'm going to help Constable Larsson nail this killer! She murdered my father. She murdered my girlfriend. And I dare any one of you to show some balls and come with us."

"Hey, man, that's badshit land. Taboo—" Caleb started saying.

"You," Jamie pointed at Caleb, "and me—we broke taboo already. We robbed the graves of forefathers."

"For a good cause, man. That ice road—"

"Is what? More important than *this*? Mindy could be alive. That woman is evil. You want to let evil hide in the badlands? Then there will always be evil in the badlands." Jamie plunked his butt back on the seat and said, "Go, Constable. Go get her."

Damien revved his engine, and pushed suddenly forward ahead of Tana's machine, taking the lead into the badlands with Wayne tucked in behind him. Emotion walloped through Tana. These guys, these townsfolk, they were her team, her tribe. In spite of their differences, they were one. United in this goal.

"Whoa!" she screamed out after Damien, then hit her sirens and lights so he'd hear, see, stop. And he did, bringing his machine around to face hers.

"Listen," she called out over the wind. "I can't ask you guys to do this. You've seen what Heather is capable of. It's dangerous."

"Then we do it without you, Constable," Damien yelled over the roar of his machine. "Caleb? You with us?"

Caleb hesitated. He rode a machine solo.

"You want to turn back, you go. Jamie, me, Wayne, we're going in with or without Constable Larsson here. Me? I'm doing it for Crash. And Mindy. For Crow, and Selena, and Regan and Dakota."

"Fine. Fine, okay. I'll go. I'm not the fuck staying here by myself." Caleb revved his own sled and pushed ahead of them all into the badlands, sticking on MacAllistair's trail.

About an hour into the badlands, the going got steeper and navigating the sleds over uneven terrain grew increasingly challenging. Damien came to another sudden halt, and once more his hand shot high into the air. Tana tensed as she came up behind him.

"Her sled! Over there!" he yelled. "She's abandoned it. Taken off on snowshoes up that incline. See?" He panned his handheld hunting spotlight up a steep ridge ahead of them. The imprints of large snowshoes were clearly visible, tracking at a diagonal across the slope and up toward a ridge.

Tana stared at the tracks. Why had MacAllistair done this? She wanted them up there on foot for some reason?

"Boulder garden," Wayne said, panning his own light across the ridge. "I reckon it's up top of that ridge."

"What do you want to do?" Damien said.

Tana considered options, and none of them felt good. "If Crash was right, Mindy is up there, and she's the bait. I think Heather will be waiting."

"Maybe we best split up," Wayne said. "The garden can't be too wide, and if she's waiting, my guess is she's on the opposite side."

"So how come *she* can make it across a boulder garden without her legs slipping between the rocks and breaking?" Tana said.

"Look at the size of her snowshoe prints," Wayne said. "They're those massive old gut shoes that she's using. Like boats on the feet. There's enough snow now, and if she knows a generally safe route across the boulders, those shoes are going to stop her going into cracks if she makes a small mistake. The snowshoes we brought are way smaller—technical things. Nothing like the good old traditional shit."

"Okay," Tana said. "But if we can see her tracks, we can also see where the safe route across the boulder garden lies."

"But she'll be at the end of her tracks. Waiting."

"I think Wayne is right," Damien said, still studying the slope with his spotlight. "I think Wayne should go up the slope on the far right. And I'll go along the bottom of the incline to the left, then up. We both come up at the far ends, and try to circle around behind her, take her by surprise. Wait for our all-clear whistle before coming up and following her tracks into the garden, because once you guys are out in the open, you'll be sitting ducks."

It was a gamble, but the best they had. They all strapped on snowshoes, and readied weapons and lengths of rope for self-rescue in case anyone fell deep between giant, slick boulders. Tana, Caleb, and Jamie watched as Wayne and Damien moved like shadows across the base of the incline in opposite directions, and then disappeared into snow and darkness.

Almost an hour passed, and the cold settled deep into Tana's bones. Worry knifed in with it—something had gone wrong. They were taking far too long. Mindy wasn't going to survive this. Suddenly a crack split the air.

They all jumped. Another. Then another. Gun battle.

They began to start frantically up the ridge, sliding at least a foot backward in soft powdery drifts for every few feet they climbed forward. They neared the crest and crouched, waiting.

All had fallen silent.

They waited some more.

Nothing. No whistle.

Then suddenly it came. A long, shrill blast.

"Go!" she said. And they clambered over the top. Breathing hard, Tana surveyed the scene. The boulder garden was a sea of smooth mounds of snow. She could see MacAllistair's trail across it almost instantly. Panning her spotlight along the trail, she hit on a shape lying in the middle of the expanse.

"Mindy," she said, peering through the driving flakes. "Trussed up in canvas like Crash was." She turned to Caleb and Jamie. "You guys wait here. I'll go slowly across, and test the route. If it's a trick, then only one of us breaks a leg. If I give the all-clear whistle, you come. If I go down between the rocks, you play it safe and see if you can throw me a rope from a secure position."

"Got it," said Caleb.

Tana started into the boulder terrain, tentatively testing each step with her snowshoes before transferring weight. Each time she felt a slip, she'd reposition her snowshoe and test again. It took several painstaking minutes to reach the canvas bag lying in the snow, and when she did, she wondered where Damien and Wayne were, why there'd been no sign of them by now. Nerves jangled.

She crouched down beside the bag. "Mindy?" Tana rolled the bag over, and Mindy's exposed head flopped back. Quickly, Tana removed her glove and placed her fingers against Mindy's neck. Her skin was ice cold. Tana could feel no pulse. A wave of emotion slammed through her. "Mindy, please, please." She moved her fingers to a different position, just to be certain she wasn't missing a faint pump of blood under skin, and that's when she saw the shadow. Coming fast. The fog and falling flakes created a curtain so dense that the shape was already almost upon her.

Tana panned her spotlight fast around to face it. *MacAllistair.*

Dropping her spotlight Tana reached for the rifle on her back, but she didn't have time to put stock to shoulder before the woman was right on her, face ghost white, her mouth open, as she brandished a clawlike tool high in the air. In her other hand was a sharpened birch stake. With a scream she swiped the claw down on Tana.

CHAPTER 46

Tana rolled onto her side as MacAllistair's weapon came down. The tips of the claws tore through the fabric of her snow pants at her hip. Rage, raw survival instinct, exploded through Tana's body as she tried to scramble backward, but her snowshoes hooked her up, and her arm slipped down a crack between boulders. Her face hit rock as she went down. Pain sparked along her cheekbone. Pulling her arm free, Tana grappled in the snow for her gun. But MacAllistair heaved her tool up into the air, and sliced it down again with another banshee-like scream. Tana rolled again, and the blow struck snow, going through to rock with a clang. Tana's rifle clattered down between boulders. MacAllistair was caught off balance by the fact her blow had missed its mark, and she stumbled over her giant snowshoes, dropping her wooden stake as she flailed to keep her balance.

Heart jackhammering, sweat running down her brow, Tana pulled her sidearm from its holster. Lying on her back, she aimed, trying to curl her thickly gloved finger around the trigger, but MacAllistair swung the bear-claw tool across the front of her body, hitting Tana's Smith & Wesson and sending it flying into snow.

Your baby, think of your baby . . . you're not going to let this woman kill your innocent child . . .

Tana writhed toward the fallen birch stake. It was about five feet long. She grasped it and rolled away again as the bear claw was swung at her again. The tips of the claws caught her upper arm, raking through her jacket and flesh.

She swung the birch stake at MacAllistair's legs, smashing it across her shins. The blow made MacAllistair stumble backward in her clumsy snowshoes, bringing her to the ground. Tana tried to scuttle backward and get to her feet, but the pointed rear end of her right snowshoe jammed fast between rocks. She was trapped, vulnerable on her back. MacAllistair was back on her feet, stumbling toward her, swinging her claw up like a baseball bat. Tana rammed the flat end of the birch stake against the rock next to her waist. She put her arm around it, clamping the base of the stake tightly against her body using her elbow. She fisted her hand around the stake pressing her forearm against the length of it. As MacAllistair lunged forward, Tana kicked at MacAllistair's snowshoes with her free foot. Their snowshoes connected in a clashing tangle, pitching MacAllistair forward over Tana.

Tana brought the stake into position just as her assailant came down on top of her. The tip plunged deep into the woman's belly bringing her to a juddering halt. Tana grunted with the impact. For a moment Heather MacAllistair hung there on the end of the stake, her eyes wide, staring into Tana's. Then blood began to drip from her lips, and the stake cracked, buckling in two with the weight impaled upon it. MacAllistair slumped onto Tana, a dead weight, thumping the air out her lungs.

For a second Tana couldn't breathe. Her mind screamed as she tried to absorb what had just happened. She felt the wetness of blood leaking onto her.

She'd driven a stake into the heart of a monster.

Struggling to push the weight of the dead body off her, her snow-shoe still wedged between rock, Tana reached for the whistle around her neck. It took her a moment to gather enough breath, to stop her hands from shaking enough, to put the whistle between her lips, and issue three loud blasts.

CHAPTER 47

The chopper materialized from dense cloud and falling snow, a shimmering silver knight in shining armor. It was a big military beast equipped like an ambulance inside with paramedics on standby as it came in to land on the small Twin Rivers airstrip. A blizzard roared in the downdraft as trees bowed, and pinecones and bits of debris hurtled across the strip.

Tana stood by the waiting gurneys, shielding her eyes against the maelstrom of debris and wind. She held Crash's hand. It was warm, and his grip firm. Chief Dupp Peters had managed to get a brief emergency message out in the dark hours of the morning while her hunting party was limping its way back toward town.

Damien and Wayne had both been hurt in the gun battle with MacAllistair. Wayne was still unconscious, in a coma. Damien had taken a bullet in the shoulder, and he'd broken a femur while tumbling down a sheer ravine at the back end of the boulder garden, losing his whistle on the way down. MacAllistair had found the whistle on Wayne's unconscious body, and blown it, guessing she was making some kind of a signal.

MacAllistair had no ammunition left after the gunfight with Wayne and Damien, and she'd come at Tana with her last resources. Jamie and

Caleb had managed to get across the boulder garden, reaching Tana only after MacAllistair was already dead.

Mindy had not made it. Her body waited in a bag, and Tana's heart was low.

They'd managed to bundle the injured together on the snowmobiles, but they'd had to drag the wrapped bodies of Mindy and MacAllistair behind them, and it had been an unsettling experience. Tana had decided against leaving MacAllistair in situ for the crime scene investigators because she was concerned animals might destroy evidence. Snow had also been falling heavily. Instead, she'd done her best to quickly photograph the scene before wrapping MacAllistair's body in a survival blanket from one of the first aid kits, and securing her to the back of a machine with rope.

The major crimes team had landed minutes before the medevac chopper. Five detectives were already getting to work at the station. A forensics team was on the way, along with more manpower. There would be an investigation down the road, Tana knew, into how she had handled things, and an inquest into the deaths of Oskar Jankoski, Mindy Koe, and Crow TwoDove. It would be a long process. But right now she was focused on the present.

As the rotors slowed, two paramedics jumped out and came running in a crouch. Tana started to push Crash toward them. Addy did the same with Damien on his trolley. Chief Peters pushed Wayne on his gurney.

Addy had managed to stabilize Crash, treating him for hypothermia, and she'd given him antibiotic shots to stave off infection. She'd sewn up the gaping wounds across his cheek to the best of her ability, and she'd done the same for the injuries on his leg. Infection was the biggest worry now. Damien was going to be okay. He'd lost some blood, and a bullet was still lodged deep in his shoulder, but he was stable. Wayne's prognosis was questionable—they'd know more after he'd seen a neurosurgeon.

As they loaded Crash into the chopper, he gripped Tana's hand tighter, pulling her toward him with surprising strength.

"You better be here when I get back," he said, as loudly as he could manage over the noise of the engine and the rotors. "Because I need a job."

"What?"

"I need a steady pilot job," he yelled, even louder. And Tana laughed, tears suddenly streaming from her eyes. She laughed and she cried because the damn rogue still had the strength to yell, and it gave her hope that he really would be coming back.

"I'm your man, Tana. I'm your pilot man. And I'm going to have your back out here."

She stilled, her eyes locked with his. And a sob choked into her throat, stealing all words. All she could manage was a nod, and she kissed him gently on his dry, cracked, cold lips. His hand squeezed hers, and then they took him away into the chopper with the others.

Shaking with emotion, she swiped at her eyes with the back of her hand as she stepped away from the chopper. She joined Addy and the rest of the crowd that had come to see the big medevac bird taking Crash, Damien and Wayne, and Mindy's body.

Chief Peters came to her side, putting his arm around her as the rotors gained speed and began to roar. Wind tore through their hair as the helicopter lifted. The chief gave her a little squeeze as the craft banked and dissolved into gray cloud and snow.

"You did good, Tana," said Chief Peters. "We did our best. We all did."

She nodded, unable to speak. And she knew that while the road ahead was going to be rocky, she had what she'd come for—friendship, a community that had her back, and she had theirs. She'd earned respect. She'd found a tribe.

Marcie came up to her and took both Tana's hands in hers. "Crash is going to be fine," she said, her dark-brown eyes earnest. "You will see. He's a good man, Tana. He flies people safely."

She nodded, struggling to tamp down another hiccup of emotion.
"Come, Tana." It was Addy. "We need to check *you* out now. You
look spent."

Tuesday, November 27. Day length: 5:52:53 hours.

Tana stood in the barn dungeon with Dr. Jayne Nelson, a forensic psychologist from a private forensics company based out of Vancouver, BC.

The RCMP investigative team had brought the doc on board when
the sheer scope of Heather MacAllistair's depravity began to emerge,
and it became evident that they were dealing with a serial killer who
had been operating for years, both in the United States and Canada,
as well as Africa and the Middle East, while either on a military tour
of duty, or doing contract work. Several more cases of missing persons
who were later found deceased and scavenged by animals had since
been reopened.

Most of the victims in these cases were female. And the doc was
slowly piecing together a psychological picture of a woman who'd lost
her mother in childbirth, and who'd been raised by an apparently violent, alcoholic father and an older brother who'd systematically sexually
abused and tortured her since early childhood. Until the day her father
got snared in one of his own traps. This information was coming to
light via interviews with people who'd known MacAllistair's father and
brother.

The doc was in her late thirties, unconventionally attractive, direct,
and smart as a whip, and Tana had taken an instant liking to her, lap-
ping up whatever she could about the woman's field of study and her
particular fascination with female aggression.

The basement was cold, and industrial lighting cast corners
and crannies into stark relief. The techs had been through here with

fine-toothed, scientific combs, and had photographed and documented the hell out of the place before removing the contents and shipping them off to the crime lab. All that remained were the glossy, black-painted walls made of concrete breeze blocks. The "altar" table, and the iron bed at the back of the room. And the white painted scrawl on the wall above the table.

Jayne had asked Tana to come with her to see the place nevertheless, and to walk her through her impressions of that night when she and Jankoski had discovered the dungeon. Jayne was after the "feel" and the "atmosphere" that Tana had experienced, and she stood there now, her breath clouding in the cold as she stared up at the white scrawl.

In the Barrens of the soul, Monsters we breed . . . retribution our creed.

"It's from the book," Tana said.

"And the book was lying here?" Jayne said, placing her gloved hand flat on the table.

"It made me think of a bible," Tana said. "The way it was positioned with the candles on either side, and the empty jar in the middle."

"Possibly waiting for Mindy's heart."

Tana shrugged deeper into her jacket, the fur ruff soft and ticklish against her cheeks. "Why do you think that horror novel became such a big deal for her?"

"Perhaps it resonated. It gave her alter ego a point of focus, and it gave Heather a way of further compartmentalizing." Jayne turned in a slow circle, taking in the rest of the space. "This whole place did. A sort of basement of the soul cut off from her real, everyday life. We all have those—it's the place of our subconscious, where we push down the dark impulses and fascinations of which we are not proud, and that we want to hide from others. And when we do this, when we can't find a way to acknowledge and assimilate these parts of ourselves, they can seep out of the psychological cracks in very disturbing ways." Jayne smiled. "At least that's the way Carl Jung would have us interpret it. Heather could come down here, where she let out her dark demon alter ego, and when she went back up that ladder and shut that trapdoor, she could pretend to be this other functional human being."

"But something triggered her, set her off?"

Jayne met Tana's gaze. "*You* did, I think. You came into town and started looking at those wolf-bear maulings as possible murders, and you started directly threatening Heather's delicate psychological balancing act, which was already wearing thin. Like any addiction, it's a one-way slide downhill." She moved slowly toward the back of the room and looked down at the iron bed.

"There was also possible female jealousy involved. She'd had intimate relations with someone you were, from outside appearances, becoming close to. In her mind you threatened that relationship, too. You forced her to cross her own lines, and once she did that, she began to psychologically implode. Her previously controlled approach to killing began to tilt toward a violent spree, which is not uncommon with serial killers coming to the end of their so-called 'career.'"

"What about her victims—why predominantly females?"

"That's something I'm still piecing together as more information comes in. In Regan Novak's case jealousy might have been a factor as well. Her father had tried to break off his and Heather's affair to devote more time to Regan and her mother. This could have put Regan squarely in Heather's sights as a threat to be eliminated. Yet, even after killing his daughter, Heather maintained a twisted relationship with Elliot Novak, visiting him, bringing him things like cigarettes."

"That's a weird one."

Jayne nodded. "Heather's alter ego probably developed as a survival mechanism over the years, a way of compartmentalizing and dealing with the abuse she suffered as a child. And this alter ego, this vengeful 'Hunger' that she wrote about in some of the notes that were found down here, probably came fully into its own when she saw her father killed by wolves while he was trapped, and she derived great pleasure from it—watching him die at the hands of wild animals."

"You don't know this for a fact, though," said Tana.

"No. It's conjecture. And conjecture is the nature of forensic psychology. My theory is that Heather began to see the animals, the wilderness, as her ally, a retributive form of justice after it had claimed her father, who had been abusing her. She began to identify with the wild animals, eventually adopting a clawlike murder weapon. There is historical precedence to this type of pathology."

"But why focus on females?"

Jayne shook her head. "Sometimes the abused becomes the abuser—a twisted way of holding on to control, a form of coping."

Tana inhaled deeply, thinking of the attractive woman she'd first seen at the WestMin camp. You never could tell what was going on inside another when you looked into their eyes. "And the inukshuks?"

"That came from Henry Spatt's novel. I'm not sure why she was using the book as a blueprint for her kills up here in the north. Again, I suspect a fuller picture will begin to emerge once we link her with evidence to some of the other cases coming to light." She smiled. "Psychosis is rarely about logic."

As they emerged from the barn and made their way back to Tana's truck, Tana said, "And that old newspaper article found among her things, about those two cowboys clubbed to death after leaving a bar in northern Minnesota—was that her, do you think, who clubbed them?"

"That's the investigative angle right now. That case has been reopened by the FBI team working with the RCMP. Heather was in the bar earlier that same evening, and those two guys cornered her outside, and made unwanted sexual advances. She got away and they returned to drink more. According to reports the men were completely inebriated when they finally left the bar around 2:00 a.m. It appears that it could have been Heather who waited for them in the lot, and beat them to death with a baseball bat. This might have been her first successful experience with a clubbing-type weapon, which she later adapted to the claw tool."

Tana drove Jayne back to the Broken Pine Motel. It was 3:00 p.m. Shadows were long and dark already. As Jayne got out of the truck, she leaned back into the cab and said, "You should come see me if you get down to Vancouver. I can show you around, introduce you to the rest of our team."

"I will," Tana said, forcing a smile. And as Jayne closed the door, an unbidden warm feeling washed through her. She was building friendships. She was finding professional respect. This was momentous in her life. Yet, as she drove back to the station it was a complicated mess of emotions that churned through her. Addy had checked her out—she and the baby were fine, apart from bruises and cuts. Her mental state was another matter. And she missed Crash like a hole in her heart. While she'd spoken with him on the phone, and learned he was going to recuperate physically, she was filled with anxiety and worry for him. And her future with him was a giant, scary question.

It also killed her that she'd not been able to save Mindy.

Not saving Mindy was the ultimate failure. She'd become a cop to save young women like Mindy.

Saturday, December 1. Day length: 5:35:58 hours.

"What are they like?" Marcie said as she handed Tana her take-out sandwich and cup of soup to go. "The new station commander and the new constable?"

"They seem nice enough."

Corporal Mark Saggart had been posted to Twin Rivers on a two-year contract to run the station, and Constable James Weston was now Tana's new partner. It was good to finally have a team. She felt she'd get on with these guys. There were also still detectives in town, going through the old wolf mauling cases in minute detail. Tana had been brought into the investigation herself, after being preliminarily cleared following extensive interviews with the RCMP's internal division over her handling of events, and over Jankoski's and Mindy's deaths.

There would still be an inquest, and half the town was being questioned in preparation for that, but the picture emerging from Chief Peters, his band council, and his constituents, was that given the lack of police personnel in town, and the fact that an ERT request had been turned down by Sergeant Leon Keelan, they'd taken it upon themselves to hunt down Heather MacAllistair, who'd kidnapped one of their own, and who had killed Crow TwoDove and also taken Crash. According to them, Tana had done her best to mitigate things in the only way available to her while civilian lives were at stake and the clock was ticking.

"Why did they send two cops?" Marcie asked.

Because after Addy had done an ultrasound, and after Tana had learned she was going to have a baby girl, she'd finally put in for maternity leave. They'd need a spare hand on deck when she took a few months off. Tana had told a few people in town about her baby now, and she bet Marcie knew exactly why they needed extra staff—gossip moved like wind through trees in a small place like Twin Rivers. Alexa Peters had already offered to babysit. Alexa had been excited by the idea of potentially opening a small day-care center next year. She was already looking after her grandson, Tootoo, she'd said, so why not a few more?

"They figured Twin Rivers needed more attention," Tana said with a smile, holding Marcie's eyes. And Marcie grinned broadly. Yeah, she knew about the baby, thought Tana as she left the diner.

She made for the station liking the fact she had a new crew, liking the fact that it had been hinted at that once Corporal Saggart's contract was over, she could potentially be in line to run this department. It gave her a fierce new goal—to keep building on what she'd started here, to keep forging closer relationships with this community, to keep growing her policing skills. Her thoughts turned to Crash once more as she crunched through the frosted snow.

He'd called yesterday from the Yellowknife airport, saying he'd finally been released from the hospital and that he felt fine, and he was on his way to New York. He was taking his files and he was going to meet with his contact in the FBI. The Interpol guy from Frankfurt would be flying into New York for their meeting as well. Crash was also going to visit Grace and Leah. He didn't say much more than that. His flight had been about to leave.

But his absence was loud in her heart. She missed him as much as she missed Jim. And yeah, it ate at her that he was seeing Leah and Grace. She also knew it was right for him to do so. For Leah and Grace, too. Part of his healing process.

She guessed she'd see down the road how things played out now for Garth Cutter, Alan Sturmann-Taylor, Markus Van Bleek, and Harry Blundt.

Her dogs were waiting for her on the police station deck. They wiggled and wagged their tails as they saw her approach.

"Hey, guys," she said, ruffling the thick fur at their necks. "Good thing the new cops love dogs, eh?" She opened the door. Warmth and smiles greeted her, and her pooches followed her in.

CHAPTER 48

Late February. Day length: 9:32:16 hours.

"Here sweetie, it's okay, come on." Tana crouched awkwardly on her haunches in her puffy down jacket and snow pants, trying to coax the skinny old husky out from under the deck of her little cabin with some raw meat. It was a frigid February afternoon, the sun making its pale and low arc across the northern sky, casting long shadows and putting sparkle into all that was frozen.

Crow TwoDove's old dog ventured cautiously out from under the deck in a crouch. It came toward Tana's outreached hand, tail between its legs. The emaciated animal had been seen along the outskirts of town several weeks after it had apparently been set free by Heather MacAllistair. And several days ago Tana realized the dog had been hanging around her cabin, perhaps attracted by the scent of the food she'd been feeding her own dogs on her porch. She'd moved back into the little log cabin by the river when Saggart had arrived, and she was incredibly happy here, with her view over the waters of the Wolverine, and the forest and sky beyond its banks. She'd sit sometimes at night, swathed in warm gear, her dogs at her side, just watching the northern lights play across that great, wide open sky. And although the nights were still long, the earth had started its tilt toward summer.

"The curtains are opening again," Marcie had said. "Soon it will be light again—and it will all be right."

The dog took the meat from Tana's hand. She was surprisingly gentle, full of scars. Tana gave her another piece from the container she had with her. "What's going on in your head, sweetie?" she said as the dog chewed and wagged her tail ever so slightly. "Bet you don't miss being tied up, eh? But it must be hard out there all on your own." Tana stilled, besieged suddenly by a sensation that she was being watched. The dog scuttled off into the leafless, frosted scrub. Slowly, Tana looked over her shoulder. Her heart kicked.

Crash.

He stood there, shopping bags in hand, breath misting about his face. Tana came slowly, awkwardly to her feet. His gaze went straight to her huge belly, then back up to her face.

"Damn, you look good, Constable," he said as he came forward, that old Crash grin cutting into his craggy and freshly scarred face, his green eyes sparking. And her heart crunched, then kicked a burst of adrenaline, anticipation, through her blood. "Don't think I've seen you out of uniform before," he said.

She gave a self-conscious shrug. "One down jacket and ski pants is much like any other, especially in my shape."

"How long now?"

"Any day."

"You on leave?"

She nodded, heart racing. Her eyes burned. She'd hadn't dared believe that he really would return to her. She'd been too badly burned too many times, and now, seeing him here, in the flesh, was overwhelming.

He hesitated, then came forward and gave her a kiss on her cheek. She stilled, met his eyes. He swallowed. "It's good to see you, Tana," he said. "Really good. It's been too long."

Reaching up, she gently touched the new scars that clawed red down the side of his face. "They didn't do a bad job," she said.

"Didn't do a good one, either."

"You okay?"

He grinned again. "Yeah. I'm good. Who's the old dog?" He nodded toward the bush where the husky had vanished.

"Crow's. We all thought the animal was a he, but turns out it's a she, and she's been hanging around my cabin a few days now. I've started feeding her. I think she's sleeping under my deck nights, but she's always gone in the morning before I let my guys out. They don't get on."

"So where are Max and Toyon?"

"Inside. I keep them in there when I feed her so as not to spook her off."

He turned, taking in her view. "Nice."

And under the inanities so much more simmered. Tana barely trusted her own voice.

"I . . . I like it. Maybe I'll try a veggie garden when it gets warm. Don't know how that will go—I've never had a garden. It's a good place to raise Destiny, though."

His gaze shot to her. "Destiny?"

She grinned, nervously. "Yeah. Sappy, huh? But . . . it . . . it's real. She brought me here."

"A girl?"

She nodded. And his eyes glistened. "Congrats," he said, then hesitated as if wanting to say more. Instead he turned away and looked out over the river again. And Tana knew he was thinking about his own unborn baby girl. About Gracie, too. She had so much she wanted to ask him, yet she felt uneasy about just how much to pry, and where they would go from here.

"Want to come in?" she said.

"Thought you'd never ask." He held up the packets in his hand. "I told you I make a good venison stew, remember?"

She held his eyes, a whole world of emotion surging silent and fierce between them.

"Bottle of red wine for simmering," he said. "Button mushrooms, baby carrots, onions, garlic. Fresh fruit for dessert. Beer. Juice. What am I missing?"

"Nothing," Tana said, voice thick. "Nothing at all."

They sat on her small sofa in front of a crackling fire, Max and Toyon at their socked feet. The sky outside had turned dark indigo, and soft waves of aurora played over the horizon. The stew simmered in her kitchen, and Crash sipped a glass of red wine. He was warm and solid beside her. He felt good. He smelled good. She liked the look of him—the new scars and lines on his face were like a map of his past, and Tana understood people with messy pasts. They made her feel more comfortable than those with blank slates who seemed to be doing everything right. Whatever "right" was. And those fresh scars on his cheek knitted directly into her own life—made her part of him. They told of a crucible through which they'd both emerged profoundly changed.

"So, I heard Van Bleek and Sturmann-Taylor were taken in for questioning last week," she said, leaning into him.

"Yeah, a joint FBI, Interpol, and RCMP op. Cutter was also officially brought in yesterday."

Her eyes flared to his. Her pulse quickened. "So he's been linked?"

He nodded, sipped his wine. "It looks like Cutter was the leak that sent the Vancouver diamond deal sideways. He couldn't allow the marked FBI diamonds to enter the system, because he knew they'd lead right back to his involvement in the laundering operation here in the Territories, so he fed information through a fellow cop to the low-level snitch in Vancouver, who in turn fed it to the VPD."

"And Sturmann-Taylor, and Van Bleek?"

"Interpol is working through Sturmann-Taylor's finances and contacts, and it's becoming clear he's involved in the syndicate, if not the kingpin. I suspect the investigators will get there eventually. Van Bleek is being charged with some industry-related murders in South Africa, and the Congo. It appears he was setting up to run conflict diamonds through Harry Blundt's new mine, feeding raw stones into the future WestMin haul out of Ice Lake."

"So Blundt is innocent?"

"So far. He looks like he was a pawn. Sturmann-Taylor was just wooing him, and providing half the financing for the Ice Lake exploration via his subsidiaries." Crash got up from the sofa and made his way to the kitchen with his glass. He poured some more wine, and offered her some.

"I'm good with soda," she said.

He stirred his stew and tasted it. That grin of his that she was coming to love so much cut across his face again. "Now, this *is* good."

She got up from the sofa, came over, and he brought a spoonful to her mouth, spilling some on the way in. She laughed, and wiped her lips as she swallowed. "Damn right it's good."

He stilled as he watched her mouth, watched her laugh. And Tana suddenly wanted to kiss him. She looked away quickly, opened the fridge, took out a cold soda that she didn't really need but she had a desperate urge to keep busy, keep moving. To not look into his eyes right now because what she felt for him scared her. It was too soon. Too deep. Too big. She was not ready. Or was she?

She *had* to prove to herself that she was properly stable and on her own two feet. She needed to be there for Destiny one hundred percent.

"How'd it go with Grace and Leah?" she asked without looking at him as she made her way back to the sofa.

He was silent a moment, before coming slowly over to the fire, and reseating himself beside her.

"I'm glad I did it—that I went to see them."

She raised her gaze, met his eyes.

Crash inhaled deeply. "It was awkward initially. But Grace was keen to meet me. I took her out for lunch, and we walked around the city. She showed me her school." He paused for a long while. "It was a bridge, Tana. It was forging a connection between the past I'd cut off, and the present. And it's a way into the future for all of us—Grace, Leah, me—a way to put things to rest, and to keep moving forward." He raked his fingers through his hair. "I needed to do it, and I feel good that I did." He held her eyes. "I had to own my mistakes. She's going to come visit."

"*Grace?*"

"In the summer. Leah okayed it." A hesitant smile crossed his face, and something deep changed in his eyes. "I'm going to teach her to fly, like my dad taught me. I'm going to learn how to be a father."

Emotion sideswiped Tana, hard. She swallowed at the intensity coming off him, the hopeful, nervous energy she felt inside herself. She touched the back of his hand tentatively. He looked down at her fingers against his skin. "I'm proud of you," she whispered.

Without meeting her eyes, he said, "And I've been cleared to fly for the Twin Rivers RCMP detachment. I signed the contract last week."

When she made no response, he looked up into her face.

"Tana?"

She sniffed and swiped at the tears streaming down her cheeks. "Damn hormones," she said with a thick laugh.

He cupped the side of her face, and his thumb, rough, moved across her bottom lip. "I told you," he whispered. "I'm your man. I've got your back. We're going to find a way to make it work up here, you and me."

She nodded, and he leaned forward and pressed his mouth over hers. She tasted him, his wine, the salt of her own tears. Heat washed through her and her bones turned limp as she drowned into his kiss, opening to him. His hand slid down her back as he drew her close against his hard body.

The next morning Tana stood on her porch watching Crash feed Crow's old husky. The dog wiggled and licked his hand.

"I think she likes you," she said.

"I think she does."

Crash had stayed the night. They'd eaten in front of the fire, and after they'd kissed, he had not pushed her for more. And she'd loved him for it.

As much as she craved a deeper physical connection with Crash, for far too long she'd resorted to sex as a way of numbing herself. Of coping. And she wanted this to be different. Slow. She wanted it to be real. She'd fallen asleep on the sofa in his arms. Later, he'd come with her to bed where he'd just held her and her baby bump, and Tana didn't think she'd ever felt anything more intimate in her life. She'd felt loved. She'd felt trust. She'd felt as though she had nothing to hide from this man. And he'd given her everything about himself.

He came to his feet. "I should go. I've got a flight run. Later?"

She smiled and nodded. "Tonight. And this time I cook. Or . . . try."

He grinned, cast her a salute, and he started down the frosted path along the frozen river. The dog followed him.

"Hey," she called out after him. "I think you've got a friend."

He stood looking at her for a long moment, and then said, "Yeah, I do."

"I meant the dog, goof."

He dropped his hand to his thigh, and the husky sniffed and licked it. "I tell you what," he called out to her. "If she follows me all the way home, I might give her a place to stay."

Tana smiled and waved. And she watched the scarred old husky follow the scarred man into the frozen morning. Crash was picking up another stray. He was a good man. A special man. She thought about second chances, and how everyone, everything, deserved them. No matter how broken they seemed, there was always hope.

There would be challenges ahead. Giving birth. Being a mom. Her career—dealing with Damien and his gang, the community. The inquest. Learning to be with Crash—learning how to fully open herself to love, which was still, honestly, as terrifying as it was deliriously exhilarating. But it was the stuff of life. Already there'd been a community celebration of Mindy's life. Crash had phoned in from the hospital for that.

Tana had gone out into the badlands with Caleb and Jamie, and informed Elliot Novak about Heather MacAllistair's death, and her role in his daughter's death. He'd howled like an animal, and even so, part of Tana felt that he'd known all along that MacAllistair had killed Regan.

A ceremony had also been held to ask forgiveness for Jamie and Caleb's mistakes in plundering the graves of ancestors. The bones themselves were yet to be returned to the band, and when that happened there would be a huge festival, a coming together as the bones were once again laid back to rest in the traditional manner.

By then Destiny would have been born.

By then Tana would be a mother.

And as Tana watched the river mist swallowing her man and the dog in his tracks, she felt she'd done it. She'd come through the crucible, and light lay ahead.

As Marcie had said, the season was turning, the curtains were opening again. All would be fine.

ABOUT THE AUTHOR

Loreth Anne White is an award-winning author of romantic suspense novels, thrillers, and mysteries. She spent sixteen years in the newspaper business before joining the world of fiction. A two-time RITA finalist, she has won the *Romantic Times* Reviewers' Choice Award, the National Readers' Choice Award, and the Readers' Crown. She is a Booksellers Best Award finalist, a two-time Daphne du Maurier finalist, and a multiple CataRomance Reviewers' Choice Award winner. Born in South Africa, White now lives with her family in a ski resort in the mountains of the Pacific Northwest—the perfect place to escape reality. Learn more about her online at www.lorethannewhite. com.